PRAISE FO
THE EXTRAORDINARY DR EPSTEIN

'Susan Lee Kerr's debut historical novel is more than just a portrait of her extraordinary great grandfather – it's a story about Europe and America, Christians and Jews, science and superstition, and the impact of immigration, dislocation and modernity on three generations of a gifted but turbulent family. Ephraim Epstein's journey is geographic, spiritual and psychological, and it takes him – and us – from the 19th century to the 20th in this compelling, surprising and carefully researched narrative.'

– Glenn Frankel, Pulitzer Prize winning journalist and author of
The Searchers: The Making of an American Legend

'We journey around the world with *The Extraordinary Dr. Epstein* and witness his fascinating forays into farming, religion, medicine, and academia. Who would have thought that a fictionalized account of a proselytizing physician would keep me coming back for more?'

– Ronna Mandel, *Good Reads with Ronna*

ABOUT THE AUTHOR

Susan Lee Kerr inherited her great grandfather Ephraim's moveable roots. She was conceived in Australia, born in West Virginia, a Phi Beta Kappa graduate of Gettysburg College, a Mademoiselle magazine Guest Editor and a New Yorker until she struck new roots in England. She is author of two self-help books and numerous magazine feature articles. Her book *Creative Writing: the Matrix, exercises and ideas for creative writing teachers* is the fruit of her years as a creative writing tutor. Her haiku poetry is published in the journal of the British Haiku Society and has been anthologized. She is married and lives in London.

susanleekerr.com
ephraimmepstein.com

The Extraordinary Dr Epstein

Susan Lee Kerr

For Katherine Lee and Alexander Robin

THE EXTRAORDINARY DR EPSTEIN

VERITAS

This novel tells the true story of the remarkable life of Ephraim M Epstein, and I feel compelled to include a section of notes to indicate fictional v non-fictional aspects of the book. They are not footnotes, because that would interfere with the narrative flow. But for the curious or questioning reader during or after reading, a flip to the *Veritas* notes at the back, which are arranged by chapters, will give clarification as to factual elements, historical context and creatively invented elements.

– Susan Lee Kerr

CONTENTS

PART 3: THE PURSUIT OF HAPPINESS

PART 5: THE TERRITORY

PART 5: THE GLEANER

PROLOGUE: EPHRAIM SPEAKS

Considering the severe mental distresses that I passed throughout my life – religious, social, pecuniary and of family life, some of which will never be disclosed and will not terminate except in my death – all sufficient to shorten an ordinary life, considering all these, why then do I live so long?

PART 1: FROM RUSSIA TO AMERICA

1

AS WAS THE TRADITION
Belarus 1846

On the eve of Ephraim's seventeenth birthday, as was the tradition, Grandfather Shimon Ziml Epstein came to the apartment in Podriadchiki Street. He would give his patrimony to Ephraim in a family ceremony, a blessing and direction for his life. Everyone knew this, none better than the impatient Ephraim: to be on his way as a man, a great step. Most of all, it meant he would continue his studies under less of his father's control. The day was soft for March, and the maids had flung open the windows to air the rooms. The younger children skittered underfoot, excited for their big brother, even more excited in the knowledge of the sweets they would receive from their zayde, their grandfather. Perhaps even some tiny silver and gold coins would appear. With big-sisterly bossiness Eva, Pauline and Kathy shooed the little ones away from the windowsill where they clung, hoping for first sight of him. All the way from Warsaw! Two days ago Zayde's message had come by courier to Papa: the journey was going well, he would arrive in time.

No need to knock at the entrance, the children's squeals and shouts saw to it that the wooden doors were flung open and all the household hurried to line up and greet Zayde. Whoever caught his eye first felt the lucky one. His visits were usually only twice a year, to discuss the family businesses with their father, his son Yehuda. But this, the birthday of the eldest son, was special.

It was Ephraim himself who first received direct acknowledging eye contact from the tall, strong-boned old man. His broad forehead, long gray beard and full head of hair supported the dignity of his position in life – an honorary citizen of Russia who secured commissions from the Czar's chief of works, and head of a long-established family held in high respect by the community.

With the greetings came gifts of oranges and sweets for the youngsters, distributed by Zayde's liveried footman. Zelda Epstein – Mama – slipped away to supervise the kitchen, taking the middling daughters with her to help. Earlier they'd set the table with the best linens, silver, crystal and china. Soon Mama's finest feast food followed: soup, pate, baked fish, roast turkey, potatoes, carrots, onions, winter radish, dumplings, wine, brandy, nuts, apples, raisins. Zayde presided, conversing with his son, and with the husbands of Chashe and Chevah, his married grand-daughters. His eye fell now and then on Eva further down the table; only a year younger than Ephraim, she would be next to be found a husband. Ephraim himself watched the older men's faces, noting the gray creeping further into his father's beard, comparing the dark beards of his brothers-in-law and the full gray of Zayde's. He touched his cheek, still smooth, barely needing to be shaved. It was not his time yet. But he carried the resemblance of his father and grandfather: the wide brow, the gray eyes, and in due course he would bear the dark and then the grizzled beard. His younger siblings and cousins had been banished from the meal, which he found a relief, because their teasing – birthday boy! – had stopped being a joke by noontime. However, he could hear muffled giggles from the kitchen and knew the older ones had climbed up to the warmth of the stove to peep and listen to the goings on.

At last Zayde stood and all rose with him. They processed into the drawing room, a dozen Epsteins filling but not overcrowding it among the heavy dark wood furnishings with their bronze corners, and the damask-covered side chairs. Zayde took his place by the round mahogany table. Mama and Papa flanked him at a distance from the table; Ephraim shot a quick glance toward his mother and she winged a little smile to him, her blue eyes shining. He smiled back quickly and then stepped forward and bowed his head.

Zayde seized Ephraim by the shoulders, pressing a kiss on each cheek: 'Son of my son!' his voice rang with pride and possession. He gazed into the youth's face, and Ephraim returned the full, frank examination, seeing the ruddy, healthy skin, and the tiny bloodshot veins, the wrinkles in the darkened circles of the old man's eyes. Before the patriarch he felt like a washed, fluffy lamb, untried but full of hope and energy. 'Yes,' spoke his ancestor, nodding, as if reading his mind. He turned Ephraim around to face the roomful of family, keeping his hands on his shoulders, and launched into prayer: 'See O Israel, our son who pleaseth us well, who walks upon the straight road, who carries the rod and the staff in his hands, who knows the true path and who obeys the Lord's commands. Bless him, O Almighty, for he is fair in your sight and will take up our burdens and carry them forward. Emen.'

The family chorused the Amen.

Zayde turned Ephraim round again and pressed down on his shoulders, so that he knelt, now gazing at the black wool of trousers, the shiny leather of soft boots. His eyes strayed to his mother's dark skirts, the hem of her embroidered apron, and then Zayde's hands settled lightly on the yarmulke crowning his head, feeling like a caress, as he prepared to give his blessing.

'Ephraim Menachem Epstein, now you enter upon the age beyond youth, into the age of growth into maturity. You have worked and studied well, and so it shall continue, as you are a shining light, with the Lord's will, and with the patrimony of the family Epstein. And so that it shall continue in all the best of ways, we have prepared for you a bride...'

Shock jolted Ephraim and he did not hear the next words.

In a daze he was raised to his feet, in a daze he received the small, heavy, highly polished wooden coffer laid in his arms. Zayde lifted its lid, and in a blur Ephraim saw gold coins in rows and thick golden chains to the brim, as he was propelled towards the family witnesses again, displaying the treasure.

'L'chaim!' They raised their glasses, toasting him. 'Mazel t'ov!' 'To life!' 'Congratulations!' they called out, clapping and smiling.

'But I can't, Mama. I can't! I can't marry Rachel. Please! There must be a way.' Tears welled up again, but he fought them, seeing his mother's tears. They sat in her bedroom, now that most of the family had gone to sleep, including Zayde, and Papa was in his study, praying. The sing-song of his voice reached them.

'You turned so white, pale as a sheet,' she said.

He had clamped his lips tight for the rest of the evening. He had asked no questions, he had said neither yes nor no. He had accepted kisses and teasing and felt all eyes upon him. Married, a wife. It could not be. He needed room, he needed time. To grow, to understand, to become a man. To... be.

'I'm not ready to marry! It's too soon, I'm seventeen.'

'Seventeen tomorrow. It is not too soon. I was married at thirteen, and your Papa was fourteen – and look at us, we are plenty happy.' She reached out and smoothed the hair from his forehead. 'This is a good age for you. And it is what we want for you, what Zayde wants. It will be good, you will see.' Ephraim pulled away, slumping back in the chair he had drawn up next to hers, dropping his head, sullen. These traditions. It was fine for his parents to marry so young, that was then. This was now, the enlightenment had changed things, Jews needed to move on. But the elders refused to understand, they stuck with the minhag, traditional ways. He sighed.

'Is it... is it that you do not like Rachel? We considered carefully. We were thinking only of your best interests. Those beautiful green eyes, and she is a good girl – the daughter of a scholar, too.' She coaxed softly, tilting her head to try peer into his face, to catch his eyes.

'I know...' As he sighed he was remembering. A pointy chin, escaping curls. She lived far away in Minsk, they had only met three or four times.

She seemed always wary and watchful, or else eager to fit in with his sisters. That summer he was ten and crowned king of the army of boys, battling for Jerusalem with his wooden sword – she saw him get a bloody nose. She was like a sister, but he liked his own sisters better. 'I don't love her, Mama. And surely she does not want this.'

'Love will come, I guarantee that. You are both good people. And marriage according to your parents' wishes is your duty.'

'But she's my cousin!' Ephraim jumped up and paced to the window, pushing the heavy curtains aside to expose the dark glass of night. He let them drop into place, turning back to his mother. 'It's not healthy to marry my first cousin.'

'Ach, these new ideas. Cousins marry, they often do. Always have done. Even in the Talmud – ' she broke off as he flung himself down and laid his head in her lap, circling his arms around her hips. She stroked his dark curls, pressed his neck and shoulders with both hands. How easy it had been when he was her little boy to comfort his sadnesses, soothe his passions. 'You know the true reason you must marry Rachel.'

Ephraim was the darling of his parents' hearts, the darling of all who knew him. The first boy-child after three girls, he was the treasured son who would sing the Kaddish over his father's death. No matter that the older daughters had found good husbands, that two other sons were among the younger six children, Ephraim was the joy and hope. And he was the most scholarly, the liveliest and the best-looking boy in all the Epstein circle of family and friends. No one could resist his good humor, his charm, and at the same time his honesty, his modesty and good intent. He was deeply serious about his faith, as was the entire Epstein family, and he was obedient to his parents. Religious duty and parental word were law, exercised in the Epstein household with strongly loving discipline. This ethos structured a strength of character and will which, combined with intelligence, had stood all the family in good stead over generations.

Even at sixteen Ephraim consciously valued this rich, purposeful life, but at the same time he had drunk in the awakening of nineteenth century Russian Jews: the enlightenment. He thrilled to the knowledge that his father had actually met and talked with the great, the famous, Dr Max Lilienthal who had come to Belarus to implement Czar Nicholas's instructions: from living turned in on themselves and their faith, Jews would loosen their nearly medieval ways. Education would no longer be limited to Hebrew and the Talmud. They would learn to read and write Russian, even German and French, literature, natural science, mathematics, philosophy. Ephraim and his brothers-in-law and his best friend, Abraham, had cultivated the results. They and the young men of Brest-Litovsk acquired textbooks, shared lessons, debated interpretations. Papa, back then, welcomed these changes – a chance for Jews to make better contributions to society, a broadening of permissions into the wider world.

But from his father's restrictions and temper now Ephraim could hardly believe that he had ever approved of the Jewish enlightenment. Papa stormed and sorrowed, appalled by the growth of free thinking, the dilution of the life of faith. Thoughts of Papa's disapproval and Ephraim's hunger to be himself streamed through the heads of mother and son. But this did not mean that they agreed. Ephraim's stomach churned. Yes he wanted to study, yes to excel in the Talmud, and in due course the mysteries of the Kabbalah – his aptness for these inner, esoteric approaches to the most divine had been hinted at by his teachers. But he wanted to know more of Goethe, of Shakespeare, Pushkin, Cervantes, Milton... and of the solar system, the circulation of blood, the workings of oxygen – it was all, all of God's making, and all so compellingly fascinating.

Finally he lifted his head, pleading, 'Of course it is my duty, and the wisdom of my parents, but...' His mother was blonde and blue-eyed, and to him still the most beautiful woman in the world. Their special bond, the unspoken, understood current that flowed between them, had begun the moment he had been laid in her arms at birth – or perhaps even before, they each privately speculated.

'I see you do not know the true reason. We thought you would grasp it.' She paused, hoping he would fill in the void, but he shook his head. 'The dowry. Your grandfather requires us to keep Rachel's dowry in the family.'

'Money!'

'She is of the age she needs to marry.'

'And I am not!' Anger finally broke through his dazed resistance.

'You are the right age for her, a good match.' His mother's voice took on a practical edge, and Ephraim sat back mouthing the word money again in disbelief. 'You know how it has been, my son. Times can be good and times can be bad for us Jews. They are not bad now – but remember when they were better? Our wonderful house... and Papa's factory...'

Ephraim was eleven when the Czar's decree demolished the old district of Brest-Litovsk and commenced the building of a great fortress to stand guard over the city's vital river-ways and cross-roads. Their spacious, elegant yellow house, with its Venetian windows, gardens and silver poplars had been one of the last to go, but the Epsteins, like the Jews of all classes who lived in the district, had had to move to the new town three miles from ancient Brest. The compensation had not yet arrived. And their new apartment, though generous, could never be as gracious as their house.

He was a child then, but not so childish that he had been fooled by his parents' brave faces about the move. Though an upheaval, the creation of Russia's new fort meant a huge construction job that provided lucrative contracts for the Epstein brick factory, and other business for Yehuda

Epstein to negotiate. But for Ephraim's father, as a respected leader of the Jewish community, the blows of the great move had badly winded him.

Ephraim nodded and waited for Mama to say more – he didn't need to be reminded of Papa's change, so solemn, so strict, so hard on everyone, especially on Ephraim. 'How many people in our family, Ephraim?' she asked gently and went on. 'The twelve of us here, and then... have you ever counted up?'

He thought of the visits, the festivals, the weddings, brises, bar mitzvahs: uncles and aunts, cousins, relations of all ages in households spreading from Brest to Warsaw to Minsk, easily thirty or forty, and then another...

'Seventy,' interrupted Mama. 'Your Zayde is the head of these seventy of us... there is not only the dowry for Rachel to provide – and you know her father, praise him, has no wealth but his soul and wisdom – but there was our own Cecilie's last year, and Eva's coming soon. Next will be Pauline and Kathy. Then there's Aaron's Esther. And babies coming...'

Ephraim felt again the weight of the dowry – part of the dowry – he had held in his arms hours before. He had seen his older sisters at their weddings adorned with their own ropes of pearls and gold chains, this wealth and more bestowed on them and their new husbands. He didn't know their bride prices exactly, but he knew that as an Epstein, highly educated and the first son, his worth as a groom would be thirty thousand rubles, maybe more. 'He wants to keep the dowry in the family,' Ephraim said dully.

'It is a burden, so many people,' Mama acknowledged. 'And a joy and privilege.' She smoothed the hair from his forehead again, smiling, and then the smile faded: 'As well, who knows what lies ahead. The Czar can do... anything.'

'Oh, Mama.'

'So you understand.'

2

THE COUSIN-BRIDE
Belarus 1849

At the start Rachel was a docile wife, but her demeanor continued as a kind of obedience that came to offend Ephraim. The first skirmish was on their wedding night in August 1846. After the dancing and singing, drinking and eating, teasing and laughter, when at last they were shut in their bedroom alone, she was miserable.

'Don't look at me! Don't look!' she cried out, dashing over to sit on the edge of the bed. Ephraim, startled, turned from the door. She buried her face in her hands. 'I said don't look!'

'If you like. But why?' Perplexed, he decided that she was shy. In all the six months of their betrothal they had scarcely been alone together. Closing his eyes he shuffled across the carpet until he bumped into the bed.

'If I like,' said Rachel bitterly. 'You don't like me. And now,' she sobbed, 'they've made me so ugly!' Tears and sobs broke from her.

'You are not ugly! You are very pretty!' Ephraim ignored her original command and came to stand in front of her. What should he do to make his wife happy? He should try, as he would with anyone. 'Look at me.' He gently pulled her hands from her face and she obeyed him. 'Those beautiful green eyes.' He smoothed away the trails of tears. 'Your skin, like cream.'

'But my hair, it's all gone! You'll hate me, you'll hate me!' Her wail returned as she yanked the white silk scarf from her head. Her thick, dark hair was cropped to only an inch long.

'Shh, shh, shh.' Ephraim sat on the bed beside her, taking one of her hands in his. True enough, her hair was a shock, like a boy's or even shorter. The last he'd seen was a glimpse during the ceremonies of luxuriant waves flowing loose over her shoulders. She sniffled. He had seen his sister Pauline unreasonably distressed over a small slight once, and how stern Papa had been with her. He decided he would not be like his father. 'Lialke, little doll. That's what you look like, a pretty little doll. It comes to all brides on their wedding day – you know that.' He squeezed her hand and she weakly returned the pressure, and sighed.

'Lialke. Am I really pretty? But you don't love me.' Her voice veered from tremulously hopeful to speculative calm.

'Of course you are pretty. Any man would think so, -- ' he hesitated, not able to say the word love. 'A husband respects his wife. It is the mitzvah, the law.'

She pulled away and flung herself down on the bed, crying out. 'You don't love me, you don't even like me! You hate me. I didn't want you either, but they decided.'

'Rachel! I do not hate you! I forbid you to say that – or even think it.' He put his hand on her back, feeling her sobs. 'I want you to be happy. I want us to be happy.' And Mama had said love would come – but he didn't say that. He comforted her weeping that night.

For months they attempted to love each other, Ephraim dutifully gentle. Rachel tried to please him, but soon she began to annoy him. She wanted something – attention, forgiveness, praise – to remove the humility of marrying for duty. Ephraim did not pretend to be in love with her, yet he tried to be kind and to bolster her pride and self-worth. But because he too wore the yoke of obligation she would not believe his attempts to reassure her. Their mutual disappointment grew into undercover warfare. Every now and then she would commit a small act of defiance. A glass of tea too cold, or too hot – with humble apologies. His pencil lost – and then found in a gap in the floorboards. He was certain these acts were intended, but they were tiny. How could he reproach her for such subtle and insignificant things? It would only make him as petty as she was. So he fumed and prayed for patience, she acted the obedient wife, and they both played their roles for the sake of everyone.

His parents supported them, so that he might become a rabbi, an honor to the name of Epstein. Ephraim did at least delight in his married status for the new freedoms he gained for studies, and he was genuinely grateful for Rachel's dutiful support, running their household, caring for his needs, as he grew ever more absorbed. But as his appetite for learning increased, his chafing against his father also increased. Papa retreated more and more into the Talmud, and harangued Ephraim about time spent on natural philosophy, Latin, Greek, Russian, French, German: he was to be a scholar, how dare he waste his energies? Ephraim fought back: even if he became a rabbi, he wanted to be a rabbi with a profession – in Russian law, perhaps, or teaching in university, or in medicine. This was the purpose of the enlightenment, to take Jews out of their limited world. Finally, his father forbade these free-thinking, worldly subjects. Finally, Ephraim was forced to study them by stealth. And then began the siren call of America.

In his liberal studies Ephraim had heard news of American freedoms, the astonishing, revolutionary experiment of democracy. Even at fifteen he'd been fascinated: so many possibilities, such openness. Lately his group of enlightenment friends circulated a German-Yiddish newspaper that published articles sent back from the new world by emigrants. A hot new inspiration began to stir in Ephraim: oh, to break away from the rules, the restrictions, the old ways. But how? And... Rachel.

A solution arrived in the middle of 1847. Within the bosom of the family an uncle on his mother's side visited, the genial, mysterious Jacob Finkelstein. Called uncle by courtesy, he was in fact a nephew of Ephraim's mother's much older cousin, a relationship lost in time and distance, for though born in Belarus he had grown up in Constantinople. Small and stocky, with a high, rounded forehead, his face was framed by a white beard and fluffy white hair, so everyone called him old Uncle Jacob though he was only in his forties. A gem-trader, he had travelled his whole life – India, Jerusalem, France, England, all over – and to the United States twice.

He had visited the Brest-Litovsk family every five or six years, so Ephraim was only twelve the last time he'd seen him. 'Will o' the wisp,' Mama cautioned, now that her son was an adult. 'Never settles for long, always chasing a new stone, a better gem, a different source. He said he was married, but we never met the wife.' Without words, his father conveyed a similar dubious regard for this adventuring relation, but all Ephraim's ears heard was America, America, America.

At the apartment of his older brother-in-law Ephraim joined Uncle Jacob's evenings by the samovar. Others gathered as the traveler spun his stories. New York, Cincinnati, Charleston, Mississippi, Shenandoah... the names intoxicated Ephraim. The young men plied Jacob with questions.

'Yes, it is so. In America, a Jew can vote.' Jacob's raisin-brown eyes shone and his cheeks and forehead creased with his smile. 'A Jew can own land anywhere – so much land for sale!'

'How can we get money to buy land? We have none to spare,' said Ephraim.

'It's free there!' Jacob stopped and laughed. 'Not land of course, not money either – it doesn't grow on trees. But a Jew is free to work in any job. You can work at what you like, Abraham,' he said to Ephraim's best friend. 'And you, Ephraim, you can have any career you wish.'

'What about synagogue, shul? About yeshiva – the Talmud? Do they keep kosher?' demanded Abraham. The others nodded with his query.

'Every big city has Jews, the community is there, the Talmud is there.' Jacob sipped at his tea. 'America can be a good life! Listen, I'll teach you one of their songs.' He searched multiple pockets in the interior of his black coat. Like a conjurer, early in his visit he had extracted from it ribbons and buttons as gifts for the girls of the family, and exotic coins for boys. This time he drew out an odd tube of wood and metal, 'They call this a Suwanee whistle. Sounds like klezmer to me.' He blew and slid its piston, producing an up-sliding note that made the whole group laugh. 'And this is *Yankee*

Doodle Dandy.'

A jaunty tune, even without the English words to sing Ephraim loved the liveliness that smacked of American optimism. Jacob announced he was returning to United States in the autumn, and he would be happy to travel with anyone who fancied to go. Ephraim, elated, began to hope: America was the answer to everything. He would go, he would earn money, get a university education and return as a professor of... of what he wasn't sure yet. The freedom would help him decide. Perhaps he would send for Rachel if conditions were very good. He would promise to return, of course.

Ephraim closeted himself with his mother and begged and badgered her to bless his decision. Eventually, reluctantly, with pained love, she agreed, 'America! So far, so different! Your studies! And Jacob, you know your father thinks he's meshuge, a little bit crazy.' Not blind to the difficulties in her dear son's marriage, she promised to join him in persuading Papa and Zayde. Perhaps the separation would bring the young couple closer together. But first she insisted he get Rachel to agree.

After Shabbat, after Mama lit the candles and prayed the blessings and the whole family around the table broke the bread and ate the meal and had the day of synagogue and prayer, in the renewed peace of the start of a new week, Ephraim called Rachel to him at his study table. She had grown toward womanhood since their marriage. A few curls of the lengthening hair only a husband got to see showed at the edge of her head-covering. When she sulked, she irritated him, but when she smiled she was startlingly attractive.

'I have some news for us,' he stood up as she entered the room. Fearful that today was a sulky day he hurried on, 'Someday you and I will go to America.'

'America?' Rachel repeated the bewildering word.

'After Sukkot I will go with Uncle Jacob. When I can bring wealth back to the family I will come back.' There, he had said it.

'America! What will you do!' Her voice sharpened in alarm. 'What about me?'

'At first, I will teach at a shul. Uncle Jacob says there are many. And I will be a tutor, which will allow me to study. I will go to university. When I am settled you will come. Then we will come back and I will be a professor.'

'You really do hate me,' she said, strangely calm. 'This is just a plan to get away from me.'

'That is not true! You cannot think I hate you. I want you to be happy. I want us to be happy. America will be good for us. It is the new world, lialke, just think...' he reached out to touch her arm, but she pulled away.

'America, so far away.' She spoke dreamily, smoothing the front of her apron, not crying or sulking, so he felt encouraged.

'It will take a few years before we can be together, but we are young. There are so many opportunities... it would be good to have your permission.' They both well knew that as husband he could do as he wished, but agreement would look best.

'I have some news for us, too,' she said abruptly. 'I am going to have a baby.'

A conflicting lurch of disappointment and pride hit Ephraim. Of course he would have to stay. In Mama's eyes, and Rachel's and his own, it was the right thing to do: the dream would have to be postponed.

When he bid farewell to Uncle Jacob that October, Rachel hoped Ephraim would forget the new world. America will still be there, she teased. A vain hope, he assured her, and this battle made a cover for the worries he did not share. He waited out her term in trepidation: the offspring of first cousins, would it be whole and healthy, or would this close breeding produce a flaw?

As he endured that anxiety, he struggled with a deeper anguish. While trying to keep a smile on his face, inwardly he feared he hated Rachel for conceiving a child. He had never hated anyone before, not even Papa or Zayde when they forced him to their will. He felt he might even hate his child, an unborn innocent. The preposterous illogic tormented him. He could only blame himself, yet his whole being was accusing Rachel of purposely interrupting his new life in the new world. Why had he not controlled his physical needs? Why, why, why... it wasn't her fault, it was his. The agony of resenting his wife and unborn child made him grim and thin – these were God's gifts, this was life itself. He could not forgive himself for feeling this way. His childhood attacks of tonsillitis re-appeared, keeping him in bed for days. Within weeks of recovery, he would be devastated by headache, another familiar ill. He could confide in no one, not even Mama. He could turn only to the Lord. He read, he prayed, he threw himself into his studies.

Suffering, impatient, anxious, by Chanukah, when Rachel's belly was great with life, Ephraim felt he might explode. Evening by evening, he joined the family for the lighting of the menorah, pretending to be glad, tasting but not tasting the latkehs and honey, roast goose and sweets. Only when he joined the younger children at their games gambling with cards for copper coins was he able to give himself up to fun and laughter, the Ephraim of old. He caught Rachel watching him, smiling with all the radiance of her pregnancy. On the final night, when the eighth tiny oil-filled jug on the silver filigree lamp was lit, his closest sisters challenged him to dreidel. They spun the little leaden top in turns: nun – Pauline lost; shin – Kathy left her stake in the pot; heh – Eva got half the pot; gimel – goor!

Ephraim won the whole pot! Triumph swept him into glee and magnanimity. With all the family cheering he scooped up the heaps of coins and poured them into Rachel's already overfilled lap. She spread her skirts to catch the holiday riches, beaming at his generosity.

That night, in his prayers before bed, the text was from Jeremiah. Ephraim knew it well, as he did all the prophets. 'O Lord, you have enticed me, and I was enticed; you have overpowered me, and you have prevailed.' The flame of the candle he read by wavered and he gazed into the dark heart of it, seeing it flicker and multiply into the eight flames of the menorah. But these were steady in faith. The light burned in his heart, the knowing: you have enticed me, Lord. Suddenly a painful joy filled him. The words were the same but the message this time was different. He saw clearly: his anger at Rachel was anger at himself, and it was more – he had been wrestling with God. With relief and praise, he submitted. The Lord was stronger. The implacable logic of God and life had held sway – at seventeen he had been full of all the natural needs of a healthy male of that age. And Rachel was irresistibly made for fulfilling desire, with her innate elegance, her clear white skin, her luminous eyes. They had married under the canopy, he had stamped on the wine glass wrapped in white cloth, she had revealed her nakedness to him, he had committed himself to be her husband before God, family and friends. No one could blame him for consummating the marriage, not even himself; he would have been at fault for not consummating it. All this logic he had known in his mind, arguing with himself, but this realization was different; it was direct from the Lord to his inmost soul. Ephraim gave himself to it and his stone-weight of anger ebbed, he could begin to forgive himself, and accept: this was God's will.

He held his newborn for the first time on 21 January 1848, tremulous with amazement at the morsel of humanity. His heart beat with fear. Though mother and baby had been declared well and strong, not until he saw for himself would he believe the risk of cousins marrying had not touched this child. Taking the bundle to the pale winter light at the window, he unfurled the wrappings and took a tiny pink and white foot in his hand. Those toenails, each one, each toe, the little heel, what a miracle. Humming and cooing, as his wife and mother looked on seeing only the awe of a new father, he assessed each limb, felt the tiny chest, nuzzled the back of her neck. The baby's eyes, squeezed shut against the light, opened wide as Ephraim kissed her forehead and held her up so they regarded each other eye to eye. She blinked, he laughed. 'She's beautiful, Mama! She's perfect. She has blue eyes like you.' The final shadows of his churlish resentment and breeding fears melted away, replaced by joy and thanks for the gift of the Lord that was his daughter, Sarah.

But her arrival did not change his intentions. In February he was just beginning enquiries about passage to America when rumors came that Uncle Jacob was returning. How Ephraim's heart lifted, it was a miracle! His uncle had not crossed the Atlantic after all. Full of tales – deals in Amsterdam, waylaid in Hamburg, contracts in Liverpool, stuck in London – he had come back to do business before departing for New York. Of course Ephraim wanted to show off his daughter. Sarah-meydle, princess-girl, the old uncle called the baby, and he astonished the family gathering by crooning a gentle tune to her, 'Durme, durme, mi alma donzella...' The crowded sitting room had fallen silent by the time he finished, and he looked around, a little embarrassed. 'A lullaby of the Sephardic Jews, from Constantinople,' he explained. 'She must have liked it, or maybe not – she's asleep!'

Naturally Jacob renewed his offer to any who cared to join him; and so Ephraim's departure in April was inevitable. Despite Rachel's hopes, he held to his decision. All this while no one had breathed a word of America to his father. Mama now prepared the way with Papa who immediately shut himself at his desk for two days, only silently going out to synagogue. Mama was silent too, until she came and found Ephraim and said, 'We cannot rend the cloth of this house,' telling him to go to his father.

He went, reining in his defiance yet refusing to appear meek. Papa's disheveled beard and hair, his hard, offended gaze shook Ephraim. 'My son, I cannot pretend to be happy about your desire.' Yes, Ephraim nodded. 'You must be aware of how unhappy your mother is.' Alarmed, Ephraim heard his father's voice flare angrily and then sag into hurt. 'But you are a man now, with a wife and daughter and you have the right to do this. So with sadness – and with hope that Jacob will help you survive all the dangers and that you will return to us unscathed – I give you my blessing.' Then, strangely to Ephraim, he chanted the words of the final prayer of the prayers they said three times a day, the Hebrew strong and familiar: 'Aleinu l'shabeach la'Adon hakol... It is our duty to praise the Master of all...' But he stopped before the ending, at the words: nor is our destiny like all their multitudes.

As he was dismissed, doubt entered Ephraim for the first time. So much pain he was causing, so far he was going, into foreign lands, alien ways. But within twelve paces of closing his father's door impatience and determination surged back. He would make his way, he would not be trapped, he would find his own fortune. No daughter of his would ever be forced to marry for reasons of dowry. Even Zayde conceded this reasoning, and Rachel – especially Rachel – accepted it too.

And then, in March, revolution broke out in Berlin, quickly followed by spontaneous rebellions in Paris, Vienna, Rome, in Belgium, France, Austria, Saxony, Bavaria, Hungary. Even the ever-optimistic Jacob insisted there was no question, in 1848, of unnecessary travel across Europe. While the mobs voiced ideas of liberalism and the rights of common people to have a say in their own government Jacob went off to Constantinople, tormentingly vague about when he might return. But at least from the depths of his many-layered coat Jacob pulled the parting gift of a child's English primer, a pledge to the future. By now the old traveler and the young seeker had grown close, Jacob's easy-going, wry practicality a good fit with Ephraim's sociable, eager intelligence. In common they had an indefatigable ability to hope.

His American dream in suspension, the crushed Ephraim could only wait, increasingly irascible. He had one consolation – seeing his baby grow from squalling, sleeping infant to gurgling winsomeness and first steps into toddling. He delighted in her golden curls and blue eyes, and in watching her tumble and play with her cousins. Sarah was a happy bond between Ephraim and Rachel. With Sarah, and in public with the family they played their parts. In private, the tension grew. They both could not forget the burden of duty that had brought them together and not been obliterated by love. He made it clear there was no question of sexual union; and he would still go to America.

Ephraim dived into his studies, avidly read emigrants' articles from America and devoted himself to the primer and then, with Johnson's Dictionary, tried to master a book of English poetry by Byron. Rebellions ebbed and flowed all over the continent for more than a year. The Czar stepped up controls in Russia, and Ephraim grasped for straws of news. The only ray of sunshine came from across the Atlantic: gold had been discovered in California. Ephraim crowed to Rachel, 'You see, the streets of America are paved with gold after all! If you dig or pan for it.'

'You have never worked a physical day in your entire life, Ephraim Epstein,' she scoffed, irritatingly sensible. 'Besides, think of the Talmud and minhag – no Epstein will ever grub in the earth.'

'But there is gold there,' he insisted.

In the summer of 1849, as if lured by word of gold, Uncle Jacob returned with rubies and turquoise, bearing gifts of shawls, stories to tell and a restless air. Ephraim cornered him where the women of his life could not hear, eager for a report fresh from the outside world.

'Peace is breaking out all over, Ephraim. That Garibaldi's been chased out of Rome, stuck up in the mountains. Paris has another Napoleon in charge. It's a good time to get going.' He spoke seriously, without his usual wry humor.

'Is it safe?'

'Safe? Nothing is safe in this life, Ephraim-ben-Yehuda.' He gave a philosophical smile to his nephew-son-of-Yehuda, face creasing under the snowy halo. The familiar Jacob returned with a shrug, 'But it's worth the risk. With the Czar sending soldiers to put Franz-Joseph back in charge of

Vienna, who knows what next. And I need to be in America before the winter storms set in. How is the English? Are you still coming?'

And so, after a flurry of preparation, Uncle Jacob now waited in the foyer, cart ready in the street. Mama had been brave. All the tears had gone before, both Ephraim's and hers. He'd begged for a snip of her blonde hair, a precious token of her very self hidden from the world under her head-wrap. He carried it – and a lock of Sarah's – in the secret pocket of his belt, tied around with red thread and wrapped in a piece of black silk he got from Kathy, the sister he felt closest to. Mama was waiting by her window to wave him off. Ephraim steeled himself for the final good-byes. He had told Rachel to stay indoors with the baby, but they were down there, wrapped up against the autumn chill.

Ephraim closed the door and touched the mezuzah, a farewell to home. He was twenty years old. A sudden fear that he was abandoning all that was right shook him to a standstill, alone in the hallway. But this was his duty, to seek a new life. He would kiss Rachel and the baby good-bye, for who knew how long, promising again to write. He hoped Kathy would be there by the cart. She'd be brave for him, she'd hold Mama and Rachel together and keep his memory fresh for Sarah.

3

THE PERILOUS JOURNEY BY LAND
Hamburg 1849

They halted on the pavement. What a house! Tall windows, colored glass in the door, intricate brickwork, shining brass – his sister was living in even more comfort than Grandfather Epstein. In Warsaw they had rested at Zayde's house, here in Hamburg Ephraim's married sister would give them a place to recover before the next stage of the journey. So, you do have to leave the old country to secure new wealth, Ephraim took satisfaction in this confirmation of his decision.

Jacob started swiping at Ephraim's shoulders and batting at his sleeves to get the dust and mud off.

'Do me! Do me!' he ordered Ephraim. 'Smooth your hair!'

'What's the panic? It's our Cecilie.'

'And her Herr Lipman,' Jacob said darkly.

They mounted the scrubbed stone steps and Uncle Jacob pounded the door knocker, a sphinx's head. 'Ha! The Jews delivered out of Egypt and now they decorate their doors with its riddles. Napoleon, the little emperor who trampled all over Europe and Russia as far as Moscow, at least he brought us that.'

Ephraim saw that the mezuzah high on the side of the lintel was of fine silver filigree, just like at home, the message on every doorpost: Shema Yisrael, Hear, O Israel: the Lord is our God, the Lord is One. He was yearning for a hot bath, clean white sheets, down-filled coverlets and family love. Enough of adventure, fleapits and anxiety, rough roads, railway cinders, bad food, suspicious soldiers, passports, bribes on demand. The word emigrating had become not full of excitement and promise but empty and lonely. Yes, a fine dinner on china with thin glassware and silver cutlery and candlelight would be paradise. Jacob knocked again and immediately the door opened. A tall, red-faced man in waistcoat and dark fitted jacket said, 'Tradesmen to the lower entrance,' and made to shut the door.

'Who are you?' exclaimed Uncle Jacob. 'It is I, Jacob Finkelstein, and Ephraim, your mistress's brother.'

Ephraim raised his chin. 'We may appear ragamuffins, but we are family. She knows we are coming.'

The butler looked them over unwillingly. 'Step inside and wait.'

He left them, fearful, Ephraim was certain, that they would steal the silver candlesticks that gleamed on the ebony cabinet. Ephraim was relieved to be able to scratch his armpit where the lice were worst. He caught himself at it in the pier glass of the vestibule and noted how this German house was light-filled. From glimpses along the way, all the newly built ones were like this. And yet for all its wealth – the black and white tile floor, the brass chandelier, the red tapestry at the door – this was still a narrow townhouse and warehouse. Ephraim felt far from Belarus and the rambling timber and stolid brick houses he knew. He realized he was tapping his foot. Where was she? What kind of welcome was this! But Jacob, patient as ever, and to distract Ephraim, said, 'I wonder what has happened to the old butler, he was a good chess player.'

Then they heard a bustling and through the draped doorway came Cecilie, big with child, dressed in gray and warm with smiles and hugs.

Entering the nursery Ephraim felt the hollow thud of homesickness. Cecilie bent down to Lisabet, kissing her, and introduced Uncle Ephraim and Uncle Jacob.

The little girl assessed both men. 'I bemember the old uncle. He gave me a ribbon.'

'And I have another one for you,' said Jacob. He pulled a length of pink embroidered ribbon from an inner coat pocket and waved it in ripples to her delight, letting her catch the end.

Ephraim squatted next to Lisabet. 'My little Sarah will grow up to look like you, I think. She has blonde curls, too.'

'So your daughter takes after our side, not Rachel's?' Cecilie took Lisabet onto her lap. 'And are they well?' she inquired as if he had seen them only yesterday instead of a month ago, a long and perilous month.

On this subject, his wife, his child, the decision to emigrate and the journey so far, there was far too much to say right now. So he nodded, yes they were well, and then exclaimed on the magic lantern nearby, 'We have one of those!' He examined it more closely, and Lisabet joined him, explaining the silhouettes. Horses were her passion and Uncle Ephraim, sitting next to Cecilie on the couch, crossed one leg over the other and offered the child a ride. She climbed aboard the foot of her handsome young uncle, and off they went, Ephraim jigging his leg at a slow, then fast and then faster pace, chanting the game in their Belarusian-Yiddish of the nursery. Cecilie and Jacob joined in: This is the way the troika goes – on the snow, over the ice, over the rutted road! Faster and faster! Gliding and sliding. Faster and faster! Bumping and riding. Fast, fast, fast!

29

Lisabet shrieked in delight, demanding more amid the adults' laughter, and another wild round began.

The nursery door banged open: 'Nein, nein, nein! No Yiddish in this house!' David Lipman glared at the culprits, and then stormed off.

Lipman had aged since his wedding day. He had much less hair and much heavier jowls. Ephraim had been fifteen then, awed that his sister was leaving home for a far off place, a foreign life. Now he hated seeing Cecilie dominated by her husband's whims and orders. Without him, in the nursery, during the day when she took Ephraim and Jacob in her carriage to the parks, squares and cafes of Hamburg, she was gay and droll as he'd always known her. But in her husband's presence she was restrained. Ephraim wanted to challenge the way he squashed her, but as a guest and brother of Lipman he could not. And thinking of his own marriage, he could hardly be the pot that called a kettle black. That first night he could tell that his host had little time for them, nor apparently for any aspect of the Epsteins. When Jacob and Ephraim spoke the particular Russian the family used in Brest he frowned, cleared his throat and finally glared at Cecilie. With an apologetic look she said to her brother: 'Herr Lipman prefers us not to speak Brisker in the house. German is better. Or French.'

'Bien sur,' Ephraim smiled, hating him for trampling his sister's spirit. 'Mais, c'est mieux pour Jacob en Deutsche, ja?'

'Oui. Ja. Das ist eine gute Champagne,' said Jacob, sipping and smiling.

And so they continued in German, with Lipman promising that Champagne was perfect to drink with their next course. At his signal the servant placed on the table a silver platter of oysters bedded on ice, their pale flesh and white shells glistening in the candlelight amid a waft of fresh sea smell.

Ephraim recoiled – treif! Shellfish, absolutely unclean! He shot a look at Cecilie but she deliberately concentrated on Jacob, vivaciously telling him the difficulty in getting the lemons they needed for the oysters. Lipman smiled and nodded, slurping an oyster from its shell, enjoying the moment in full. Ephraim saw that Jacob, too, was taken aback. Then with a shrug and down-turned smile, the old traveler partook of the unclean food. Cecilie and her husband by now had had three oysters each. Ephraim's spiritual heart reeled as his stomach revolted. Shellfish.

Jacob slurped down another. 'Hmmm. Oyster. It reminds me of something...'

'Sea, fresh sea,' said Lipman, and ordered the servant to pour more Champagne. 'But I think our younger brother does not care for it.'

Ephraim sat slack-faced, waiting for the torment to end. Kashrut, kosher, treif, clean, unclean. Following the dietary law, the rules of mitzvot and minhag, was woven into every fiber of his life, as natural as breathing.

He knew some liberal Jews thought the food laws too extreme, but this! Was this the enlightenment his parents feared? Perhaps they were right after all. Lipman's free thinking had gone radically far. And he was forcing Cecilie with him.

Conversation moved on and so had the food – turkey, clean and safe, unless the whole kitchen was contaminated. Ephraim recovered himself to hear Lipman scoffing, 'Adventuring off to America. Expecting the streets to be gold.'

'I have been there and they are not,' replied Jacob calmly. 'But it lies on the ground in California. And everywhere there is work to be had, and freedom of work.'

'A clever person who works hard can make money anywhere,' said their host.

'Not where there is persecution and army conscription. Not where there is restricted education, restricted professions, limits on travel. Not in Russia, not Prussia, not even here in Hamburg,' Ephraim said.

'There is no persecution of Christians.' Lipman smiled knowingly. Jolted again, Ephraim looked from him to Cecilie, and she lowered her eyes. Surely not!

Despite Lipman's radical and domineering ways, he honored his family obligations, for one of his ships was to provide their passage to America. He reaped his reward in their reports on their journey so far, grilling them closely as they sat in his office in a corner of the loft warehouse. Ephraim liked the high view over Hamburg's bristle of ships' masts, and the thump and squeaks of the crane loading bales of fabric onto a barge in the canal below. Above the desk was a map of Europe, now a Europe of shifting, dubious borders. Conditions had been terrible for Lipman's trading during 1848, with few goods to ship across the Atlantic. Everyone knew Franz Josef was in charge of Austria again, bullying Ottoman Turkey to extradite that Hungarian rebel leader. Otherwise, reports said calm had returned elsewhere. But how were things really, on the ground?

'From Brisk to Warsaw, muddy ruts and thin nags. But not too bad,' said Jacob, using the familiar nickname for Brest-Litovsk. He had traveled the route many times. 'Warsaw to Berlin, worse. Terrible transport, military stop and searching, stupid customs officials, abandoned villages.' He shook his head.

'We had to walk miles and miles,' Ephraim spilled out some of the shock of the experience. 'We slept in the forest and in barns for a week. I never felt safe.' He had seen simple rural living all his days, and poor people in Brest, but never poverty like this. 'So many people so hungry and hopeless, begging in the towns, fighting over scraps of bread and bones.'

Lipman sagged. 'I thought it was over.'

'Ach, ja,' said Jacob philosophically. 'I saw it like this in the thirties. And think about Napoleon – worse, much, much worse. I was only eight, Ephraim, but I can still remember. However, it is passing.'

Ephraim gritted his teeth, having heard from his uncle a hundred times already on this journey how much worse things had been in the past. Or, sometimes, how much better. Jacob's equanimity provoked Ephraim's usual impatience to irritation, though he had to admit the disarming manner had slid them through some dangerous encounters. He was talking about Berlin now, how things seemed nearly normal, and the rail journey from Berlin to Hamburg, 'Just like the good old days. Except we didn't have trains then! So even better!'

'We saw burnt-out warehouses though,' Ephraim qualified the enthusiasm, 'and lots — ' but he had to stop, because pounding footsteps on the stairs heralded a breathless young blond boy who interrupted the men. He thrust a note at Herr Lipman, saying, 'Bitte, please, Captain Wagner asks you to read this, schnell!'

Lipman read it and groaned. He dashed over to the workmen by the goods crane, shouted orders, then came back and wrote a few lines across the captain's note for the ship's boy to take back. To his traveling relatives he said, 'England and France – sailing to defend Turkey against Russia and Austria. Everything's changed!'

Distraught, Lipman went to the crane hatch and thought out loud as he stared toward the hundreds of moored ships, then turned, bumping into Ephraim. 'My cargo... the ship has to leave now, before the chance of British blockade. Quick, I must be quick!' Ignoring his guests, he patted the pockets of his coat to check their contents, then unlocked a desk drawer and took out three small canvas sacks which chinked with guilders.

'Tell my wife I will not be home until late,' he barked at Jacob and Ephraim as they followed him down the stairs. 'And pack your bags. The *Howard* is your passage, not the end of the week but today.'

4

THE PERILOUS JOURNEY BY SEA
The Atlantic 1850

Looking up to the broad, taut sails, awe filled Ephraim at the power of wind, the power of the Lord. The air on his face was a blessing. Then his gaze shifted to the half-deck above him where a dozen or so well-dressed gentlemen took the air by the turned wooden railing of the area for cabin passengers. They may have puked and suffered like us from the sea, he thought, but not in our circumstances. It shouldn't be like this. He and Uncle Jacob should be up there with them.

They had set out as cabin passengers, relishing their six foot cabin fitted grandly with mahogany paneling, two built-in berths, a cupboard and porthole. On deck they strolled and savored the peaceful progress down the Elbe and out to the rolling North Sea. Other passengers were few, because the *Howard* had debarked so hastily, now bound for Liverpool before New York: merchants, businessmen, a manufacturer and his wife, German, Portuguese, British. The food was reasonable, their cabin was a retreat in which to study and pray, the general conversation was interesting, and Ephraim had a chance to practice his English. A British couple made certain that he was on deck to admire England's gleaming white cliffs as they navigated the Channel, and even more, to have him marvel at the approach to the magnificent port of Liverpool. Where the choppy Irish Sea mingled with the Mersey River, huge stone piers and granite-edged docks stretched for miles along the east riverbank, like fortifications containing lake-sized calm waters thronged with ships, bustling with activity. Despite the damp cold of January, Ephraim hung agog at the railing until he was ordered out of the way as the *Howard* slid in to Albert Dock.

The captain requested that his two passengers to America remain on board for the few days of cargo loading. Ephraim chafed, eager to explore this astonishing place.

'Docks, sailors, stevedores, thieves, rats, sharpsters. Take my word for it, this is no place to go wandering,' cautioned Jacob. 'I should know, this pool of liver I don't recommend, if you want to get to our promised land.' So they bid adieu to their shipmates and settled for watching the noisy, ever-changing scene from the comfort and safety of the *Howard*. Massive brick warehouses lined the shores which rose, densely built, to the rest of the city. Hundreds of ships and craft of all sizes filled the quays, loading and unloading, others crossed the waterways in constant traffic. The whole place seethed with rugged men hauling, climbing, shouting amid the clutter of cranes, ropes, masts and rigging. Ephraim described the chaos in letters home, trying to convey the din of hammers, bells, hoots, gulls, the smells of river and sea, of tar, timber and rot. Jacob pointed out nets of oranges landed from Seville, casks of rum and molasses from Jamaica, raw cotton from America, and they caught the whiff of coffee and spices spilled and crushed. On their own ship, Lipman's small cargo of compasses and telescopes was buried somewhere in the hold with other merchants' wares. The blockade worry had come to nothing and now Captain Wagner alerted agents to find merchants with further goods to fill the *Howard*'s unexpected void: printed cloth, buckles, rifles, ax-heads, pumps, ceramics, furniture, whatever the great British engine manufactured that America could want.

By the fourth day in Liverpool Jacob had paid the ship's purser to get their letters ashore; the activity of stevedores and crew increased. Planks went down a main hatch and the two travelers heard hammering and the rasping of saws. They saw live chickens and goats loaded on, barrels and crates. 'Water and provisions. So, soon we'll sail. America is calling,' said Jacob.

The next morning the purser came to them as they sat with their coffee and bread in the snug, tidy dining room. In his familiar blue coat and white cravat, the officer's red face seemed more harassed than usual. 'Passengers coming aboard tomorrow. You will have a change of berth. All deck cabins are filled and you will travel below.'

'Below – where?' said Jacob. 'Are there cabins below?'

'With the other passengers.' He paused, avoiding their eyes. 'With the Irish. In steerage. Unless...'

'This isn't right! Herr Lipman reserved our cabin! We paid.'

'Things changed. Captain's orders, with his regrets.' At last he looked at them. 'Now, Mr Finkelstein, Mr Epstein. If you can double the fare that the upper deck passengers will be paying, perhaps something can be arranged. If not, I suggest you send out for additional provisions for yourselves, as conditions will be... rather different. Or, of course, you are welcome to depart the *Howard*. Today.'

'Well, at least they're new,' said Jacob as they pushed further along the hold. The cargo space had been converted: ten bunks on each side, stacked two high, between them a long table, bench and stools cluttered the central area. 'And so is the straw bedding. And we get first choice.'

He was wearing his philosophical face, a recovery from his anger and Ephraim's shock at being cheated. Nephew and uncle had quickly retreated to their cabin, raged, debated, discussed, decided. If they left and sought another ship how long would that take, how much would it cost? If they paid an immense fare what would that do to the rubles that already had reduced alarmingly? So they would travel with the poor Irish escaping from the potato famine, a paying human cargo for the unscrupulous Captain Wagner. It would be three weeks, they could endure.

'Up here is good.' Jacob put his pack on a top bunk half-way along. 'Here stays cleaner.'

'Aye! That's my place!' A woman's voice snarled out of the darkness from the bunk across. Somehow she had got in before them.

'Pardon, madame, we didn't – '

'Who says it's yours?' Jacob's brusqueness strengthened Ephraim. He looked closer at her: thin, a few pointy teeth gleaming in the dim. She muttered and dropped back into the depths of her lair as Ephraim added his bundle to the bunk he and Jacob had to share. He soon saw that this was no hardship: whole families of five had to share a single bunk. And they were better off than their fellow-passengers in other ways, too, for the food on the voyage was to be only seven pounds per person per week, and only one cooked meal a day. He and Jacob had bought provisions of pickled herrings and hard black bread, but most of the Irish were too poor to bring extra. A phrase in Hebrew from the traveler's prayer came to Ephraim: make us reach our desired destination of life, gladness, and peace. America – I hope you are worth this for all of us.

Out of Liverpool, the rocking had started as soon as the sight of land fell away, and became heaving. Passengers turned green with seasick, and the vomiting began. After five days they grew used to it, even as the Atlantic seas rose higher. A storm hit, and the hatch had to remain closed. Water ran down from the decks, the ship mounted and dropped, leaned and wallowed. No air circulated, the toilet buckets overflowed, made worse by diarrhea. Ephraim lay next to Jacob, gripping the bed frame, going deep into himself, escaping into the rooms of his childhood, visions of his mother, of Sarah, the words of psalms, all the passages of the Tanakh he knew by heart.

At last had come this quieter morning. A grizzled sailor turned the forty steerage passengers out of their quarters and enlisted the younger men to swill out the space with salt water. Up and down the ladder Ephraim went with bucket and mop, into the biting wind and bright light, then back to the stench and dim. Each time he emerged he praised God. His companions hunched on the deck in the cold. Some women washed diapers and sick-stiff clothes and hung them wherever they could on pegs and ropes. The handful of children ran and played, relishing freedom.

He paused for a moment to chafe his reddened, raw hands; the hardest labor they'd ever seen was when he'd dug up worms and chipped at logs to find subjects for nature studies. He ruefully acknowledged Rachel's comment on his unfit state for physical work. Cecilie's white linen and fine crystal felt a paradise long past, and his own home, kept scrupulous by Rachel, a fantasy. As he watched, resting, Ephraim heard the name Reverend Hamilton called on the deck above. Well-dressed passengers gathered around a gaunt, sandy-haired man in a clerical collar. He spoke briefly, the words snatched by wind, then all sang. A few phrases – worship the king, ancient of days – he heard, then a second verse reached his ears loud and clear, 'dark is his path on the wings of the storm.' The words struck and turned him to watch the blue blackness of ocean heave like a breathing beast. He praised the mightiness of the Lord again – and took some pride in his growing understanding of English.

He listened harder, curious to hear them sing to their God in English. All he'd personally experienced of Christianity was resonant liturgical chants of the orthodox church, when Jews and Christians in Brest shared civic ceremonies. He was curious to hear more but a prod from the supervising sailor interrupted his reflections: 'Get on with the cleaning. It'll stir again.'

The sky loured with clouds. The heaviest storm season in these northern waters had begun, and the swells and heaving of their ship on the vastness of the ocean increased. When the gusts hit, down they went to their hell hole still reeking of urine, feces, vomit, rot. Ephraim focused on hope: how long, how long to America, the promised land of opportunity?

They were confined to steerage for a whole series of storms with barely a let-up. Then came the worst of all. It started in the night, lurches in incredible swings so that Ephraim just managed to save himself from pitching out of his bunk. It brought him wide awake amid people's cries of fear. Moments later came another huge swing. He felt the ship must be horizontal to the sea. It then rose up up up, pressing Ephraim into the berth's wood frame, then dropped for centuries, producing sheer animal terror. Again it happened. Again.

'Y'hi ratzon milfanekha Adonai…' Jacob began to recite the traveler's prayer in Hebrew and Ephraim joined him, 'May it be your will, Lord, our God and the God of our ancestors, that you lead us toward peace…' Others were praying to their Father, their Son and their Holy Ghost, and to Mary and Joseph, to Saint Patrick and Saint Christopher. In between they whimpered, all in complete darkness. The ship creaked, banged, thundered. 'Barukh ata Adonai… Blessed are you, Lord,' Ephraim raised his voice louder to out-shout the panic and as he prayed some small remote part of him wanted to clamber out to witness the storm, to see waves like mountain peaks. He thought of Rachel and Sarah, widowed and orphaned, left with only his last letter from Liverpool. They would never come to the freedom of America. He would never send home gold. He would die, his future would die at the age of twenty. His new world would be with these wretched souls, and Uncle Jacob, at the bottom of the sea. No one would survive this.

The hatch burst open to cries of panic. Murky daylight appeared, and hurling water, and a silhouette. They had reached dawn.

'My brothers and sisters, let us pray!' Reverend Hamilton descended the ladder with a lantern, raised his Bible and began. 'Lord deliver us from the powers of the ocean. Lord God Almighty we praise and adore your greatness, we petition you through Jesus Christ your son to lead us through this mightiness and save our souls.'

'Go to hell with your protestant prayers!' screamed Ephraim's neighbor. 'Hail Mary, Mother of God, pray for us sinners, now and at the hour of our death...'

'Hail Mary, Mother of God...' The chorus of others rose.

'Your will be done, oh Lord Jesus Christ,' the preacher resumed his bellow. 'We pray the devil is behind us and we spurn all his ways – ' The ship rose up and keeled to the side, forcing cries of terror.

'The devil is in here with us!' yelled the vixen. 'It's those Jews!' The ship righted itself. Ephraim hoped the preacher would ignore her.

Hamilton advanced toward Ephraim and Jacob, clinging to the bunks as he went, Holy Book and lantern in hand. 'The Lord sends punishment. The devil sends torment. Let us pray together, brothers and sisters,' the preacher drew breath. 'Jesus we beseech you to look upon these two Jews.' A few repeated the words after him. 'And bring them to the light.'

'Even an Orangeman's light,' someone called, and Amens supported him. Creeping horror and sickening curiosity washed through Ephraim: he was being prayed for by Christians.

The preacher reached their bunk and, struggling to maintain his balance, fixed his eyes on Jacob, then Ephraim, who glared back. 'Shalom,' said Ephraim, 'Peace,' with venom in his voice. Hamilton flinched, but kept his eyes on the young Jew.

'Brothers, the Lord God our Father loves us all. Repent your sins and be baptized in the name of Jesus Christ!'

Ephraim answered in Brisker Yiddish, 'Can you pull in leviathan with a fishhook? Don't think converting two Jews will stop the Almighty's storm.'

'He's saying a curse!' a male voice said.

Reverend Hamilton looked at Ephraim and they locked eyes. Even as the ship dropped again and involuntary cries came to their lips he and Ephraim stayed engaged: one's burning determination, the other's fierce defense. Hamilton transferred his gaze to Jacob. 'Be it on your souls, if you go to your deaths without being saved,' he spat out. 'I will pray with the others.' He went along the bunks touching heads or clasping prayerful hands, when the ship shook with a thunderous crack. They felt her swerve and the winds buffet from another direction. The hatch banged open again and the salt rain and spray blew in even as far as Ephraim's face as wails and sobs renewed.

The Christian assault was not over, because when he finally got to the ladder Hamilton stood silhouetted again and raised his Bible, saying, 'Sisters and brothers, may the Lord Jesus Christ bless and save you *all*.' He loaded the last word with meaning, leaving Ephraim as furious as the storm.

Four weeks in, seven days after the scheduled date of their arrival in blessed New York, the mainmast had fractured, they learned. The only solution was to head for the nearest port – in Newfoundland – for repairs. This would at least give the ship a chance to buy food; it had brought only enough for the promised three weeks and already they were on rations and tainted water. Between them Ephraim and Jacob had one loaf of black bread and a smoked fish remaining, and that only thanks to the experience Jacob had gained on his previous voyages. This crossing, he said, was the worst of the worst.

The ship was marooned in dock for a fortnight. Although they were safe from the seas, the weather continued icy cold and foul, and the regulations of Newfoundland trapped steerage passengers on board. Water and the meagerest amount of bread, and dried cod and hard sausage were brought in. Under purser's orders a steerage stew was cooked in one common pot. The sausage was of pork, treif, unclean. Though famished, Ephraim balked. But Jacob persuaded: 'Remember the rabbis' wisdoms. When our Jewish conscripts have to break kashrut in the army, they tell them – put the first bite aside for the Lord. Then eat the rest.' So, revolted but also curious, Ephraim tasted the unclean – fatty, like goose; spiced, like hot peppered herring; meaty, like cow – but none of those. It was pig.

When at last the mended ship departed no one cheered; grim determination was the only emotion, and simmering toleration between the utterly dirty, hungry Catholic steerage emigrants and the weary Protestant cabin passengers and the two Russian Jewish travelers. Nine weeks after leaving Hamburg, the battered ship *Howard* dropped anchor in New York harbor. At the red granite circular fortress called Castle Garden Ephraim Epstein set foot in America on 11 March 1850.

5

NEW YORK, NEW YORK
New York City 1850

How to start in this amazing, thriving, bustling city? With a tour by Uncle Jacob, of course, setting out from their boarding house in the Jewish area. This lower East Side section reminded Ephraim strangely, sharply, of home. Not old Brest-Litovsk, but the new part where the family now lived, with its orderly grid pattern of streets, built when the ancient quarter was razed to make way for the fort. Brisk buildings were mostly wood, except for a few apartment blocks like the Epsteins', but here neat brick tenements were jammed together side-by-side. On Canal (no water in sight, and Ephraim learned not to say Canal Street) as uncle and nephew headed west to Broadway the uniformity broke into a higgledy-piggledy mix of roof-lines, flat or gabled, one story to four. Wood houses squeezed between brick store-fronts, workshops and offices. Narrow and wide, some buildings had porches or entry steps, some were flat to the pavement, many sported awnings. The cacophony of styles was as boisterous as the streets themselves. Uncle Jacob halted at the corner of Canal and Broadway which was indeed broad – but unpaved, just like a rutted country road. The Yiddish, German and Russian of their neighborhood had given way to raw Yankee English, and to horse traffic shouts and rumbles, the hawking and spitting of men, the barking of dogs. Ephraim translated the signs on the buildings: College of Health, Wright's Fancy Dress Goods, Watches and Clocks, Photographic Studio... his spirits rose with the energy of it all: work, America, freedom!

'Up is right, that's north. Left is down, back to the harbor,' instructed Uncle Jacob. He was alert, and at the same time distracted, like a dog sniffing out territory. Over time Ephraim had seen him in modes from tough to fawning, but never quite like this. Amid the carriages and single riders on the avenue, horse-drawn omnibuses off-loaded and took on passengers. He anticipated Ephraim: 'No, we save the penny. I have to see what's new from last time. The richest man in America has been building.'

So up Broadway they walked in the bright late winter chill, Ephraim peering into shop windows and taverns, puzzling out signs, noting the popularity of shaggy mustaches and goatees, negotiating ladies' wide crinolined skirts. The busy-ness continued for ten blocks until they reached a cross avenue: Houston, said Jacob: 'Right is east, left is west. Walk either way and you hit a river.' They kept on straight, but suddenly entered a new world. Broadway widened out to a handsome triangular plaza and an enormous gleaming white temple, or so it seemed. Gracious stone houses and an elaborately spired church lay beyond it. 'There you are. John Jacob Astor's theatre. Nice tchatchke, yes? A little knick-knack.'

'It's wonderful! Beautiful! As fine as any opera house in Europe!' And when the saplings so regularly spaced around it grew into stately trees, even finer, Ephraim thought. The whole effect was splendid, but raw and new. 'He can even afford paving, but it's not gold,' Ephraim teased his uncle.

'No – land is gold here. He bought it up piece by piece. Wait til you see his hotel.' Uncle Jacob started walking west again along elegant townhouses til suddenly they emerged into a large, pleasant square. 'Nice one!' Jacob approved. 'Last time I was here it was a parade ground, Yankee soldiers marching up and down.' He pulled a face. 'Much better, this.' Iron railings provided a central sanctuary of lawns and pathways for ladies and gentlemen, nursemaids pushing perambulators, children rolling hoops. Ephraim could see mansion blocks stretching away in one direction, but Uncle Jacob said, 'Do that on your own, Fifth Avenue, where the rich people live. Today, from Washington Square we go south again – to City Hall.' And so they did, away from the peace of the residential area to the jostle of Broadway again. Smells assaulted Ephraim now, whiffs of cigar smoke, horse dung, roasting chestnuts on charcoal braziers, sour beer. When trees came into sight the street atmosphere began to change, and New York transformed again. In a handsome park a water jet shot high in the center of a round pond. Beyond the bare branches of mature trees rose a massive, creamy stone edifice complete with pillars, pediments, and a tower. The red stripes and blue field of the American flag rose and fell in the March breeze.

'What a place! What a country!' Charged with excitement, Ephraim resisted his uncle's urge to move on, intoxicated by the sense of freedom, of possibility. Jacob led him to a bench where they sat in silence, watching people. The rumble of traffic mixed with the rush of the fountain and the aura of business everyone seemed to carry.

'So, now. You've got the lay of the land,' said Uncle Jacob. 'From here it goes straight down to Bowling Green – nice houses, fancy people – after that, Castle Garden – you'll recognize it! Think you know the way home from there?'

Ephraim thought back to their walk just yesterday from the immigration depot to their boarding house: narrow criss-crossed streets, some important-looking buildings, some ordinary houses, crowds, confusion and his wobbly sea-legs. He began to shake his head, it was all too new.

'See that over there?' His uncle pointed to a grand, pale stone five-story house that took up a whole city block. 'That's his house, Mr Astor – but now, a hotel! Smart man. Nothing but the best. There's gas-light in every room, bathrooms on every floor! Some day, for you and me, hey!' Ephraim and Jacob shared a rueful smile. Last night they had washed away the filth and lice of their voyage in a rough Turkish steam bath, and their boarding house room was the size of a cupboard. 'So, you're on your own now. I'll see you later.'

'What!' Ephraim looked around, alarmed.

'Think about it,' said Uncle Jacob gently. Ephraim looked where he gestured: Broadway. Of course. If he followed Broadway down to the harbor he could then follow it straight back up to Canal, turn right and get to their street – easy! Jacob watched Ephraim working it out and prompted, 'You can always get your bearings from St Paul's steeple here, and the new one down further, see? Trinity Church.'

'Yes, I can do it – Lord willing!' The suddenly empty place in Ephraim filled once more with hope and determination. 'But where are you going?'

'Business – I'm here for business! And you are here to make a new life. Tomorrow we find you work.'

Ephraim's brain was his strength, and so was his faith. Uncle Jacob agreed, but his tune had changed: 'Scholars are a dime a dozen, lots of good boys like you here.' He bewailed his connections in these spheres, then said, 'However, we can try,' returning to his optimistic self at Ephraim's crestfallen expression. They started at the Brisker schtiebl, the little prayer house where Jacob took Ephraim in any case to give thanks for their safe arrival, and to arrange for mikvah, the ritual bath to purify themselves after the long, unclean journey. Regarding work, however, the rabbi and elders of B'nai Avraham had no help to offer but prayers.

So together Ephraim and Jacob knocked on the doors of three synagogues. Next day, when his uncle went off to do more business, Ephraim found another three congregations with yeshivas, the schools of the Torah and Talmud. In this new world Judaism came in dozens of flavors: German and Polish, Ukranian and Romanian, English, Dutch, even Greek. Not only old country languages but favorite rabbis and variations in the minhag and mitzvot – rites and rules – splintered followers. The range intrigued and stimulated Ephraim – at home in Brisk there were four different congregations, and his father's domination, but here, now – he felt his mind and soul expanding. Once he was settled, so many choices! Orthodoxies as conservative, and more, as his household he would avoid; he would find a liberal Judasim, though he would not, he thought, go as far into reform as Lipman pushed Cecilie. But there was a price for all this variety: instead of a single elaborate synagogue like the one being re-built by the community in Brest-Litovsk, New York's split Hebrews gathered mainly in make-do buildings or upstairs rooms. Except for one, Anche Chesed, a fantastical new red brick Gothic style synagogue on Norfolk Street. Ephraim goggled: fifteen hundred worshippers could fit inside! But its German congregation, like the rest, only gave teaching jobs to its own. It was hard, hard to be humble and beseeching, hard to be rejected. Against his father Ephraim could rail and argue, with friends he could debate and challenge, with Mama he used persuasion, against Rachel he could freeze or simmer – but how to fight this?

His rubles had converted to forty-five dollars, and New York was costing him three dollars a day; he needed work fast. Clearly it would not be teaching, and his uncle could offer no hope in the New York gem trade where jobs went strictly to sons. In a stroke of inspiration Jacob persuaded a colleague in peddling to hire Ephraim – 'He's smart, he's good looking! And charm? Look at him, he can charm the birds out of the trees... the cash out of the ladies' purses.' Marcus Goldman dubiously gave the brilliant nephew a chance to sell lace, shoe strings, needles, stove polish and sundries from a barrow. He sent Ephraim to Broadway a mile from the lower East Side where, said Goldman, our own people don't spend enough money. What crazy English these Yankees spoke! Ephraim's book-learning of a psalm, his careful please and thank you and good morning were little use. His potential customers had strong accents, with words in twangs and flat vowels, phrases that forced him back to saying 'Bitte?' or 'Je ne comprends pas.' When Mr Goldman came by he watched, he checked the undepleted stock on the tray, he shook his head – 'You need better English. Talk faster! And you need to be more American, hustle them, sell, sell!' The day ended with an invitation to try again in a few months, with better English. Ephraim knew he said this only as a favor to Jacob. Yes, of course, his English had to improve, it would improve, he worked on it daily, but he needed to earn now.

The next day Ephraim invested three cents in the *Herald*, devoured the help wanted columns and raced off to Mulberry Street, then on to Pearl, then Broadway. Two were a shipping agents, one a clothing manufacturer – each needed a young man of intelligence who could wield a pen in a back office. But each time there were a dozen other hopefuls with better English or with experience. By day's end he had a new outlook on the new world: opportunities, yes, and opportunities to fail, too. He dragged his failure to prayer at B'nai Avraham. It was above a dry goods store, up narrow stairs, a dim little room with battered furniture. The shabby place was, at least, a refuge. The cantor was from Brest, the rabbi from Kobrin so the Brisker accents gave the comfort of familiarity, even if the conservatism of discussions reminded Ephraim too much of his father's way of thinking – the men even wore peyes, the earlocks now forbidden in Brest. Strange to think that the famous freedom of America made space for a retreat to backwards, unenlightened ways.

The sixth day in New York was Ephraim's twenty-first birthday and of course they went to Shacharit, morning prayers. Davening near Jacob, Ephraim gave over to the concentration of prayer and rocking as he began to chant the essence of his faith. 'Shema Yisrael Adonai Eloheinu Adonai echad... Hear, O Israel: the Lord our God, the Lord is one.' On the bone-deep service went through the nineteen blessings of the Amidah, the Torah reading, the Aleinu, the Kaddish of the mourners.

Emerging from the depths of thanks, praise and beseeching Ephraim and Jacob withdrew to a bench in a corner of the little beth midrash, the room for Torah study. Despondent, he could not help flashes of that fateful birthday eve four years ago breaking through. If Zayde had not insisted, and Mama and Papa too, if he hadn't married Rachel... Would he be here struggling for a new life of freedom? Should this be cause for rejoicing – or regret?

Jacob reached out and adjusted Ephraim's yarmulke, a tender gesture. 'Mazel t'ov – twenty-one years old! What – what's this in your hair?' He snatched his hand away.

'What!' Ephraim clapped hand to head, panicked.

'Praise be, incredible!' Two glittering gems, each the size of a young green pea, lay in Jacob's outstretched palm. 'I knew you had brains, but to get these out of your ear!'

Ephraim looked up from the sparkle of the stones, wary. 'Uncle Jacob, what is this?'

His uncle's face crinkled into a smile. 'For your Rachel. A good-bye present from me to you. And birthday. Here, hold them up to the light.' Ephraim did, and in their facets saw a flicker of the light of Rachel's eyes, the creamy skin of her neck and earlobes. But – why? Good-bye? Jacob now dangled a small black velvet pouch before Ephraim who automatically dropped the diamonds into it. His uncle pulled the yellow drawstring tight, pressed the bag into Ephraim's palm and closed his fingers over it. 'I leave for California tomorrow. I made good trades: Bombay sapphires, Columbian emeralds, Amsterdam diamonds. So these are for you. For your wife. Or...' he shrugged, 'or sell to one of my friends for your ticket back to Belarus, if it comes to that.' He laughed, 'Don't look so confused!'

At the corner of Delancey and Allen Ephraim hesitated before picking through the mud, hoping for a way to cross without further dirtying his boots. Appearances mattered. Not that his clothes had made a difference yet. Today's lead to work copying ledgers had gone to nothing, or rather it had gone to the boss's cousin just landed from Minsk.

Less meticulous pedestrians charged into the flow of buggies and wagons without thought. Another whole week of searching had passed. How could it be, among all this teeming city, that no work existed for him? He gave up the idea of keeping clean boots, and just as he made the plunge he heard a call: 'Ephraim? Ephraim!'

He raised his eyes to see the waving arms of – could it be? Benjamin? Benjamin Berman? Dodging a harness of horses pulling a coal wagon, Ephraim crossed and leaped into the hug of a young man his own age. Benjamin, once his khaver, his best buddy, once inches shorter, now a lanky beanpole, but unmistakably Benjamin, with his springy hair, jutting jaw and bright narrow eyes.

'All these years, all these years – and here you are!' Ephraim's heart surged. Uncle Jacob had been a good companion, but more than twice his age. In the boarding house, in the congregation, any young men Ephraim met were busy or exhausted from working, and many were not his caliber of education and background. Except for his thoughts and prayers and landlady he was alone in the world. But now: a friend! A friend from home.

Over the samovar in the room he shared, Ephraim and Benjamin exchanged stories of their gap of eight years, and of their venturing since arriving in America. Benjamin, here for more than a year, had succeeded where Ephraim was failing. When his family had left Brisk for France his parents had seen that he acquired a practical skill, and a portable one, as a crafter of wind instruments. Benjamin had completed his apprenticeship in the famous Muller workshop, with its links to the Paris Conservatoire. When he fled the 1848 French disturbances, music made connections and he had arrived in New York with a position waiting at a manufacturer of instruments. 'People want music all over the world. There's nothing like the voice of the clarinet.' Benjamin smiled and sipped his tea, and pretended not to be appalled by his friend's surroundings – beyond the curtain that made the corner private a woman muttered as she swept the floor; Ephraim had moved down here to save money. 'And what is your plan, your idea for America, when... when....'

'When my English is good enough.' Ephraim tried to turn his bitterness into a joke. 'Rich man, poor man, beggar-man, thief... Uncle Jacob told me the rhyme. That was back at home when he said you could be anything in America. I was thinking, a lawyer, after all I'm good at arguing the Mishnah. But that's very tied to the laws of one place or another. Business, trading... maybe, but maybe not my talent as proved by Mr Goldman! A professor, maybe – of Hebrew perhaps, or German. Or doctor...'

'People will always get sick. Doctor Epstein will make them better!'

'Then I can go back –'

'If you go back.'

'If I go back,' Ephraim nodded. He had shared his frustrations over his father's orthodox insistence, reveled with Benjamin at the freedom here for Jews and every faith. You could see all sorts of people succeeding at all sorts of occupations. There was the lack of soldiers and petty authorities, too – how many times, in Brest, under the Czar, anywhere in Europe, had they had to show documents, get permission to travel, pay for official stamps, negotiate bureaucracy. Depressing as his situation was, the idea of going back to that atmosphere of restriction had begun to feel unreal. 'But I need English, strong English. And I need money to apprentice myself to a doctor – a good doctor. So my plan, ha!'

Benjamin slapped his hands to his thighs, dispelling gloom. 'Something will work out!'

'Might you know of... anything for me?' Ephraim stared into his tea-glass. Asking, asking, he was getting hardened, but still, it pained. 'I could do accounts, maybe. Or transcribe, or translate... I could even sing!' he brightened and looked at Benjamin. His boyhood friend had been present at Ephraim's recital in Brest in honor of Crown Prince Alexander's marriage, Ephraim chosen for the purity of his voice.

'Your voice has broken since you were twelve, old man! Are you a tenor or what?' He paused, considering. 'Do you read music?' Benjamin had described his New York life. Unencumbered, earning decent money, he had frequent access to concerts and chamber performances. Indeed he played occasionally at private gatherings for a few cultured, wealthy patrons. And he enjoyed the camaraderie of the mixed world of musicians. But Ephraim could not read music to a professional standard, and besides there were plenty of singers looking for work. 'I can try, but most likely you'd be singing for no pay.'

'For the sheer joy of it,' said Ephraim morosely.

6

AMAREKA
New York City 1850

Down to his last nineteen dollars, the seeking continued. After a morning's effort Ephraim would hole up in a coffee house and study the *Herald* to improve his language and to learn this country. There were German and Hebrew papers too, borrowed from the boarding house. Twice he went back to Castle Garden. Outside the immigration depot agents touted job introductions for two dollars, but inside, the intelligence department kept a register of situations at no fee. How confidently he and Uncle Jacob had spurned the officials' offers of help on arrival. Now Ephraim studied their lists for possibilities, and even followed some up – but he couldn't be a tailor, couldn't butcher meat, craft a chair, cooper a barrel, drive a team of horses, and jobs like waiting tables required good English – and experience.

Day jobs were listed too, and he was lucky to earn a dollar trundling bales of cloth from a dock to a cart. He earned blisters, too, like he had on the ship. But next day the foreman refused to recognize him. Sagging, he had gone back to the public garden and leaned against a tree to watch the small boats arriving at the pier laden with their hopeful passengers from the big ships in the harbor – mainly they were Irish. In his third week now he could detect Irish from Scots, English from Yankee English. He listened to snatches of German, Polish, Russian. Though depressed he spoke to some of the Russian Jews, giving directions to his neighborhood where they would find kosher food and places to worship, and maybe relations waiting for them with a job.

Ephraim longed to talk to Mama – how her strength, her faith and gentleness had bolstered him all the years of his life. The lock of her hair nestled deep in his waistcoat pocket where now the diamonds hid. Home. The sweet aspect of the bittersweet times with Rachel called to him. And Sarah. Purim had come and gone, the festival of Esther with its playacting, pot-banging and excited children running about. Ephraim thought of Herr Lipman at his fine table declaring, 'a clever man who works hard can make money anywhere.' Suddenly Ephraim wanted to lash out at Uncle Jacob – of course America's streets weren't made of gold, but there was no way to make money! It was all the old fool's fault, making him believe in America. There was a phrase he'd heard the elders at shul use when bewailing the values of this land of too much freedom: AmaReka... sounding like America, but in Hebrew it meant hollow people – the so-called good life, all hard work and no respect for the old ways. Hollow indeed – if I get hard work I will thank the Lord, Ephraim vowed. He started a second letter to follow the one that announced his safe arrival after the nightmare voyage. They must believe! He set out telling some of the astonishment that was America. But after three lines he faltered, more depressed than ever. He tore off the strip of paper and crumpled it, carefully saving the rest of the sheet.

Another day of defeat, another Sabbath approached. At least he had Benjamin, who two nights ago had treated him to the vaudeville, up on Broadway. The theater had plush curtains, gas-lit chandeliers and gilded woodwork, but the floor was littered with peanut shells. They'd sat at the back in cheap seats, surrounded by raucous men – women, too – who laughed, cheered, catcalled, sang along with favorite numbers. Ephraim gleefully joined in singing *Yankee Doodle Dandy*, proud to know the words, relishing Benjamin's surprise. Loud, rude and full of life, the show and the audience were so good natured that they caught Ephraim up in the mood. He was getting to own this place, making it his. And he was listening, learning all the time, watching the rough and ready American manners, the brash confidence, the informality, making conversation to practice his English.

But what use? The awfulness of his situation bore down – Ephraim knew the time had come when he should inquire about passage home. Eating just once a day, walking everywhere, he had enough money for three or four days and then – he could borrow a little from Benjamin, who had not much to spare, but soon... the diamonds, his insurance. To sell one, or both? To sell and go home, to sell and stay on – he couldn't bear the thought of either. He imagined sharing his discoveries and woes with his friends and brothers-in-law, the welcome from Mama, holding Sarah. And then he imagined his father. Rachel. Never. Never would he slink home defeated.

Restless, he went from prayer to a long walk for the mindlessness he needed. He strode along Grand to the edge of the East River where ferries, schooners, and small steamers criss-crossed about their business. He gazed over to the heights and church towers of Brooklyn, made out the docks and settlements of Long Island. What hope, what hope, what hope for him? He turned north and followed the river, only stopping when a sturdy railing blocked his way. The land swept left. This must be Kip's Bay – because there was a huge and sturdy granite building four stories high, wings stretching either side of the center. So this was Bellevue hospital. Any sea voyager found sickly on arrival in New York was sent here to recover, or to die. Uncle Jacob had told him of its fearsome reputation: prisoners, lunatics, filth, mortality. Its surrounding farmland was supposed to provide food for patients as well as isolation – along with the location on the river – to keep typhus, cholera, yellow fever, smallpox and Lord knew what from the rest of the city. But ten years ago outrage had triggered reform. Ephraim gathered from the newspapers that Bellevue was now a model of modernity, run by the most distinguished physicians and surgeons in New York. Doctor, lawyer, Indian chief, the children's rhyme taunted Ephraim: could he ever get an introduction to a good doctor? The conclusion had been growing in Ephraim: people more than want medicine, they need it. And he had another, deeper reason for setting his dreams on healing. But the obstacles... standing at the railing a heartfelt prayer swept through him from the daily Kaddish, Yehe shlama... hayyim tovim... May there be abundant peace and good life.

As he headed back to familiar territory Ephraim stopped once more, this time at a building under construction, his way blocked by some workmen sluicing trowels in a trough, finishing up their day. Two stories were built, and it would grow to four, like the narrow handsome house adjacent. He came closer to appreciate the design and workmanship – good red brick, molded lintels, the Federal style – which really was classical Roman style, amended, adopted and Americanized.

'Whaddarya, pavement superintendent?' A red-faced burly man in a top hat called from the empty doorway.

'Just... admiring. The brickwork.'

The gentleman, if that's what he was – Ephraim as yet found it hard to distinguish between classes of Americans – picked his way down the few steps and around the bricks piled ready for the next day's work. He positioned himself next to Ephraim so together they assessed the building. 'Yep. Pretty good – betcha ain't got anything like this back in the old country.'

'The design, not quite.' Ephraim chose words carefully, not only because of his hesitant English, but so as not to offend the man. Americans, he had observed, believed that their country, their ways were superior to anything anywhere. 'But the bricks. My father had a brick factory.'

'No kidding! Where's that?' The manager or developer, which he must be, Ephraim guessed, because of his proprietorial air and the way the departing workmen had tugged their caps at him, turned to the young man with interest.

'Russia. The fort at Brest, you know it? More big than Castle Garden fort, every brick stamped with our initial.'

'Ruski, eh. Fresh off the boat?' He talked over Ephraim's murmured reply. 'Lookin' for work?' This time Ephraim spoke his reply loud and clear. 'And you know about bricks. Don't exactly look the type to me.'

'I will do anything. My English is not too good yet. But I have German, French, Russian…'

The man put down the brick he'd picked up, dusted off his hands and extracted a watch on a gold chain from his waistcoat. 'Tell the truth, I'm fed up with these Irish. Friend of mine has a brickworks, just lost some men.' He clicked the cover closed after checking the time. 'You look like a good fella to me. Go round and see him tomorrow.'

Ephraim floated home. Work, a job, at last! Twilight softened the city, merchants had rolled back their awnings, street vendors trundled away. Workers streamed homeward, ladies and gentlemen dawdled enjoying the mildness of the evening, for spring seemed to have arrived. Next morning, following the directions he'd been given, he chose to walk straight up Fifth Avenue, past new mansions and churches, past building sites until a board fence blocked him. Beyond it, copses, hills, clusters of shacks, smoke rising from wood fires, and the smell and bleats of goats, chickens, geese, pigs. The really really poor squatted in this shanty town. But this was not a day to dwell on penury. Toward the Hudson along 23rd he went, then upriver until the huge enclosed yard and the sign over a gate declared – Brown & Sons Brickmakers.

Ephraim entered in hope with Mr Robinson's business card, practically giggling to himself when he thought how outraged his father would be if he knew his scholar son was working in the offices of a brick factory. And he left at the end of the day with his tail between his legs. Bloodied hands, an aching back, his good suit ruined and two dollars he'd gained, but no job. Mr Brown did not want a desk-worker, his sons did that. He wanted brickmakers. He need men who could haul water, coal and sand, stoke kiln fires, knead raw clay with hands and feet, shift lumps to the brickmolder, off-bear the molds, re-sand and return them to the team chief. A man who knew the procedure, how to pile green bricks onto palettes, sound them for readiness, assemble them into a kiln. Ephraim's heart sank as he listened to the overworked Mr Brown's diatribe – he knew nothing about actually making bricks. He'd been to the factory as a boy two or three times, looked at his father's workers, asked a few questions and turned his mind off. His destiny from birth was never, ever to soil his hands with physical labor. He pleaded with Mr Brown, swore he'd learn the craft, and gained a day's trial. At the end he was dismissed: 'You're willing but not able. Can't teach you in our time – too busy.'

But he did come away with one profitable realization: he could use his body to earn a living – if he learned a skill. Beyond scrubbing decks, hauling bales, selling wares, there was the sheer miracle, a kind of pride, at delving, sweating and straining to make something – bricks – out of nothing: the Lord God's given earth, water, sand, heat. Something else, too. Falling in with the men making bricks he felt the cooperation between them, rough as they were, and appreciated their brute expertise.

That same night Ephraim had been due to meet Benjamin at Waverly Place where he was playing in a Mendelssohn concert piece at the home of a well-off client of the wind instrument factory. He was a Sephardic Jew, head of one of the most distinguished old New York Jewish families, among those here when America was a colony, supplying General Washington when this country was born. Perhaps Ephraim might get a chance to sing... no money would come of it, but he was willing, curious to see how wealthy New Yorkers lived. Besides, any kind of enjoyment would be welcome, including hearing good music and seeing his friend perform. But now, aching, filthy and completely disheartened, he would not go. He limped back to the boarding house and the sight of him was all the persuading it took to get Mrs Mandel, the landlady, to heat water and set up the tin tub in the kitchen. This was only his second full bath in three weeks, and as Ephraim lay back after scrubbing he gave way to complete despair. What could he do? Uncle Jacob had promised to say where he was, but it was too soon. The diamonds, his last resort – he found he had entirely ceased thinking of them as Rachel's. He could sell or pawn them and follow Jacob. Take the voyage around South America to San Francisco – even farther from home but guaranteed to have lots of opportunities – maybe even finding gold. That reminded Ephraim of the day just spent with clay and sand... grubbing in the earth. It was not that he was afraid of the work, just that he didn't know how to do it. There was no point to anything. And the idea of being a doctor... the idea that he would send money home... the idea of his father and of Rachel, gloating in vindication – should he laugh or cry?

Ephraim ate Mrs Mandel's watery cabbage soup, grateful that she had taken pity and put in a second morsel of corned beef and bonus half potato. And then he went to bed, falling into a hard sleep even though his neighbors on the other side of the curtain were playing checkers and bickering.

Benjamin's voice and urgent touch jolted Ephraim awake. In tails and an exquisitely starched shirt, bright eyes shining, he sat on the bed talking all the while. 'Why weren't you there! Are you sick? You missed a great chance!'

'Sorry, sorry. I just... couldn't.' Ephraim pulled himself up, wincing at his muscles. 'Was it good?'

'Not that! I mean, yes, it was good. But listen: Lilienthal was there!'

Ephraim rubbed his face and cleared his brain. Lilienthal. 'Dr Lilienthal, the reformer? From Russia?'

'Russia, Germany, I don't know. But he was there. He is here in New York. Now he would have connections for you, wouldn't he?' Benjamin's enthusiasm still hadn't fully woken Ephraim, but the roommates groaned for quiet. 'He knew your father, right? He's for the enlightenment, right? So here you are, enlightening yourself in the new world – he's bound to help you!'

He was a little man with well-kept wavy white hair and pince-nez glasses. He looked all the slighter for sitting behind a huge mahogany twin pedestal desk. A stiff-collared secretary, sheaf of papers in hand, stood to one side and neat stacks of papers covered the desk. Ephraim advanced over the deep Turkey rug toward Dr Max Lilienthal and waited to be noticed. Leather-bound books filled shelves around the room, and a sofa and armchairs gathered convivially by the marble fireplace. The great reformer's host was obviously a man of learning and taste. Ephraim hungered to browse the spines, pick out a book and sit down to read, read, read.

'From Brest-Litovsk, you say.' Lilienthal barked. 'Son of Reb Yudl Epstein.'

'Yes, sir. He met with you in 1842.'

'I know. I remember. Sit down, Herr Epstein.' They spoke in German, Lilienthal's native language. Ephraim chose the leather brass-studded chair to the left, away from the hovering secretary. 'And then your father went the other way, so I hear. Back to a closed mind.' Lilienthal removed his spectacles and massaged the bridge of his nose. He flapped a hand at the secretary who removed himself to yet more papers at the other side of the room.

'Yes, he did,' said Ephraim, 'but my brothers-in-law, Samuel Feigish and David Ginzburg, they continued to study. We had to sneak. And the others –'

'Ah! Samuel! Bright boy. And so, why are you here?'

'I need work. I have Greek and Latin, besides German and Russian and French. I did natural sciences too. And some literature, German and classics. My English is progressing now that I am here. At home my teacher's teacher was Rabbi Yisrael Salanter. Ramchal says...'

Lilienthal gave that dismissive hand gesture again. 'But why are you here – in America.'

'Because of my father. I want to learn. And because of Russia. I want to learn and be something besides what a Jew is allowed, and what my father will allow. I cannot do it there.' Ephraim stumbled in his plea. He had prepared his speech but had not expected to have to explain the reasons for coming to America to the champion of enlightenment. Lilienthal stared intently at him, waiting impatiently for some answer to a riddle that Ephraim couldn't guess. He had to fill the silence. 'I cannot do it here either, until I earn money. Or, or… or someone helps me.'

'You are short of money.'

'I cannot get work. I have tried everything. Even manual labor.' He said this proudly, knowing Lilienthal would approve. As reformer of the Jewish faith, he did not hold with the denigration of physical work for educated Jews – that thinking belonged to other eras, not the new age of the nineteenth century.

'Huh. You should have stayed in Belarus.' Ephraim started back in shock. 'To help the reform,' Lilienthal continued.

'I want to help it here!'

'I have no extra money. And plenty of scholars.' Lilienthal signaled the secretary. 'And no use for young puppies. You came to America to make your own way. Make it yourself.'

7

THE COUNTRY BEYOND
New Jersey 1850

Ephraim reached for the warmth and heft of live flesh, soft, full, ready. He gave himself over to it, kneading round the teat until the milk-source's stiffness begged for release. She shifted her bodyweight, he heard her breathing, she gave a low moan. He pressed his forehead against her flank and stripped his fingers down the length of the first teat to hear the stream of milk hit the bottom of the oak bucket. His hands were strong now, and hardened with calluses. If Papa, Mama, Zayde could see me... he thought of the yellow house of his childhood, felt again a fool to remember how he took milking for granted, believing any peasant or dairymaid could do it. Eyes closed, lost in the rhythm, he could see the daily pail brimmed full of milk and cream, the tub of churned butter, mounds of cheese, the family at the table of the Sabbath meal.

The cow shifted and snorted. He moved to the next teat, its obscene length long since familiar, the milk now squirting with a rewarding squitch into the depth already gained. It had been a battle but he'd won. His mind went back to April: Farmer Ackerman, looking him over in the Hackensack labor bureau: 'Never plowed? Think you can milk? You can, you say.'

'Ein wenig.' A little. Ephraim hedged, detecting the farmer's German accent. 'And I learn fast and work hard,' he continued in German. 'You are from Hamburg, I think?'

'Ja.' Ackerman's watery blue eyes sized up Ephraim. 'But now, I am American,' he said in accented English. 'And I need a farmhand with experience.' He moved to the next man, in his late twenties, vigorous looking. Ackerman asked him about milking, plowing, sowing seed. Spring wheat had to be sown, maize and barley, vegetables planted. Ackerman moved on. More New Jersey farmers worked along the row of ten hands for hire, asking a few questions. Ephraim was third in the row, and picked up the gist of their needs, same as the bureau man who'd quizzed him, same as Ackerman asked. With a shrug and a sigh the barrel-shaped agent had allowed Ephraim to join the line of work-seekers, one only a boy of fifteen, the others older than Ephraim. The farmers clustered on the other side of the bare room, fitful sun lighting their corner. They kept glancing over to the farm hands. Ephraim looked at the posted advertisements on the wall, making out the English, mentally speaking it: Maid of all work situation available – must be able to sew fine seams. Notices sought mill-hand, tanner, stable boys, shop clerks – he'd tried for a day, but it was the same as New York. Another poster headlined Spring Hiring Fair, farm hands wanted – this event, his realistic goal, today. Ephraim had learned from the men at the brickworks that New Jersey farmers at this time of year weren't too choosy. They'd mentioned Hoboken, so the very day of Lilienthal's rebuff, over Benjamin's protests, he'd taken the ferry to New Jersey, found a boarding house, and grimly started anew. He was acting on his other lesson at the brickworks: he could dirty his hands in soil – it was honest, and as close to the Lord as any other work, despite what minhag said. And by the Lord he would dirty his hands with good reason: this is my new land, my country, I will learn it with my body.

One by one the farmers spoke to the agent, bargaining back and forth in bursts of controlled passion like the scholarly disputes of the Mishnah in shul. The agent spat his tobacco juice onto the floor and walked over to the waiting workers. 'You, twenty dollars a month, with him,' he pointed a sturdy man to a tall farmer across the room. 'You two, eighteen a month,' to the next seekers. On he went, picking from the row until Ephraim's heart dropped; only he and the youngster remained, and one farmer in the corner. The agent glanced back at Ackerman, then addressed the boy, 'Squire Ackerman's offering ten.'

Before the boy could answer Ephraim spoke, 'Nine. I will take nine dollars a month.'

Anywhere, anything, to get a start. Barukh ata Adonai… shehecheyanu… Blessed are You, Lord… who has kept us alive, sustained us, and enabled us to reach this season. The prayer of Shehecheyanu was meant for thanks on special occasions, and that first job had called it forth. Ephraim used it often as the seasons and the miracle of nature moved through spring, summer, into autumn. It was a battle and he'd won. But it was not enough. Just as Ephraim came to this conclusion he found he was out of work again – Squire Ackerman declared he could not keep a farmhand over the winter. Ephraim resumed his search for a new life in America.

'Good day, Mr Epstein.' The blind judge extended his hand in Ephraim's direction. The older man placed his left hand over Ephraim's. Six months of labor he is feeling, thought Ephraim, horny skin, scars of a hundred minor injuries – from plow, thistles, wire, splintered posts, horse bits, corn stalks, hammer and nails – the hundred ways for toughening a scholar into a farmer.

The physical assessment seemed acceptable, for Judge Sherman invited Ephraim to sit, and feeling behind him, guided by a light touch from his wife, he took his own chair by the hearth. This was a finer house than any Ephraim had yet seen in America, except for the rich man's library in New York and the gilded hotel lobbies he'd peeked into, and the red plush of the vaudeville theater. In any case this was a home, its chestnut floorboards close-laid and gleaming. Turkey carpet softened their steps, white paint picked out the doorways and windows. It was a real home and he almost wept from the feeling of welcome.

'You have a letter of reference?'

'Sir, I do.' Ephraim handed the folded paper to Mrs Sherman. He was ashamed of it. Not the words, but the way it was written.

She read out: *Ephraim Epstein is a hard worker and he larned fast. I larned him good and he followed. Your obedient servant, Johann Ackerman, Esquire, Ackerman Farm, Hoboken County, October 1850.*

'Tell me about Squire Ackerman's farm and your work,' said the judge, cocking an ear now in Ephraim's direction. So he did: a full season of plowing, harrowing, planting, reaping, mending, of milking, calving, going to market, slaughtering, butchering, salting. 'And what was the thing that gave you most triumph in learning? A strange thing to ask you may think, but questions like this help me to know a man's character. Without my sight I and my wife and daughters could be at the mercy of anyone.'

What should he say? Filling the milk bucket for the first time? Seeing the green-sprouting barley in the rows he'd at last got straight? 'Sir, I think – learning English.'

A laugh lit the judge's face. 'Not from Squire Ackerman, I'd guess.'

'No, sir. By myself, from the books and the newspapers, and from talk to others when possible, in the town.'

'What country did you come from, and what brought you here?'

'Belarus. I came to make a better life than I could there.'

'So Mr Epstein, you are a Jew? Do you speak Hebrew?'

'I am, and I do. Hebrew, Latin, some Greek, French, German. Russian, of course. And Polish.'

'A scholar! Your English is already impressive. Tell me, is the life better here?'

How to explain the contrast – home, family, knowing his place in the world versus the struggle to find his own way in complete freedom. 'It is honest and it is free. Free of persecution by government. Free to get work and to read and learn.' Ephraim paused. Had he said too much, not enough? 'Life is not easy but it is better.'

'This farmstead needs a strong manager with good sense. Tell me what you made of the farm as you came in. I have not been able to see it these last five years, only to hear what others say.'

Ephraim hesitated. Here was a man in his sixties, clearly knowledgeable about farming; he feared sounding foolish. 'Prosperous, sir. The low-lying fields a little sog-ridden maybe. Woods encroaching on the hill pasture. More livestock could be supported. I read the agricultural journals. Also, the fencing must take a good deal of attention.'

'Mmmmm. And you'd be content to bring your farm-larning to us and improve your English here?'

'Very much, sir! I still have much to learn.'

'You seem a suitable and upstanding young man, Mr Epstein. I am willing to hire you at twenty-five dollars a month, as well as your board, from next week. I am mindful of your wish for betterment on all sides. You are also a learned man. Perhaps, Mrs Sherman, Mr Epstein might sit with us one evening a week for the sake of his English?'

As the judge's wife agreed Ephraim did too, with enthusiasm. Triple the pay! A chance to save something, to send money to Rachel – and such fine, intelligent people. He rose to seize the judge's right hand to shake it.

'One more thing, dear boy, if I may... may I see your face?'

Ephraim looked to Mrs Sherman, unsure, and she explained. 'He wants to see your face with his fingers, Mr Epstein. It helps him to know a person's character.'

Ephraim agreed and knelt by the judge's chair. The white haired man with the clouded blue eyes reached with both hands towards Ephraim's face. First one, then the second hand touched his forehead, smoothed the eyebrows, circled the eye sockets. Ephraim felt the fingers mold his cheekbones, his nose, sweep over his lips, lightly stroke his mustache and chin whiskers, grown American style.

'Your hair is dark?'

'Yes.'

'And blue-gray eyes, Judge,' said Mrs Sherman.

The judge lifted his hands and rested them on Ephraim's head for a moment. The weight of his worries melted and Ephraim felt, for the first time in America, acceptance.

8

I WILL PUT EPHRAIM TO THE YOKE
New Jersey 1851

It was spring, and Ephraim's English had progressed by leaps and bounds. His English, and his confidence. His heart gladdened to see wheat greening the fields he himself had plowed behind the judge's two horses. Plowed and sown, a little raggedly to be sure, because Ackerman had never let Ephraim sow, saying he would be like the Lord's parable in Matthew, letting seeds fall by the way side and stony places. Ackerman had added that being a Jew, Ephraim probably didn't know what he meant. Your Lord is not my Lord, Ephraim refrained from saying, and I don't care about your parable and Matthew, but I understand your meaning. He'd let it pass, and similar comments too. He needed the work, and besides he was not sure if the German farmer was deliberately offensive, or just stupid. But now Judge Sherman's field was growing, for Ackerman's old nag had at least been good training for the ease of managing the judge's two good workhorses. The corn was planted in its mounds, the turnip for winter feed set in rows. Today he had put in potatoes, their eyes white and hopeful, now snug in the loose brown soil. The judge was blind but he knew his acreage and knew the sandy loam of his north-most field was the one for potatoes.

Ephraim finished scrubbing his hands and slicked water over his hair. The dinner bell clanged from the back porch and he and Amos, the cowherd, fell in together, remarking on the mild evening, the hopes of weather to come.

Yes, it was good, this life he was making. Ephraim was coming to know American ways, and the range of Yankee society. He thought of that boy sometimes, the one he'd beat to the job, and hoped he'd done well elsewhere. Squire Ackerman had been a lowly, ill-educated miserly start, but, Barukh ata Adonai, Blessed are you, oh Lord, a start. Amos the cowherd by contrast was a simple soul but kindly, and though he was not strong in intellect, he was wise and skilled with creatures. Judge Sherman and his wife and two daughters were a different cut altogether: educated, bright, curious. They put Ephraim in mind of his own home and indeed, very soon after his arrival, they had invited him into the bosom of their family.

After Amos returned to his quarters Ephraim stayed on for an hour or more in what quickly had become a mutually rewarding regular habit. The judge, starved of the pleasures of reading, delighted in his immigrant farmhand's learning and opinions. Mrs Sherman, Miss Sherman and Miss Grace generally sat with them, listened, served coffee and joined in the talk. Comfortable as this felt, nostalgia occasionally pained Ephraim. Perhaps because the judge was old, or blind, or was of such a high station, the Shermans together were cool, polite and restrained with each other. Or just plain whey-faced, Ephraim found himself thinking uncharitably. Where was the noise, the laughter, the teasing and games as in the Epstein household? He missed the shouting, and the sing-song of religious study and prayer. But the Shermans were certainly kindly. And if authoritarian, the judge at least was not a tyrant. Ephraim wrote some of these musings to Mama. To Rachel, he made much of the joys of farming life and his new physical prowess. 'Ephraim is a trained heifer that loves to thresh,' he quoted the prophet Hosea. 'So your Ephraim has a yoke on him.' Let his father make something of that. And of the little drawing he'd made for three-year-old Sarah, of chickens and their chicks.

'Aren't the peas brave!' said Miss Grace as Ephraim took his accustomed place on the stool by the judge's wing chair.

'Brave. Courageous.' Ephraim considered. 'I think first of soldiers with this word.' Before she broke in to explain he went on, 'But, yes, to grow from a speck of seed through the darkness to be a curling leaf-ed thing. Brave. Braving the world.'

She nodded, her brown curls dancing, excited that he had caught her meaning.

'Then braving our teeth and gullets,' said Miss Sherman as she entered. The elder of the two sisters, tall and fair, she was the dry realist; Miss Grace was the romantic. When he wrote home Ephraim called them spinsters, to allay Rachel's worries. Now that he knew them better, now that he was twenty-two years old, he'd begun to realize that thirty years of age – Miss Grace – and something not far beyond that – thirty-five, perhaps, Miss Sherman? – was within the age of hope for an American woman.

By now the whole family was gathered, the candle brought close and Mrs Sherman handed Ephraim the Bible. Besides Wordsworth and the *Autobiography of Benjamin Franklin*, they had set on a course of reading the Old Testament aloud to improve Ephraim's English. Judge Sherman was avidly curious about his employee's Hebrew insights.

'Exodus, Chapter Three,' Ephraim began. His voice was pleasantly deep, come from the sounding board of good lungs, and he rarely stumbled over words and knew to let the punctuation guide him in expression of meanings and feelings. He read the text like a small drama. But his r's and u's were still strongly Russian. He was fascinated by the translation of his familiar holy writ into English. It seemed fresh, new, as if just written. A new holy book for a new life. Yet familiar and safe, the same Lord God he knew, the same forefathers, Adam, Abraham, Isaac, Jacob, Joseph. And women, Eve, Leah, Rachel, Rebecca. The same Israelites. Six months ago they had started with Psalms and Proverbs, many of which the Shermans and Ephraim had by heart, but more recently they had begun at the beginning, with Genesis. They read for half an hour most evenings, except when calving and lambing interrupted. The judge plied Ephraim with questions, and their discussions reminded Ephraim of home. Tonight's reading was about the burning bush, a favorite of Ephraim's from childhood: how could a bush burn with fire and yet not burn? Was an angel made of fire? And here was the Lord speaking to Moses, and Moses speaking to him! Could that be? Even as he wondered at this he read out confidently:

...when I come unto the children of Israel, and shall say unto them, The God of your fathers hath sent me unto you; and they shall say to me, What is his name? What shall I say unto them?

And God said unto Moses, I AM THAT I AM: and he said, Thus shalt thou say unto the children of Israel, I AM hath send me unto you.

'I should like to hear that in the Hebrew,' said the judge. More and more frequently, the judge asked for the language he believed the first Christians prayed in.

'From when God calls?' Ephraim paged through his Tanakh, glancing up at Miss Grace, knowing she was intrigued by the front-to-back, as she called it, of the Hebrew Bible. His fingers knew the pages, his eyes found the place.

'Further on,' said the judge, 'after the land flowing with milk and honey, where Moses asks God what his name is.'

In the guttural ancient language the phrases rang. He had to chant it, he could not help himself.

'Ah! That's the part,' the judge broke in. 'Adonai Elohenu Adonai. Now I recognize that, Adonis, adonai, Lord, from the Latin and Greek. So Elohenu – is that I am that I am?'

Ephraim hesitated. He pointed to a block of four Hebrew letters on the page, thinking of the yad, the finger-pointer the reader used in synagogue for the daily portion of the Torah scroll. But because the judge could not see, he showed the page to Mrs Sherman. 'These letters are the name of God.' Ephraim sounded out each one, 'Yodh – He – Waw – He,' and did not join them together in a word. 'His name is too sacred to say aloud. So we say instead Adonai, Lord. And Eloheinu means God, as you use it.'

Silence fell, except for a spark popping in the hearth-fire.

The judge stirred. 'Now, Mrs Sherman, turn to Matthew five seventeen, and Ephraim, read from that.' She handed him the Bible and he read out loud:

Think not that I am come to destroy the law, or the prophets: I am not come to destroy, but to fulfil.

'The Lord Jesus Christ was a Jew, that's him speaking, remarkable, isn't it! You are closer to him than we Presbyterians are.'

Ephraim laughed. 'If you say so, sir!'

'I do! You should come to church with us of a Sunday and see.'

'Papa, don't tease,' said Miss Sherman.

'I am not meaning to embarrass him. Ephraim would be most welcome. Will you?'

Ephraim looked away from the blind, inquiring face, down to the New Testament on his lap. He thought of the odious reverend on the ship during the storm, daring to bless him in his Christ's name. And yet he liked the Shermans' freedom of enquiry, intellect and religion. If Russia had this... a longing for home suddenly pierced him. Home, and his mother lighting the Shabbat candles, speaking the words, Hear, O Israel. 'Thank you, but no, if you will forgive me.'

'Not at all. I hope you are not offended? No doubt it is against your scruples, perfectly understandable.' Fascinated by Ephraim, the judge wanted to display this bright young Jew to the other elders of their church. Miss Grace jumped up to brush a cinder back into the hearth, and Mrs Sherman reached for her knitting, anything to smooth over this awkwardness. Ephraim assured the Shermans that he was honored by the invitation and they bid their good evenings.

Was it against his scruples? He didn't want to be an object of curiosity, but in fact he was himself curious – how did American Christians worship? Ephraim briefly imagined his father's reaction to this invitation: disdain, distrust, apoplexy. All based on strength and faith – and fear? Fear of thinking, fear of questioning the Lord? Fear of retribution perhaps. Or of letting in a single chink of challenge – that was why the orthodox clung to every iota of their laws and traditions, one false step and everything might crumble. Yet Ephraim keenly missed assembled worship, the chanting of prayers and blessings, the Talmud disputations. He got by with his own prayer book, the siddur, and the Tanakh, and with occasional trips into New York. Time off had been hard to get from stingy Squire Ackerman, who allowed only the Sabbath – the Christian Sabbath. Keeping kosher had, of necessity, become impossible; the labor made Ephraim ravenous and Ackerman served pig meat often. Judge and Mrs Sherman had been more accommodating, providing an alternative when they ate ham. And monthly they let Ephraim visit Manhattan on a Friday to arrive before sunset and to return on Saturday night. It was good to pray at the shabby B'nai Avraham, and of course to meet with Benjamin.

By the candle in his own room he read from Exodus again, and then recited evening prayers, moving his lips but issuing no sound so as not to wake Amos through the thin partition. His body rocked to the rhythm of the chanting sunk deep in his being.

As he went to sleep Ephraim decided to ask to go into New York on Friday. He wanted to be among Jews.

9

THE ROAD TO METUCHEN
New Jersey 1851

The hay was in, the summer was sweltering and Judge Sherman had agreed to Ephraim joining Benjamin on a week's walking tour to the seaside of New Jersey. Ankle deep, the ocean surged and retreated around Ephraim's feet, the silky wet sand washing away from his toes with each ebb. With trousers and shirt sleeves rolled up, the brown of his field laboring showed sharply against the whiteness of the rest of his skin. Several days into their adventure, Benjamin's milky city flesh was pink with sun exposure. He knelt up the beach, constructing a sand fort.

Ephraim thought about this Atlantic at his feet. It had carried him to America. Three ships lay on the horizon, one a great sloop with full sails, and two with plumes of smoke, coasters from New York down to Baltimore probably, or further south, Charleston perhaps. He wished one was sailing straight for him, with Rachel and Sarah on it. A wife, a child – but no living yet to provide for them. Even such a wife as Rachel would make them a unit, anchor him. Could she ever be a farmer's wife? A hard thing to ask her. Especially as he was no farmer. He was as yet nothing.

He knew he should want her with him, it was his duty. But in his more secret heart, Ephraim admitted he was glad to be free. Free of the burden, free of temptation: cousin and cousin, the blood too close. Rachel's letters said Sarah was bright and pretty, so at least this generation's breeding was unscathed. The Lord be praised. But it was because of being the Lord God's chosen people that he'd been forced to this marriage in the first place. He wiggled one foot, disturbing its depth in the receding flow. His restless nature did not like dwelling on the past; he had accepted what was accomplished, he was glad here and now to be alive. He inhaled the sea air deeply, pleased that he was a year and a half into doing something positive, moving forward, even if slowly. The past could not change. A length of vivid green seaweed wrapped around his leg and Ephraim plucked it up: 'For your fort, Benjamin!'

'Twenty-two and playing like children.' Benjamin sat back and happily admired his building.

Ephraim knelt and spiraled the shiny ribbon of weed around the tower.

'You need a flag,' he said after a serious appraisal.

'An American flag would be good. No chance of that. But how's this!' Benjamin snatched up a dried reed stem and bent it in two places. A triangle resulted. Ephraim found another reed and did the same. Benjamin jammed them, point up, point down, into the sandy tower: the star of David.

Yesterday's castle they had trampled on with glee. Today, when it was time to go back to the boarding house for dinner they left the fort whole for a child to find or high tide to claim.

From the seaside the next morning they began their return walk, first inland away from Long Branch and the sea, then northwest. Though a different route to their walk down, it was just as pleasant. Woods and fields alternated, the land was gently rolling, and to the west low hills rose in a bluish haze. The region, settled first by the Dutch, then the English and the native Indians even before the Dutch, was scattered with hamlets and larger towns. Tall grasses bordered the road, now and then a brook babbled over rocks or became a narrow quiet stream, and there were lakes, small and larger, and occasional marshy areas. Ephraim felt it could have been Belarus, but for the knowledge – or was it the actual scent? – of the sea within five or ten miles, and the spice of the whole wide country of America lying further west. They ate their bread and cheese and melon in the shade, drank water from streams, slept through the midday heat after their dawn start and then set out to reach a town to sleep the night. Metuchen, named for an Indian chief, was two days off, then they'd turn north east for the last leg to Hillside and the Shermans.

Sometimes as they walked they talked, and spoke in English, the more to practice it. Benjamin explained the construction of the clarinet and his mentor's radical invention of stuffed leather pads to close the keyholes. Ephraim expounded on the finer points of different corn seeds, and recounted some of Judge Sherman's tales of court cases won, lost and judged. They rejoiced again in the absence of laws against Jews and laughed ruefully over the golden pavements they had hoped to find. Uncle Jacob had reported in a letter that finally reached Ephraim eleven months after he set out that the streets of San Francisco were paved with mud. And that its streams ran with: sand and mud. But Jacob rejoiced to write that his trade was good, for as sure as the sun rises in the east, gems and gold have an affinity – and some prospectors indeed found gold.

'This country, so full of promise!' Ephraim stopped and spread his arms wide in the sunny country lane. He sighed and his arms dropped, 'Would you ever go home? Do you miss it?'

'No. My home is here – ' Benjamin pounded his heart with his fist – 'ever since we left Brisk. I advise you to be the same, Dr Epstein.'

A shadow fell on Ephraim's heart – to be a doctor, how could he ever… anger flared. 'Easy for you to say! It's different for me.' He walked ahead, cross to have his mood spoiled. He had left home of his own will, and part of him was still there among friends and sisters, a child and a wife – and his mother. Home and heart and future: he brooded. Benjamin walked a mile in silence until he saw that Ephraim was once more noticing the scenery, and had returned to his usual self.

In other conversations on their way, Ephraim recounted to Benjamin some New Testament stories he could remember from evenings with the Shermans, and chewed over some of the discussions he'd had with the Judge, the reading back and forth between the Torah and the English language Bible. They were reading Devarim now, what Christians called Deuteronomy, full of Moses, from the Shema Yisrael bedrock of Ephraim and Benjamin's faith through the intricate and often peculiar laws of the mitzvot: the 613 commandments of Jewish law and ethics. The prohibition against wearing fabric combining wool and linen, for instance, puzzled Judge Sherman. But more than that he wanted Ephraim's elucidation on the Bible's slavery laws. An abolitionist, he wanted answers to pro-slavery landowners who quoted the Old Testament's acceptance of it. This had taken several of their evening sessions – no longer by the hearth but in hot weather on the side veranda of the comfortable house – and Ephraim shared his interpretations with Benjamin as they strode through the New Jersey countryside. Both young men had been horrified by the vile selling of Negroes that existed in the American south. Benjamin approved Ephraim's tack: the different interpretations of Hebrew words, and the customs in Biblical times: a slave was a servant, indentured perhaps, but not owned body and soul. Slavery did not exist any more, for Jews; it went back to Egyptian times, Babylonian, Canaanite, medieval times. And even then it was about how to treat them well, and when to free them; it was more, perhaps, like serfs in Russia, who belonged to their owners and the land, but were never auctioned in public, and in any case now had more freedom.

'I drew on all the scholars – from Maimonides on – for so many of the mitzvot. But in the end for some of the laws, unfortunately, I had to use our fathers's explanation,' Ephraim confessed to Benjamin and swiped at a clump of grasses with his walking stick.

They chanted it together, in Hebrew: 'Some laws we understand, others are there for us to obey without reasons, for who can understand the Lord God Almighty?'

'Is he trying to convert you?' Benjamin asked. 'These Christians can be mighty convinced.'

'I doubt it. He is genuinely interested in the Hebrew language. Like any

THE ROAD TO METUCHEN

good Jew, he wants to learn.' Ephraim walked ahead dodging overhanging branches that closed in on the path. He laughed shortly, 'Here we are discussing scripture, just as when their Christ appeared to them on the road to Emmaus. Perhaps he is among us now.' He shaded his eyes and pretended to scout the trees and bushes. 'They didn't recognize him, you know.'

'But aren't you worried? He's out to get you.'

'Judge Sherman? No! He likes me as a Jew.'

They walked on. The road crossed a stream by a mossy wooden bridge. The echoing knocks of a woodpecker rattled the afternoon peace.

'The ideas interest me, however,' said Ephraim.

'What!'

'Purely intellectually.'

'Why? What is so intellectual about a false messiah that was executed! Who failed to save the Jews!'

'Oh, Benjamin! It's just the idea of – ' he wanted to say the possibility of a loving, living God, how close this was to the Kabbalah, but balked at saying the mystic aloud – 'just the idea.'

The afternoon shadows had lengthened and they let silence take over as they forced their pace; according to their directions a good place to stay lay two miles after the wooden bridge. The way was wider here and they easily walked abreast, thumping their improvised walking sticks, walking fast in the competitiveness of friends.

'Have you ever been into a Christian church?' Benjamin asked.

'No. They asked me but I declined.'

'Because you don't dare?'

'Do you dare?'

'You don't – you're afraid!' Benjamin crowed.

'You think my faith cannot hold its own? My intellect? How can I possibly give credence to resurrection?' Anger made Ephraim's voice harsh, and then ironic. 'I dare say I can emerge from a Christian service unscathed, unlike Saul of Tarsus.' He told Benjamin another road story from the Shermans' Bible: how Saul the Jew became Paul the saint. And so they made a bet. On the next day, which was Sunday, if they found themselves in sight of a church, they would attend it.

Over the next hill, a mile along the valley road, pink in the glow of sunset, two white steeples rose from the town of Woods Landing.

The church was plain inside: white painted walls, dark plank floor, clear glass windows pouring the daylight in. Ephraim wondered if all American churches were this simple, or if he and Benjamin, by deciding on the one their landlady had said was the largest, had chosen the style most preferred. At home and on his travels he'd seen churches and even had glimpses inside. He held an impression of muted light and rich colours – reds, green, blues – in the stained glass windows. Soaring height, too, arches, columns and carving. They seemed not unlike the great synagogue of Brest-Litovsk, except for the crucifixes, statues and paintings of Jesus's mother and others. But this Baptist church was total simplicity. The second jolt was to see men and women seated together, whole families in fact. Judge Sherman and his wife and daughters went off to church together, but he hadn't imagined them actually sitting side by side. When Ephraim worshiped, the men had the main body, women were in the balcony, or curtained off. What would it be like, he marveled, to stand and chant the nineteen blessings of the Amidah next to Mama in synagogue.

A single wooden cross stood on the altar, which was just a table covered in white cloth. Now they were standing to sing; a balding man, seeing the young men's confusion, showed Ephraim the open pages of his hymnal so they could find their place in the book they'd been handed as they entered the church. Out of politeness and curiosity Ephraim joined in the singing and Benjamin followed. It was about celestial seas, reminding Ephraim of a psalm. A brown-haired woman in a straw bonnet played an upright piano to one side at the front, leading the singing with rousing rhythm. Ephraim threw himself into the song, breathing deep into his chest, raising his voice with the others. Praising God for his creation was good in any language, any religion. He glanced sideways at Benjamin, also singing lustily.

The congregation sat down and a priest – was it? He wore no robes, no special collar, no hat, no gold cross or chains – went to the uncarved, undecorated pulpit. 'Our reading today is the prophet Isaiah: 'Behold, I will do a thing; now it shall spring forth; shall ye not know it?' Ephraim had not yet read the books of Nevi'im in English, but he recognized the passages about making a way in the wilderness. 'Amen' all said together at the end. A different man took the stand, announcing he would read the Gospel, which Ephraim knew from the Shermans meant the stories of their Christ. This passage Ephraim did not know, despite the judge's frequent calling on Matthew. In it Moses and the prophet Elijah stood on a mountain talking to Jesus. A quick sense of outrage piqued Ephraim: how dare these Christians make so direct a reference to the Lord appearing to Moses on the mountain! But then it struck him: at the time Jesus really was a Jew, whatever Christians claimed for him now. Following the general Amen yet another gentleman went to the pulpit and began to speak, this time without a book.

'Brothers and Sisters, how blind are you? How blind are we all to Lord Jesus in our life today. We sow and we reap, we toil, we do our duty to our neighbor – but do we? Do we really live this life as our Lord meant us to? No, we do not, we are not filled with love for one another but filled with sloth, envy and sin. We pursue the wrong pathway and the destination is:

damnation! We are on the road to perdition but – like Paul – we may yet be saved. You know the story of Paul.'

Ephraim and Benjamin exchanged a startled glance, this was the story from yesterday, the basis of their dare. The preacher continued, 'Saul, as he was – a righteous man. Oh so righteous. Proper too, a citizen of Rome. And a Jew. And he did everything right. Oh yes. He hated those Christians. He pursued them, hunted them, tracked them like a bloodhound. They were preaching against the law, the law of the Romans and the Jews. He believed they were stirring up trouble. Trouble! He didn't know what trouble was but he sure found out. You know what happened. He was blind to the truth, the truth of Jesus, and he got the message. Yes, you know, just like YOU have to get the message in your own hearts. You know what happened. There he was on the road to Damascus, in hot pursuit of some Christians up there, then Wham!'

Ephraim flinched at the shout. He thought of the horrible Reverend Hamilton on the ship, but this preacher's face offered pure warmth and concern as he leaned over the lectern towards the congregation

'Yes! Wham!' he banged the pulpit, paused, then continued conversationally, 'The Lord Jesus appeared in a blaze of light and spoke to him: Saul, Saul why do you persecute me? And Saul from that moment recognized Jesus, and fell to the ground blinded and prayed to the Lord, prayed for forgiveness.'

'Amen!' someone called out. The preacher nodded, his eyes fixed on the people. Finally he spoke again, in a calm, confidential tone. 'You know what happened next. He went on to Damascus, he was taken in by Christians, the very ones he was pursuing. They saw, they knew, they believed, he was a changed man. And he changed his name to Paul.

'No matter where you are or who you are,' his volume began to rise again, 'if you have already seen the light, or if you are a sinner who hasn't yet, you are on the road to Damascus. Get ready for change, get ready for the Lord Jesus Christ and let the scales drop from your eyes and live the way of the Lord!'

Voices murmured, male and female: 'Amen! Amen! Praise the Lord. See the light!' Ephraim's heart burned within him. This burning, this was joy! Or was it pain? This appeal, to live by the light of truth. He looked at Benjamin and saw that he was trembling, his skin pale, knuckles white as he gripped the song book. Ephraim had time only to think What is happening? before the congregation followed the preacher's order to pray the prayer Jesus taught. He had heard it on the ship and caught some of the words: father in heaven, daily bread, forgive trespasses as we forgive... temptation... deliver us from evil.

Immediately after the Amen the piano struck up and the preacher called out 'Hymn number one hundred and thirty, *Rock of Ages*!' And the voices rang out, men's deep tones, women's high notes in unison right through to the final Amen.

Somehow Ephraim and Benjamin made their way out with the others. They nodded to the churchgoers, shook hands with the preacher and avoided his eye, explained they were passing through, just visitors from New York.

Ephraim's mind and heart were shaken, stunned. In the church he had felt something he'd never felt before. This wasn't a decision. It was not an act of will. He felt – he KNEW – it was sheer simplicity. As simple as the plainness of that church. Jesus was the Lord God's son, truly God on earth, a human being. And the Lord God in Jesus was love. No argument, discussion, rationalizing could change that, nor prove it true. It just WAS. As simple as the Christ's commandments – honor and obey the Lord, pray for sustenance and against wrongdoing, forgive wrongdoers. No antique rules or blind obedience. It was so simple.

Wrestling with the surge of feeling and thinking, the young men remained quiet on their return to the boarding house, taciturn as they collected their belongings and bid goodbye and set out again. Two hours into their silent walk toward Metuchen, the road forked right. They took it and as they approached a small wood, Ephraim said, 'Well, Brother Benjamin, I feel a call to pray.'

'Is this the road to Damascus, then?' Benjamin said in a small voice.

'Amen. So it seems.' They swung down their packs in the shade, washed their hands and faces in the brook they'd found, and drank of it. Ephraim felt excited, yet also grim. Exhilarated, yet determined. What had happened? Jesus had happened.

'But what about your faith! You said you couldn't possibly –' Benjamin turned away from Ephraim's shining face. 'You said he was a false messiah! And resurrection is impossible.'

'Benjamin, it is about love! You saw it, you felt it. The Lord Almighty's love – he gave us his son, a new deed.' Ephraim gave a wondrous laugh, 'How strange that I work for a blind man and I did not see. And then I hear about a man blinded – by the vision of Jesus! – and I see.'

'I did feel something, I heard what he said, I was trembling. But, I can't – what about the Torah? We would be apikoros, apostate... I don't know.'

'It doesn't matter! We have new faith. Other things will follow.' They began to talk about their church experience. The several revelations of each had come at different times – the first hymn for Benjamin, the Gospel reading for Ephraim, the sermon for both. It was all so peculiar. But also undeniable. And the question arose: now what?

'It will surely be easier to be a Christian than a Jew,' said Benjamin. For although they savored America's political code forbidding religious discrimination they also, now and then, had encountered anti-Jewish jokes, jibes, cartoons and social chill.

Ephraim studied his friend's sharp, solemn face in the dappled light: 'You can't be doing this as a matter of convenience.'

'Tell me it didn't occur to you.'

'No! Well, yes – only afterward. But that's nothing to do with it!' Ephraim's conscience was troubled by even having had the thought. Convenient? Probably. But also difficult – what to do now, and what about everything he'd ever known. The Torah, synagogue, the mitzvot, Shabbat, Passover, Sukkot, Yom Kippur, his parents, his family, all this was – as nothing? He felt lost, in grief, angry at the loss. And at the same time this joy, lightness, flame of… belief. Jesus in his heart. He and Benjamin sat in silence. This was too intimate to speak aloud.

Ephraim got on his knees and clasped his hands. Benjamin resisted, and then joined him. Ephraim raised his eyes to the sky through the treetops where a breeze swayed the branches. 'Lord God Almighty, we thank you for your son Jesus Christ. We have seen the light. We pray you Jesus for your guidance on this road you have set us upon. Show us the way, the light and the truth. Amen.' Benjamin echoed the Amen and then together, faltering as they tried to recall the words, they began the prayer that the Jewish messiah had taught the Jews, 'Our Father, who art in heaven…'

10

MELIORATION
New York State 1851 – 1853

'Alleluia! Praise the Lord!' Water streamed down Ephraim's face as he shouted his joy. Through the blur he saw the congregation praying and praising. 'Amen!' Sister Susannah called back to him, smiling widely. She had waded ahead almost to the shore, her yellow hair dark and flattened down her back. Ephraim followed, helped by the preacher's assistant, the weight of the water in the robes pulling at him. The sun, the lake, the trees all about: new, now, Christ the Lord's good world. The kindly brothers and sisters reached to help him up the bank. Alleluias echoed round and he returned them, beaming. Ephraim looked back to Benjamin emerging and stretched out for his hand. Christians! 'Brother!' They embraced. The choir broke into *O Happy Day* as these last three of the new flock went to the changing tent.

It was September now, but the summer had been a long struggle. On first returning to the farm Ephraim's heart was elated, but his mind still questioned. He realized he'd hoped for a dove, the word of God, a sign, a sureness. With Judge and Mrs Sherman he had been lit with joy, amazed, and eager to declare: 'I will come to church with you! I went away a Jew and have come back a convert.' They welcomed him warmly, and proudly brought Ephraim and Benjamin to their Sunday service. The pastor, well-pleased, told them of an organization ideal for their transition: the American Society for Meliorating the Condition of the Jews. Ephraim balked at the title and the thought of being actively proselytized – but he desperately needed to understand what was happening to him. And Benjamin, going back to Manhattan alone, wanted their introduction to the Christian world. Both young men began to warm to the idea because for a Jew this was a frightening, dangerous crossing. They risked the horror and condemnation of fellow Jews and family, the cost of becoming outcasts: apikoros, apostates. To be Jewish was an engulfing world, indeed sometimes suffocating, but also supporting, an element like the very air they breathed.

Ephraim and Judge Sherman and the judge's pastor spent hours discussing, praying, learning from each other, praying yet more. And then, sponsored by the judge's church, the Melioration Society offered Ephraim and Benjamin a fortnight in their upstate New York camp where they would be with committed, enlightened Jews like themselves, Jews who had walked the same path to recognizing the Messiah. So after the autumn harvest was in, Ephraim boarded a train north and west from the city, eighteen months after he'd crossed the Hudson to New Jersey in desperation.

Benjamin laughed at Ephraim's enthusiasm for the railway carriages – passengers sat on bench-seats in rows, like an omnibus, instead of in discrete compartments, as on European trains: 'Typical of America, the people mix together, so democratic!' Speeding through villages and towns, past virgin forest, woodlands, farms, lakes, rivers and glimpses of the new canal network fanned his enthusiasm – what a country, what a future! God bless America: God the Father, Son and Spirit. From the rail hub at Syracuse they changed trains to Oswego and finally on foot they arrived at the campsite of cabins and tents among woods beside Lake Erie. They were greeted by a broad, dark-bearded man, the director, Solomon Levi. He was a German Jew, now a Hebrew Christian, of middle age, settled in America for twenty years. An instant bond was formed when he told Ephraim his story – orthodox upbringing and oppressive father in the old country, the break for hope and freedom, early struggles and conversion, new faith and commitment. The same journey – but without a wife and child.

Christ's victory was not lightly won. Ephraim's spirit knew but his intellect had to be convinced, and he had to be absolutely certain in mind, heart and spirit that his new faith was not a whim, not a yearning for an illusion, not some sort of inverted homesickness and certainly not influenced by convenience. He had pored over the Torah and found many things he had not seen before. The knowledge burned in his heart, yet he could not understand his way through this mystery: God's own self a man on earth, the crucifixion, the resurrection. It was a concept he could think around all sides of, but not penetrate. It was a truth he had to accept, or reject, without fully understanding. Yes, this was the Messiah, yes, he was the Christ. Finally, finally he accepted. It was impossible but true. The insight had come not like a dove, nor a thunderbolt but in a whisper, a surge. Nothing could be proved but now that it had happened the insight could not be denied or un-done. The final realization came: this search and questioning – this itself was faith. With confidence he had at last put himself forward for baptism.

'They look like angels,' said Susannah happily as the newly Christened walked towards the picnic spread. Ephraim agreed: the white robes they'd worn, hung on lines between the trees, lifted and fell in the September breeze, dazzling in the golden sunlight. She was sixteen with pale skin and blue eyes and a quiet way about her, the Italian Jewish daughter of a whole family baptized today.

'I have a sister at home. You make me miss her.'

'Is she like me? How do I remind you?'

'In fact, I have seven sisters. But I am thinking of my favorite.'

'He means Kathy, yes Ephraim? Is it still Kathy?'

'And am I like her?' Susannah appealed. But Benjamin had left when Kathy was a girl, so he couldn't say.

'Yes, in coloring. And pleasantness,' Ephraim said. He meant prettiness, but reined in to bland politeness, because he was not intending a flirtation. Any hint of flirtation he had to stamp on, and he could see that Susannah, though innocent, was learning to flirt, hoping for flattery and... who knew what else. He was glad when they reached the picnic tables and greetings of the congregation.

After blackberry pie he dared to look toward Susannah again, her hair now dried to pale golden blonde. Benjamin caught the sight line. 'It is Rachel you are really thinking of, isn't it?'

'Sarah and Rachel and... everyone.' Ephraim's heart suddenly expanded. He wished all of them here, here, all right here by the lake, one big safe and loving family, joined in joy and harmony under God, Father, Son and Spirit. Benjamin had no family: sad, but fortunate in the circumstances now. He did not have to face Ephraim's problem – what, when, how to tell the family. For a brief moment Ephraim mused on persuading them to see the light. He quickly dismissed the notion. His father would be stricken, Rachel would rebel, his brothers-in-law would argue. It was his mother, most of all, Ephraim dwelt on: he feared how she would take his conversion. He had seen Jews utterly cut off for turning to Christ. His news would bring pain, but at least his mother would never do that. He reassured himself in speaking to his friend, 'Soon I will tell them. We have so much work to do, so much to study and learn about the Jewish Jesus, his words, his thoughts, his message.'

'Amen, God willing,' Benjamin concurred as he devoured another portion of pie, and then set off to see what kind of pie they served at Susannah's table.

I will wait, Ephraim decided, for the Lord Jesus Christ to show me the way and the time to tell the family.

Over the next two years the way continued to be the Melioration Society. The community Ephraim found among his intelligent, free-thinking, argumentative fellow Jews – now Christian Jews – provided a support and companionship he'd not known since the youthful days with his brothers-in-law and khevre, his gang of friends. Ephraim bid goodbye to the wise, kind Judge Sherman, his wife and daughters and with their blessings joined a group of newly baptized Hebrews in a venture the society had recently launched – a farm in Harrison, twenty miles north of New York City along the Long Island Sound. Benjamin had gone back to his woodwind crafting in Manhattan where he found new Jewish Christian friends from the society, which was active in the city. They supported him in the wrench from ingrained ways and from former friends who reviled his apostasy.

Meanwhile, Ephraim's farming skills, though still raw, were welcomed with almost as much joy in Harrison as his erudition and possibly even his conversion. The Jews who had seen the light of Christ were, most of them, as inexperienced in physical labor as Ephraim had been, and the society's vision of a self-supporting farmstead where Jews could live and receive instruction in Christianity needed more than faith and prayer. The idea was even, eventually, to form a colony for converted Jews to come directly from the old country. Ephraim fell to working the land gladly. He could only be amazed and grateful for having failed to find work in New York, for being driven to learn to farm – it was all to a purpose. Side by side with Brother Solomon and others he worked the hundred acres, and enjoyed the freedom of the five hundred acres of woodland, the orchard, the good horse and barn, and the proximity of the Sound with its ample fish and fowl. All the while, every day, every evening, they studied, read, debated, interpreted. Ephraim now fully mastered Greek, the written language of the oldest, purest version of the Christian Bible. Linguistic disputation, phrase-by-phrase, sometimes word-by-word, discussion, the passionate rationality of Talmudic debate turned with all its strength to the New Testament. Debate also turned back to the Old Testament, re-interpreting it in the light of the truth, that Jesus was the Messiah and the five books of the Torah and the Nevi'im, the Prophets, actually said so, if you knew how to read them in the light of Christ. Rigid unenlightened Jews could not see the divinity of Christ Jesus; Ephraim and his fellows saw and believed. In the talk and learning, this inner exploration and pushing out of boundaries, this freedom to question everything, Ephraim experienced the pure oxygen of encouragement. No longer his father, his grandfather, the rabbis to tremble before. No longer their disapproval and outrage at his champing at the Law, his balking at restrictions to learning. Even Mama's sweet piety and obedience failed in the light of the Son of God. Ephraim's mind, heart and soul were unfettered at last.

From time to time Ephraim visited Benjamin in the city, or, as before, Benjamin came to the farm. In the summer of 1852 they returned to the Oswego camp to teach new converts, and rejoice and welcome with the Melioration Society the baptism of more into the fold. Ephraim's second year of growing faith passed, a year of celebrating Advent, Christmas, Ash Wednesday, Lent, Good Friday, the glory of Easter, alongside his lifetime's rituals, the very same commemorations that Jesus had lived, of Rosh Hashanah, Yom Kippur, Sukkot, Chanukah, Purim, the Seders of Pesach, Shavuot. A year of Sunday service and the Eucharist, bread and wine, body and blood of Jesus Christ as he commanded in remembrance of Him, and the comfort of Friday evening Shabbat candles and meal. All this while he sent little drawings to Sarah and wrote home only about new friends on this new farm, his Jewish year, and said nothing about his Christian life.

By the following summer Ephraim's future came into question. His English was now perfect, his knowledge of the Gospel deep and passionate, his preaching, his arguments an undeniable union of Old and New Testament. Was he to continue his learning, his teaching of newcomers and valuable work on the farm? Or would he better serve the Lord, and the melioration of Jews, by another path? The society had ideas, and so did Ephraim, who girded himself for the challenge at the start-of-camp interview.

Paul Cassel, the president of the society, sat with Solomon Levi behind a trestle table piled with texts and notebooks in the log cabin where Gospel studies were held. He was a lean man with piercing dark eyes. Ephraim admired his preaching, but did not know him well, and was in awe of his faith and charisma.

'So, you want to be a physician, Brother Ephraim,' Paul said abruptly the moment Ephraim took his chair.

He startled but leapt to a response, 'You see me as I am, you have heard me and you know my deepest heart. Yes, I believe I can best serve the Lord Jesus Christ as a physician.'

Solomon leaned to murmur something in the president's ear. Paul smiled at Ephraim. 'We believe that ourselves.'

'The college of medicine in New York is the best in America,' Solomon said. 'And the course is now three years long. Would you agree to that?'

Joy flooded Ephraim as he nodded yes. Yes to three years of medical training repaid by three further years of missionary work for the society. Yes, yes, to be a physician and to reach out to unenlightened Jews, yes, with all his strength. He managed to contain his tumult with a smile and a phrase of gratitude to the Lord. But he said no more, because of the conflict within him, a barrier he had to confess.

Paul continued, 'One of our brothers there, Dr Cable, has heard of your intelligence and faith and wants to sponsor you, to begin this fall, if he deems you ready. Will you meet with him?'

'No,' Ephraim heard himself say, and paused while he confirmed this in his pounding heart and watched the baffled expressions on their faces. He hastened, 'Or rather, not yet. Dr Cable might deem me ready, but I am not. To follow this path is everything I want, but something more is demanded of me.' He hesitated before revealing himself – they could reject him, declare him arrogant, or greedy, or foolish. Or unfit. They could withdraw all support and turn him out into the world as a lowly farm worker again. But he had to ask. 'I am called to further learn in the Lord and serve him by attending seminary. To be a pastor as well as a doctor, if the Lord wills.'

Astonished, irritated and eventually bemused, the director and the president heard Ephraim's plea: his years of intense Judaism needed to be balanced by an equal intensity of Christian study. In Russia he had been groomed to be a rabbi; well, now he would be a minister. He kept to himself the pleasing irony that he was fulfilling his parents' wishes – in the wrong religion. It did not matter to Ephraim that he would owe the society six years of service: all the better, to be a theologian and a medical missionary.

For an agonizing week he waited. He walked alone and prayed alone by the lakeside, putting off Benjamin's questions – he had not confided in his friend. So bold, or so foolish, a request: he could not bear to be vulnerable before Benjamin. After Sunday service, a bear hug from Solomon brought the end of his anguish. The message from the society committee: if anyone should be granted this prospect it was Ephraim, with his intelligence, his passion for learning, his evident faith, his hard work for the farm and the society – and his charm and humor. It would be the finest establishment in America – Ephraim was to write his application immediately to Andover Theological Seminary, in order to begin the three year course this September.

That night, in their tent nestled among firs and maples, when the owl hoo-hooted for the third time, Benjamin tossed under his blanket and spoke into the darkness. 'You asleep?'

'No, there's a mosquito tormenting me.'

'You seem much happier today, Ephraim.'

'You thought I was unhappy? No. Living in hope and fear – and now my prayers are answered.' He told Benjamin the whole story, and together they rejoiced. 'Mazel'tov. Medical school and seminary – no one deserves it more.' Benjamin said this philosophically. He was content with proselytizing the Jews of lower Manhattan and he admired Ephraim's drive and intelligence without envy. Ephraim, however, acknowledged to his inner self that he felt some envy toward Benjamin's capacity for contentment. Not that his friend was lazy, just that he accepted the present moment, savored it, wasn't impatient to accomplish and move on. If only his own life could be so simple.

He punched the rough pillow and settled his head again. 'Oh, but Brother,' he sighed, 'there was one condition.'

'Obviously. It is time.'

'I have been denying Christ, like Peter before the cockerel crowed thrice. I beseech the Lord Jesus to forgive my cowardice. At last today I have done it. I wrote to Mama and Papa to tell them I am a Christian. I pray it doesn't kill her.'

'Amen. And Rachel?'

'I asked her to come, with my daughter. She is five years old now, think of it! Paul said the society would help until my training is finished. A minister needs a wife.'

11

AT ANDOVER
Massachusetts 1853 – 1856

Of all the Tanakh – or as he called it now, the Old Testament – that Ephraim carried closest in his heart when he arrived at Andover Theological Seminary, it was particular verses of Psalm 2. 'I set my king upon my holy hill of Zion. I will declare the decree: the Lord hath said unto me, Thou art my Son; this day have I begotten thee.' This paean, from King David's era or even before, stated the undeniably obvious: Jesus was the Christ, the Son of God, existing in the timelessness of the Lord God Almighty. How could the Jews of the Sanhedrin who condemned the Lord have been so blind? How could all Jews ever since?

Surrounded by rolling farmland, the seminary was set in the town of Andover in the sheltered Merrimack River valley in Massachusetts. The railroad had delivered Ephraim to Boston and from there an express train took him twenty-five miles north and west to this pretty, long-established town with its several steepled churches, weathered saltbox homes, clapboard Federal-style houses and establishments. Seminary Row – three handsome brick dormitories – gazed over a great lawn, and the library, infirmary and teaching halls were dotted among pathways and plantings. It was September, the trees lightly touched with gold and scarlet. As he explored, Ephraim discovered the campus was spread over a slight hill and he was secretly uplifted to think of the king upon the holy hill. Indeed, he felt a king; it was a wonderful leap from farm worker to scholar, his natural kingdom at last. He'd begun to realize, though, that it was going to be a testing jump from the warm commonality of Jewish Christians to a new kind of loneliness in the company of born-and-raised Christians. Of the twenty-five men in his enrolling year, he was the only Hebrew. Also, he was the only one who had not been to college or university. But he was toughened to being in unfamiliar circumstances, and eager for challenge. In fact, his difference was about to stand him in very good stead.

Ephraim's other close-held verse from the second Psalm was, 'Kiss the Son, lest he be angry, and ye perish from the way, when his wrath is kindled but a little. Blessed are all they that put their trust in him.' Kiss the Son, yes he had embraced Lord Jesus, and put his trust in him. And look where I am now, he reflected as he arranged his own dozen books on his own shelf, filled the inkwell, laid out his pens and pencils on his desk. As for wrath – he still awaited a response from the family. Why had he not heard? Each time he had written home during the two years since his conversion he had pretended. He had mentioned attending churches, saying synagogues and Jewish congregations were too far away; he warmly described his new friends and their joint ventures on the farm; he referred to their scripture studies, spoke of their celebrations of Jewish holy days – and left out the Christian calendar. None of it was lies, but nor was it the truth. All that while, the worm of fear had eaten at Ephraim – dare he tell, how could he?

Psalm 2 had been the core of his revelation to his parents: 'I will declare the decree: the Lord hath said unto me, Thou art my Son; this day have I begotten thee.' He quoted it to Rachel, too, and begged her to come to America, for he sorely wished to have a family and he now had the resources to support them. He promised her that he would never try to convert her to Christianity, she could keep her faith. With what strange hope he had sealed this letter, hope and trust that the years of separation had matured her as much as it had him, that their petty warfare was all in the past. Abstinence, with the Lord's help as proved thus far, would not be a problem, and the domestic companionship of an attractive, intelligent helpmeet – and a child, his own Sarah – what joy! He kept to himself his certainty that, away from the autocratic Epstein family, Rachel would blossom and surely, slowly, she would see the light of Christ.

His letter to Kathy was shorter, for he was confident that his adoring younger sister would approve anything he did. Since 1850 she had sent cryptic reports on the marriages of their siblings, on Papa's increasing withdrawal into studies, on Mama's resistance to the secularization creeping into Jewish households in Belarus. Ephraim and Kathy had always had a bond of rebellion among the duties and spirituality of Epstein life; as he'd hoped, her practical, responsible nature had indeed helped Mama and Rachel cope with his departure from Brisk. The bond was all the stronger now, because Kathy had married Ephraim's best friend at home, Abraham Sack, fellow champion in Jewish Enlightenment. Ephraim commissioned them both now to help the family accept his Christianity. And because he was not sure how Papa and Zayde would react he enclosed in their care, not Rachel's, a bank draft for Rachel and Sarah's passage to America.

All three of these missives lost? Surely soon he would hear, and he would be looking for a little house to rent like the other married students. He felt so much freer for no longer living a lie, open and proud before family and God. He prayed, and left it in the Lord's hands.

In the meanwhile, he reveled in the atmosphere and the studies to come. The first year concentrated on the Scriptures, the second would be on theology, the final divided between ecclesiastical history and sacred rhetoric. Biblical interpretation ran throughout the three years. The whole was a miracle of freedom and intelligence, for Andover maintained a Congregational church, so democratic that the congregation ran its own affairs. The seminary faculty and students entertained many variations on the theme of Protestantism: Baptists, Presbyterians, Unitarians, Methodists, Lutherans and Anglicans prayed and studied at Andover, as well as Congregationalists. Ephraim initially found these Christian differences illuminating and sometimes comic – so like Talmudic disputations! But all the differences took place in the knowledge of God's love, through Christ, as a way to God. And the arguments happened without burdensome centuries of mitzvot and the Mishnah, without the world's oppression and Jewish communal inwardness. Protestant openness was fresh air, fresh spiritual life – for it was Protestants, after all, who had found freedom from the superstitions, ritual and power structures of Roman Catholicism. Whichever brand of Christianity they chose, Andover students were so free that they did not even have to join the seminary church, nor attend its Sabbath service, though of course Ephraim did.

The year started well. Professor Calvin Stowe was chief lecturer for the juniors, a man with a firm bird-like expression, his forehead rounding into receding baldness, his sideburns and fringe of beard a white frame to his intelligent benevolent face. Fifty years old, he was distinguished for his editorship of the *Boston Recorder*, his teaching and his political influence as an educationalist. The fit between twenty-four year old Ephraim and this mentor seemed made in heaven – this new heaven of Christianity. *Text of the Old and New Testament – its History and Identity of the Present with the Ancient Text*, this was Professor Stowe's main subject for the year, and it extended to comparative studies of language in the scriptures. Ephraim was afire with enthusiasm – at last, scripture treated as historical, academically examinable text, as examinable as any other book instead of defended as precious God-spoken words. All Ephraim's knowledge, his background and his new faith came to bear on this learning.

But there was a problem, and its name was mammon. While Andover did not charge a fee for instruction, Ephraim had expenses for his room, use of the library and lecture halls, plus his own fuel, lights, washing, and the purchase of a wood stove; on top of this he needed two or three dollars weekly for meals with a local private family or a student association. He estimated the annual total to be one hundred and ten dollars – a third of what he'd earned under Judge Sherman. But since joining the Melioration farm, he'd only had his living costs covered and occasional pocket money when needed; he had earned nothing. He'd had two hundred dollars put aside – but now that, matched by the society, was gone to Rachel's bank draft. And he would need more when she arrived. For now the Melioration Society would provide him with ten dollars a term; they had recommended he apply for Andover's charitable funds.

Could he justify this? He had two diamonds, after all. But they were enmeshed with feelings – struggle, failure, hope, survival, home – the possibility of return, the giving up of that possibility – and Rachel. The diamonds really were Rachel's; Uncle Jacob had said so. How he looked forward to presenting them to her, a reward, a surprise when she arrived. Ephraim laid it before the Lord and wrestled, torn between utter honesty and the ties of the heart. He read scripture and prayed, but, still torn, he soon knew he could not sell or pawn them. By the end of the first week of term he submitted himself for approval to the charitable board, and was delighted to see Professor Stowe among the assessors. He repeated the story of his origins and departure from Russia, his manual labor, his conversion, his commitment – he had told this in his application to Andover, but now added his passion, his quick humor, his intelligence, his demonstrable linguistic ability, his presence. Letters from the society and from Judge Sherman testified to his indigent circumstances. Some half the other first-years seemed to be applying, was he as worthy as they? To Ephraim's relief the answer came quickly: he'd won the maximum pecuniary assistance – forty dollars per annum. But this still left him short fifteen dollars a term.

So once more Ephraim would seek work – at least he had saleable skills now. Perhaps at last in this setting he would find scholar's work, for he doubted that plowing or milking would be suitable for an Andover seminarian. However, there was a problem: the seminary made clear their preference that students do no paid work during terms. The whole time should be devoted exclusively to religious learning, unless absolute necessity demanded otherwise. At this halcyon phase of his life Ephraim had no wish to rebel against authority. Chafing had been his way: against his father, grandfather, the orthodox rabbis and mitzvoth, the Czar; now, for once, he wanted to obey, but necessity dictated otherwise.

The solution came, paradoxically, from the very fact of his being Jewish. The study of Hebrew was essential for first year students. Ephraim calculated that if he could be let off these lessons he could justify taking time for paid work. He applied for dispensation: Alleluia! Better than that, he was offered a post as assistant Hebrew tutor and positively urged to accept.

It was Professor Stowe's doing; he had persuaded the seminary that Ephraim's deep authentic knowledge of Hebrew and the Pentateuch would not only benefit Andover but also by the teaching of it this Christian Jew would better understand the perplexities of Christians facing the text. When Ephraim went to thank him his benefactor questioned the young man further as to his welfare: 'And where do you board?'

'It is cheaper in the Bartlett Hall association than with a family. And the food is not bad at all,' he stretched the truth. Meals were adequate, but he had had much better in his farming life.

'You would prefer private board in a home?' Stowe smiled, appreciating his student's politesse. At Ephraim's nod and gesture of regret, he continued, 'Will you do Mrs Stowe and myself the kindness of dining with our family daily? As our guest.'

And then the blow fell. A letter from home at last, but it was bordered with black, the only words: 'O my son Absalom, my son, my son Absalom! Would God I had died for thee, O Absolom, my son, my son!' At the bottom, the signatures Yehuda Yudl Halevi Epstein, Zelda Miriam Epstein and the dates 1829 – 1853: his parents' names and the date of Ephraim's birth and his revealed conversion to Christianity. They had declared him dead.

No argument, no questions, no attempt to understand. Ephraim's stomach lurched and a wave of nausea hit him. The room spun and he gripped the sides of the wooden chair he sat in, dropping the letter on his desk. This was all? No word of tenderness, of love. He steadied and looked at the letter again – Mama, nothing from her?

This time he had to retch into a basin, and then, trembling, he gathered his scarf and hat and hurried down the staircase into the biting air of gray November. He walked fast, blindly. He tried to reason, he tried to pray. My God, my God, Lord Jesus Christ... 'Thou art my Son, Kiss the Son.' A classmate waved from across the lawn, a professor looked across from the library steps, but he sped on, driven by grief, by horror: what had he done? Jesus Christ, the light, had split his world asunder. Always he strove to break away, to get free, to find and prove his own self. He had found his own God. And now his parents had severed him.

By the time he came to himself Ephraim discovered he was five miles out of town, on the road leading to the highest hill in the area. Bleak bare trees crowded close, rain and evening darkness began. He tried to pray, but nothing, no One was there. Not the Lord Jesus Christ, not the wrathful God of the Old Testament. Even God had severed him. On the long trudge back, reason began to assert itself; reason and soon anger. How dare his father do this? How could he be so cruel and blind? Mama!

Of course he knew that conversion to an alien God, by Moses's own law, was punishable by death. Long since it had become a figurative, not literal death – a complete shunning, a shame, a crime. He had confronted this consequence in his soul during his first Christian studies; he had seen this death carried out in Brest-Litovsk. But, he now recognized, some hidden hopeful favored son part of him had been sure his parents would not do this to him. They couldn't! They loved him. And he loved them. From hurt the anger grew – for he knew, absolutely, that his mother did not think him dead. He could envision her cries and tears, her pain, and her love, and see his father standing by her insisting, watching as she signed the letter. Not letter – document. And Rachel – what about Rachel? With another sickening lurch of his stomach, he understood what would come.

Back in the dormitory he spoke to no one, went to his room, stripped off his wet clothes and got between the cold bedlinens in a fetal curl, the night un-prayed, the stove un-stoked. Professor Stowe himself found Ephraim at noon the next day – his protégé had missed dinner, missed the morning lecture, had not been seen anywhere. Ephraim did not recognize him.

The infirmary physician's initial diagnosis was scarlet fever: high temperature, swollen neck glands, stomach pains, white-coated tongue. In a day the blotches and spread of the pink-red rash would appear. It was a common enemy at the seminary and could kill; quarantine was essential. The physician administered cold sheet wraps, cool drinks, purgatives and emetics to evacuate the bowel and stomach, starvation to avoid feeding the illness. By the third day no rash emerged and a sudden acute fever set in. The doctor cupped his patient, heating the air in glass bulbs and applying them to the torso to suck poisons and inflammation to the surface. The fever continued, and now Ephraim moaned and whimpered at fierce pains in his left chest. A blood-let of four ounces on the fifth evening and again in the morning did nothing to reduce the overheated congestion. It was time to call in a consulting physician. Coming from Boston, Dr Howard declared the condition to be intestinal inflammation and Ephraim's life at risk, immediately writing prescriptions for quinine to address the fever, morphine to ease the pains and strychnine isolate for the stomach. He increased the bleeding to reduce the excess of blood and applied leeches in the heart area and abdomen to relieve the affected parts by drawing the circulation away. There was a general relaxation of the young man's system after each of these sessions, and the consultant added alternating hot and cold sheet wraps to the treatment, combining old and new medical theory. Close nursing and his expertise aided Ephraim's body, but not Ephraim's mental state. No longer at high risk, though still weak and feverish, he became intermittently delirious, praising God and cursing Him, calling on Jesus and berating Him, asking for Mama, fearful of Papa, furious at Rachel, sobbing at the pain of his heart breaking as he clutched at his body, quoting Scripture, speaking in the tongues of Hebrew, Greek, Russian, German, English, French.

After twelve weeks the delirium and chest pains abated. One late February morning Ephraim woke aware of himself alone in an unknown room, pale sunlight and bare tree branches visible through the window he could see from his bed. Everything looked strange and pure and white. He lifted his hand and examined it curiously, so thin, so pale, and his arm – so weak. Inside he felt utter, complete stillness.

Dr Howard, round and genial, came out from Boston to confirm his patient's recovery, and they had a lucid conversation about the illness and treatment. Ephraim expressed his gratitude and, a true sign of his healing self, plumbed the Boston expert about the course of his treatment. 'Heroic therapy, my dear young man!' This was no metaphor but the actual name for the severe methods used by physicians of the mainstream 'regular school' of medicine, in which Dr Howard was a highly respected figure. Whatever the crisis, heroic therapy used the best available mineral drugs – mercury, potassium tartrate, iodides and others – and administered powerful plant concentrates such as quinine, morphine, and strychnine, along with bleeding and blistering, plus vomiting and laxatives to purge the body. The principle was: to be useful treatment must be disagreeable. Dr Howard scoffed at the upstart eclectic school of physicians who used moderate doses, botanical isolates and humanitarian methods. 'Poppycock to that! The sick body needs a shock, absolutely. We must drive out the disease. Look at you, a prime example,' he beamed at his patient. 'Heroic therapy did wonders for you!' With which Ephraim, thanking Almighty God, Father, Son and Spirit, agreed. A month of convalescence was prescribed, visitors would be allowed, and a gradual return to studies.

Professor Stowe and his wife and niece, as the nearest he had to family, were Ephraim's first visitors. Soon reading was permitted, and for a gift they brought a signed copy of the novel Mrs Stowe had authored. Published barely two years before, the fame of *Uncle Tom's Cabin* and Harriet Beecher Stowe was sweeping the nation. Miss Clara Stowe, who was twenty and pretty and Ephraim's best friend within the Stowe household, offered to read to him, to help preserve his strength. For an hour a day they shared the living story of American Negro slavery, of Eliza and Tom, Eva, Topsy and Simon Legree, and discussed the abolitionist politics he'd heard around the Stowes's dinner table.

Ephraim reflected in the quiet of his convalescence and gained strength; he prayed and gave thanks. His Lord had returned and rekindled his heart. He was not abandoned, and he was doubly blessed by the friendship of this intelligent, influential, Christian couple, and the kind interest of their niece. Miss Clara gave him the feminine warmth he yearned for, the companionship of his sisters which he had missed for so long.

After they had ascertained his steady recovery, Mrs Stowe one day brought Ephraim a letter, explaining that it had arrived in December. He knew what it would be and was not distressed; the great wrench and illness had done its work. But he was surprised to see the address in Kathy's handwriting instead of his wife's. Inside, however, a folded paper bore Rachel's writing. First he read his sister's report of their father's wailing and tearing of clothes, his mother's tears and illness, of the mirrors covered over, the low stools they sat on to mourn, the solicitous visitations from relations and friends. Ephraim was dead. Kathy and Abraham themselves could hardly rejoice in Ephraim's change of faith, but said they did not condemn him. Furthermore – but he broke off and opened Rachel's letter:

My dear husband,

I write this in haste because your parents have forbidden me to reach you. You are my husband under God's blessing and I will cleave unto you. I wish to come to you but they forbid it; in time perhaps it shall come to pass. Kathy and Abraham have promised to help us, and I will try to write to you through them. I shall keep your memory alive for Sarah. She is as you would expect her to be, the bright daughter of her father at cheder.

I am your grieving widow,

Rachel

Ephraim let the letters lie on the counterpane as he conjured Sarah, the miracle of her, six years old now. And Rachel's image, at their wedding dance, on their wedding night. Her sly pettiness, her radiant motherhood.

He longed to get back to his own room and see their portraits. The rest of Kathy's letter explained that she would, with Ephraim's permission, keep safe the money he had sent for Rachel and Sarah. Under Abraham's rule and not their father's she could secretly do this, and be the conduit of correspondence between husband and wife, for she did not agree with their father's ruling over Rachel. Eventually perhaps they could help his wife and child escape to him in America. When I am a physician, Ephraim vowed, then I will have a livelihood, then I will rescue them.

He wrote as such to Rachel and Kathy. And, feeling so raw, so tender, he told Clara Stowe something of the cost of Christianity his father had imposed. He sought and received her sympathy. The next day, when she brought him a fresh-picked posy of violets, smiling, full of life, her hair shining filbert brown, her bonnet tied with blue satin, he was struck with terror. He feared he was in love with her, and she with him.

Stiffly Ephraim thanked her for the violets and made a little speech. 'I fear I am become too dependent on your kindness, Miss Clara. You must have many other calls on your time, and Mrs Stowe must be missing your help with the children.'

Rachel, in a similar situation, would have been defensive, suspicious and hurtful. Clara simply looked puzzled. 'You do not wish me to visit any more?'

Ephraim felt an utter fool. She was not in love with him. He was in danger of loving her. He touched the violets. 'Of course I do. But perhaps a little less often, as I am much stronger – I was just concerned for you.'

He began to throw himself into studies. He was God-seared now; he had been through hell-fire, been tested and survived. By March he was ready for normal life, his return to be celebrated at his twenty-fifth birthday, the Stowes decided. Benjamin managed to come up from New York, and Solomon Levi from the Melioration Society, their Hebrew Christianity, like Ephraim's, fascinating the invited students and faculty. With the Stowes's children larking and playing, the youngest his own Sarah's age, and Benjamin's lively music, and Clara Stowe to dance with (but not too often), with the good food, good company, the laughter and warmth, Ephraim felt the joys of home. He raised his fine voice in song with the others and beneath surged involuntary praise for this hard-won new grace: Barukh ata Adonai Eloheinu melekh ha-olam... Blessed are You, Lord, our God, king of the universe...

On August 7th 1856 the chorus from Handel's *Oratorio of the Messiah* soared over the audience at the seminary commencement exercises. One by one the graduates received their diplomas as their thesis titles were read out. *The Parallel Truths of Theology* came before Ephraim's, *The Internal Argument for Divine Truth* came after and Ephraim's friends rejoiced with him at his: *The Doctrine of Atonement in the Theology of Modern Judaism*. In three years of seminary he had not let a word pass without full understanding. The more he studied, the more he was convinced that the truth of Jesus was embedded throughout the Old Testament. Jesus was the Christ who brought a direct relationship to God. An inward, living Way, it was a path requiring constant self-judgment and questioning. Never ever would Ephraim regret his choice, only regret that his parents, and all Jews, could not accept the truth. Before he left Andover he sent a copy of his thesis to his sister with grim satisfaction, and with his prayers.

12

BELLEVUE
New York City 1856-57

The third-year medical students raised tankards to the first-years, gulped their ale and shouted for the rota to begin. This was Dalton's tavern on East 30th Street, a dim, beer-smelling student favorite where the newcomers, seated on wooden benches along the walls, were being inducted. Ephraim was glad to be in New York again – he was an urbanite at heart in spite of three years working the land and three years in the peaceful seclusion of the seminary. The city's rumble of traffic, the jostle, grime and busy-ness carried on just as before, and now he was a new man, embarking on a new life. The seniors chanted the new boys' names: Adams, Burns, Epstein, Frankel, O'Reilly, Schmidt... twenty in total, strangers to each other. Ephraim drank the bitter gold liquid and nodded at the student next to him, a weathered man in his thirties. 'Burns,' he said and smiled, showing even teeth through a black curly beard. Ephraim exchanged his name but before they could talk, the senior students called all to order. 'Now, the anthem! You must learn the words!' They cheered and launched into song.

> *We are off to doctor whoever we oughter,*
> *The sick, the poor but even more*
> *It is the rich we're after. Charge 'em,*
> *Charge, charge, charge 'em, hey!*

Ephraim and Burns did not laugh but everyone else did. 'Come on, sing along, it's the doctor song!' The leader, a smooth-faced blond, chivvied them. 'We have two Scots, one Hungarian, some Germans and a raggedy bunch of others, including three Jews. And we're all in it to get rich. Especially the Jews – hey?'

Burns spoke, 'The Scots aren't in it to get rich.'

'And what's your name, bright eyes,' sneered the smoothie. 'Are you the Epstein or the Horowitz?'

'Neither. Is this what medics do?'

The others quieted, shuffled at their seats and looked into their drinks.

'I am the Epstein,' Ephraim stood. 'But I am not a Jew.' The silence continued.

The blond leader glanced round at his fellow seniors. 'All right, boys? Then – drink to the Jew who's not a Jew!'

They roared approval, chinked their beer mugs to the Jew-not-Jew, and raised them to Ephraim, who stared back defiantly. Most of his fellow juniors held their ground, not giving into the bullying. Instead, Burns lifted his tankard to the roomful of men and said, 'To our health, and the Hippocratic Oath.'

'Hear, hear,' Ephraim responded, and the others along the benches joined in.

The smoothie bellowed now: 'The Oirish ones, who's the O'Reilly?' But his seat-mates pulled him down and he laughed.

'Wouldn't want to be doctored by him,' murmured Burns as Ephraim sat again.

'Hardly the conduct Hippocrates meant,' Ephraim answered.

Burns, Christian name Andrew, and Ephraim and two others went on to a chop house and traded the stories that had got them to medical school. Ephraim's was not the only circuitous journey. Burns himself had been to the California gold rush, panned enough to come back east and dedicate himself to a new life; he aimed to go west again. Isador was a New York Sephardic Jew who had studied in Paris. Teddy was fresh from college, his father a doctor, and his father before him.

As with the other two top medical schools in the United States, Harvard and the University of Pennsylvania in Philadelphia, the course of study at New York's College of Physicians and Surgeons was intensive and took three years – unlike others in America which took only two years. However, in common with all med schools, it was expected that students would get additional instruction, and a better chance of graduating, by signing up to a preceptor, a practicing professional doctor who gave individual tutoring and supervision to a score of private students. The Society for Meliorating the Condition of the Jews paid Ephraim's one hundred dollar annual fee to the college, and Dr Cable, who had originally endorsed his application to the college, offered Ephraim a preceptorship, waiving the usual further hundred dollar fee. For this Ephraim was exceedingly grateful – of course he was, because he had no other means of paying – but also because the lectures in college were sheer didactic telling, a dictation of fact and theory, each faculty member giving a one hour lecture in turn, students taking notes as fast as they could – or drooping with boredom under a mumbling, droning lecturer – for five hours a day. The college had two main lecture halls – the upper, with a skylight, was for anatomy, physiology and surgery. The lower was for chemistry, materia medica, theory and practice of medicine. In either, depending on the lecturer, subjects included skin, eye and ear, lungs, heart, gastrointestinal system, obstetrics, fractures, ulcers, blood, common diseases. The afternoons saw Ephraim next door in the lab building, training in dissection and chemistry. His entire being – even that part of him committed to the Lord – was engaged, stimulated and challenged by the pace and breadth of learning. By moments he remembered his brothers-in-law and best friend Abraham in their youth, how they had hungered for science, for knowledge outside Scripture. He thought of his father forbidding such worldly learning. He tried not to think of Mama at all.

The course ran three days a week for five intense months. On the other two weekdays students saw medical practice in action; they trailed the attending physicians on ward rounds, heard clinical lectures or observed surgery in the amphitheater of the hospital this advanced institution was connected with: Bellevue. Bellevue at last. The first time Ephraim entered the gates he stopped to gaze over its farmland toward the East River. Sails, plumes of smoke from steamboats and the whiff of river stirred his memory of standing on the far side of this hospital, yearning for a future. Yehe shlama... hayyim tovin... May there be abundant peace and good life – unbidden, the prayer he'd said then rose up.

He had wondered in those days how he would ever find a physician who would introduce him to the privilege of medical study; through Christ he had found one. No better could be had than Dr Cable – respected, successful, dedicated, and a caring but tough taskmaster. Tall, lean and blue-eyed, he had been Christian since birth because his parents had been converts, and he was born American. Dr Cable drove his students hard. After lectures and labs and in the breaks between courses, his students had to give daily recitations on the medical school lectures – but using textbooks he selected, different to the college's texts. Every day he quizzed each of his twenty students on the assigned reading, critiquing each. Cable also provided an experienced practitioner for their ten week course in midwifery. Furthermore, with his cooperative charity patients he demonstrated and then supervised his students' practice of auscultation, percussion and palpation to hear, feel and diagnose conditions of the inner organs. Entitlement included the summer courses Dr Cable gave at the College as well: physical diagnosis one year, clinical use of the microscope another, pathological anatomy another. By his second year, Ephraim and his cohort would be Junior Walkers at the hospital under Dr Cable's three-month unpaid term as Attendant Physician, and under other physicians in their turn of service.

Compared to his thoughtful, scholarly days as a seminarian, the intensity of Ephraim's medical studies left him little time to reflect on the past – to feel the pain of amputation from Mama, the bitter defiance of Papa, the regret over Rachel and Sarah. Since his daughter had reached reading age he wrote little verses for her, usually about nature, or sometimes silly ones about himself, or lines from Longfellow, tucking them into his letters to Rachel via Kathy. His sister's letters, sometimes with a line or two from Rachel, continued to come four or five times a year. He had left the lively, nurturing Stowe family life at Andover, and at first sorely missed it, living now in a boarding house with other students. The med students had occasional Saturdays or Sundays free and managed to shoehorn in entertainment – Dalton's tavern for some – visits to Judge Sherman's family in New Jersey and Solomon Levi at the farm in Harrison for Ephraim now and then. The Melioration Society and Bible study was an essential part of life, and he attended prayers at several different churches – Presbyterian, Baptist, Methodist – choosing among them by their intelligence and the level of discussion instead of committing to any one Christian dogma. He also put his language skills to use in scraps of free time, gaining a double advantage. Through Dr Cable and the college library he had access to advanced European medical texts; as well as learning from them, he earned, translating articles from French and German, charging a few dollars to other students for the translations, and even to Dr Cable for subjects of his particular interest. And there was Benjamin of course, Benjamin and his fiancée Susannah, met those five years ago at the Oswego camp since when friendship, romance and finally courtship had flourished. As a threesome they sometimes went to concerts, plays or galleries, or strolled in New York's parks and squares. In passing Ephraim could not ignore the turn of a lovely ankle beneath long skirts, the smooth skin of a pretty neck, shining hair with escaping wisps, the female voice, gentle laughter and smiles. He repressed his responses: he was not a free man. He channeled his energies into his task of learning, and of dedication to the truth of Christ.

Once his life as a medical student had settled to a routine, most Fridays Ephraim would walk two miles down to the lower East Side to meet Benjamin. There among the residents heading home to Canal, Orchard, Delancey, Broome and Essex streets to celebrate the Sabbath, the two young men handed out leaflets titled: 'The fullness of Israel.' Produced by the Melioration Society, the text quoted Isaiah, 'Arise, shine, for your light has come, and the glory of the Lord rises upon you.' Paul of the New Testament followed: the mystery of God choosing Jews as the people who believed in Christ before he came, Jews who in recognizing the messiah know the truth of their union with God. Few took the fliers, none came to the faith. When the rush hour ended Ephraim and Benjamin would go up to lower Fifth Avenue for the Baptist Bible reading, where soup and bread fed body as well as nourishing the soul. Slow work, this converting of Jews – why could they not see the light?

It was here Ephraim met a new friend of Benjamin's, Gideon Lederer, and the Great Idea was formed. A native New Yorker and a Baptist, one evening after a reading from Matthew about Jesus making his disciples fishers of men Gideon said, 'The trouble with you, Ephraim, is you think others are as intelligent as you. But they're not; you're too smart.'

Benjamin started to defend his old friend, but Ephraim said, 'Thank you.'

They were sitting at one of the long tables in the meeting house, elbows on the planks, shadows cast by the gas lamps, Gideon's spectacles catching the light. 'It is the intelligent ones who are the hardest to convince of Jesus the Savior.'

'No! It is the simple ones. They cling to their mothers' skirts, to Talmud, Moses, Elijah, the Mishna, minhag, mitzvot. It's the stories they like. The ritual. The obedience.' Ephraim spat out this last word.

'Well, but they love tradition,' said Benjamin. 'Also, it is a tie with the old country, with home.'

'This is their home now,' Ephraim banged the table with the flat of his palm. He said it in Brisker Russian, and other discussion groups glanced up startled. 'This is their home now,' he repeated in English. 'How to convince these clingy Jews? How to make them see the light, come to the Lord?'

'At camp last summer, remember? We prayed for guidance on this. Let us pray,' said Benjamin. The three men bowed their heads and Benjamin prayed aloud. Ephraim let the words wash through him. He was tired. Lung anatomy he still had to read, the cardiac exam to revise for, and tomorrow was dissection and he must be alert. He prayed to the Lord Jesus for strength of will, strength of mind.

'That's it! Praise the Lord!' Gideon startled the other two in the midst of their Amens. 'We must reach the intelligent ones! Single out the lead sheep and the flock will follow.'

'And how do we –'

'You're right!' Ephraim caught the inspiration. 'No more of this standing on street corners. We must reach their minds. We Jews, the Jews, are thinkers, the best of them, and they need food for thought. If only we could get them to a shul... but a Christian shul. If they would argue and discuss the proof of Christ in their Tanakh, they would see the light.'

'Or... get thoughts in front of them by... reading!' said Gideon, 'Not pamphlets but news. Reading a newspaper, just for them.' The idea was the Holy Spirit in action, they agreed, for Gideon worked for a printer, the same printer who produced the society's leaflets and posters. With the financial help of the Melioration Society *The Israelite Indeed* was born. A monthly newspaper, as things turned out, due to the realities of energy and money. Its declared purpose was the true interests of the Jewish nation generally, and the illustration of Hebrew Christianity, starting with Moses and the prophets. The first issue was published just before Passover and Easter, in March 1857. Editors, Gideon R Lederer, and – taking the lead from Professor Stowe, educationalist, newspaper editor and his Andover mentor – Ephraim M Epstein.

13

REVEREND DOCTOR EPSTEIN
New York 1858-59

Spring in New York arrives all in one day. Sharp greens veil maple trees, clouds of pink and white apple blossom look like brides in waiting, balmy air erases memory of winter – especially such a winter as '58. A spell of extreme cold had preceded weeks of foggy warm weather and at Bellevue a terrible number of women died of the fever that comes after childbirth. But the renewal of spring is inevitable and even busy Manhattan for a brief while becomes a paradise. Oblivious, Ephraim and his best med student friend Andrew Burns hurried through the gates of Bellevue hoping for good seats in the hospital's amphitheater. The famous Dr James Rushmore Wood – who twelve years earlier drove the reforms which turned Bellevue into a model of advanced medical practice – was conducting one of his Saturday lectures and demonstrations for those quick enough to have purchased tickets.

Two hundred students filled the stands looking down at the revolving wooden operating table beneath the skylight high above, the patient already lying under white sheets; Ephraim and Burns adjusted their sightlines from the sixth tier. What would the surgery be? The buzz of speculation quieted as Dr Wood entered, his black silk gown fastened tightly at neck and wrist – modestly black, as he had no need to display its evidence of previous operations, unlike boastful surgeons so proud of their blood-stiffened whites. In a nice seasonal touch he bore a boutonnière of jonquil and violets on his left breast. His house surgeon followed, wearing an everyday suit, its left buttonhole dangling a dozen or so waxed ligatures ready for service. Joined by three resident assistants he moved to a side table with its array of glittering ivory-handled instruments. 'Gentlemen, I bid you good day,' Dr Wood intoned to his audience. He plucked a jonquil from the posy he wore, inhaled its scent beatifically, and then let it drop to the floor. 'A good day for an amputation.' Amid the murmurs of appreciation he added, 'Of the foot. Due to latter complications of diabetes.' He lifted his hands, the room hushed, he bowed slightly to his assistants for all the world like a high priest at an ancient sacrifice. He signaled to a junior assistant who wet a wad of cotton from a bottle of ether, placed it in a cone made from a towel and folded newspaper, and approached the patient. During this time Dr Wood expounded on diabetes and on the case details, then held out his right hand for the saw and calmly, systematically, explaining as he went, cut off the gangrenous limb. At least, in this scientific age, he could take as long as he wished and three men and iron bars were not required to hold an un-anesthetized patient in place, as would have been the case a mere twenty years before. Then, speed was a surgeon's chief aim.

'After that Dr Wood nearly had a tantrum when the assistant handed him the second scalpel. Took a look and hurled it to the floor and cursed the maker for its badly mounted blade – I could see the man cringing in his seat.' Ephraim embellished Burns's account of the operation to their fellow students the following Monday. They were on the way from materia medica lecture to lab.

'Then Wood launched into his lecture and generously revolved the table for all to see the stump while his house man did the sutures. The tourniquet assistant practically had to gallop!'

Someone among them began to compare observations of a foot amputation he had seen by Dr Alonzo Clark, of their own college – but all too suddenly they were at the laboratory; general conversation had to halt. Materia medica was a challenge virtually opposite to surgery, requiring finicky deliberation instead of flair and emphatic decisiveness; Ephraim liked it. Not all student doctors would do surgery, but every physician had to learn to write and make up medications – Dr Cable drummed this into his students and Ephraim took it on board. In due course, once practicing, they could choose to have pharmacists produce them, but still each prescription had to be written for each particular patient. Certainly standard formulas existed, as well as dubious patent medicines, but for a specific person in a specific case a specific Rx was the physician's job. Today they were increasing their repertoire of purgatives. Ephraim moved with confidence along the shelves selecting powder of senna pod, ground magnesium sulphate, fennel oil, and for the other formula, oil of castor plant, an egg, syrup of ginger, cinnamon-water, along with plain boiled water. The Latin labels and ranks of brown, blue and clear glass bottles, the porcelain jars, boxes, and rows of drawers, the tomes of the American Dispensatory and the U.S. Pharmacopoeia pleased his orderliness. He went to fetch mixing vessels and bottles for the finished products, but then noticed that Burns, whose station was adjacent to Ephraim's, had already laid these out for both – counting on Ephraim to gather the ingredients.

After concentrating on weighing and measuring ingredients and starting the maceration, their usual quiet banter began, centering on a hypochondriacal Miss Pringle they had devised. 'Besides needing a purge, the poor lass is complaining of dysmenorrhea,' Burns reported.

'She's not after laudanum again! I fear she is becoming an opium fiend, Dr Burns.'

'Indeed, like many a sad physician, Dr Epstein. What shall I say to the young lady?'

'Quote our master Dr Cable to her.' Ephraim straightened up and orated: 'The use of morphine at proper times is one of the greatest boons of suffering humanity, but its misuse is one of the greatest curses.'

'She'll soon forget her monthly pain with this double dose of purgatives,' said Andrew, breaking the egg and adding its yoke to the castor oil mixture to begin emulsifying. 'A truly explosive treatment, heroic therapy would do the trick! Or kill her off entirely.'

Ephraim laughed, then added seriously, 'It saved my life, you know.'

'Along with hot and cold compresses, isolation, cleanliness, the good Lord and your strong constitution,' Burns retorted.

He knew of Ephraim's Andover illness, for the med students had long since compared notes on their personal medical crises and expounded opinions on the cures effected. The college taught 'regular school' methods, including the time-honored heroic therapy. However, some highly placed physicians, including Ephraim's own Dr Cable, had growing faith in the new eclectic methods which used botanicals and minerals in gentler doses. Burns took the eclectic side; Ephraim would once have leapt to it too, for its science seemed sound and he trusted Dr Cable's wisdom. But he could not deny the success of his heroic treatment, ghastly as it had been. Which kind of healing was best?

Ephraim couldn't be sure, because beyond his Andover cure he had even older doubts about medical wisdoms. Way back in time, right after his bar mitzvah, Mama's pains had begun. Once a year she was devastated by a gastric attack that sent her to bed for days. When the pains were very bad she wouldn't even let Ephraim read to her or pray with her. Then at her lowest she would begin to mourn Anna. Anna was her first-born, the child of her heart, but Anna had died. She was seven when it happened, years before Ephraim was born. Mama still could not forgive, not forget the horror of the doctor who had let her precious one bleed to death because of poorly managing the use of leeches on her abdomen. The event became a kind of myth for the young Ephraim, a child's death and a doctor's incompetence a faint shadow among the general happiness of the family. When his mother fell to these attacks Ephraim in his helplessness cursed the doctor – he must have been a cretin, a charlatan; it was heroic therapy gone murderously wrong. He wished beyond logic that he had been there to cure Anna, wished he were a doctor and could relieve Mama's pain. Their current physician had been useless in the other extreme. He did nothing but say, 'Drink tea, and wait. Wait and pray. It will pass.' Which kind of healing was best? The conflict in medical theories sharpened Ephraim's passion for learning; he was undecided, he would trust everything and nothing, he would find his own way, take the best from all theories, with the Lord's help.

On a more immediate scale, Ephraim had another personal medical puzzle to solve. Though fully recovered from his illness, occasionally its remnant, an excruciating pain in his upper left mid-chest, would strike, last for a minute, then disappear. In studies and dissection Ephraim sought possible reasons and drew a conclusion – the pain came from something in the cardia, where the esophagus meets the stomach. What triggered it he could never determine, but he had come to know that if he didn't drink some carbonated water – for its relieving burps – he'd be exhausted for half a day. Benjamin had long given up teasing about the episodic belching, but Burns and fellow students under Dr Cable mercilessly called it Dr Epstein's gaseous remedy.

By his second year Ephraim and his cohort had attended the wards of Bellevue as Junior Walkers, taking orders from the physicians or surgeons, dressing and bandaging wounds, administering bloodletting, copying cases into medical records. In his third year he was a Senior Walker, dressing fractures and dictating the case histories, all the while continuing lectures, labs and Dr Cable's extra studies and daily recitations. In entering the gates of Bellevue Ephraim felt no longer the novel thrill of privilege but the familiarity of professionalism, though never forgetting in his morning and evening prayers to praise and thank the Lord for this grace. He also had the blessing of a weekly clinical practice in a dispensary, an advantage not allotted to all under Dr Cable's preceptorship, but given to Ephraim in light of his aptitude and his Melioration mission. Senior students and even graduates normally paid to gain this experience, for unlike their hospital work it offered a pace and frequency of patients, a range of ages and infirmities closer to what they would encounter in general practice. This was a Presbyterian dispensary, next door to a church on Fourth Street. For working class and charity patients, it drew members of the congregation and other Christians and – sometimes – the Jews the society was trying to reach. As well as *The Israelite Indeed,* Benjamin distributed Fourth Street Dispensary fliers and acted as clerical assistant to Ephraim.

So they came, the Jewish poor who heard about the free dispensary. There were Jewish charities, but they generally treated those from their own kinds of Judaism, their own countries of origin; families who didn't fit or didn't go to synagogue were helped last of all. If this dispensary's doctor was a Christian Jew would he sprinkle water on them and turn them into Christians? Never mind, if he could cure their boy, their grandmother, the sick wife, the breadwinner, they'd risk it. Some cases Ephraim referred to Dr Cable but mostly he was on his own. It was all practice, readiness for the next step. Was this selling Christianity by false means? If he had to be honest with himself, and he did have to be, yes, probably it was a kind of bribery. He prayed that God forgave him.

One Tuesday in April, tapping the chest of an eight-year-old boy, Ephraim could hear the hollow and then the solid resonances of tuberculosis. 'He needs to go to the country,' Ephraim said to the thin-faced mother. She looked at her husband, an exchange of despair. Ephraim felt the boy's shoulder bones through his coat. There would be more like this when he went on mission. 'May I pray for him?'

'No medicine?'

'The medicine he needs is sunshine, clean air, eggs, meat, fish, vegetables, oats.' He kept his voice measured, trying to be the wise doctor, concealing his despair. Faith in the doctor was as important to the case as any medicine. Neither eclectic nor heroic therapy would save a child at this stage of the wasting disease. What hope for him, with his cough and too bright eyes, pointy chin and patched coat? Nothing but the Lord God's healing love would do it, and sometimes this did happen. But usually it did not. Nevertheless Ephraim's own faith in the Lord remained staunch. In Christianity, the boy had the promise of everlasting life.

The father said, 'Pray then,' and in Yiddish muttered, God knows, it's all we have. They sat and linked hands around the table. The sounds of others waiting, talking to Benjamin, shuffling their feet, coughing, penetrated into the curtained area. The boy's thin cold hand in his, Ephraim began, in Hebrew, 'Barukh ata Adonai Eloheinu melekh ha-olam.' Then in English repeated the words, 'Blessed are you, Lord, our God, King of the universe...' and the words of the Lord's Prayer, 'Our Father, who art in heaven, give us this day our daily bread...' After the Amen he added, 'These are the words of the Lord Jesus Christ, the messiah, beloved son of the God of love who gave his life so that you may live. Amen.'

'He may live?' the mother asked.

'If God wills it through Jesus Christ his son.'

'If we pray to Jesus he will live?'

'In my Father ye shall have everlasting life,' Ephraim quoted. He took a pamphlet from his black bag. 'Read these words and pray. Bring the boy to me in a month. Keep him warm, go for walks three times a week in the fresh air of Castle Garden. Can you give him an egg every day?' They were silent. 'Well, try. I will ask Benjamin.' He scribbled a note and gave it to them, saying, 'I think the funds can help for eggs.'

'Thank you, Doctor Epstein, thank you!'

'Read, pray, walk.' Bidding them goodbye, he looked into the boy's face, smiled and addressed him by name: 'Mordecai, have faith.'

'Give them six Bibles?' Benjamin's head poked through the curtain.
'Bibles – it's too soon.'
'That's what it looks like.' Benjamin waved the note at Ephraim.
'Eggs! A half-dozen eggs.'
'Medical handwriting, Dr Epstein! Right, money for eggs.'
'Ephraim!' A new voice called and a head peered in: Uncle Jacob's
wreath of white hair, his face leathery brown from sun and weather.
'Jacob!' Ephraim jumped up and hugged him. 'Where have you come
from?'
'That's for me to know and you to find out. What's this you are doing
here?'
'Solace for the sick and poor of heart. And body.'
'The Briskers at B'nai Avraham told me. I saw your newspaper, too!'
Jacob said. 'Mazel t'ov, you're a writer, and a regular snake oil salesman.'
'Shalom, Uncle, peace be with you,' he smiled, acknowledging the
teasing critique.
'Your patients are dwindling. When do you eat?' Indeed the noise level
of the waiting area had dropped. Ephraim checked his pocket watch, at
which Jacob raised his eyebrows. 'Nice tchatchke.'
Ephraim beamed. 'Essential for a doctor. A gift from Judge Sherman.'
He packed his lancets, bottles of purgatives and prescription paper into his
bag.
'Essential for a doctor's dignity most of all!' said Jacob as they set out
with Benjamin to dine and catch up on their news. In the last nine years
only six letters had passed between uncle and nephew. Distance was the
chief factor, as the route between California and New York could take five
months or more, but their communication was further slowed by
forwarding, for both had changed locations often. And then there was the
individuality of each. Jacob's passerine approach to life meant that he made
his home wherever he found it, and did not bother himself much with
writing to faraway family and friends, confident they would always be there.
Ephraim, for his part, had used the gaps in their correspondence to put off
revealing his radical conversion to Christianity. Finally he had told his uncle
at the same time that he'd told the family; a reply arrived in Andover when
he had long recovered from his illness. With trepidation he'd read Jacob's
letter, still shaken by his parents' response. Only at the end, after
descriptions of flourishing trade, of gold-bearing quartz and the queer
sensations of earthquakes did his uncle write, 'The Talmud says if you have
the chance to taste a new fruit and refuse it, you will have to account for it
in olam ha ba, the world to come. So, you tasted. As for me, I'll bend my
ear to your messiah-talk the day I hear Jerusalem is rebuilt. In the
meanwhile, Shalom.' And so Ephraim knew that one elder of the family did
not spurn him, even if he could not be persuaded to Jesus Christ.

There was a last summer for Ephraim at the society's upstate New York camp in Oswego. One last chance to sleep among the trees, among friends, to educate Jews newly come to Christianity, to study and debate and practice preaching, to swim in the lake, enjoy the sunshine, walk the trails, clear his lungs of the city. This time it felt different. Ephraim had a final short term of medical school to complete, and then... what? Staying in New York was unlikely, because the society had many members there, people tied to work and family, whereas he, Ephraim, was a free agent, about to be an MD who could practice anywhere, unencumbered by wife and children, to his continuing regret. He held to the faith that he and Rachel could somehow make their marriage work and he so much wanted to be a real father to Sarah. He had kept up his quarterly letters routed through Kathy, describing life in New York, sending some money, enclosing rhymes and wisdoms for Sarah. But before any possibility of being together he was at the behest of the society. He thought they might send him to the mission in Boston, because Andover was nearby. Or perhaps out west to Cincinnati where there was a sizable Jewish population. His highest hope was for Charleston down in South Carolina. Jews were long established there, too, but in addition he hoped for the chance to aid the abolition cause; if he could argue intelligently enough to convert Jews to Christianity perhaps he could also persuade slave owners to emancipate their Negroes. He even dreamed he might become a station for the underground railroad, linking the network for escaped slaves directly to Mrs Stowe's connections.

There was another reason for the difference this summer: he'd lost his tent-mate. But the loss was Benjamin's gain, for just before coming away to camp Ephraim had stood as his best man at Trinity Church in New York City. Benjamin Berman and Susannah Cuneo wed at the church of her family's chosen Episcopal Christianity, a more formal and elaborate form of the faith than Ephraim had yet known. New York City sparkled on that bright and happy day, and Ephraim, Jacob, Benjamin's musical friends, Melioration Society friends and Susannah's family showered the happy couple with rose petals outside the church amid the bustle of Broadway. Oswego was an extension of their honeymoon, and the new Mr and Mrs Berman's tent was set in the married couples' area.

Benjamin and Susannah believed in Ephraim's zeal and silver tongue; they speculated that his mission would be in Germany, Russia or even home, Belarus. The society would ask him to reach Jews not only through medicine but by recruiting them to emigrate, promising places at the farm in Harrison.

'Belarus? A prophet in his own land,' Ephraim gave a wry laugh. 'Not likely. Even Jesus wasn't heeded in Nazareth.'

'You spoke so well today, Ephraim,' Susannah tried to banish his doubts. They were bidding each other good night outside the main meeting tent beneath a crescent moon.

'Not too simple for the purposes? It's hard to judge. In church it's all Christians, so I have to inform and educate them about the Hebrews. Here it's all for Jews – drop the Hebrew, increase the Christian.'

'You had them eating out of your hands. I can just see you preaching in the square in Brisk,' said Benjamin, only half-teasing.

Ephraim stuck to the teasing mode, but couldn't help an edge of bitterness: 'Surrounded by Epsteins. Now there's a vision. Especially when I am a dead man to them.'

'Truly the resurrection when a dead man sends dollars to his so-called widow.'

'Not very many dollars, not yet. But at least I am keeping to my side of the agreement.' Ephraim thought again of the two diamonds he still held. When he knew his future, maybe he would sell them and send for Rachel and Sarah. Replies via Kathy now came only once or twice a year, with very brief notes from Rachel, and none from Sarah. He was sorry, knowing how difficult it must be for them.

When the society's decision came, Charleston receded; so did Boston, New York, Cincinnati. Ephraim learned he would be going both near and far. In the log cabin where six years earlier they had granted his destiny, Solomon Levi and Brother Paul Cassel, president of the society, in the name of Christ set him on his next path. When he had his medical degree he would take a steamer a mere hour's journey across Lake Erie to Kingston, Canada. On first hearing this Ephraim had to fight back a surge of disappointment – Canada? But then the plans unfolded and a mighty Alleluia lifted his heart. Kingston, capital of the British colony of Canada, was home to the outstanding Queens College Medical School. He would have three months of further medical training, learning the newest practices directly from English and Scottish physicians and surgeons. Even more important, he would be ordained a Presbyterian minister. That is, if the good people of St Andrew's Church, Kingston, approved of him. And then – before the year was out – he would be on his way as a missionary of the Presbyterian Synod of Canada to the Jews in Saloniki, European Turkey.

'We believe this is eminently suited to you,' Solomon said, smiling beneficently through his dark beard, appreciating Ephraim's astonishment at such a cornucopia of blessings. 'Dr Cable speaks plainly and with unaccustomed enthusiasm for your powers of observation, your natural sense, your dexterous management of patients, your energy, courage and patience in the face of obstacles and negative outlooks.'

The society's president spoke: 'We put our faith in you – your high character, your intelligence, your gift of languages, your Christian faith and passion. We also think,' and now he smiled too, 'that European Turkey is close enough to Belarus that you may be supported in your mission by the presence of your wife and child.'

PART 2: THE MISSION AND THE VICTORY

14

A MAN SHALL CLEAVE UNTO HIS WIFE
Saloniki 1860

Ephraim halted at the apricot seller and bought a pound of the dried fruits. He could understand the responses to his questions better and better. Yes, the apricots were plump. They came from the hills to the southwest. Fifty miles away. They came in by the old Roman road. Yes, he would like to see the blossom in the spring when the snow was still on the mountains. He, the Doktor, would be honored to visit.

The language was unlike others he knew but after four months he could get by in Turkish. He strolled off down the market with his packet of apricots, past the vendors of figs, pistachios, olives and oil, into the street of ceramics, and entered the gate to the Jewish quarter of Saloniki. Here again apricots, herbs, chickpeas, lamps and more filled the market, the men in black fezzes, in shirtsleeves and waistcoats. At the sweetmeats stall Ephraim bought dates stuffed with almonds, and now he was addressed in Ladino as M`edico. His mission among these Sephardic Jews meant Ephraim had to learn yet another new tongue, Ladino. Fortunately he knew a smattering already, for long ago Uncle Jacob had imparted some phrases, a vestige of his misty past. The Castilian-flavored Hebrew and Aramaic had come with the Jewish community when they were driven out of Spain and Portugal in 1492 and evolved since, a fascination for Ephraim's natural linguistic sensibility.

Dr Epstein entered his favorite cafe, and though rewarded by a familiar greeting, he tried – and failed – to forgive himself for not progressing faster. Four months, and he had won no souls. 'The end of a matter is better than its beginning, and patience is better than pride,' Ephraim could hear his father quoting Ecclesiastes; how hard he had drilled him to learn the Torah, what chastisement at Ephraim's own despair at ever being as perfect as he wanted to be. Patience, patience and faith, he told himself now, patience will win belief in Christ. Ephraim sat with the tiny cup of syrupy strong black coffee before him. Impatience was a familiar foe. Twice a week for three weeks now he had waited at the pier for the arrival of the big passenger boat from Athens, scanning the gangway for two dear, dear figures, his wife and twelve-year-old Sarah. The original welcoming sweetmeats he'd bought for them were no longer fresh, so he had replenished. Surely this time? Ephraim checked his pocket watch and departed through the winding streets down to the port, blind, for a change, to the minarets of the Ottoman Mohammedans, massive ruined Roman arches, domed Byzantine basilicas.

The steamer was already in sight. He hoped the voyage had been easy for his two women, although it was long. His own crossing from America had been smooth, the idyllic opposite of the hellish journey he had shared with Uncle Jacob. What would Rachel and Sarah think of this land? The ship docked, stevedores in baggy trousers secured ropes and gangways, fezzed porters in kaftans jostled for positions. It was more foreign than anything in America. America, even Russia, was more European than Saloniki. The heat for one thing. This Turkish heat was searing and dry, and Ephraim did as the residents did, resting, even sleeping, during the hottest part of the day and going about his business – at the missionary clinic, to the European chapel, on medical visits – in the mornings and evenings. Ephraim stood on a bench, the better to see and be seen. Many women with dark hair lined the railings; his heart leapt: a blonde child.

They were moving, shuffling toward and then down the ramp. He lost track of the pair he'd spotted, jumped down and pushed through the crowd, waving his top hat high, one of the handful of western-dressed gentlemen, the easier for them to find him.

'Mrs Epstein! Mrs Epstein!' he called and suddenly, 'Mrs Rachel Epstein,' he dropped his voice. There she was, 'Mrs Rachel Epstein.'

'Doctor Epstein.' She chose to speak English in response to his Belarusian. She smiled, 'Mein Mann. Schauen Sie sich den Bart!' My husband. Look at your beard! Not English, German. They clasped hands. She wore dark green, and a lighter green bonnet, dark curls at her forehead, that creamy skin, hardly any wrinkles, those shining eyes. People surged around them.

Ephraim startled and looked to her left, to her right, tried to peer over her shoulder. 'The porter promised to bring all the luggage,' she said in the Belarusian of their youth.

'But where is Sarah?'

'In the end, she did not come.' Rachel watched his stunned expression. 'I am sorry. They kept her.'

Ephraim had difficulties with Brother Albert Jeffers right from the start. The Presbyterianism of his fellow melioration missionary was of the dour, Calvinistic sort. Born and raised Christian, his father was an English Presbyterian but his mother had been a Jew – hence his calling to the cause.

Some souls, according to strict Calvinists, would never be among those predestined to be with the Lord; only the Lord God knew who would be saved and who not – so everyone, including Jews, had to be brought to the light. Ephraim had encountered a few like him at St Andrews Presbyterian Church during his six months in Canada. Like them, Jeffers's faith was dogma-ridden, unintellectual; his preaching battered at the Jews. Ephraim preferred to persuade in the words of Jesus Christ himself, and the irony of Hebrew logic: the Jews regarded themselves as God's chosen people – perhaps they were already saved? All they had to do was to recognize Jesus as the Christ, God's son, a gift of love. Jeffers's advantage: here for a year he spoke Ladino quite well, and he had none of the middle European Ashkenazi Jewish tradition that might interfere with his understandings of Sephardic ways.

But the year's head start in Saloniki was another part of the problem. The Reverend Jeffers was a pharmacist, sent with a doctor from the missionary training college in London to set up a free clinic for the benefit of the Jews. They had made some progress and then the physician had fallen ill and been invalided home. Left alone Jeffers lost heart. Gloomy, discouraged, discouraging, he provided no warm welcome for Dr Epstein, little hope that their mission would flourish. Ephraim's first work had been to rouse his brother in Christ from this slump; and it was still a challenge, for the sandy-haired man seemed morose by nature.

In the salon they shared, up one flight of stairs from the ground floor clinic, Ephraim presented Reverend Jeffers to his wife, and they found their way to French as the language all three could speak.

'J'espère que vous serez très heureuse ici, Madame, dans notre petite maison,' Jeffers gestured around the simple room.

'Moi, aussi, merci,' said Rachel. 'C'est très, très … Turkique.' Yes, thank you, she too hoped she would be happy in their little three-story house. Happy with its bare wooden floors and coarse Turkish rugs, its wooden settee and stiff, cane-seated chairs, with the glare of that fierce sun bouncing off the white building opposite. With sharing quarters with a complete stranger, a Christian stranger. 'Puis-je…' she turned to Ephraim and changed to their native tongue, 'May I adjust the shutters? The heat…'

'Bien sûr!' Of course. Ephraim hurried to slant the louvers more sharply, explaining that the cooler part of the day was just beginning, but the housekeeper had opened them early for this occasion. A muezzin's call wafted from another quarter, and he urged her to their room to rest, relieved that his pharmacist had been cheerful, joyful to be in possession of a wife at last. And deeply, quietly seething at being denied his daughter.

That evening Reverend Jeffers discreetly chose to see a friend from the consulate, leaving the couple to dine alone. To catch what small cool came with night Ephraim pulled the table near the open windows and after their meal of fish, rice and greens, bread and fresh figs, conversation deepened. The steady flame of a pottery oil lamp threw its glow on Ephraim's modeled cheekbones, his gray-blue eyes, his dark beard, on Rachel's waves and curls, her green eyes, the wide white V of her skin above the bodice of her dress. So many years, so many experiences to tell. First, further details of Rachel's journey: the railway to Vienna, then Trieste, the delays in finding the boat, the storm in the Adriatic; nothing, of course, like his first sea voyage, she made haste to assure him, no fear of death, no lack of food.

'You remember that!' Ephraim was charmed.

'Every letter. I read, and re-read. Some are in tatters.' Her voice thickened, 'Soaked in tears.' He stretched a hand across the table to her, and hesitantly she put her hand in his and gazed at him, tears glittering in her eyes. 'I was lonely, so lonely. I was a widow in your family.'

'I am sorry.' He bowed his head. He had begun their supper with a prayer of thanks to the Lord in Hebrew, and to Christ Jesus. 'I can imagine my father. But Kathy and Abraham, they were good to you. And Mama, too.'

'Oh, yes. She talks of you almost too much, every prayer, every day.' Rachel withdrew her hand to tuck away two stray curls that had fallen from the combs of her hairdo. Ephraim thought for a moment of the diamonds – but this did not seem the right time. Instead, having earlier complimented her on her uncovered hair, he said again how good it looked, how pleased he was that the enlightenment had released her from the Orthodox practice. 'The Czar's decrees forced it,' she added, with a shrug. 'Your mother was distressed at first. But Kathy and I were happy.'

'I need to hear all about Mama. Papa too, and everyone, and everything. But tell me about Sarah. You had her for comfort and company at least. Why did they keep her, how? How dare they!'

'You see the power they have. I told you it was hard. Even writing to you I had to do in secret.' Rachel sipped the last of the water from her glass and Ephraim refilled it. 'When you qualified as a physician Papa finally had to admit the arguments of Abraham and Reb Isaac, "a man shall cleave unto his wife". He could not deny. With Sarah... it was different. I have brought a new daguerreotype of her. You should be proud. She's pretty, and intelligent, too. All that worry about cousins marrying,' she shrugged again, and smiled. But Ephraim looked away and she continued. 'She is living and playing and studying with her cousins, at your parents' apartments. She is well, she is happy. I try to keep you in her memory.'

'This is unconscionable.' Abruptly Ephraim got up from the table and looked down into the dark quiet street 'I will demand to have her with us. I will write to father tomorrow.'

'Ja, mein Mann,' she said, savoring the words. My husband. Ephraim felt his response stir, thought of the marital bed upstairs. He sat again and their conversation resumed with her report on Pauline's wedding, on Kathy and Abraham's move to Heidelberg, on the older brothers-in-law, on Samuel and David. On Zayde too, hale as ever at the age of eighty-eight. What could Ephraim tell her of America? He described the brashness of manners, the pride in democracy, the confidence in striving and building. He said nothing about his conversion. Instead he outlined plans to show her Saloniki, told her more of its history ancient and modern. In thinking of her days, he promised he would take her to the one Ashkenazi shul for prayer – the Sephardic Jews even had a different name for synagogue, esnoga. She had met the Jewish cook-housekeeper, Deena, and he hoped that as well as visiting the market together Rachel would in turn share some of her own kosher traditions – if this was what Rachel wanted. He explained the mission's strategy in hiring a local Jewish woman to cook, a small but important way to gain the trust of the community. Besides, the food was different here, so much was different. 'So you gain trust through the stomach,' Rachel said. 'And through women. This is interesting, how your Christianity works.'

Ephraim regarded her, uncertain. Was this a challenge or genuine interest? Surely, it was too soon to introduce the Savior. He decided on a simple response – if and when she was ready to learn more, she would ask and ask again, as he had done. Patience, patience. So he answered, 'Yes. Food, women, children, medicine, learning. This is the way we show Lord's love, just as in Judaism.'

Soon it was time for bed. He suggested she precede him up the stairs with the oil lamp, and he would follow shortly. They agreed that she was tired, everything was so different and strange. He sat alone in the dark by the window for ten minutes seeing the sharp shadows cast by the nearly full moon, he thanked and praised the Lord for Rachel's safe arrival, and prayed for a new and happy married life. Upstairs, he opened the door to the small front bedroom which was to have been Sarah's: the little wooden chest, the table, the pretty turquoise and red tile he had bought for her, the single bed empty except for a slant of white moonlight.

One step across the landing and he opened the door to the glow of the small lamp. Rachel had left it on his side of the bed, and she lay, eyes closed, under the white sheet, her hair in a loose plait. He tiptoed in and turning his back to the bed, removed his clothes down to his undervest. 'I'm not asleep yet,' she said.

'Shhh. Go to sleep, you are tired.' Ephraim blew out the flame and took his place, feeling the strange weight of another body next to him on the mattress.

'It is so hot.'

'Yes.' Head on the pillow, he lifted the cotton sheet and let it waft down again over them both and realized Rachel was covered neck to wrists to toes in her white nightgown. 'You can... you will be cooler if you take that off. We just sleep under a sheet when it is like this.'

'I don't know what you want,' Rachel said meekly.

'Take off your gown, get into bed. Be comfortable.'

She slipped out and pulled off the gown, dropping it on the floor, the whiteness of it and her body picking up what little light came through the shutters. He looked away as she climbed back into bed. This time it was she who wafted the sheet over their bodies to create a brief breeze. 'Thank you, Ephraim.'

'Sleep well. Shalom, lialke.' Peace, little doll, he used the endearment from long ago. He lay quietly, listening to her breathing, thinking over the whole day, hoping for the days to come. Rachel sighed, and he felt her hand move on the bed towards him, nearly touching his thigh. He took it in his own and they lay holding hands. He thought of a print he had seen of the tomb of a Crusader knight and his lady wife, side by side in marble. The Song of Solomon came to him: 'my beloved is mine and I am his.' Of the words from Jeremiah, 'Lord, you have enticed me.'

Ephraim positioned the bleeding bowl below his patient's forearm and lanced the vein. They both watched the deep red blood flow. When it reached the first line engraved in the pewter, Ephraim said, 'One ounce should be sufficient.' He unbound the upper arm and as the blood slowed, pressed a cloth to the neat incision.

The mustachioed man looked doubtful. 'Is enough?'

'More in two days if your headaches do not change.' He slipped the lancet back into its tortoiseshell cover and returned it to the leather case. Joaquim had come to the clinic every other day for weeks, always looking worried, always with headaches. The emetics Jeffers had made up seemed to do no good, and two weeks' breathing of blood to relieve congestion also had no effect. Yet the forty-year-old was not debilitated by his headaches, and Ephraim had begun to suspect that the problem was not physical. 'Your name means "God will judge" '.

'Si. God will judge,' he answered listlessly as he rolled down his sleeve. He remained seated, although another patient waited outside. 'The blood. You Christians, you drink the blood.'

At the counter across the room, Jeffers stilled his grinding of cinnamon bark and caught Ephraim's glance. He nodded and returned to the mortar and pestle. Ephraim replied to Joaquim: 'Wine. Do this in remembrance of me, Christ said. Just like the wine of Shabbat, he blessed it and said that.' Ephraim spoke gently, slowly, though his heart pounded and his soul leapt up; indeed Joaquim's problem was not physical. 'God's son gave his life, his blood and body, to save us from God's judgment. To save you.'

'Why?' Joaquim looked directly at his doctor, his brown eyes begging for a reason.

'Because you are good.' But Joaquim turned his head, gesturing No. Ephraim continued, 'Do you know Eliazar's café? Come to me there. I will tell you where it is written in the Tanakh, the love of the Lord through Jesus was promised to the Jews long ago.' But he was torn, for tonight, of all nights in this fortnight since her arrival he had promised Rachel a walk by the harbor, an evening under the stars, a raki at a café, watching the parade of Turkish life. And then, and then...

But here was a soul in torment, ready for the Word. Why tonight? Resentment leached into him – his wife or his Lord? Well, of course, there could be no question. Of course – and what's more Jeffers had marked the opening. The opportunity could not be delayed. Oh but the taste is bittersweet, Lord God, Lord God, you are testing me, Ephraim prayed, and tried out ways to tell Rachel. He continued with the remaining two patients.

And so Ephraim left his wife alone after their evening meal yet again. On Tuesdays and Thursdays the medical missionaries preached downstairs, turning the bare clinic into a chapel, welcoming their little flock, growing their faith, educating those who, like Ephraim himself, would be fishers of men as Jesus had said to Peter. On other evenings they followed local custom in order to reach out. The cool of night was when men of the households came out to socialize over coffee or puff a nargile, so Brother Ephraim and Brother Albert would cross to Eliazar's café in the Jewish quarter. Sitting with cups of coffee they encountered one or other of the new Christian Jews and discussed, shul-style, various points of Torah, Nevi'im – especially Isaiah, and Ketuvim, most especially Psalm 2 – all the written words of God Almighty that proved Jesus as the promised Christ. True to Hebrew tradition their debates became lively and loud enough for others to overhear... and thereby spread the gospel of Christ. Even more than in America, Ephraim believed his mission to Jews here would win converts because its plain Protestant directness offered so much more clarity than the elaborate ritual and dogma of the Eastern Orthodox Christianity all around them. Ephraim carried in his heart the simplicity of the first church he had attended, how he had been touched.

Ephraim admitted cowardice to himself, having chosen to explain the disappointment to Rachel under cover of Jeffers's presence. She gave her husband a short smoldering stare, but then accepted the apology gracefully. He pledged the next night and thanked her. Walking down to Eliazar's after praying for Joaquim, Ephraim and Jeffers reviewed their plan of discussion, but in the background he found his thoughts upon his ordination. What a contrast to this heat: the crisp October blue skies, brilliant red and orange foliage, fresh wind off Lake Ontario – oh, but the fire in his heart. The congregation of St Andrews had welcomed him with joy. Old Reverend Machar admired and made full use of Ephraim's Judaic and Christian theological knowledge and insights. His strong Greek and Latin sealed the church's sponsorship of his mission, his prospects of success enhanced by his many other languages. No sooner had Ephraim settled into Queen's College Medical School and clinical rounds at Kingston Hospital than his preceptor there, a deacon in the congregation, urged the elders to proceed with Ephraim's ordination. And so he had prayed, and delivered his discourse, and been given the firm blessing of the Presbytery, said his vows, and full of the love of the Lord Jesus Christ, preached for the first time as a pastor.

Back later than usual, and exuberant, Ephraim found Rachel in bed, but not asleep. She was reading a book from Ephraim's collection, a practice begun because she had so little else to do, and one he was glad of, the more for them to share. He smiled down at her, pleased that she had decided to wait up tonight.

'So, it went well,' she said, keeping her eyes on the book.

'Yes, praise the Lord.' But for a change, Ephraim waxed no further. 'What are you reading?'

'Goethe.'

'Kennst du das Land, wo die Zitronen blühn?' He was undressing and stopped, his white shirt unbuttoned, to turn and quote the famous words of yearning for the sun, the light, the golden south, Do you know the land where the lemon trees bloom?

'There, there, with thee,' Rachel spoke the haunting refrain and then broke into tears. Ephraim was with her in an instant, arms about her, murmuring into her hair, kissing her face, comforting. She melted into him and wept.

'My dear, my dear – are you so unhappy?'

She shook her head, and turned her face up to his, and he kissed her tears, and then her lips. And then, as the volume of Goethe fell to the floor, the thing that he had planned would happen tonight after the stars and harbor and raki, did happen. And he praised the Lord yet one more time for leading him to be a scientist and doctor from America, with a knowledge of and access to the new preventative made of Mr Goodyear's patented rubber.

15

THE TASTE OF LEARNING
Saloniki 1861

Before long, to Ephraim's deep satisfaction, Joaquim accepted Christ and began preparation for baptism. Two others hovered on the verge: the medical mission was beginning to reap a harvest. On the domestic front, Rachel, escorted the first time by Ephraim, attended synagogue. How strange, how familiar it was, as he had waited outside, to catch the male Hebrew voices, Shema Yisrael Adonai Eloheinu Adonai echad... Hear, O Israel: the Lord our God, the Lord is one. They would be standing to daven, so different from his way of praying now. He still had his prayer shawl and yarmulke buried among his things, an attachment to his mother he could not bring himself to break, for by birth he was forever her son, forever Jewish under Jewish law. Impatience and frustration stirred again: Hear, O Israel – if only all Jews would continue to grow in their faith and accept Jesus as the Messiah, the Christ. But Ephraim refrained from proselytizing with Rachel. He was pleased indeed on Fridays to see her light the candles for Shabbat, to hear her pray, Barukh ata Adonai Eloheinu melekh ha-olam, Blessed are You, Lord, our God, king of the universe. He was happy to be the Epsteins sharing with Reverend Jeffers the prayer and food of the ancient weekly ritual that bound all Jews together, including Jesus Christ. Of course he framed this meal and all others with Christian prayers, praise and readings as normal, confident that they would subtly work their influence on his wife. He rejoiced in full marital life, and was pleased to see Rachel mixing with the women of both Ashkenazi and – via Deena the housekeeper – Sephardic communities. This was especially important because his work meant he had to leave Rachel alone frequently. With their daughter they would have been be a real family, and he still was determined that she would come. His hope lay in pressure from Kathy's Abraham as his own letters of demand had gone unanswered. But at least Rachel was forming friendships here; Ephraim's hidden hope was that in her these Jews would see the joys of Christian life reflected.

It was a good and peaceful year, but for the lack of Sarah. However, among all the goodness, there was still something missing. On the first anniversary of his arrival in Saloniki, after much prayer, Ephraim found the answer. Medical help reached out through the physical; now the mission needed to reach the intellect. The mission needed a school. At first Jeffers was not convinced – who would teach? how to support it? The Presbytery's money was stretched to the utmost. And who would attend? The Jews would be just as suspicious of a school as they were of physicians. But Ephraim pressed until Jeffers agreed to join his signature to Ephraim's in a letter of proposal to the English Presbyterian Synod, and another to the Melioration Society and one to the Canadian Synod as well.

Just as our fathers rained down sweets upon us when we learned our first Hebrew letters, so the sweetness of learning the languages of progress and the tools of science, and thereby the truth of scripture, will bring light to the Jews who remain in ignorance...

... he wrote his plea. Surely this would stir the elders, the brethren, to provide funds. As for teachers, at first Ephraim and Jeffers would teach, they would make the time, somehow. Even Rachel could teach the beginnings of French and German. Oh, to have bright, hungry minds to stimulate, Ephraim harked back to his youthful desperate quest for enlightened learning.

Of course it would take weeks for responses, and both Synods had to agree, so the wait for a school might stretch to months. In his impatience Ephraim went further. He would make his regular 'Our Fisherman in Foreign Fields' column into an appeal in *The Israelite Indeed*. Benjamin would see that Lederer gave it prominent space. He fired the article with his passion – this was like the good old days in New York, applying his God-given gifts of language, intelligence and faith to best purpose in reasoned, persuasive articles.

As medicine relates to all physical health, so does mental science relate to theological health. From the time of Nebucadnezzar, Hebrew tradition has suffered rabbinical wrappings and the degeneration of superstition. The un-Christian Jew cannot look to his scripture for the Word of God – the Word which names Christ – as an historical document, because he has not been educated to do so...

He ended the piece in a hurry, intending it for the Tuesday ship that would get it to New York in a fortnight. Rachel looked up from her sewing as he bustled about folding and sealing the letter. 'Shall I walk with you to the ship's office?'

Ephraim hesitated and looked at her, her eyes wide, trying not to plead. He had reason for not wanting her to come, but felt sensitive to the fact that she could not share his work as physician, preacher, mission worker, writer, and would not as yet share his faith. He wanted, after all, to be responsible as a husband. 'That would be pleasant,' he acceded. 'Would you like to stop and see the mosaics of the rotunda again?'

'To test me on my history lessons,' she mocked, but she was teasing.

'Well, they are Byzantine! Ancient, beautiful!'

'Yes, yes,' she fetched her hat and went on indulging his enthusiasm. 'Among the first in Christendom. See? You are a fine teacher. What was it again Saint Demetrius did?'

On the way, descending to the sheer pale turquoise of the harbor, he curried more support from her, talking of his plans for the school, her part in it. Sometimes he knew she was amused by him, tolerating his passions – passions mental, spiritual and physical. Most of the time he was struck by her sincere dedication to him. She would soon see the token of his husbandly regard. The other errand he had intended was to the jeweler's street to collect the diamonds he'd had the goldsmith mount as earrings. Should he give them to her for her birthday in July, or wait until their wedding anniversary in August?

But everything was about to come tumbling down. In his half year of medical training at Kingston Hospital, Ephraim had deliberately focused on childbirth, knowing that he would be called to this in his mission. The terrible year at Bellevue when four hundred women died from childbed fever haunted him. In Canada the hospital's Scottish physicians supported the disputed hypothesis of Semmelweis. In the 1840s this physician in Vienna General Hospital required his interns to wash their hands with chlorinated solution before examining each woman. The practice reduced cases of fatal post partum fever from ten per cent to only two per cent. Eventually Semmelweis insisted that all disease came from lack of cleanliness, leading to his dismissal in 1850 – the theory was radical, ridiculous: medical science had long established that diseases came from varied causes, abetted by imbalanced humors and foul miasmic air. Since then, journal articles and medics pro and con had debated the issue throughout Europe. Ephraim himself was convinced; he had seen the success of it for himself in Kingston's maternity wards.

In his own practice he rinsed his hands and made sure always to praise the kosher cleanliness of the Jews when he visited to attend births. In Saloniki most women managed with only the midwife, but when trouble arose, or among the more educated families, M'edico Epstein was called. And so he had the ever renewing joy of delivering a new son, a new daughter to a mother and father. Not all was joy every time; there had been a cleft palate, a strangulating cord, a stillbirth, a hemorrhage, a mis-formed foot – the risk of life brought the risk of death or damage. He was careful always to offer prayers and consolations in Hebrew, and go gently with his

Christian comforts. It was on a happy occasion, however – the safe arrival of a son after two previous daughters – that Ephraim's upheavals began.

After he had examined the infant and declared him healthy, after the midwife had swaddled him and put him to the breast of the exhausted, exhilarated mother, as he washed his hands preparatory to joining the celebrating father he listened to the women crowded into the next room for their own celebration. Old and young, family and neighbors, they were sharing tales of labors, births, marriages, betrothals, the familiar female gossip at these times. Among this he heard laughter, and his own name and familiar Hebrew words. 'Brit... mohel... Jesus...' He delayed, listening harder: a giggle, Mrs M'edico Epstein named. The subject was the circumcision of the boy child. The ceremonial operation would take place in eight days. But M'edico Epstein would never perform it as mohel because – giggles again – he puts el prepucio back on his schlang when he and Mrs M'edico do tashmesh like all Christian men do.

Ephraim's stomach heaved at the humiliation of his wife revealing the intimacies of their marital life. Icy with rage, he forced himself to smile and praise his way through the congratulatory gathering for the father and excused himself as fast as he could. Little did he know worse was to come.

He sat by the window of their parlor the better to see Rachel coming down the street, Bible on his lap, so angry that he could not bring himself to open it. Righteousness blocked him from God, anger piled upon anger. The day faded. His wife still had her hat on when she entered, exclaiming at Ephraim sitting in the dimness. 'You'll go blind, trying to read like that! Here, let me – ' and she lit the lamp, chattering all the while – 'What good news, I heard it was a boy! And the birth went well, she's well? She must be so happy.'

'Mrs Epstein. You are no longer to go among these people.'

'Ephraim?'

'You are the respectable wife of a respectable doctor and pastor. It is not right and proper to give cause for gossip about our intimate life.'

'What gossip,' Rachel said flatly and unpinned her hat, turning away to lay it down.

'You may continue to help in the clinic. You may go to your own synagogue among our own Jews. I will see to getting another housekeeper.' He was standing now, looking toward the hat on the side chair, not at her, his voice low, steady and sad. 'I will be sleeping in the other bedroom.'

Her cheeks flared red. 'I am the respectable wife of a Christian doctor, who puts a rubber cover on his penis! For Christian sex!'

He raised his voice in response to her hiss: 'It is nothing to do with Christianity and you know it. We are cousins. We cannot risk another child.'

'Sarah is beautiful, she is fine! We could have children. You just hate me!'

'No. I thought I could love you. The Lord knows I have tried.' They faced each other. 'But I cannot. You have lied.'

'It is not a lie! And anyway, it's just woman-talk, nothing that really matters.'

'Respect matters, by the Lord Jesus Christ!' His voice rose, and then dropped again. 'But there is more. I got a letter from Mama today.' Rachel sat down, knowing what was to come. Ephraim resumed his quiet, sad tone. 'I've come back from the dead – wonderful, the first letter from her in eight years. But also terrible, because now I know you betrayed me. You said it was my parents who made Sarah stay behind with the family. But to them you said I did not want Sarah to come, a complete untruth. You have denied Sarah to me.'

If Jeffers noticed the new sleeping arrangements he said nothing, of course, and he accepted Ephraim's explanation of the other changes: his wife had found the languages and customs just too difficult to tolerate. In public Ephraim and Rachel were civil. In private they spoke not at all. He was shocked to discover that until this point he had still held a dream of the two of them making a real marriage. Instead they were worse than back to the warfare of their early married days. Ephraim's bouts of gastric chest pains became more frequent. He spent time in the little bedroom studying, writing and praying. Rachel worshipped at the Ashkenazi synagogue more often, and joined its charitable work among those Jews. The ever-morose Reverend Jeffers continued to train her in the production of pills and syrups and actually praised her skills. She comforted children and their mothers at the clinic under Ephraim's watchful eye. She ceased to attend the evening preaching and Ephraim hoped that Jeffers assumed this was to do with their religious differences. No decent Christian could force anyone, not even a wife, to come to the love of Christ.

He prayed for patience, more patience. He must trust in the Lord to find a way through this impasse. Send Rachel back to Brest? That would be so cruel – but then, she'd been cruel, perfidious, in preventing Sarah from coming. Why? To hurt him? To beat him in one of their petty battles? He could hardly imagine the possibility that she wished to have him all to herself. Perhaps it was to punish him for the years of so-called widowhood. After all, he in the first place had left them behind. But when it came to 'in the first place' it was his grandfather, Zayde, who had made them marry and created this mess. The buts and ifs and accusations chased through his head and he knew he would continue to tolerate Rachel. He had to, it was his duty. She was bearing up well, out of guilt because she knew she had done wrong, he surmised. But meekness was not in her nature, it would not last long. When the mission school opened her energies would be diverted into teaching German and French; she could do little harm there, and she would be happier with more to do. And therefore easier to live with. As for the diamond earrings, never, ever would they belong to Rachel.

At least one benefit had come of this pain; Ephraim delighted in being in contact with Mama again. He was relieved that his father had relented enough to allow the letters. He did not stoop so low as to reveal Rachel's lie, simply made sure to clarify the reasons he supposedly had for keeping Sarah from Saloniki – the heat, disease, her education. He described the Turkish people, the port, the ruins, their little house. With regret (and furious anguish he kept between himself and Rachel) he had to say there was no question of sending for Sarah at present. He continued to write short, colorful notes to Sarah, as he had been all along in care of Rachel, via his sister Kathy. Now, at last, he could send them directly in care of his mother.

It was May, 1861, approaching the anniversary of Rachel's arrival in Saloniki. Despite the baptism of several whole families, Ephraim chafed to move forward, to do more in the name of Christ Jesus. There was still no reply from the Presbytery Synods about founding the school. Some donations arrived from the Melioration Society and *The Israelite Indeed* articles, along with news of a different sort: war in America. The southern states had broken away to form an independent confederacy, the north fought the rebels to maintain the union of the United States. Over dinner on the day they'd read of the war in the English newspaper, Ephraim told Jeffers and Rachel about Harriet Beecher Stowe and the inhumanity of Negro slavery. He told them too about the ravages of civil revolution he seen as he'd crossed Europe in 1849. They prayed in both faiths for an end to the fighting. Ephraim that night wrote to Benjamin and wondered where in the world Uncle Jacob was now.

Finally, the longed-for letter from the senior Synod arrived. Instead of coming by ship's post Jeffers brought it home from the English Consul. Addressed to Dr Epstein as head of the mission, both men were pleased to have this official channel used for their new endeavor. It connoted recognition of the education project. But within moments of scanning the letter Ephraim's face fell. 'Smallpox. We are ordered to Monastir immediately. And there is to be no school.'

16

EPIDEMIC
Monastir 1861

On the three-day coach journey to Monastir, Ephraim thought and thought again about his decision. The ancient Ignatian Way took them inland, southwest, climbed through a mountain range, then descended to take them north through a wide flat vale with hills in the far distance on either side. The country was fresh and green with spring which receded as they travelled north, the vistas were punctuated with farming hamlets, Byzantine-style chapels and occasional mounds of Roman ruins. In other circumstances Ephraim would have exclaimed, asked questions of coachmen and fellow travelers, explained significances to Rachel. She sat beside him, watching the land through their jolting progress. But Ephraim had not relented in his response to her perfidy. The silence gave him full reign to brood over a greater insult. He fumed each time he ran the Presbytery's letter through his head. How could it be that arrogant, bull-headed authority had interfered in his Christian life? Could they not see that a school was the way? They were wrong, and the whole mission in European Turkey would fail.

Reverend Jeffers had not been surprised at the rejection of the proposal. He led prayers to assuage their disappointment, seeming almost to enjoy acquiescence. This stoked Ephraim's outrage. Hurriedly, before their departure, he dashed off an impassioned letter to the senior Presbytery in London and set out the case more firmly, not even bothering to get Jeffers's support. He wanted to say he would resign if a school was not founded, but held back – would this do the Lord any good, or the mission, or himself? Perhaps it was a test; he would keep the threat of resignation as a last resort, for truly, the Lord knew, Ephraim knew, a school would win souls to Jesus Christ. Nevertheless, Ephraim dared to disobey one aspect of the order. He left Reverend Jeffers behind in Saloniki. The mission was just beginning to make headway, timing was crucial. To abandon it now, a folly. Much better to keep Jeffers fanning the flickers of new faith; Rachel could do as much as the pharmacist when it came to smallpox. The only care for the horrible disease was good nursing – and prayer of course. Any medicines would be of the simple kind that Jeffers had taught her; if more complex prescriptions were needed Ephraim would make them up himself or find a chemist in Monastir.

He glanced at his wife and found her looking at him, and hastily looked away. Teaching would be the best use of her time and energies. Until then, he hoped the nursing would keep her busy. For the first time since he had come to Jesus he found himself wishing he were still Jewish, for under Jewish law he and Rachel could divorce. But the God of Christ – and his theological training, the Melioration Society and his ordination as a pastor – did not sanction divorce. The words from Benjamin and Susannah's marriage ceremony reverberated: That which God hath joined together, let no man put asunder.

Just as his onslaught of emotions and thoughts was calming and Ephraim was beginning to speculate about the situation in Monastir itself, Rachel, sitting opposite, exclaimed, 'Snow!' He twisted round to see the highest peak of the Baba Mountains ahead, in the direction of their travel. The other four passengers took turns at the windows to get a good sight of Mount Pelister. Soon the city at its foot would appear. Ephraim's memory of the classics spoke – Macedonia. This kingdom had grown up seven hundred years before Christ, it had been ruled by Alexander the Great and centuries later it had been a Roman, then a Byzantine province. Now it was part of the Ottoman Empire. Their way was the old Roman road that connected the Adriatic coast with the Aegean. Monastir was at the meeting point of routes north, south, east and west. Saints had followed the road, bringers of the gospel, and now he, Ephraim trod in their paths. The same expulsion that had brought Portuguese and Spanish Jews to Saloniki had brought them to Monastir, the same Sephardic Jews he needed to convert to Jesus Christ. But at present he needed only to be their physician through this crisis of smallpox.

As the provincial capital and second largest city in the region after Saloniki, Monastir had been chosen for mission to the Jews by the Presbytery of England some five years before, run by a highly experienced missionary. The city was rapidly transforming into European ways under the influence of trade, war and diplomacy; the population was open to new ideas. Ephraim very much looked forward to meeting the respected Reverend Blackstone who won converts by his preaching alone; as yet there had been no further development into medicine. Or schools – Ephraim felt the light of Christ leap within him: here, this, would be the place for a school. When health returned to the town, he would institute education here instead of Saloniki. The Lord works in mysterious ways, he frowned, perhaps this was all meant to be.

118

One hundred and two people had died, fifty were ascertained ill with various stages of smallpox, and twenty a day added to this number. Until people in these unenlightened parts of the world gave up their superstitions, believed in and had access to vaccination, the scourge of smallpox would strike and strike again. Outbreaks had come before to Monastir, but this one was overwhelming. The main street was like a ghost town. City officials had closed the famous huge covered Bazaar and all but the most essential of the workshops and markets in the sprawling alleys. They were grateful for any medical help: English, Austrian, French, Russian, Christian, Muslim, Jew or Hottentot. The scale of the disease and the work to be done sidelined the catastrophe that had greeted the Epsteins – Reverend Blackstone had died a week ago. Not of smallpox, for no missionary would be unvaccinated, but from a fall. Ephraim and Rachel had found their way to the mission, a big, pleasant Italianate building just off a small square, to find no one, and no explanation. Leaving their bags and boxes they walked the narrow side-streets and quickly found the Jewish quarter and some of the Christian Jews, including a convert couple who had helped Blackstone in his house and mission. The Monastir converts had had no idea that a mission doctor was on his way, and Ephraim's arrival seemed truly miraculous. That very evening Reverend Doctor Epstein led prayers and preached to the orphaned flock. The fact that he was a pastor, a physician, and married, for Reverend Blackstone had been a widower, was all the more miraculous. Rachel threw herself into her role as the good, obedient and authoritative wife. She unpacked pharmaceutical supplies, surveyed the understocked house, requested supplies from the mission's followers, made use of her Ladino to gather information about the smallpox outbreak from the local women. If the little congregation noticed that she did not attend prayers, they assumed she was supervising medical preparations. In fact, she was seeing to it that two bedrooms in this comfortable house were prepared – one for her, one for Ephraim.

After meeting with the English consulate and two exhausted local physicians, Ephraim drew on his time at Bellevue to manage the smallpox. As at the great New York hospital, isolating existing cases was paramount; elsewhere in the city some physicians had begun to do this and Ephraim urged support for the movement. For use as quarantine hospital he was offered a mansion surrounded by a walled garden; it belonged to an Austrian merchant who had fled the epidemic. He and the other doctors recruited helpers who had already had smallpox. They set up beds, carried in the sick, and, under Ephraim's direction Rachel and the helpers ministered to them, sponging, cooling, getting liquids into them. There was no point in bleeding or cupping. At first ten a day died. After a week this slowed to four a day. By the end of a month, it was four a week. Those who survived were scarred, usually disfigured with pitted pocks all over the face where the vicious disease always manifested most strongly. Some were blinded by smallpox, some crippled by its effect on joints, but when it took the hemorrhagic pathway fatality was the outcome. Overall a third of those infected would die. Among children Ephraim knew eighty per cent would die.

Most of the patients were Mohammedans, of course, and many were Christians of the Eastern Orthodox kind, and some were Jews. So the feverish moans mingled with callings out to Allah, to the Lord, to Jesus, to Mary, to saints Ephraim had never heard of. He had no one to share his proselytizing with; nevertheless, he kept his Bible and prayer book always with him. Murmuring for permission, speaking of Jesus Christ, savior of souls, he baptized the dying who expressed hope – some Jews, some Mohammedans – that the Christian Lord would save them. For those who expressed no such hope he prayed in Hebrew, in Greek, in Ladino, in Turkish to whatever god they called upon. Uncle Jacob's accusation of snake oil quackery taunted Ephraim in his tiredness at night, in his helplessness at women's ululations of grief, at men sobbing and tearing their beards.

And then it ended. On a June afternoon the etesian winds arrived, unusually late, blowing in from the north clear, dry, warm weather after weeks of gray drizzle. No new cases were brought in, the ill could be nursed more closely, survivors began to go home. The crisis passed, and the Epsteins began to sleep at nights, to bathe and eat meals regularly, to live something of a normal life. But there was the final death, a little Jewish girl of seven named Sarita. Rachel and Ephraim had taken turns tending her, each knowing the other thought of their own Sarah. Together they attended the funeral at Monastir's Jewish cemetery and joined in the burial Kaddish. Ephraim had spoken the Christian funeral rites in sad solemnity many times over the last month, but this time the sorrow nearly overwhelmed him and he barely heard the words as he recited the Jewish rite, 'ul' ahay metaya... ulme 'quar pulhana nukhra'a m'ar'a, where He will give life to the dead... and uproot foreign worship from the earth... Shalom alenu ve'al kol yisrael, peace for us and for all Israel... Amen.'

After the family's week of sitting shiva for the child her older brother came to Ephraim in the mission residence, to thank him, it seemed. But to do more: to ask about the Christian God. If his sister had been Christian, would she be alive today? But of course Ephraim could not and would not promise that.

'Why did the Lord take Sarita and not me? How can he be so cruel? I was just as ill, I nearly died, but – why! Why did I live and not die?' He was seventeen, dark-haired, light-eyed, intense, wracked with grief and anger. Ephraim listened, not trying to stem the anguish. He waited and thought of himself at the same age, full of questions and anger. Now he was nearly twice that, still full of questions and passion, which had taken him far. He hoped he had learned some patience, some wisdom, some worthiness before God. The youth went on, 'I would rather be dead. If I could have died in her place... It can't be right.'

'You expect the Lord to be right? To be fair? The Lord does not operate on our terms.'

'The rabbi says that. My father says that.' He clasped his hands together, staring at the floor. He unclasped them, balled his fists, re-clasped them. 'I hate being alive.'

'No, you must not. God is also love.' Now Ephraim used the full word, in Hebrew, Jehovah, Yaweh – in the Jewish faith of the young man an unsayable word. He was making a point: the God of the Torah was the same Christian God of the Old Testament. 'God sacrificed his own son, his own living selfhood, for love.'

'What kind of love kills?'

'The love of all mankind. This love, this suffering and death, once and for all time, forgave all sinfulness. If you can find that in your heart, then you are saved.'

'And Sarita? It is too late for her to be saved,' the seventeen-year-old said bitterly.

'We cannot know. We can pray for her.' And Ephraim began to pray for the soul of Sarita beloved of her brother Teodor. He prayed also for the community here in Monastir and for the world. He prayed for the light of Christ to enter the hearts and souls of all. And he returned at the end to Sarita and her everlasting peace. He repeated this last prayer, eyes on Teodor who had sat through all this praying, listening, watching. At Ephraim's eyes' urging Teodor hesitantly joined in the repetition of the Christian prayer for his sister.

After a silence, Ephraim said, 'Do not despair, Teodor. Jesus Christ is with you.'

'If only I could believe that.'

'You can. Come to see me here again tomorrow. We will talk.' The work was beginning again.

Ephraim decided that he had to continue at this mission, at least until further orders came from the Presbytery. No messages had come from Jeffers this six weeks, but nor had any news of smallpox in Saloniki so there was no urgent need to return. They had said no to a school there – very well, he had come to Monastir as a physician and here he would stay. He had to join the city's other physicians in conducting a smallpox vaccination program. There was a congregation of new converts who needed a minister, and a population of primed Jews to bring to Jesus. He and Rachel had already set up a room in the mission building as a clinic. He would explore the establishment of a school, which would be most welcome. This he knew for certain from the little flock here and from the city officials who thanked Dr Epstein effusively for his achievements in helping to manage the smallpox epidemic.

As for Rachel, Ephraim had seen her in a new light during the crisis. She had been strong, capable, reliable. She had not complained even at the dirtiest and saddest of work. She had mixed, rolled and cut up pills, brewed syrups, administered medicines, supervised helpers, comforted the sick. She had followed his orders without demur. He could never forgive her for denying him Sarah, but perhaps in this new setting of Monastir, and with a school, perhaps their partnership could be successful. At least successful enough outwardly and tolerable enough privately; perhaps they even could send for Sarah. Tentatively, after thanking her for sharing the burdens of the emergency, and praising her good work, he hinted at this truce. Without rancor she agreed, saying the climate here near the mountains was much more bearable than the fierce heat of Saloniki, and the shops, cafes and markets were so cosmopolitan, so lively now that normal life had resumed in Monastir. She mildly added that she preferred to be with him than being the so-called widow of a shunned kofer, a heretic.

It was on Shabbat, the Saturday, of that first calm week of renewal, that everything changed. Ephraim came back from the poste-restante perturbed and shut himself in his study to pray. When he heard Rachel return from shul he called her to come to him. Which news to break first? He held up two letters briefly and asked her to sit down. He chose the blow bitterest to him.

'The replacement for Monastir is on his way. He is a physician and the mission here is to expand, with a pharmacist they have selected. I am to return to Saloniki.'

Rachel took this in. 'I'm sorry. We liked it here better.'

'There is more. I am reprimanded for leaving Jeffers there.' Ephraim raised his voice, 'And there is to be no school. Not here, not there, nowhere in European Turkey. The fools!' He flung the letter onto the desk. Then he heaved a great breath and with the other letter in hand said, 'But there is something else. Zayde has died.'

'Zayde!' Rachel gave a startled cry and put her hands to her face. The patriarch, the one who had always been there, an implacable mountain, gone.

Ephraim sat down in the straight chair next to her, sharing the strangeness. He did not feel sad, but only as if a huge gap had been broken through the thick stone wall of a giant fortress, revealing a wide landscape. 'Mama says we should come to Heidelberg, to Kathy and Abraham. It is decided in law that because we obeyed and married and kept the dowry in the family we must inherit Zayde's legacy as husband and wife together – a great amount, ten thousand rubles. Mama says we should come to receive it. She says she will be there, Papa and she will be there. We will meet – I can see her again!'

17

EPHRAIM FEEDS ON THE WIND
Heidelberg 1862

Pale, small, frail, for the briefest of moments Ephraim did not recognize her, and then – 'Mama!'

He flung his arms around his heart's balm, bowing his head to kiss her tear-wet cheeks as she murmured his name. They pulled apart and Ephraim extended his hand towards his father, seeing his rising unease at the outpouring of emotion, and then surprised himself by hugging Papa, too, and found the hug returned. He had aged, wrinkles etching his fine skin, beard gray, but he was still robust in figure. There was Kathy next, recognizable as his little sister, but a handsome, mature woman now. Their embrace turned into mutually curious smiles of assessment. Greetings with Abraham, his khaver, best pal of youth, and now brother-in-law, had been exchanged joyfully at the train station when he collected Ephraim and Rachel. As can happen with early soul-mates, they immediately felt easy, talking during the carriage ride home as if they'd seen each other only a month ago. And then, hovering half-hidden behind Kathy, a graceful, blonde, blue-eyed fourteen-year-old, Ephraim's daughter: Sarah. Rachel had followed her husband along the semi-circle of gathered family but now pushed forward to kiss Sarah on the cheeks and draw her toward Ephraim. Astonished by her beauty and natural elegance, he could find no words.

'Papa,' she bobbed a little curtsy and blushed.

'My dear, dear girl,' he pulled her close and kissed her forehead. 'I knew from the daguerreotypes you were beautiful, but they do not do you justice. I look forward to spending hours and hours with you.'

'So do I.' She smiled and then looked away and blushed again, not comfortable at being the center of everyone's attention.

Suddenly the room bustled with movement as four of Kathy's children came forward and she and Abraham and Mama – granny, Bobeshi – introduced them to Ephraim and re-introduced Rachel to them. Adding to the happy chaos, the youngest, not counting the baby asleep in the nursery, clung to Sarah's skirts clamoring to be picked up.

To embrace the family he loved, to be embraced, and not in Belarus but Heidelberg – it was like a dream. The journey from Turkey had been long, not only in miles but in Ephraim's inner pathway. Initially he and Rachel had stayed on at Monastir for the arrival of the replacement physician missionary. She continued to be biddable, and he had relented in his silent treatment – although they still slept apart. The prospect of a solid amount of money and Europe and family seemed to lighten the burden between them. He chafed, still, at the utter dismissal of education for the mission's work. During this waiting period, with prayer and contemplation, he reviewed his two years in Saloniki and his few converts, his work as a physician, his temperament and his faith. He was a man of Christ, most definitely, but he felt – Ephraim finally admitted to himself – a failure as a missionary. Not that he would fail if they allowed him to form a school! He owed a great deal, so much, to the Melioration Society: three years of seminary, three years of medical school, ordination, brotherhood. But to cloak preaching under medicine had begun to feel tainted, for himself at any rate. His portion of Zayde's money could free him of his obligation.

What would he do instead? He was a man of science as well as a man of God. Continue as a physician – and perhaps one day he would teach. Stay in Europe? Vienna, Warsaw, Berlin? Not Belarus – too discomforting to the family now that he was Christian, and too much at the whim of the Czar. More likely back to America, land of opportunity. He would pray for guidance. In these wispy possibilities he did not see Rachel at all, but what he was to do about her he did not know. Only that the money that long ago had forced them together would somehow make their situation easier. Ephraim wrote his letter of resignation to the Presbytery, and wrote to Brother Solomon of the Society, to Benjamin, to Reverend Jeffers. Rachel knew of his bitter disappointment about a mission school, so he told her only that he was resigning the Saloniki post, but not that he had decided to give up being a missionary altogether.

Heidelberg is a small city with an ancient provenance and Ephraim was enormously curious to see it, and to see how his brother-in-law had settled in here. The same enlightenment that had set Ephraim on the path to America had resulted in Abraham Sack succeeding as associate professor of chemistry in the medical faculty of the famous University of Heidelberg. Among Europe's oldest educational institutions, the university was founded in the 14th century, its handsome buildings centered on a square in the heart of the old town. Nearby, the well-kept market square bustled with prosperity in the shadow of the city's massive gothic church, and just beyond lay the old red brick bridge across the River Neckar. The area abounded in cafes, bookstalls, student inns, drinking taverns and students themselves, flush with exuberant intellectual energy. The university had a theology faculty as well, harking Ephraim back to his student days. But the ethos at Andover had been austere and earnest, and in New York the school of medicine was new and striving while here he felt caught up in the atmosphere of a pure, relaxed and confident heritage of learning. Goethe himself had once strolled and talked and thought in the gardens of Heidelberg Castle, its battlements rising above the city, its rambling ruins even older than the university.

'Abraham, Abraham – so, you are happy?'

Ephraim's friend, with the same mild, restrained manner he'd always had, nodded. 'Happy in my faith, too. Lord willing, you are in yours?' This could have been a barb, an accusation, but his tone was natural and gentle and he continued, 'Very wise of you to arrive after Yom Kippur and Sukkot. Although your mother…'

'I arranged it – impossible for all of us otherwise. So far, it's all right, don't you think?' Ephraim took another bite of apfelstrudel, another swallow of hot chocolate. They sat at a café off Universitatsplatz on Ephraim's impulse, a wish to spend time among students. Abraham had shown him through the venerable institution, introduced him to colleagues in the chemistry laboratory, opened doors into lecture halls and libraries, and stood with him for a half hour at the top tier of the medical theater while the university's leading professor of surgery conducted the removal of a gallstone. The brothers-in-law took pleasure in comparing the practice and teaching of medicine in the new and old worlds. Now the talk turned to family.

'Mama shouldn't be traveling, I can see it tires her, and puts Father completely out of sorts. Why come all this way? They could have made us to go to Brisk for the inheritance and the paperwork.'

'You shamed them, Ephraim. Better for them to come here.' Abraham hesitated as Ephraim bowed his head. Then he went on, 'But there is more. It was closer for you, and they were afraid you might refuse the money. Or even refuse to see them. You are the lost sheep, the heretic, apikoros.'

'Kofer ba-Torah.' Ephraim refined the word his friend chose for the particular one of nine kinds of apostate he was: not a denier of God or Moses, but a Nazarene, maintaining that in Jesus the Lord has given a new covenant.

'Kofer, yes. They don't know you anymore. But she is so longing for you. They are courting you, Ephraim, can't you tell? The money's an excuse. It is their last rounds, visiting each of their distant children – Pauline, Cecilie in Hamburg, Eva in Warsaw, Kathy. Your mother – do you see how pale she is?'

'But she's only…' Ephraim thought of her age, and then thought again of her appearance. 'She's not…' he couldn't bring himself to say it, and he had been unwilling to see it: his mother was declining into mortal illness, her health worn down by eleven births, the first at age fourteen. 'No, no, she will soon be better, we will send her to a spa, we will find the best one for her.' He denied the facts, and knew the truth. He quietly voiced the next obvious thing: 'I know what she wants and prays for. But I can't. I know Jesus Christ is the Messiah.'

Abraham left a thoughtful silence as Ephraim gazed unseeing across the café, out through the window to the passersby so full of life and direction this bright October day. He came back to the present moment with new thoughts. 'Isn't Sarah a fine girl. She is lovely with your children.'

'They are very fond of her. Kathy thinks Sarah is very special. Your parents have done well by her, raised her like one of your own sisters.' In both men's minds Rachel arose, but the troubled marriage was not a subject either would broach. They stirred their chocolate and drank. Ephraim commented that Abraham no longer kept strictly kosher, nor did he wear his yarmulke outside prayers.

'I have escaped orthodox mitzvot... old ways, old rules. Superstitious nonsense,' he replied. 'But there is much that is good. Much.'

They parted, Abraham back to his work, Ephraim to explore the city. So he said, but in fact he was desperate to find a church. Thus far, to avoid paining his parents, he had only prayed in his bedroom – once again shared with his wife, for propriety's sake. He thirsted for hallowed ground, the crucifix, the unison of worship, the words of Jesus Christ spoken aloud, for the joining together of female and male voices in hymns, too, for he found much joy and meaning in Christian sung praise. He needed to pray, needed the support of his faith to guide him through the onslaught of his return to Europe, the presence of his parents, meeting his nearly-grown daughter. So many ties, so many pulls. The soaring gothic red-brick bulk of Heiliggeistkirche – the church of the holy spirit – drew him. Inside, white and pale pink was the overwhelming effect: high pointed arches, pale pink stone, fine rib vaulting, delicate fan vaulting, exquisite narrow arched windows illuminating all. Light and airiness lifted his heart. Ephraim paused at the west end of the nave adjusting to the cathedral-like space and became aware of a mutter and hum far forward to the left, a call, 'Dominus vobiscum.' And response: 'Et cum spiritu tuo.' Latin: The Lord be with you. And with thy spirit. Then he noticed the man-height wooden partition that began a few steps in and ran straight up to the choir and high altar far ahead. Half the church was Catholic, half Protestant, a sharing begun some three hundred years ago in this land where Martin Luther had stirred the reformation of Christianity. Ephraim advanced to the righthand, quiet, side. He knelt and prayed for half an hour, then sat in contemplation.

The first few days had indeed gone well. His father, as usual, went to synagogue daily and retreated to his room to study and pray, but even he lingered with the family over meals to hear Ephraim's descriptions of American people, industries, cities and countryside and the tale of the terrible sea voyage with Uncle Jacob. Every afternoon Ephraim delighted in strolling out with Sarah; how wonderful it was to say 'my daughter', to tuck her arm under his and walk and talk and to learn each other as she emerged from her initial shyness. They would return to sit round the samovar, Mama and Sarah an enraptured audience, listening and asking. He told them about American politics, laws, freedoms and rights. He shed light on the northern and confederate states and the war, told them about Mrs Stowe and the underground railroad that helped Negro slaves escape. He avoided religion, keeping to safe topics: some of his medical experiences, the recent smallpox drama, the Roman ruins in European Turkey.

In turn, gradually he learned from his parents about life in Belarus: grandfather's decline and death, news of Ephraim's siblings from Chenye at the top to Helene, the youngest, plus the education and health of all the grandchildren, details of betrothals and weddings, struggles and successes of the Epstein brick factory and other family businesses. His father also clarified the worrying stories of changes since Nicholas I had died and Alexander II became Czar. Yes, the law to emancipate serfs had been published, all very well, but despite his liberality Alexander was determined that Polish peoples, Lithuanians and their own Belarusian area should be directly governed Russian-style. Last year had seen scores of demonstrations, and finally the Russian army had put the Polish under martial law. Unrest was building. Of course the Jews of these regions had always lived under the Czar's diktat, but what troubles would come from all this, what difficulties in Brest?

Rachel came and went, having heard it all before, pleased to be back in Europe, back in an Ashkenazi Jewish household. Although Ephraim and she could not hide a certain awkwardness between them she was still on good behavior, reveling at last in her due and proper role as wife and mother within the family. She busied herself helping to put the house back to rights after Sukkot, supervising Sarah's lessons and sewing, entertaining Kathy's five children. What matter that he was kofer, her husband at least was a physician, handsome, intelligent and talented. He'd left the Turkish missions, his parents were talking to him at last, and now they had a sizable nest-egg between them – who knew, anything could happen.

In several sessions Ephraim had his longed-for time with his mother, quietly alone in the Sacks' front parlor. She plied him with questions on his illness in Massachusetts: what symptoms, what treatment, who cared for him? He told her about the heroic therapy's success and his lingering gastric symptoms. He found himself expounding on the new, less harsh school of medicine, and confessing his worries about her health, and the influence on her – and him – of that long-ago death of her first child. He described the intelligence and loving nature of the Stowes and their family, even sweet Clara. She wanted to know about Benjamin. Her sympathetic, listening nature brought Ephraim to tell her of his dreadful despondency, loneliness and fears in the early days. Finally the feelings and thoughts he was free to expose in the comfort of her presence lead to the as yet unspoken subject.

'I am grievously sorry that it pains you, Mama. Please think of it not as a new faith – it is a continuation of our own faith. Don't you see?'

'I see that you have left the community, you have broken mitzvot, so many laws. Above all, the first. Shema Yisrael Adonai Elohenu Adonai echad,' she said sadly. Hear, O Israel: the Lord our God, the Lord is one.

'But even Moses himself, even in the second Psalm, the Lord hath said – Thou art my Son; this day have I begotten thee. Jesus IS his son, Adonai Elohenu Adonai, he is the Lord our God. He IS the messiah. Some Jews recognized it then. And some still do not. It is the same faith, can't you understand?'

She covered her ears and shook her head, eyes filling with tears.

Ephraim gently pulled her hands away and held them. 'Please, Mama, listen. It is a new covenant – there was Noah... and God's promise. There was Abraham, and God's promise. There was Moses, and God's promise. There was David, King of the Jews. And there was Jesus, another new covenant from God.' He pleaded urgently, his eyes too filling with tears, and he pressed her hands in his. 'Don't you see? God grows and changes, mankind grows and changes and – in history – God renews Himself.'

She freed her hands and sighed. 'How does our Rachel take this? Is she turning apikoros too?'

'Rachel,' he said flatly. 'No.'

'Things are not well between you,' she said. She acknowledged his chagrin at the transparency of their relationship with a light shrug and continued, 'It has been hard for her. For all of us, but especially for her. And I wish you had written to your daughter as well.'

'You knew that we wrote letters?'

She gave him a wise woman's reproachful smile, 'Of course. A marriage, even a troubled one, must be lubricated by contact. We just had to keep your father from knowing. I had to obey him, so I could not write, but Kathy and Rachel and I found a way. You were good to send money. You kept to your promise. But Sarah, she needed to hear from you, too.'

At this, Ephraim was flummoxed. 'In every letter to Rachel I put in something for Sarah. I didn't want her to forget me, or to think I had abandoned her forever.'

'Then when you changed, when you became kofer ba-Torah. When you found Jesus,' his mother's gentle voice turned briefly acid. 'Then you did abandon her. What could a child think when her father stops sending her letters?'

'But I didn't stop! I stopped sending little drawings when Rachel said Sarah had started to read. I sent poems, and verses from the Tanakh – not even anything about Christ.' For the first time with his mother Ephraim raised his voice in protest. They both sat back in silence, and then in dawning outrage: Rachel had withheld Ephraim's loving notes to Sarah.

A special family outing had been arranged for the afternoon, so Ephraim had to maintain his cool façade with Rachel. Annually, Heidelberg took advantage of its mild climate by holding a version of the Bavarian Oktoberfest, a crafts and harvest festival. Abraham and Kathy always indulged their youngsters in a visit and this year their guests would come too. Music, dancing, rides, puppet shows, sweets, pretzels, beer, displays and even a horse race were part of the fun. Ephraim and Rachel strolled with the others, appearing a normal couple delighted to see their Sarah shepherding her cousins onto the carrousel, to see her laughing as it turned, to see her toss quoits at a games stall and almost win a china figurine of a water-nymph. But Ephraim wanted time alone with his daughter and after the family stopped for cakes and apple juice he asked if she would like to come with him to the agricultural tents.

As they walked away from the frivolities to the main road and the river bank, Ephraim felt especially aware of Sarah as a person. Her head was nearly to his shoulder, she wore her blonde hair long, its sides fetched up in combs with a plait to the back. Her eyes were as china-blue as his mother's, her neck and limbs graceful as Rachel's. She was almost a woman, but still a girl. He felt suddenly shy, and could tell she did too. He scanned the cluster of spacious tents, telling Sarah he wanted to see the dairy cattle, and followed his nose toward the sweet grassy smell of fresh hay and undercurrent of cowpats. Inside the temporary stable a dozen beasts in individual stalls, some with calves, stood placidly chewing, occasionally shifting their weight, rustling the yellow straw underfoot.

'What a fine lady,' Ephraim crooned, drawn to a patterned cow more brown than white, leaning on the rail to assess her. 'Do you see her cowlick?' he said to Sarah, 'A fine swirl. And look at those haunches, how broad she is! The udder, heavy – time to milk soon.'

'Where is her calf?' Sarah asked, stepping up on the bottom rail to peer into the corners of the stall.

'Taken away already, I expect. The better for milk production. The earlier they separate the calf the kinder it is for both of them.' He read the information notice, 'Friesian, twelve thousand pounds of milk a year.' What he had just said – separating soon after birth – reverberated. 'I'm sorry... sorry you did not win the little china sprite.'

'It's all right, Papa. Besides, I love the tulip tile you brought me. I wish — ' she stopped and he waited, hanging on her every word, his own daughter, his own flesh and blood daughter, gazing dreamily at the cow, lost in a wish. What poison had Rachel sowed in her against him? Sarah turned with a teasing, impish smile. 'I can't imagine you milking cows, my father the doctor. Did you really?'

He laughed and assured her, yes he really had, and tucked her arm through his as they walked on to see other cows. He repeated in more detail, and at more expense to his dignity, his trials of labor as a farm worker. He told her, too, that he was proud of what he had achieved for Judge Sherman and for the Melioration Society's farm in New York state; he said he loved the land, loved to make things grow. Sarah told him she still treasured the sketches he had sent to her in his letters home when she was little, of fields and American barns and farmhouses, of the American robin, so much bigger than in Belarus. And the one of New York City, too, with the fountain. The natural flow of conversation dried, the past intruding again. Ephraim fleetingly prayed to God the Father through Christ his Son for strength to prevent himself from poisoning Sarah against Rachel.

Father and daughter had wandered through the dairy tent and stood outside now, by the pen of a massive white bull. 'Maybe some day you will see America,' Ephraim said tentatively.

'You and Mama would want me to come?' Sarah's eyes welled with tears, telling Ephraim two things. First, the dear child believed Rachel's painting of a rejecting father. Second, it seemed he would in due course be returning to America, a decision he did not know he had made. There was a third thing too — Sarah in herself, whatever the wounds of separation and misdeeds of her father, forgave him.

He drew her to him and kissed her cheek. 'There is war there now. And I must re-establish myself.' He held her tight for a moment, head full of unknowns, then with a sigh, released her. 'If you wish to come to America, you shall, when the time is right.'

'I hope so,' she replied with a shaky smile.

'Here we are, fine sleek cows and a river,' he said as they paused by the Neckar flowing steadily north-west to the Rhine. Then in Hebrew: 'And Pharaoh said unto Joseph, In my dream, behold, I stood upon the bank of the river.'

Sarah continued, 'And behold, there came up out of the river seven kine, fat-fleshed and well favored; and they fed in a meadow.'

They walked back to the market square alternating verses of the story of Pharaoh's dream and Joseph's interpretation, seven years of plenty and seven years of famine, greatly pleasing Ephraim that his daughter could so easily quote from memory the first book of the Torah, Bereshith, the book he now called Genesis.

18

THE GET
Heidelberg 1862-63

It was time to lance the boil. The next morning, another warm October day, Ephraim asked Rachel to walk out alone with him to the park around the castle which rose above the old town. They made a fine couple strolling up the winding path, Ephraim in his top hat and square-clipped dark beard, Rachel in her new bonnet and the red and black parasol she'd acquired in Saloniki and was pleased to flaunt here. They had been to the gardens with the family, so there was little need to exclaim over the broad, romantic view down over the town, the river and the wooded hills on the other side of the river, nor the flower beds and intricate pathways, nor the brick and stone remains of castle walls and turrets. Besides, they were well-used to not talking to each other. Ephraim led them through one terrace, then another, hesitated at a cul-de-sac, walked on, and finally settled on an alcove of myrtle well off the main pathways. With a gesture he invited Rachel to sit on the timber bench and sat himself a little distant, angled towards her.

'I will be returning to America.'

'To convert the Jews of New York again. At least it will not be so hot as Turkey.'

'No. I have given that up.' Ephraim looked away from her out to the glimpse of hill and sky afforded by this secluded spot.

'Given up Christianity!'

The shock and relief in her voice forced his eyes back to her, and he explained. 'No, I have given up missionary work. I have arranged to pay off my obligation to the Society with Zayde's inheritance.'

'What? That is our money, my money! How much?'

'It's from my half.'

'What will you do there?' Rachel's voice softened into curiosity, moving on from outrage to consideration of married life without proselytizing.

'Medicine. I will open a practice. Somewhere. But we need to talk about Sarah. I want her to come. She wants to come.'

'Feh! What can she know.' Rachel turned her furled parasol on its point where it rested on the ground.

'Very little of her father,' Ephraim said through thin, stiff lips, and then could not keep from raising his voice: 'How could you dare to keep my messages from her?'

She whipped her face toward him, raw at being caught out. A flash of guilt: 'They were not good for her.' And then claws of defense. 'How could you dare leave her and me behind!'

'I did it to save us,' he bellowed.

'To save yourself. To let your Jesus save you.' Rachel shouted just as hotly as he, words tumbling. 'How dare you spend our money on getting yourself out of your own fiasco. You were hopeless as a missionary. They laughed at you. You think you are full of love and righteousness and the Lord – you are arrogant, proud, selfish, deluded. A selfish, selfish man. I don't want to go to America. I don't want to live with you any more. You hate me and I hate you.' She drew a breath. 'I want a divorce!'

Ephraim closed his eyes and let his head drop, shoulders sagging.

Convinced of her words, Rachel continued, the frustration held back for years flooding out. 'I am completely within the law for a get. For one thing, you turned kofer. That alone is enough. For another, you refuse to lie with me naturally – that also, alone, is enough.'

'Yes.'

'You owe me all of Zayde's money. You are getting free to make a living in America. I am alone here, with my daughter.'

This stirred Ephraim from his slump, but he controlled the urge to shout in the face of her hysteria, keeping his voice low. 'My daughter, too.'

'I brought her up, not you. Now you prefer her to me!'

He let this pass and said quietly, 'Do you still have all the notes that I sent to her with the letters to you over the years? She should see them.'

'If I did I wouldn't tell you.'

'Rachel! You are unnatural!' He leapt to his feet in anger.

'You are unnatural. The beth din will know that!'

In a turmoil of anger dark and exhilarating Ephraim escorted Rachel back to the house. At last they both agreed – if that word could be used – that the marriage was irretrievable. But he needed to think. The procedure for the get, the bill of divorce, would have to begin, the beth din, the rabbinical court, arranged. Scribes, witnesses, costs, and, his feet faltered, the ketubah. The financial settlement specified in their marriage contract. Rachel had paused at his slight stumble, then moved ahead, outpacing him, but now he caught up. She was partly right, he would owe her all of the dowry. Never mind, the Lord would provide, he had a profession, he was able-bodied. What would it be to be free, free of this unhappy, impossible marriage, this wife – he was thirty-three, he'd been married to her half his life. Father could arrange rabbis for the court, he would know how to proceed, and despite their wide differences Ephraim felt his parents would not oppose the get, especially not Mama. But it should happen here, as soon as possible, to end the misery and falsity, to start a free life again. He needed to talk to Abraham before anything else. At the door to the Sacks' tidy three-story house, Ephraim said, 'Please don't say anything yet to my parents.'

'And why not? It is my right to seek a divorce.'

He ground his teeth and reined in his irritation. 'Do you wish for the get here, or to wait until Brisk?'

Rachel considered. 'It will take a long time. It will be gossiped about for months – I have already been the butt of gossip because of you. Here will be better, and faster. Cleaner.'

'Then give me time to see Abraham, see what he can arrange.'

She nodded agreement, and just at that moment Kathy opened the front door, saying, 'There you are! Mama was worrying.' Beyond her in the entry hall stood Ephraim's parents, his mother's eyes red and weepy. She saw Ephraim and Rachel appearing to be in accord, and caught her son's eye, questioning. He shook his head slightly, and said that he must go into town, he would be back in the afternoon.

The tang of acid and eggy smell of sulfur lingered in the chemistry lab, but the benches had been cleared, apparatus cleaned, and Abraham stood chalking something on a blackboard with two students. He beckoned to Ephraim hesitating at the doorway and dismissed them.

'Ah. Precipitation of arsenic,' Ephraim scanned the formula. Then urgently, 'Can we speak?' Abraham led the way to his cluttered, wood-paneled office. They sat, and Ephraim explained, as delicately as he could, the hidden sides of his marriage, and his request. Would Abraham be willing to help them divorce?

'A get. I'm sorry. But all the family has guessed how it is between you two. So sad. It means pain for everyone. Yet to stay like this will only bring more pain and damage. Sometimes, divorce can lead to happiness.'

'Just freedom will be enough,' Ephraim replied grimly.

'There is something you have not directly mentioned which you must take into account. The beth din will consult Sarah, but whatever she wishes it will explain that she must stay with her mother while young.'

'I know.' Ephraim drew breath. 'Jesus told his disciples that they had to leave their families. Which I knew when I answered his call. I am afraid of what it will do to Sarah.'

'From what I know of her, I believe she is wise enough to understand that her parents are unhappy.'

'Just seeing her again… she has forgiven me thus far, a miracle of love – it must be Mama's influence. My hope and consolation is her age: soon she will be an adult, able to do as she pleases. She has asked and I have promised she can come to America.'

'That would distress Rachel,' Abraham cautioned. Bitterness and revenge surged in Ephraim. He pushed it away and murmured that it was several years in the future and he hoped all of them would be happier by then.

'Come,' Abraham squared up the papers on his desk. 'This is very good timing. I am dining with Dr Lieb – I mentioned him to you? – he might be the other righteous witness we need for the get. He's all a-buzz about old Bronn's new translation of Darwin. Become acquainted, then I will ask him afterwards.' For a little while, in the high intellectual atmosphere of the university's dining chamber, Ephraim put his worries aside and plunged into discussion of *On the Origin of Species*, the just-published version he longed to read.

Kathy caught him at the entry and gestured him into the parlor where his parents waited, shut the door and left them alone. His father stood by the hearth in his prayer shawl, with siddur, prayer book, in hand. Ephraim nodded a greeting to him and crossed to his mother where she sat on the horsehair settee by the samovar. She looked up when Ephraim kissed her cheek, tremulous, smiling.

'Has Rachel told you we want a get?' He faced them both.

'She says you are no longer apostate! You have come back to us!' his mother said ecstatically.

Ephraim braced his legs and raised his chin, standing in the center of the room. 'I have NOT forsaken Christ. I have ceased to be a missionary. Rachel is – Rachel is being Rachel again. I am Christian, Mama.' He watched her slump, putting her face in her hands. 'We want to divorce.'

'This is no surprise,' said Yehuda Epstein. 'Your mother suspected. There is cause.'

'We agree on that. It should not have been in the first place. And other causes under the law.' Ephraim hoped that his apostasy and the breakdown of their marriage would be sufficient evidence, but he knew that his restrictions on their conjugal relations were also cause, and might well come before the court, because physical agreement was a condition of Jewish marriage. To reveal this would be embarrassing – he would be labeled mored, a sexual rebel within marriage. But it was the truth, an exposure he was willing to endure. All he craved was relief. 'Abraham is speaking to his chief rabbi this evening.'

'So soon?' His mother cried out. 'Oh, my son. Divorce Rachel, yes. But come back! If you hadn't married you would still be with us. If you hadn't gone to that terrible America.' She broke into high-pitched crying and sobbing, repeating his name and Aleinu l'shabeach la'Adon hakol, the opening of the thrice daily prayer: It is our duty to praise the Master of all. Ephraim held his stance, feeling tears choke his throat, fill his eyes, spill down his cheeks. He saw his father's eyes spilling with tears too. And then before Ephraim could stop her, his mother threw herself at his feet, clinging to his legs. 'Please, please. I have not long to live, come back to us, come back. Ein od.' The end of the Aleinu: There is no other.

Ephraim knelt to catch and raise her up, and held her close, then saw his father also on his knees by the hearth, cheeks streaming with tears, eyes begging.

He arrived at Heiliggeistkirche as the evening service was ending, in time to join in a psalm, *Soweit der Osten vom Westen* and the dismissal. The words rang in his ears: as far as the east is from the west. He remained kneeling alone as the Protestant men and women of old Heidelberg departed for their homes. The distant drift of Latin, bells and incense reached his quiet half of the huge church. Not prayer, only pain filled Ephraim's heart, mind and soul: I can't, I can't, I can't. I cannot forsake you Lord Jesus. Am I a Judas? His mother's heartbreak and even the long begrudged duty to his father told him he should obey, he should respect their love and faith, he should honor his father and his mother. He loved the clarity and truth of Christ's message, he was sworn to Christ. But he was sworn to God the Father, too, the Messiah's own Father. Take this cup from me, Ephraim begged, and then recoiled from his blasphemy. Jesus in agony in the Garden of Gethsemane was sacrificing his divine life. Ephraim was sacrificing: Jesus himself. Or sacrificing Mama. Which faith, which truth, which God? He groaned in the dimness. Far ahead in the shadowed altar a candle glowed.

His mind turned to the divorce. The light of Christ is the grounds for divorce. Am I using Him as the means of getting free of Rachel? Ephraim recoiled from this too – to cling to Christ as a mere way out, had it always been this? Out of marriage, out of orthodoxy, out of narrow minds. No, no, Christ was the Truth, and the marriage was wrong from the start. In Jewish law, the divorce was undeniably justified. Under Christian law – his mind froze. In the law of the land, Heidelberg and Brest-Litovsk, the civil divorce would be arranged in due course. But in the Christian faith, would it be recognized? Will I ever be able to marry again in the eyes of God the Father, Son and Holy Spirit?

My god, my god, my god. Which god am I praying to? Here in this church of two faiths, Ephraim recalled the glittering mosaics and votive-blackened icons of the Greek Orthodox churches in Saloniki and Monastir, the silver, gold and tassels of synagogues, the Arabic calligraphy of mosques and muezzin calls from minarets. He felt a sudden longing for the simplicity of American churches, for the first church he'd ever entered, in New Jersey. But then, how free and bewildering he'd found the disputations between the many Protestant churches, their arguments about salvation, so like the Mishnah. What is God, who is right, how to live, what to believe? It's the message of the Messiah himself – essence is what matters, truth. Who matters most? The decision came to his heart: Mama.

Ephraim, accompanied by his father and Abraham, went to the mikvah for the ritual bath. The emergence from the waters echoed the total immersion of his baptism in Lake Erie, haunting his return to Judaism with a strangely Christian feeling. The ablution, though not strictly required, was to restore purity after his years of exposure to traif, the unclean, unkosher. It came after days alone in meditation and prayer – teshuva: repentance. Because his transgression was not against man – Ephraim had not stolen, cheated, slandered or otherwise sinned against a human – his confession, repentance and atonement was not public. In Jewish law he had sinned against God, and only God could forgive him. He had only to regret his sin and resolve not to repeat it.

Ephraim deeply suffered his betrayal of Jesus Christ. The barb of doubt he carried from medical missionary proselytizing was nothing compared to his self-accusations now. Nevertheless, for his mother, it had to be done. He had not lost faith in Christ, but he had to live with compromise. He was borne up by memories of his years with the Jewish Christians of the Melioration farm, how they had lived as Jesus himself did, as Jews... with faith in the Christ's message. He could not – nor did he have to – speak against or think against Jesus. He had just to believe in the same Lord God that Jesus had, accept the five books of the Torah, obey the commandments of Moses and rejoin the community of worshiping Jews. And live with his promise to his mother: not to worship as a Christian, not to return to America.

'Aie, my son! Oh, my Ephraim!' Mama's joyful tears and cries at his decision had shaken him more than her grief had done. He bore his pain and rejoiced in the reward of her happiness when she saw him don the yarmulke and drape the tallit over his head and shoulders, the very same prayer shawl of white wool with black stripes he'd been given at thirteen for his bar mitzvah.

On Friday evenings, when Kathy lit the candles to welcome Queen Shabbat he was one with the family in custom, word and deed. He kept glancing down the table at his mother's peaceful expression, his daughter's attentive, shining face and thanked Lord God indeed for this treasure. On the very night of his decision he had told Rachel of his plan to revert to Judaism. Her eyes gleamed for a moment with triumph and vindication, but she had the sense to hold back comments. Even she allowed for his pained pride and felt no need to make it worse. Returning to the fold did not mean he was coming back to her of course – both knew, all knew, the divorce had to be.

Where Ephraim thought he might feel resentment, he discovered a new tenderness towards his father at their first attendance together at Abraham's synagogue. He worked hard to keep his heart open as the morning service began: Shema Yisrael Adonai Eloheinu Adonai echad, Hear, O Israel: the Lord is our God, the Lord is one. On through the eighteen blessings of the Amidah, the reading from the Torah, on to the Kaddish, standing and rocking to pray. The bone-deep pattern was no hardship. Only the closing Aleinu bit into him, its ending expressing hope that the world will recognize the true Lord God and abandon idolatry.

It had taken weeks of introspection before Ephraim's first attendance at synagogue, and further weeks for the divorce preparations. Being apostate was no longer an issue, marital physical intimacy did not need to be exposed: their mutually agreed unhappiness was sufficient grounds for divorce. Documents were submitted, papers scrutinized, suitable witnesses validated, the date arranged. Seeking calm, once started Ephraim found himself going to synagogue several times a day, accompanying his father in silence, anguishing internally, pleading with Jesus and his own mind to forgive, allow, understand. Trying to forgive himself. Daily he also went to the university, sitting in on lectures, reading the Darwin translation, moving in Abraham's academic scientific circles. The only true happiness and light in this miserable time was Sarah and her young cousins. He played soldiers with the youngsters in the nursery, worked jig-saw puzzles of the world, told them stories of his travels. He read out loud from English newspapers about the war in America, recited Longfellow's *Hiawatha* and told them what he knew of American Indians. He even materialized a Suwanee whistle, taught them *Yankee Doodle Dandy* and helped them put on a show for the family. Finally came Chanukah. Evening by evening the family lit the menorah, and he joined the children to gamble with cards for copper coins and spin the dreidel, re-living the fun and laughter of his own childhood. In this setting he once more knew himself as the best beloved child of his mother and basked in her contentment. And for the first time since childhood, felt his father's approval.

But away from the family nest he was miserable. He had promised Mama that he would not go back to America. Worse, he had promised not to practice Christianity. When she died – an awful, evil, terrible thought he tried to un-think ... how could he wish her death? But he knew, because a vow like a voice had come, that he would return, as a Christian, to the United States. For now he was trapped in Judaism. So he would stay in

Europe and further his learning, and once he had built up contacts he would practice medicine here, in Heidelberg perhaps, or maybe Vienna.

Ephraim opened a conversation with his brother-in-law to explore the possibilities for his future. He seized Abraham's offer to continue the talk in the solitude of the Philosopher's Walk. Across the river, rambling paths climb the wooded hill opposite Heidelberg, a place where the professors and philosophers of the university walked and talked and gathered inspiration from nature and the perspective on the city over the river. The trees were bare this time of year, the air chill and grayed with river mist. They strode in silence til halting for a view directly across to the great bell tower of Heiliggeist Church.

'Do you miss it badly?' asked Abraham.

Ephraim nodded. 'But there is comfort in following Christ's own faith. Oh, but I wish... the Lord hath said unto me, Thou art my Son; this day have I begotten thee. Psalm Two. You only have to read Saint Paul – sorry.' He stopped, then gave a wry laugh. 'You know the ridiculous thing is that they have as many differences about beliefs as we Jews do. That's mainly what makes coming back possible, it's the message of the Messiah himself – essence is what matters, truth. Judaism, Catholicism, Protestantism – it's all split, split, split, when really the Lord is one, all one and the same.'

They began to walk again. 'So, tell me, the Trinity, what is it, exactly?'

Ephraim laughed. 'Abraham! I am a Baal teshuva. You want me to go back on my repentance?'

'Think of it as a scholar. I hear they worship the Lord Almighty as three gods, but I don't understand how.'

'It is not so hard. You are Abraham my friend, you are Abraham also my brother-in-law, and you are Abraham husband of Kathy, Abraham father of five children, also Abraham ben Isaac. All these Abrahams, yet one Abraham. There is Adonai Eloheinu Adonai, Lord God the Father Creator of all. There is Adonai Lord God His Son, sent to renew us all. And Lord God the Holy Spirit, the living life that moves in and of us all. Ever three, ever One. Trinity. Consubstantiales, coaequales – consubstantial, co-eternal.'

'Amen,' said Abraham.

'Amen,' responded Ephraim involuntarily, then looked at Abraham with raised eyebrows.

'Listen, I will tell you about mussar.' Abraham smiled at Ephraim's surprise. 'We strive for the Divine in everything, inside everyone. Inner truth, inner meaning. From the Kabbalah. The essence, if only we can reach it.' He put into Ephraim's hands a journal, *Tevunah*. 'It's dedicated to the mussar movement. And you'll never guess: published by Rabbi Yisrael Lipkin Salanter, remember his name from home? He lives in Germany now!' The normally mild, sensible Abraham radiated quiet joy. 'It is a path, a way, a discipline; it is wisdom and ethics. Your father does not know, of course, none of the orthodox approve.'

'Abraham, you amaze me. You are hiding from Papa like we did at home. The Haskalah, the enlightenment, Salanter, Ramchal – why didn't you say?'

'You had your Christ.' He laughed gently. 'There was no reason to tell you. But now you worship as a Jew. And we are both old enough.' Abraham confided that the deep and mystical mussar path was gathering followers – including many of his university colleagues. Judaic, but also universal, mussar was a way of contemplation and spiritual discipline leading to inner light. A tiny spark flared and faded in Ephraim's anguished soul.

Finally, when the waiting periods and the paperwork were done, and the divorce petition heard and granted, Ephraim closeted himself with his mother to confer about what he would do next. He received her blessing, and then informed Rachel, but he had still to tell Sarah. He found her with Kathy, checking bed linens for need of repair.

'It's a cold day, but would you care to join me for a bit of air?' He had his cloak and hat in hand, and hers as well. A quick apology to Kathy and they were on their way, through the streets and up to the by now familiar castle gardens. He liked her willingness to walk in all weathers, recognized a kindred spirit in her eagerness for adventure. Few were about on this drear February day, but Ephraim found himself on the winding paths to the shelter of the evergreen myrtle alcove where divorce had been the subject months before. On the way, father and daughter talked about the views over Heidelberg, about the weather, about Sarah's visit with her grandparents to Bad Bergzabern so that grandmama could take the waters for her health.

'I will no longer be going to America, I'm afraid, Sarah,' Ephraim said, once they were settled on the bench.

'Because of the get?'

'No, your mother and I are free now to do as we wish.' He hesitated. 'I'm very sorry we cannot be together, you and I.'

'Papa, we never have been together, so things will go on just the same,' she said practically. 'But won't you ever go to America?' Her wistful note recalled to him their conversation in the dairy tent.

'I have promised your grandmother that I will stay in Europe. I plan to go to Vienna to work and study as a physician.'

'So I may see you! It's not so far from Brisk, easier than Heidelberg!'

'Let us hope. We will try. When I have established myself, when you are an adult, if you wish… In the meanwhile, you must continue your studies, and continue to be kind and good to your mother and grandparents. And continue to grow and be as beautiful as you are.' Ephraim hugged her. 'I have a gift for you to remember me by.' He reached into his coat pocket and produced a black velvet bag with a yellow drawstring.

When Sarah saw the diamond and gold earrings, intense with white light even on this dull day, she could only murmur 'Papa' and look at him with wonder. He told her how Jacob had given him the diamonds that long ago birthday in New York, how important they'd been – having them had strengthened him. And now he hoped the strength would be hers too.

She listened with full attention, then holding an earring at each earlobe she beamed, 'How do I look? Will Mama let me wear them in St Petersburg? She says I can put my hair up – we are going to a ball with Eva! Oh, thank you, Papa!'

'So, you and your mother are going to Petersburg! You'll have a wonderful visit. I shall think of the diamonds and you, dancing.' He smiled at her excitement and determined himself to speak to Mama, to be sure Rachel allowed it.

'But what can I give you?' Sarah cried out. Before he could demur she had found an answer, standing up to break a twig of myrtle from the green wall of shrubbery that sheltered them. 'Here! Press it and keep it in your siddur… or maybe,' she teased, 'in your Darwin.' It was a fitting token, one of the four sacred plants of Sukkot, the feast of huts, from the time when the Israelites wandered the desert in exile. The sharp, green, resiny fragrance brightened the air as she tucked the sprig into his breast pocket.

After all the arrangements were made, after the packing, the prayers, the promises, the tearful farewells, Ephraim, alone on the train to Vienna, found one memory burning paramount. In the rabbinical court, Rachel cupping her hands palms open as instructed, and he, Ephraim, holding the get above them, careful to have no physical contact as the beth din required. And his recitation of the words, 'You are now permitted to marry any man.' The clear image: letting go of the ritually folded document, seeing it drop into her hands.

19

FIERCE AS A LEOPARD, LIGHT AS AN EAGLE
Vienna 1863-66

Ephraim arrived in Vienna a lost soul. He was forbidden Christianity, yet he believed and prayed to Jesus in his heart. He was uncomfortable in Judaism and its archaic rules, yet responded to its prayers. He felt tentative about the mussar movement.

Mechanically he set about installing himself at a boarding house in the 9th District of Vienna, as his brother-in-law had recommended. Then with a dull heart he followed up the two offers that had resulted from letters sent by Abraham to his network of connections in Vienna. The professional passion that normally drove Ephraim to seek the best was in abeyance. Here he was at Europe's leading teaching hospital, yet any post would do. He chose the post of junior assistant in the First Obstetrical Clinic of the great Vienna General Hospital. This was the very place where Ignaz Semmelweis – whom Ephraim had learned of in his Canadian training – had instituted the washing of clinicians' hands in chlorinated solution for patient examinations. Physicians here at the obstetric clinic had adopted the practice, but Dr Semmelweis had long ago been sacked for taking his theory of cleanliness too far. Through passion and righteousness a man who should have been a hero had become an utter fool.

Ephraim went about his work circumspectly. Instead of wanting to shine, he wanted to fit in. He saved his charm and human warmth for patients, learned what he could from his colleagues and superiors, attended lectures, read avidly and kept himself to himself. He wanted to curl up in darkness, to stay in his quiet room, alone, where he could talk to Christ in his heart. He hungered for the bread and wine, the body and blood remembrance that gave direct communion with Jesus. So changed and isolated did he feel that Ephraim expected to be stricken with a great illness, as had happened in Andover. But shoring him up was the freedom from his cousin-wife, a raw, dazing freedom. Even more, he had the comfort of his beloved Mama and his daughter. He honored his promises, writing weekly to his mother: yes, he went to synagogue, yes, he kept kosher. He wrote weekly to Sarah, too, and it was this that began to rouse him from torpor. Her letters made clear how dazzled she was by her visit to St Petersburg with Rachel, its elegance and diversions, though she kept discreet her disappointment that her Mama had said she was too young yet to wear diamonds. It seemed that Rachel had decided to stay on in Petersburg; competitively Ephraim rose to her challenge to impress Sarah. He woke to Vienna in order to describe the wide new Ringstrasse boulevard, the gas-lit streets, the pocket-parks, the grand parks and palaces, the Danube. He reverted to little sketches: the giraffe at the Tiergarten, a bird's eye view of the vast Vienna General Hospital marked with the clinic where he worked, the zig-zag patterns of blue, white and yellow glazed tiles on the steep roof of the famous Stephansdom cathedral. Addressing the envelopes directly to Sarah was a small, sweet pleasure, as was receiving her carefully composed missives once she was back at home in Brest-Litovsk. She entertained him with news of her studies, her grandmother, the cousins, aunts and uncles. In reply he tried composing poems for her, but inspiration failed so he quoted verses from the Tanakh or lines from his favorite English language poets – Wordsworth, Byron, Longfellow – to help her English for the day when she might come to America.

These activities, and time and his natural vitality gradually brought Ephraim back to something like his old self. A further spur came from worship at the Lithuanian synagogue Abraham had suggested, for here he found a few men with a Jewish spirituality that interested him. Through them he learned more about Ysrael Salanter and his mussar movement. Its origins lay in the Kabbalah, Jewish mysticism. At twenty, when he left Belarus, Ephraim had not reached this esoteric level of spiritual understanding; though mentioned in his studies it was permitted only to mature men. Ironically, he had learned something of it as a Christian, for in Hebrew history at Andover he encountered the Zohar, the ancient kabbalistic text said to go back to Moses and Abraham. The Zohar had led to Ysrael Salanter's mussar: the word meant correction, or instruction. Salanter was a rabbi from Lithuania who in the 1840s had actually told Jews to violate mitzvot when life and health were at stake. This was just as Jesus had done! What mattered, both Salanter and Jesus said, was right living, right doing, not just following rules. Mussar, Ephraim determined, could be his way to keep faith.

Embarking on the search for new truths reminded him of the joys of Andover when he had delved into scriptural interpretation. The Torah, which he thought of now as the Old Testament, had so many layers of meaning. Ephraim had grown through his childish, literal understanding, on to allegorical, then theological meanings. Now he learned hidden, mystical meanings, complicated codes for divine light in all things. Keeping Christ in his heart, Ephraim joined in chants meant to bring light into his interior darkness. Sometimes he found a faint flicker of it. But mysticism was one thing – what purpose, what good would it do?

Mussar practice provided an answer, a clear, step-by-step way to work on the inner self and so to bring more blessings on the world. It was *Mesillat Yesharim*, Path of the Just, a hundred-year-old text written by the brilliant thinker Ramchal. It set straightforward virtues – including awareness, enthusiasm, purity, humility – and the ways to work toward them. Ephraim's Christian American life echoed, for this code and practice of character improvement was very like Benjamin Franklin's Thirteen Virtues, which he had read and discussed with the Shermans on those New Jersey evenings so long ago. Order, resolution, industry, sincerity, tranquility, humility… each day, Ephraim focused on one particular quality, each evening he wrote an assessment of his achievement or failings. Though it was not a happy time, he felt his casting back to Judaism was at least a field worth tilling. The work was far too deep to communicate to his mother or daughter, but he did send one Ramchal quote on the trait of zeal to Sarah: 'Be fierce as a leopard, light as an eagle, swift as a deer and strong as a lion to do the will of your Father in heaven.'

As he returned to himself Ephraim began to accept the overtures of the men at the synagogue. Being Jewish, he had to BE Jewish, which means being part of the community – he had promised his mother. He was invited to their homes for Shabbat and high festivals. A number of his mussar friends were quite cosmopolitan, despite their mystical and moral devotion, for they were freer-thinking than the strictly orthodox. To them, the divine permeates all the world; and all Jews hold that life is to be lived – God's gift should not be denied. Through these friends and through his medical colleagues Ephraim began to attend dinners and parties, lectures, concerts and dances. He had looks, intelligence, bright liveliness, he was a linguist, a scholar, physician, he told fascinating tales of America and Turkey… and he was unmarried. He was introduced to sisters and daughters whenever he socialized.

He met pretty women, and intelligent women, and pretty, intelligent women, but though he laughed, waltzed and conversed, he was not drawn to anyone. He still was not settled, not established enough. Furthermore many of the women were Jewish; he knew in his heart he was Christian, and he would not progress a romance with that secret. As for Christian women, his Jewish faith, and his mother, stood in the way. Finally, he carried the memory of the get. Though it was the wife, not the husband who must not remarry for ninety-two days, and though three times that many days had passed, Ephraim realized he had lived so long as a married man with and without Rachel that he did not know how to fall in love.

Half way through the next year, in 1864, news of Louis Pasteur's dramatic lecture at the Sorbonne was all the talk in medicine, and even in other intelligent circles. His experiments established that micro-organisms came from exposure to outside sources. Infection, in other words, came not because of poor humors, or chance or God's punishment, it had a direct physical cause. In Ephraim's view the theory was proven and made perfect sense; but throughout the medical world and right here at the Obstetrics Clinic many practitioners remained skeptical. To Ephraim this was utterly unenlightened; he argued the point with colleagues. On the day his supervisor asked if he was defending the ridiculous Semmelweis's theory of all contagion by touch, he decided to look for another post.

If his opinion was not welcomed at the clinic, it was, at least, sought after in his social circles, not only on Pasteur but on America. Terrible news continued as General Sherman led the northern forces through the south. In the Vienna drawing rooms and balls as newspapers brought new developments in the American troubles, listeners clustered to query Ephraim on the union and the confederacy, to hear his tales of Harriet Beecher Stowe's underground railroads, and his first hand accounts of the famous author whose table he had shared. A small musical evening at the home of a fellow physician threw him together with an American of about his own age who had his own tales to tell.

'Mrs Stowe was surely the little woman who started the war,' said this tall, dark-haired man, 'but I have already fought and won one against slavery – in Bleeding Kansas.'

'You were there in Kansas! Were you one of the Yankee freedom settlers?' Ephraim had recognized Stephen Wright's New England accent.

'Summer of '55,' Wright nodded. 'And we called our rifles Beecher's Bibles – because that's how we got them shipped into Kansas. Crates labeled as Bibles!' Laughter drew others to the group listening to the two men. 'Of course that's not your Beecher Stowe, it was her brother.'

Their conversation became a kind of entertainment, Ephraim warming to the clean-shaven gentleman, plying him with questions and providing explanatory asides to their audience. As the son of a railway magnate, he had traveled America's uninhabited west assessing routes for new railroads and in 1854 had seen the newly opened Kansas Territory flooded with slave-holding settlers. An abolitionist, he, along with others, could not bear to see slavery established in this virgin land. He joined a throng of settlers from Massachusetts determined to populate Kansas as a free state. Hostilities between slave-holders and abolitionists led to a miniature early civil war lasting six years.

'I surmise, Mr Wright, that you were involved in the skirmishes?' Ephraim gestured towards Wright's leg, a made of wood below the knee.

'Well observed, Dr Epstein. Cost me a foot and a collapsed lung, and...'

he saluted, smiling, revealing the loss of two fingers on his right hand. 'A small price for the free manhood of human souls.'

'A cost indeed. Well done, sir,' said Ephraim, and rounded out their lively lecture by explaining to their listeners that in 1861, just before the slave-states formed the confederacy, Kansas had been admitted to the United States as a slave-free state.

Dr Epstein and Mr Wright relished their double-act and continued to see each other, deepening their acquaintance into a warm friendship. Mrs Wright, with her smooth brown hair and calm, sweet manner, reminded Ephraim of Miss Clara Stowe, an intelligent American woman of the finest sort. Wright himself was an earnest, honest Christian businessman, recalling to Ephraim the best aspects of the Epstein family as entrepreneurs in timber, brick, road and canal-building. The couple had come to Vienna in search of further recuperation from his lung condition, and to observe continental railway technologies to adapt at home. In contrast to his muted relationships with medical colleagues and his mussar Jewish companions, Ephraim felt free and natural in the freshness and enthusiasm of these Yankees.

Meanwhile, the Vienna salons bubbled with talk of political struggles and military actions all over Europe. Russia enforced its rule over the Polish, Ukrainians, Lithuanians and Belarusians, even banning their native languages. France was intent on maintaining the borders of its Empire under Napoleon III, wary of Russia and Austria. The regions and city-states of Italy had united into northern and southern kingdoms, chafing for complete unification and willing to deal with any power who would help win Rome from the French, and Venice from the Austrian Empire. Late in 1864 the biggest buzz was Austria's success, with Prussia, in defeating Denmark to win two prized North Sea duchies as part of a united Germany. The hero of the victory was flagship commander Wilhelm von Tegetthoff and even Ephraim got caught up in the fervor, writing to Sarah about the three-hour running gun battle and Tegetthoff's promotion to Admiral.

Increasingly irritated with his supervisor's attitude to Pasteur, and ready to expand himself, Ephraim managed to secure a new post at the Vienna General Hospital – in the Third Surgery Clinic. He did not intend to train as a surgeon, but as a physician in surgical wards he would learn from managing diagnosis and recovery, and gain knowledge of bladder, kidney, stomach, tumors and all manner of ills, along with amputation for crushed or septic limbs. What path he would follow next he could not know while he was trapped here, honoring his promise to his mother.

Between the jobs Ephraim visited Heidelberg to see Kathy, Abraham and their children. They said that Rachel was thriving in St Petersburg and he felt only relief. In the beth din, at the end of the divorce proceedings, the rabbi had announced that the get was not the end, but the beginning of a new path of contentment for each of them. For himself, Ephraim could not claim content, but he was glad for her, and for Sarah to have a happier mother who had chosen to settle far away. From Kathy he gained confirmation of Sarah's and Mama's reports that the tightened conditions in Belarus under Russian rule were bearable, though they could only speak their Brisker tongue at home, and had to use formal Russian in public.

With his brother-in-law he shared his mussar pathway, discussing and praying together over the discipline and hard work of Ramchal's *Mesillat Yesharim* virtues. Impatience was still Ephraim's bête noir. And now he knew humility was an equally impossible task. Surprisingly, he often failed at enthusiasm, for he fell prey to depressions – due to his betrayal of Christ. His inner clinging to Jesus he did not reveal to Abraham, though he let him guess it between the lines. Out of the same misery Ephraim, having already alienated the Melioration Society, had completely cut communications with his Christian brothers and friends in America. Only to Benjamin and Susannah had he written, only to say he was divorced, that he had reunited with his mother and daughter, and that he was staying on at the clinics in Vienna to further his medical knowledge. Though he signed himself 'yours in Christ' he said nothing of faith. Let them read between the lines.

In April 1865 Ephraim was with his friends the Wrights, their guest in the Schonbrunn assembly room gleaming with gilded paneling and crystal chandeliers. On returning Mrs Wright to her husband after a waltz, he instantly saw something was wrong. Wright's face, his whole body, was stricken, and those around him looked solemn, worried. The American spoke in a daze: 'Lincoln's been shot dead!'

The shock and loss shook Europeans and Americans alike. The waste, with the war so close to an end: Lee had just surrendered to Grant at Appomattox, the other confederate forces would surely soon follow. But a courageous, right-caring, right-living man, killed, against reason. The cost of Lincoln's leadership was death, and Ephraim immediately thought of Jesus who made the ultimate sacrifice – willingly – one life for the good of all. Courage. Ephraim began to question himself, and found he almost envied Stephen Wright his injuries. His nightly mussar self-examination turned to: What kind of test in battle could I endure?

'War,' said Ephraim's chief surgeon, 'the only good thing that comes of it is medical progress. And opportunities,' he harrumphed to his team, 'especially for doctors.' Talk among the medics turned from the massive losses of the American war which pitted brothers of the same nation against each other to the horrible losses of only a decade past in the Crimean War. Thousands had died in this conflict for influence over the Ottoman Empire. The resulting medical advance: hygiene. Overcrowding, weak ventilation and poor sewers, finally dealt with by a sanitary commission, had proved to be the main cause of death. Since then, and since the pioneer nurse Florence Nightingale had published her book *Notes on Nursing*, Vienna General Hospital had adapted to this new knowledge. The obstetrics clinic might still be recoiling from the Semmelweis debacle, but here in surgery Ephraim found less hostility to Pasteur's ideas. At the very least, while the violences of heroic medicine still continued alongside more humane therapies, Ephraim saw the embodiment of the new premise that, beside medical knowledge, the virtues of good hygiene and nursing were essential to prevent and to heal disease.

Ephraim heard Pummerin, the huge boomer bell of Stephansdom, ring in the Christian new year: 1866 – a year that would change his life in most surprising ways. Political conversations in Vienna turned from the resolved American war to speculations about the schemings of the Prussian Chancellor, Bismarck. Ever since the fall of Bonaparte in 1815 both the Kingdom of Prussia and the Austrian Empire had joined in a loose German Confederation. This had grown to a patriotic idea of a totally unified Germany. But where would the capital be? Bismarck's Berlin, in the north, or the Emperor Franz Joseph's Vienna in the south? As a symptom of the power struggle they quibbled for a year over sharing the Danish territory they'd won in Tegetthoff's famous sea battle. Then, outrageously, Prussia marched and took all the disputed area. Austrian troops headed north to confront Bismark's men. It was war.

As rumors built and news broke Ephraim's personal interest grew. He saw younger physicians and surgeons seeking military commissions, heard his superior recount experiences in the Crimea. Here was the chance – a test of courage in battle conditions, a gain of medical experience, an escape from claustrophobic Vienna, a justifiable fight against the betraying bully Bismarck. And, he had to admit, a way to forget his Jewish-Christian dilemma. Dare he do it? Had he the courage? The right? What of Mama and Sarah, what if he died or were maimed? Conferring with no one, Ephraim prayed for guidance. He received no answer. Then came the lightning thrill and alarm: in an alliance with Prussia, the Italian navy had attacked Austria in the south. It was war on two fronts, threats by land and sea, and no other nation would come to Austria's aid. This was the answer for Ephraim; a call and a determination he'd not felt since his decision to go to America and his conversion to Christianity.

The urgency of war melted formalities. Ephraim's chief surgeon at Vienna General Hospital gave him a glowing letter of introduction to his comrade, the chief medical officer of the Imperial Navy. But even in the heat of the hour Dr Epstein's medical experience, his scholarly abilities and American degrees were not enough. He must take the exams of the

University Academy of Vienna. Reining in impatience and pride Ephraim skimmed through the syllabus, which demanded classical knowledge and German literary excellence. All those years of wide reading, his ever-growing library, his insatiable intellectual quest served him well. He passed. After a whirl of uniform fittings, good-byes, and letters home, Dr Ephraim M Epstein was commissioned ship's surgeon on board the *Feuerspeier Battery*, off Venice.

20

BATTLE
Adriatic Sea and Vienna 1866

No sooner had Surgeon Ephraim M Epstein gained his sea legs on his first ship than he was transferred to the corvette *Seehund*. What different circumstances to that voyage across the Atlantic in the bowels of a leaky merchant ship: he was in uniform in his rightful place among fellow officers. The Adriatic, below summer's clear Mediterranean skies, surged deep marine blue and, near the shoreline, the same brilliant turquoise he'd known in Saloniki. Ephraim stayed on deck as much as he could to savor the taut sails, the wind, bird life, the dolphins playing alongside. And the grand sight of the ships of the line as they together patrolled the coast off Venice.

But suddenly now they were sailing and steaming southeast with purpose to join the fleet directly under the command of Admiral Tegetthoff himself – for the Italian navy had commenced besieging the island of Lissa, defense outpost for Austria's key naval base midway down the Dalmatian coast. The *Seehund* sailed alongside large vessels, often darting and tacking, a small, single-gunned wooden warship nipping among the tall-masted frigates. Tegetthoff's fleet hove into view. There was *Habsburg*, *Salamander*, the two-decker *Kaiser*, and then, with the admiral's flag flying, the new half-armor-plated wooden frigate *Ferdinand Max*. Painted sleek, threatening black, in total they were twenty-six ships, and seven of them were ironclads. Word came: bombarding of Lissa's port had begun. Further word: the Italian flotilla was twice as big as Austria's. Worse, twelve of these were modern ironclads, nine even had iron-hulls.

On the morning of 20 July 1866 Tegetthoff ordered Austria's armada into three divisions – his ironclads at the front, then unarmored wooden ships, then smaller gunboats and auxiliaries, including the *Seehund*. Ephraim readied his implements and bandages, then led prayers in the surgery with his assistant – Christian prayers, for here he was among Christians. How good it felt, and right. Peace Mama, he sent her a prayer too, and silently recited Y'hi ratzon milfanekha Adonai… the traveler's prayer that he and

Uncle Jacob had called upon during the great sea storm: make us reach our desired destination of life, gladness, and peace. Firing began and they went on deck until they would engage. *Seehund*'s orders were to stay on the fringes with the other smaller wood-hulled ships.

On the fringes *Seehund* remained, for after the crackle and boom of initial cannon fire, amid thick clouds of gunsmoke the two lines of ironclads closed, imperial Austrian black against Italy's grim gray. In moments, Tegetthoff's *Ferdinand Max* led his ships straight through a gap in the enemy line. Once through, each Austrian vessel turned to barrage the Italians broadside-to-broadside in rolling, repeated roars. Through the blaze of gunfire and smoke, Ephraim and the *Seehund* crew made out the *Ferdinand Max* rushing full speed ahead at the ironclad Italian *Palestro*, heard the blow, the crunch and creaks as Tegetthoff smashed her stern and set her on fire. The admiral pulled away and hunted another – his tactic, outnumbered by ships, men and guns, was, against the odds, to ram the superior Italian fleet into defeat. Could Austria possibly succeed?

The *Seehund* hung back watching, hoping, ready to dash in at a signal. The *Ferdinand Max* scored a glancing blow against the *Portogallo*, then went to defend the big wooden *Kaiser*. Off to the sides Austria's smaller warships engaged sections of the Italian fleet, luring them away from Tegetthoff's best vessels. Sea breezes cleared vision momentarily, a sailor high up in the *Seehund*'s rigging shouted down reports. Freed by an Italian ironclad's withdrawal, the *Kaiser*, despite its lack of metal cladding, followed up Tegetthoff and rammed the *Portogallo* again – wood against metal, sheer madness! But brilliant fighting spirit. Nearby the enemy flagship *Re d'Italia* had stopped in the water. Tegetthoff charged full speed ahead, and with an almighty crunch the *Ferdinand Max* hit her amidships. Her iron sides gave way, her tall masts toppled, she sank in a whirlpool of spars, ropes, canvas, metal, blood and men.

Cheers and shouts of triumph mingled with screams and cries and continued gunfire. Surely the Italians were beaten, their flagship gone. But before their loss was fully registered a massive burst of flame and roar of explosion overwhelmed all other noise of battle – the Italian ironclad *Palestro*, the first ship rammed by Tegetthoff, had blown up. She sank as the Italian fleet began to retire in disorder. Austria claimed its victory, sailing into the harbor of Lissa.

It was a magnificent battle, valiantly fought and won in two hours. This was naval history – an under-armed force trouncing double its size, using classic ramming tactics against the newest designs in naval strength. The daring and courage, the leadership – Ephraim was moved and thrilled, full of pride and admiration. He was sobered, too – the Italians had suffered appalling losses. Even from outside the fray he'd seen and heard the injured, dying and drowning men, the scrambles for rescue. The *Seehund* took on some of the wounded, including many from the Italian fleet, for their casualties ran to hundreds and hundreds. Austria had only thirty-eight lost, 138 hurt. It was time to work. Like other naval Surgeons, Ephraim combined all three branches of medicine. He was physician, diagnosing and prescribing; he was apothecary, preparing and dispensing medicine; and he was surgeon, performing operations. He completed two amputations, six extractions of bullets and set two broken limbs. Burns and gashes needed treating too. From his Austrian patients, as he worked, Ephraim learned more about the triumph: how proud the men were of their Admiral, how he had drilled and drilled them, in maneuvers, in gunnery, how he planned the ramming even though the ship armoring was incomplete. Most of all, he showed he loved his men, he believed in them and their morale. He proved it by commanding not from his favorite frigate, the wooden *Scharwzenberg*, but by shifting his flag to the new, unfinished *Ferdinand Max*. And he personally led the fleet into battle and fought it all the way through. 'He must be charmed. Bullets were flying all around,' one sailor said. 'I saw him, just kept moving on the bridge, calling out commands,' said another, 'God is with him.'

In the quiet, late at night, Ephraim thanked God for the victory. Exhausted and exhilarated by all he had witnessed and by the devotion of the men and officers to the great Admiral, he began to compose a description of the extraordinary day. After some thought, he chose to write in English verse, for the variety of rhyme and rhythm that language offered.

Tegetthoff led, flag high above the fray,
Our Admiral on the bridge, directing all:
'Close with the enemy and ram everything gray!'
His commanders and men rose to the call.
Decks slippery with blood, Ferdinand Max held sway.
'Full steam ahead,' he ordered through gunsmoke pall.
It made a scene men do not soon forget;
For they remember battles, fires, and wrecks,
Or other times of glory and regret,
That make or break hopes, heads, or necks.
Then rose from sea to sky the wild farewell –
Then shriek'd the timid, and stood still the brave,
And the sea yawn'd around her like a hell,
And down she suck'd with her the whirling wave.

It took two days to complete the one hundred lines. He titled the poem, *The Victory of Lissa*, and dedicated it, 'To the great Admiral and man, Vice-Admiral Wilhelm von Tegetthoff.' Before the week was out, his

Captain having read and then charged Ephraim to read out and translate his poem to the *Seehund* crew, a missive came back to Surgeon E M Epstein. The Admiral himself sent thanks and praised the poem, signing the letter in his own hand. To be recognized by the man himself! Ephraim was thrilled: his degrees and successes had come of long, hard effort, but this honor was born of sheer inspiration. He wrote out the poem again, proud to send it home to his mother, father and Sarah.

The battle had been won – however Ephraim soon learned that the war was lost. On the very day after Lissa the Austrian army, having in June defeated the Italians in several land battles, lost to Garibaldi's troops near Lake Garda with huge casualties. Worse, on the northern front the Prussian army in early July had decisively defeated the Austrians with enormous loss of life. Even before the Battle of Lissa Austria had begun negotiating peace with Prussia. All fighting ceased by August: Austria and Germany were now two separate countries. Nevertheless, there remained a great Austrian empire, and while all this was transpiring in the larger world, Ephraim received a new commission. He was to report to Pola, Austria's port in Croatia, as supervisor of the naval smallpox hospital.

Fresh from the triumph of Lissa, an officer in sole charge, dealing with a foe he knew well, Ephraim was in his element. The land welcomed him, green-clad mountains rising above the harbor town, the blue sea dancing in sunlight. Two-story buildings with terracotta roofs reached toward the foothills. The smallpox isolation hospital lay on the very tip of the harbor's point. Ephraim took the briefing from the acting assistant surgeon in charge. He examined the patients: sixty, ten severe. The care had been good thus far, but too many had died, and the number of cases had been increasing. He commanded canvas shelters to be constructed on the east side of the building and, to the doubtfulness of the orderlies, had the most ill moved outdoors.

'Fresh air, breezes, sea air, this is nature's way. It is the most we can do,' Ephraim told them. He joined his staff in applying plain cold water to the pustuled bodies and urging high fluid intake, the simple nursing remedies that were all they could offer. Ephraim, in his tiredness, could almost see Rachel beside him, his able helper in that intense time in Monastir. At least there was none of the hemorrhagic and malignant smallpox he'd seen there, forms that were nearly always fatal. Here, confluent rash was his direst worry, when all the pox blisters joined together and detached layers of skin from the flesh, like an extreme burn. Some of these patients he did lose. His hospital was filled with native Croatian sailors, mostly, and their Christianity was mainly Roman Catholic or Eastern Orthodox, with some Muslims too, but no Jews. Ephraim went among them with the Navy Chaplain, repeating prayers and reading Bible passages.

Within a fortnight he'd trained his staff to his satisfaction and could take up a more normal schedule, although new cases came in as steadily as recovered patients departed. The disease was ever-present in this part of the world, and the populace, as in Turkey, had a medieval fear of vaccination. Ephraim began to muse, and then to fume. He conferred with the assistant, and then, in his naval uniform, he walked about Pola and observed, he spoke to vendors in the market, to several priests and a rabbi. Finally, he went to his senior medical officer, Physician rank, at the main naval hospital. Ephraim had a cause again, a righteous cause, a proven cause, for the good of all, to save all, and it would benefit the Navy and Austria too, to prevent the spread of smallpox. 'The people must be persuaded of vaccination. They are ignorant anti-vaccination fanatics. We know it is safe. We have healed local men, so the people will trust us. I myself will direct the program.'

Austria was licking its wounds, there was no war to fight, Ephraim had reduced mortality to less than one per cent at the smallpox hospital. Permission granted. Dr Epstein, the Navy Surgeon, thanked the Lord for this opportunity. In Pola he went to the synagogue for Shabbat – and posted letters to Mama and Sarah, getting back to the routines of land life. He kept up his mussar self-examination and dared to discover, with humility, he hoped, that he had developed in the virtues of industry, sincerity, tranquility. The latter, admittedly, was still challenged by his old nemesis, impatience. He rejoiced to welcome Jesus in his heart when he prayed with the chaplain. Then, just he readied himself for the first vaccination session in the town came an astonishing letter. The Emperor Franz Josef commended Dr Ephraim M Epstein for his poem of the Battle of Lissa, forwarded by Vice-Admiral Tegetthoff. Dr Epstein was to be awarded a prize of 600 florins from the Emperor's own purse and he was to present himself at the Hofburg Palace two months hence to receive the honor. In the meanwhile, he was commissioned shipboard Surgeon on the *Dalmatia* with immediate effect.

A tumult of response swept through Ephraim – awe and joy at the award, irritation at the loss of his vaccination project, bemusement and anticipation at his new posting. He wrote quick letters to the family in Brest-Litovsk and the Wrights in Vienna and packed his kit.

The *Dalmatia* was a side-wheel steamer, an old-fashioned cruiser that had been one of the first generation of steam-powered warships. She was aptly named, for her task was to ply the Austrian Adriatic coast. Tegetthoff was determined to protect the lands of Croatia, Bosnia, Herzegovina and Montenegro in order to keep and develop the empire's naval bases. Back and forth they swept, but the patrol met no challenges. With no battles there were few men for the ship's surgeon to attend to, and those were dull cases indeed – a festering boil, the clap, a damaged finger, tooth ache, a wasting condition, malingering. Tedium began to eat at Ephraim. Peacetime naval medical life provided him no chance for scientific exchange, no forum for learning. He discussed literature and natural science with some fellow officers, but they lacked his own deep training and wide background so the talk was not stimulating. His religious practice was solitary and of little comfort, a different spiritual loneliness to what he'd known on land. However, he was warmed by Sarah's thrill that he might meet the Emperor, by his parents' congratulations and by the Wrights' delight in his good fortune. He counted the weeks, then days, until his return to Vienna.

How Ephraim wished his mother could have seen the presentation. To enter the grand and ancient Hofburg Palace by imperial invitation was to partake of fantasy. For her and for Sarah he drank in the glittering of epaulets, swords and scabbards ranked below crystal chandeliers, damask hangings, pastel plaster scrollwork and cherubs. Gigantic oil paintings of glorious battles hung in gilt frames, including Tegetthoff's earlier triumph in the North Sea. The Emperor was not there, but the Admiral was, and Ephraim had the pride of hearing his poem read out to the assembled. All cheered at his rendition of the victory, and praise came from the lips of Tegetthoff himself. Ephraim saluted the great man after accepting the award, and was saluted in return. A score of officers received medals at the same ceremony and all were guests of honor at a ball the same evening.

As the poetic ship's surgeon he was much remarked on, and Ephraim felt it necessary to dance with the sisters and wives to whom he was proudly presented by his fellow officers. Stephen Wright and his wife were Ephraim's invited guests, a momentous opportunity to repay the hospitality of his kind friends, and again to dance with the gentle Mrs Wright. In his happiness and pride, Ephraim thought of home long ago. He closed his eyes briefly as he moved to the music and recalled the gracious yellow house of his childhood, his sisters: Cheyne, Chashe and Cecilie, so grown up, Eva, serene and blonde like Mama, his closest sisters, Pauline and Kathy, his little brothers, Aaron and Isaac, and Helene, the baby of the family. The cousins and friends: David, Samuel, Abraham, Benjamin; even little Rachel, the giggler. How they ran and played in the gardens, how they sang. Gliding and swirling in the waltz he wondered if he dared to dream of having a warm and happy family life.

Mama was never to know the glamour of the court presentation. Two days after he dispatched his description to Brest-Litovsk Ephraim received a black-bordered letter from the same place. Despairing, he knew what it meant. Sarah, demonstrating the considerable sensitivity, intelligence and maturity of her eighteen years, and the wisdom and love she'd received from her grandmother, gave her father details of his mother's final days and hours, and of the funeral and the week of sitting shiva.

Gone! Alone! In the quiet of his room where Ephraim had taken the dreadful letter to open, a cry broke from his heart. Numbly, urgently, he found an under-vest among his clothes, and as he tore it and put it on for keriah, the mourner's Kaddish came to his lips. Slowly, deeply he began: Yitgaddal veyitqaddash shmeh rabba, May His great name be exalted and sanctified is God's great name. But then he had to change the next lines to the burial Kaddish: 'In the world which will be renewed and where He will give life to the dead and raise them to eternal life.' Tears choked his throat, and even as he spoke the Aramaic, he thought the words of the Gospel of John: 'For God so loved the world, that he gave his only begotten Son, that whosoever believeth in him should not perish, but have everlasting life.'

What to do, what to do... in pain and sorrow he thought of going to a church, because now he was freed to Christ. Instead he went to synagogue praying for his mother. He was lost once more. As a serving surgeon he had to report for duty, but a telegram from Kathy the next day urged Ephraim to come to Heidelberg. He applied for leave. The full thirty days of mourning still had three weeks to run, he would wear the torn vest over his heart all that time, he would not cut his hair or even shave. To be with family and express his grief was the only way.

'At least she knew of the Emperor's award,' said Ephraim to Stephen Wright over coffee at their favorite cafe. 'I take comfort from that.'

This was the sixth or maybe tenth time that the bereaved Dr Epstein had repeated his self-consolation, and Wright soothed yet again: 'And so good that she saw the poem itself.' But his friend also needed stirring. 'When will you see your daughter?'

'First I have to decide.' Ephraim was still circling, delaying. But finally he was no longer paralyzed with grief and remorse. The weeks of mourning at Kathy and Abraham's had been a kind of hell, his pain sharply mingled with joy in Christ Jesus. He was near ecstasy when he walked to Heiliggeistkirche, knelt below its soaring fan vaulting and partook of the Eucharist. Bread, wine and blessings were at the heart of the Shabbat meal, but Jesus himself had said, Take, eat, this is my body; Drink, this is my blood of the new covenant – do this in remembrance of me. Ephraim savored and embraced Christ, at peace within his sorrow.

In Vienna when the Wrights encountered him at their Lutheran church they welcomed and comforted him. They knew something of his conflicted religion; they understood – he had returned to Christianity, to the Protestantism of his conversion and training. Ephraim resigned from his synagogue and his mussar group, a painful second betrayal, but he did not shirk his honest duty to bid farewell. He was kofer ba-Torah again, an apostate Nazarene. He hoped his faith in Christ would illuminate his fellow Jews. Bearing their disapproval was his sacrifice: he deserved it. He offered it up to Jesus.

The gate of freedom had swung wide open, choices were his to make: Jew or Christian, naval or civilian, doctor or pastor, Europe or America. Ephraim had had time, meandering the Philosopher's Walk in Heidelberg, to think deeply. And time in Vienna, to talk things through with the Wrights. Did he have a future as a naval surgeon? Medicine was his true calling, with the help of God. But not medicine for clap-ridden sailors and medieval peasants. Private practice in Vienna or Heidelberg? Though rich in culture European society was stifling, and there was another fact: once a Jew always a Jew here, even though he was Christian. As he mourned and pondered Ephraim began to yearn for the clean white clapboard churches of America, the new-built steeples, the mud of the roads, the open spaces, the virgin woods – and the freedoms. Everything new, raw and full of possibility.

So he applied for dismissal to return to the United States; his honorable discharge was forthcoming. He would practice medicine in America. But where? New York, so crowded, so… Jewish, the New York he knew. New Jersey, New England… having abandoned missionizing he shrank from meeting meliorating activists. California perhaps, or Charleston, Cincinnati, Chicago, other burgeoning cities.

Yes, said the Wrights, America needed him. And Leavenworth in the new state of Kansas in particular needed him. He made the decision. He did not see Sarah again, dispatching instead 200 florins from his award and the promise he would send for her as soon as he was established. To her, and to his father, he said nothing of returning to Christianity – Mama's death released him from all promises, that was understood. In January 1867, with Stephen Wright's letters of introduction in hand, Ephraim set sail for America for the second time in his life.

PART 3: THE PURSUIT OF HAPPINESS

21

AMERICA REGAINED
Leavenworth, Kansas 1867-69

Ephraim unpacked his crates of medical texts, literature and books of faith, and commissioned a signboard. What finer place to be than Leavenworth, the gateway to the West! Through Stephen Wright's kindness and connections he soon met the very best people of the city. Attorneys, bankers, manufacturers and merchants were among these civic-minded citizens, aspiring, sincere, self-made men. He shared their belief in America as the land of opportunity, and caught their enthusiasm for America's duty to civilize this great continent – its manifest destiny.

As promised, there was certainly need for physicians in Leavenworth. Back in 1855 when Wright had joined abolitionist action the outpost on the west bank of the wide Missouri River held two hundred residents; now it was a boom-town twelve times the size, and still growing. Wright's closest friend, another railway man, had directed Ephraim to a recently vacated doctor's house, complete with consulting room and housekeeper. Called back East, the man's patients were satisfied to be attended by the 38-year-old physician fresh from European clinics. More came Dr Epstein's way from the letters of introduction. Yet more patients came from his church, for having been welcomed by the Wrights' Lutheran congregation in Vienna, Ephraim exulted in his renewed Christianity and sought continuation among the Lutherans in Leavenworth.

Within two months he felt well on the way to establishing himself – until struck by the realization that Kansas was a terrible mistake. At first Ephraim had thrilled to the novelty of the frontier nature of Leavenworth. Street names of the city's grid alone told the story: Dakota, Cheyenne, Pawnee streets crossed 6th, 7th, Broadway. His practice was on Walnut Street, near the busier thoroughfares of Choctaw and Cherokee streets. Indians themselves did business down by the river around the quay, some in fringed leather leggings, a few in military jackets, wearing long hair and beads. They were a minority among the bustle of cowboys, mule drivers, soldiers, recently freed Negroes, riverboat workers, pioneer families.

In letters to Sarah he tried to capture the raw and optimistic atmosphere. He chose a viewing point to give her the flavor: 'I stand by a blacksmith opposite the best freighters in the west, Russell, Majors and Waddell. The continental telegraph and the railroads have taken over from the Pony Express and great wagon trains, but some still roll. What a sight! A dozen canvas-covered wagons, each pulled by six yoke of oxen, rumbling out of Leavenworth bearing settlers and supplies. I cannot help but think of the Israelites setting out for the Promised Land.'

She wrote back, eager to know when she could join him, but he said the time was not yet right. Indeed it was not. Ephraim's shining vision of the United States had begun to tarnish. The disillusionment started on the journey from Vienna to Leavenworth. Choosing to avoid old friends, old haunts, he set out on his new life by arriving in Charleston, South Carolina. Though he'd known of General Sherman's swathe of destruction through the South he was shocked at its viciousness. As he journeyed towards the Mississippi for the river trip north he saw burnt-out buildings, dead trees, scorched fields. To be sure America's indomitable spirit prevailed in the rising timber frames and bricks and mortar of reconstruction. But the scars were unhealed and the Southerners he met, once they established that he was a foreigner, spoke openly and bitterly about the rapacious Northerners, both during the war between the states and now. What had his America become?

Religion, too, took on shadows. No longer tied to the intensity of the Jewish melioration brethren, Ephraim in Kansas soon found Christian freedom sullied. In seminary the variations in Protestant faith stimulated him, but now, away from the atmosphere of theological study, instead of intelligent, spiritual fresh air he encountered petty disputes, personality politics and sectarian snobbery. He found the Lutherans here were more simplistic than those in Vienna, and after a while he began to attend occasional other services. He liked the Baptists' straightforward approach, the Congregationalists' democratic organization, the Unitarians' inclusiveness, the Episcopalians' ritual. But each had flaws. Some lone pastors had their own quirky variations and preached in tents and hired halls. There were Jews in Leavenworth, too, quick to welcome him, assuming his faith by his surname – and Christians made the same assumption. What's more, he soon learned that the church he attended greatly mattered to his well-off connections who lived in the brick mansions along the esplanades overlooking the river. So, though it chafed, he continued as a Lutheran out of obligation to the upper echelons among his clientele. How strange, he thought, that now with perfect freedom to worship his God, he could not find a denomination in which to worship perfectly. He carried on reading, praying, writing and thinking in solitude.

Finally, the awful truth was that along with the earnest and civic-minded the gateway to the West drew hustlers, con men, failures, cheats and criminals. Living near the center he was called out to saloons where drink, cards and cockfighting routinely led to fights. A different class of patients seeking his predecessor began to turn up needing treatment for gun wounds, knife slashes, bloodied faces. They were the dregs of society, worse than any he had encountered in the navy, Turkish ghettoes or New York slums. He was sickened by their lives and godless codes. Of course he told none of this to Sarah, but his revulsion expressed itself physically and he literally fell sick in his first sweltering Kansas summer.

Severe gastritis kept him bedridden for a month. His income plummeted, but as bad as this, his inherited housekeeper took it on herself to nurse him closely. Clean and hardworking, but garrulous and dim-witted, Mrs Murphy had a monotone voice that nearly drove him mad. She yattered about the neighbors, about the laundry, about the chickens, the corn, the rain, the sun. In his illness she became possessive, shooing away the ladies of the church who brought him nourishing treats and diverting conversation. Through one of these kind Christians he discovered a new treatment for his old gastric complaint, Hoffman's Anodyne: a heady ether-based liquid taken in water, it relieved the pain and promoted the belching that always helped. When he recovered he still sipped at his old remedy, carbonated water. Somehow he remained curiously unable to rid himself of Mrs Murphy. Even when he made it clear he wished to dine alone, she would hover at the door, and break into commentary on food, health and digestion.

In the autumn, out of the blue came a letter from Cincinnati, Ohio — from Uncle Jacob. Since Ephraim last saw him a decade ago in New York the gem trader had wandered the world, returned to California, wandered again. Brisker gossip had told him where Ephraim was in America. 'Hold onto your hair, if you still have any,' he wrote, 'your ancient Uncle Jacob's traveling days are over.' Business was good in Cincinnati, the city cultured. 'I'm not as rich as Mr Astor yet,' he wrote, 'but my house has gas-light and a bathroom! Why not come? You'll keep me company, like before.' There was a teaching hospital, and plenty of scope for private practice, he promised.

Ephraim assured Jacob that he still had a head of thick, dark hair, and expressed amazement at the moss that must be gathering on his uncle's balding pate. He gave thanks for the Cincinnati offer, but rejected it. Indeed it could be a more civilized place for Sarah, but to accept would mean reneging on his commitment to America's great western destiny.

Winter came on, just as hard as the dreadful hot summer. Fierce winds howled off the plains, the Missouri froze over. There was no shipping, no bustle on the streets and the rowdy frontiersmen went stir-crazy, brawling and feuding. How could Sarah ever live in Leavenworth? But then treating his patients, socializing, leading prayers, Ephraim wondered if he was being over-protective: the good citizens were brave, hopeful, inspiring, and he knew by now that Sarah shared his openness to adventure. Still, something felt amiss; he delayed sending for her.

By the time spring arrived another Leavenworth problem emerged: women. As in Vienna, he was assessed as a good catch. Popular at social events, in the city's genteel circles he felt that his every dance, every conversation, every smile was being watched and interpreted. Some ladies found community or charitable matters as reasons to come visiting, a few even came with imagined ills as patients. He enjoyed knowing that he was attractive, but felt smothered by these attentions. The women were too coy, too earnest, too desperate or... too American. He was not yet ready for a wife, not in his heart, and not financially either. Even after a year he simply was not bringing in enough money. He had to learn through losses how to bill and collect from patients, how to keep his books. Sarah kept writing and hinting, Ephraim kept saying he needed to be more established.

Uncle Jacob wrote again, embroidering the opportunities: Cincinnati, established and thriving for nearly a century, close to the West but not of it, ideal for him, suitable for Sarah. Tempted, Ephraim declined again out of fear he was using his daughter as an excuse to leave Kansas. But intellectually, professionally and culturally he yearned. He was no longer an innocent, hopeful twenty-year-old immigrant, but a grown man with a place in society. He had mastered the learning of two disciplines, had survived personal and spiritual betrayals, had saved lives and brought life into the world. He had lived in Russian, American, Ottoman and Germanic cultures, he had farmed and sailed in battle and been received in a palace. Idealism was fine, but could he really spend all he had become on a muddied American dream? After Heidelberg and Vienna, Leavenworth was a desert of learning, and he thirsted keenly. In Cincinnati, with a medical school and large hospitals a physician would serve on a consulting rota, hear lectures, grow his private patient list, have paying students. Here, there was only one modest hospital run by nuns. Here, Ephraim was one of only two physicians who had practiced in Europe. A few others were all right, but some were from the desperate side, drunks, or with dubious qualifications or, worst of all, addicted to morphine. To extend his learning he had to rely on medical journals by post and exchange professional ideas by contributions to their letters pages. He continued his habit of self-examination: by staying on was he being stubborn? Or principled?

Early in 1869 came a startling letter from Sarah: Rachel was remarrying. The image of the many-folded get flashed through his mind. And then a prayer – he wished her well, and felt a weight lift. But there was more. Sarah stated clearly: she was now twenty-one, and she requested, begged, indeed charmingly demanded to be allowed to come live with him. She would not be a burden, she would teach French and German, she could teach piano too. She would keep house for him – they would be together at last. And she so longed to see America. She enclosed a pressed sprig of myrtle, reminder of their closeness and his promise in Heidelberg.

At last Ephraim sent a telegraph to Uncle Jacob: 'Accept your kind offer – STOP – arriving to practice three months hence – STOP – Daughter to follow – Dr E M Epstein.'

Sarah's moving appeal was one reason he finally accepted Uncle Jacob's blandishments. The other was the prostitutes. They had recently found their way to him and it was his Christian and medical duty to care for their pregnancies and botched abortions, injuries from beatings, their syphilis and gonorrhea, which he treated with mercury and silver nitrate. They came at night, in shame, and he administered to them clandestinely and tolerated their laudanum habits. He talked to them of Christ, who had forgiven the woman who sinned, and prayed with them for as long as they would listen. To have his daughter in this setting – it simply was not possible.

Reflecting, as he packed up his books once more, as he briefed his replacement and bid farewell to the good citizens of Leavenworth and (with great relief) to Mrs Murphy, as he boarded the steamboat to St Louis, then the train to Cincinnati, Ephraim concluded that Leavenworth was his first true defeat. Other situations he had quit because he sought a better way driven by righteousness. Certainly choosing to set up home with his daughter was a fine and good thing, but larger than this was the fact that he had failed to live up to Kansas, or it had failed him. Perhaps the wild West was a question of too much freedom. Perhaps simply – at age forty – he was putting away childish things, and seeing no longer in black and white, but perplexing shades of gray. He had no shining truth to urge him on. He accepted his need for civilized surroundings. He chose now the mature path of simple joy in family life, and a return to the high exchange of professionalism and ideas.

Ephraim reckoned he had salvaged one benefit from his time in Leavenworth, and that was brotherhood – Masonic brotherhood. Stephen Wright's introduction had borne a between-the-lines recommendation that Ephraim be considered a candidate for initiation into the organization of like-minded, well-intentioned men from all walks of life. As he had socialized, set up his practice, participated in church and community gatherings, lectures and events he was recognized as one of their own. For the Masons there was common belief only in a single Deity, and in the need to aspire to be and do the best that fulfilled and reflected this, the Architect of the Universe. The many strands of Christianity, even Judaism or Mohammedism were not an issue. Not even the heated divisions between

Democrats and Republicans mattered. No dogma, no orthodoxy, no arguments, free independent thought and truth: Ephraim had found true fertility of mind, good will and purpose among the brotherhood in Leavenworth. In turn, they deemed him worthy of being the lodge's senior warden. He rejoiced in this lifelong, universal brotherhood; he was already in touch with the Masonic Lodge of Cincinnati. All the rest of Kansas he was glad to forget.

22

HOME SWEET HOME
Cincinnati 1869

Once again, Ephraim arrived in a new city to start a new life and this time it was an easy, comfortable beginning. Cincinnati, the lively, pleasant city along the banks of the Ohio River, greeted him with open arms, starting with a big bear hug from Uncle Jacob. Still garbed in layers of black, wrinkles multiplied, a frizzle of white hair below his black homburg, he rushed Ephraim from the bustling train platform out to a cab.

'Look around, look around! They call this city the Queen of the West,' said Jacob once they were under way. 'What do you think?'

'Very different from the west I've just come from, I'm glad to say.' Ephraim peered out at a splendid square white-domed building opposite a pillared, pedimented edifice, both flying the Stars-and-Stripes high on their flagpoles.

'Court House, town hall... everything you could want! A good place to make a life.' Jacob pointed out other highlights as they continued along busy streets lined with three and four story brick and iron buildings, describing the layout of the city as they drove away from the center. Ephraim felt himself unfurling, letting go of bodily and mental tension he'd been unaware he held. They passed a groomed park, churches, a high school for girls; wooden three- and two-story buildings appeared, some were businesses, some residences, then the road turned up hill passing handsome brick houses. Then, slightly down hill, the road was lined on either side with smaller wooden white-painted houses.

'Is this where you live? They remind me of dachas in Belarus,' Ephraim said just as the cab stopped by one with window boxes brimful of yellow crocus.

'No,' said Jacob. 'It's where you live. We found a home for you, come see!'

In his astonishment and in the unloading of baggage and fare-paying Ephraim paid no attention to the word 'we' until the front door opened as they walked up the path. A tiny, beaming woman with auburn hair called out, 'So this is the famous kofer nephew! Welcome to your house, Dr Epstein.'

Jacob hurried forward. 'Esther, I present my nephew. Ephraim, my fiancee, Mrs Tobleroff.'

'Your fiancee!' Ephraim put down his suitcase. 'Now I know why you stayed in Cincinnati. Mazel t'ov! Mazel t'ov!'

'Yes, I persuaded him,' she bestowed an adoring smile on her intended who gave Ephraim a sheepish grin, reached for her hand and kissed it. 'My Jakey,' she said fondly, showing Ephraim a large diamond on her finger. 'But enough of this schmaltz, come in, come in, Dr Epstein!'

And so the story came out, of a long late courtship of the red-haired Cincinnati widow and the easy-going peripatetic gem trader. How they'd met at the San Francisco boarding house she owned, how she'd saved his life in a fire, how she'd returned to Ohio and he had later visited... Over coffee in the kitchen of what seemed to be his own house Ephraim realized that Mrs Tobleroff's upswept hairdo with dangling corkscrew curls was in fact a wig. This, along with her calling him kofer and a mention of kosher food, told him she was an orthodox Jew, a curious choice for the freewheeling Jacob. As the conversation continued Ephraim managed to control a giggle at the pet name Jakey. In his sixties, it seemed his uncle wanted – or had succumbed to – a doting, capable woman of his own age. Her wrinkles matched his, and her gritty energy balanced his easy-going pragmatism She declared their kave klatch over with the business-like words, 'So Mr Finkelstein, let's introduce the doctor to his home. It's very empty, you need to hurry to make it ready for your daughter.'

A tour of the handsome little house beyond the kitchen and entry hallway revealed a back parlor for everyday use, a front parlor for more formal occasions, a flanking front room to serve as consulting office, and four upstairs bedrooms. Ephraim was nearly overwhelmed by the helpful proposals: paint, wallpaper, furniture, bedding, she knew what he would need, where to get things. He was moved almost to the point of tears by the perfect possibilities. Suddenly Sarah's presence in his own life was a reality, father and daughter, together. 'A piano,' he said, 'We will have a piano for her, in the front parlor. And I will have shelves for my books in the other room... and she shall have this bedroom, looking down on the...' he paused, peering closer, 'Ah, it's a cherry tree!'

'Tell him the rest, Esther,' said Jacob.

As the three of them stood by the window, the tree below still winter bare, she told him about the cook-housekeeper Ephraim was to interview tomorrow. Mercy Johnston, a Negro freed long before the Civil War, would come daily from her own quarters. 'Of course, she will not cook kosher. But I have told her you will give instructions for your daughter's requirements. You haven't forgotten what is kosher, what with you and your Jesus, I hope.'

'Now, Esther, you promised no kvetching,' said Jacob mildly.

'Kahsrut, treif, of course,' Ephraim hesitated, recalling the vision of Jacob slurping down oysters at Cecilie's house. He had counted on the liberal approach of Uncle Jacob to ease the gap between Sarah's Jewish practice and his own Christianity. Now he had to accept this loving bossiness. 'Such a woman, Uncle! She thinks of everything. I thank you both so much.' Esther beamed and he led the way out and down the stairs, pausing again in the front room where he would see patients. Work was the next challenge and he was eager to hear Jacob's leads.

'She will come to us for Shabbat, and to synagogue,' Esther happily intruded as they returned to the kitchen table. Ephraim felt a cold hand grab his heart. Sarah: indeed he had planned that she would attend synagogue with Uncle Jacob. But he had held visions of Sarah as queen of her own Shabbat table, with Uncle Jacob here and which even he himself would join, as Christ Jesus had joined in the Friday meal every day of his life. It would be like the early years he spent with the Jewish Christians, a mingling of both ways. Through this he might even gently, naturally, bring his daughter to Christ. Was he going to gain Sarah only to lose her? Stiffly he said, 'Thank you, Mrs Tobleroff. Sarah knows I will not fail in my promise to her and the family and the beth din to support her Jewish faith.'

'Oh, just call me Tanteh Esther. It's our pleasure!' She patted Jacob's hand. 'Now, Jakey, talk more to him about work. I'm going home to make us all a good meal.'

With domestic matters under way Ephraim left concern over his daughter's religious practice to the Lord in order to concentrate on Cincinnati's medical world. Jacob arranged meetings with several physicians, Tanteh Esther saw to the printing of Dr Epstein's cards and the painting of his sign board, the brotherhood of Freemasonry extended helping hands. Ephraim's faith helped, too. He made a point of going to several different Protestant churches before attaching himself to two: Baptists and Methodists warmly welcomed the erudite, accomplished, well-travelled physician into their midst. Within weeks Ephraim's references, his New York training and his Viennese clinical experience won him a post as visiting physician at Cincinnati University Hospital. In this role, for an unpaid annual three month spell he would daily attend a ward overseeing the care of patients. The system benefited the community, and allowed him to practice privately the rest of the time – and to spread his reputation. He settled into his profession and enjoyed overseeing preparations for Sarah's arrival – in only two months! What would she be like now, would she really be happy in America? Would he, could he live up to her expectations and be a proper father – he laid this before the Lord in his nightly self-questioning.

Finally came a sparkling April morning, with Cincinnati's cherry blossom at the peak of its ethereal glory, when Ephraim set off for the railroad station. He rejoiced in his blessings, praised the Lord God and could scarcely believe that he was established and waiting for his daughter. As he searched the faces and figures of passengers descending from the train, Ephraim harked back to that time long ago in Saloniki when he had waited to see Sarah disembark and been so bitterly disappointed. Then suddenly here she was, and he pushed through the crowd to embrace her, thrilled at how she had grown into full and beautiful womanhood.

'Papa! You look just the same,' she pulled back to take in his top hat, waistcoat, trim dark beard. 'Not like a cowboy at all!'

'And you! You look... you are all grown up!' His Sarah was small and gracefully built, her blonde hair swept up in a mop of curls framing her forehead, long locks at the nape. A frivolous hat of maroon velvet perched atop her coiffure to match her full-skirted travelling costume. He was touched that she wore his gift of diamond earrings, and astonished at how her fairness reminded him of his dear mother.

She spoke in excellent English and they laughed, then fell into the family's particular Brisker Russian as they talked about her journey while he supervised the handling of her trunks. The carriage jogged over the cobblestone streets and Ephraim took her gloved hand in his two hands. He described the passing sights and delighted in her interest as she peered out.

'Next to New York this city is spacious and clean – but I liked New York. There seems to be so much energy in America,' Sarah hurried to dispel any hint of criticism. His old friends Benjamin and Susannah Berman had greeted and hosted her, and father and daughter spoke of them until a clamor and odor intruded. 'Pig yards are that way – they used to call this Porkopolis.' She wrinkled her nose, and then asked about the smoke stacks in the distance. 'That's your American energy again,' he answered. 'Industry is thriving here. I can show you this side of Cincinnati, too, if you wish.'

'I want to know everything about my new country,' she said, sitting back happily in the cab.

'My dear daughter,' he patted her hand and beamed, his gray-blue eyes lighting. 'We are of like minds, seeking, questioning.'

Sarah's religion was the chief matter to settle as far as Ephraim was concerned and he intended to make it their first discussion over tea once she had freshened herself and unpacked a few things. But he could not. Sarah first praised her pretty pink-painted bedroom and they gazed together at the cherry tree, then she insisted on seeing every room in the house, and ecstatically sat at the piano. They laughed as she dashed off a few bars of

Yankee Doodle Dandy. Finally they sat down in the back parlor, where Sarah exclaimed over her father's tea served American style in a china pot, with china cups and saucers. She also praised the cherry pie he cut and served, and asked him to tell her more about Mercy. She said she was eager to meet the cook-housekeeper who had been such a blessed relief to her Papa after the tormenting Mrs Murphy he had entertainingly sketched in letters. At last, clearing his throat and changing to a serious demeanor, Ephraim came to the subject he'd been chafing to open.

'Dear child, you know that I will support you in your Jewish faith. The divorce will in no way impinge upon your practice.' She listened attentively as he detailed the arrangements with Uncle Jacob and the new Tanteh Esther.

Sarah looked at his grave face and thanked him, paused a moment and said, 'I would prefer to go to church with you, Papa.'

'Are you sure of this?' Ephraim's soul leapt with joy, but he maintained a stern front.

'You will teach me about your Jesus Christ and I will become Christian. If you agree.'

'I am grateful to the Lord, but this is so fast, am I reaping a whirlwind?'

'I have been thinking and even praying about it ever since our time in Heidelberg. I am determined: I will be a Christian. Of course Mama does not know.' She glanced over to the Bible she had noticed on the sideboard, its spine embossed with a gold cross.

'My dearest girl, if you think you are certain... nothing could give me greater happiness. We could begin, a little, right now – with a prayer?' He clasped his hands, and she followed, and he uttered words of thanks and praise. Then he reached for the Bible and opened it to the New Testament and read:

As the Father hath loved me, so have I loved you: continue ye in my love.
If ye keep my commandments ye shall abide in my love; even as I have
kept my Father's commandments, and abide in his love.

And then he handed the book to her, pointing to where he had stopped, so that she could continue:

These things have I spoken unto you, that my joy might remain in you,
and that your joy might be full. This is my commandment, That ye
love one another, as I have loved you.

'Stop here,' Ephraim said quietly. 'So you see, Christ speaks of the commandments, the same commandments of Moses from our Torah. But the greatest commandment of all, he says, is love.'

'Yes, Papa.'

'You have brought me such joy.' He patted her hand which still lay on the open Bible. 'Each day we will read together, and discuss. Bless you, my dear.' He stood and kissed her on the forehead, and sighed deeply and happily.

'Mazel t'ov, Ephraim! You have won one for your fold, back to proselytizing!' said Uncle Jacob that evening. Ephraim had arranged the dinner as a welcome for Sarah, which it was indeed, but now it was also an occasion for disappointing the old adventurer and his red-wigged fiancee. Father and daughter endured Jacob's complaints over the loss of a pretty guest at their Shabbat meals. Esther Tobleroff's teasing barely veiled her disapproval: 'So, a fast worker, Dr Epstein – when I marry into this family I better be careful.' But she smiled as she spoke and moved on to ask Sarah about Brest-Litovsk. 'Your uncle never tells me enough – what was he like back then?'

'He was a magician! He got a silver coin out of my ear. I was ten years old when he came. He'd been all over the world!' Sarah's voice turned introspective and dreamy, 'He told us about gold nuggets in California. Of course I wanted to know everything about America, because my Papa lived there.' She smiled shyly at Ephraim.

'Twice I opened pathways for him,' Jacob boasted jovially.

'But you left me all alone in New York!' Ephraim protested.

'And look at you now, Dr Epstein, with a prize from an emperor, too.' The banter led to the re-telling of their legendary perilous crossing, and Sarah and Esther demanded more stories about their early days in America, even though they'd heard them before. Ephraim basked in his daughter's adoration, the family warmth echoing his days as the lively charmer among his sisters at home in Brest.

There would be no question of Sarah earning a living, according to Ephraim. He owed her all those years of fatherhood; she should have time to enjoy American life, and to improve herself. Sarah objected, saying she longed to be independent, wanted to try her talents in this new land, wanted no more than his love and encouragement. Ephraim, at first surprised and then indulgent, saw in her his own willfulness; they agreed on a delay, during which time she would study her chosen new faith, practice piano, do needlework, read and write letters. And would she like him to give her lessons in Greek, so that she could read the New Testament in its early, true form? Yes, she would, and she also insisted on sharing some domestic duties. Once she had penetrated Mercy's southern drawl, the doctor's daughter and the kindly cook-housekeeper soon were exchanging recipes: latkehs and Bobeshi's borscht for pumpkin pie and hominy grits.

Sarah was determined to know American ways beyond the house, and for this too Ephraim had prepared, proudly taking her to community socials, concerts and lectures. Her declaration for Christianity meant they saw less of Uncle Jacob and his Mrs Tobleroff than they might have, but the gap was filled by the community of Ephraim's Baptist and Methodist churches. As an ordained minister he occasionally guest-preached in other Protestant churches, too. Before long his strikingly pretty daughter turned tables and was introducing him to new people. One particular favorite of hers was a young woman who looked so like her they could have been sisters. They shared interests: both played the piano well, read widely, enjoyed simple family pleasures of long walks, picnics, croquet, card games, ice skating. Ephraim was delighted that Sarah shared in Helena Greyer's church choir, a further and youthful exposure to the Christian faith. Languages were another bond – both knew French, and spoke German, too, for Helena's family had emigrated from Hanover when she was little. And there was another element in common: they were daughters of physicians. Helena's father, Dr Wilhelm Greyer, was an ear, nose and throat specialist at University Hospital.

Their friendship bore fruit, for the Epsteins and the Greyers – a household of five children – enjoyed each others' company. One further mutuality affected the Epsteins. George, the eldest son of the family, was beginning to study medicine and asked Ephraim to be his preceptor. In this role Dr Epstein would guide the young man's studies and drill him in clinical routines; as well as a compliment to Ephraim's professionalism young Greyer provided useful additional income, and having this one student led to two more and increased satisfaction, for Ephraim loved teaching.

The closeness of the two families enchanted Sarah, and even led to a new name for her. Partly as a teasing Americanization, and partly out of convenience, because the littlest Greyer sister was also Sarah, Helena began to call Sarah Epstein by a nickname: Sadie.

'I'm not sure, it sounds so American,' said Ephraim to his daughter as they walked home from a shared family evening of music-making.

'I like being Sadie!' she insisted. 'It makes me feel like I belong.'

Fondly he patted the arm she had tucked under his. 'You do belong, you belong to me.'

'No, but I mean... when I was growing up and you weren't there, and you were apikoros, I was... it made me different. Like an orphan, or even...' by now they had stopped their companionable walking, and she averted her head so he could not see the tears forming.

But he heard the tears, and the whispered word outcast. Barbed by her statement of his failure as a father, he tried to forgive the wound he felt by pulling her close. 'You are dear and courageous. Now we are as one, in home and in Christ. And you shall be Sadie, if that is what pleases you.'

23

SADIE
Cincinnati 1870-71

Over the months Ephraim and his daughter settled into a pattern of life. In the evenings if not socializing they sat by the iron stove and read, or she played piano as he listened or refined a medical or theological article. They enjoyed the Greek lessons, for she was an apt student, a natural linguist like him; they studied the Bible and prayed twice daily. Her plans to work remained dormant, although the Greyers insisted on paying her to teach piano to little Sarah and a friend. Ephraim saw patients in his consulting room in the mornings, or conducted correspondence with journals, then after mid-day dinner he called on patients, did hospital rounds, met his students or conferred with colleagues. Now and then, and only in fine weather, Sadie – as she pressed him to call her – came with Ephraim on visits to patients. She had asked and he agreed: she would wait outside in the horse trap and witness stations of American life other than their own. Some visits were to gracious brick houses in Mount Auburn on the hill looking out towards the Ohio River, some to new-built mansions in Walnut Hills, some out to farms a few miles from city center, some to crowded tenements near the manufacturing districts. He enjoyed her company as they jogged along in the trap. Not only did she alleviate the solitude of a physician's practice, but also he could share with her observations on his patients in a Christian, pastoral light. One day Sadie suddenly asked, 'Papa? Will you marry again, do you think?'

Ephraim hesitated. He was aware that he was a focus of female speculation, and he at last had begun to entertain the idea of marriage. His life was so rich now, all that he lacked was a bride, a helpmeet, a true partner in life. The terms of the get and the thought of Rachel remained with him. They each had been bid to new contentment. Was his cousin-wife now content? Was he truly free in the eyes of the Lord Christ Jesus to have contentment in marriage? Yes, the time was ripe. But although he had met some fine, educated Christian women in Cincinnati none had yet spoken to his heart. And he had wondered how Sarah-Sadie (he could not yet easily use her new name) might feel.

Sadie filled the silence. 'I'm sorry, it is too impertinent of me.'

'No, no. It is a reasonable question for a daughter to ask.' He glanced at her sitting beside him on the bench. 'I would dearly love to have a wife. I am so sorry that your mother and I...'

'I was wondering – you don't mind my saying?' A shake of his head encouraged her to continue. 'I was thinking you could make Miss Pettifer happy.'

'Miss Pettifer!'

'I've noticed she is very eager to study Bible with you. She's accomplished and... pretty.' Sadie looked up at his profile.

'Out of the question,' Ephraim said abruptly. Good heavens, what a thought. The woman was nearly forty. He had felt his daughter flinch slightly at the vehemence of his denial, so he pretended to consider. 'She is kind... and clever. But I have never thought of her that way.'

'Oh, good! Because I like being your hostess.' She smiled up at him. They had reached the stable by now, and he said she was the finest daughter and hostess any father could ever hope for, and the prettiest, too. He handed her down from the trap and led the horse away and when he returned found her pondering a daisy picked from a cluster by the roadside. 'Do you think I will make a good American wife?' she said wistfully.

He gave her a reassuring hug. 'I am sure that soon you will marry, and he will be a lucky man.' He had seen the young men clustering around his daughter and her friend like bees to blossoms. He shook his head, teasing, 'And then what will I do without my hostess?'

Ephraim entered a new phase of busy-ness around this time. His former professor and mentor at Andover Seminary, Calvin Stowe, had published a book which had been in the making when Ephraim was under Stowe's tutelage. *Origin and History of the Books of the Bible* was a work of utter appeal to Ephraim, and indeed some of his own Greek and Hebrew translations had helped its author. Now a best-seller, though not at the same level as Mrs Stowe's *Uncle Tom's Cabin*, it was one of the first widely read books to examine the Bible from an historical perspective. The divine word could be treated – respectfully, of course – with the same critical scholarship as any other ancient text. Like Darwin's *Origin of Species*, Stowe's book stirred controversy and discussion. Cincinnati was abuzz with interest for further reasons: Calvin Stowe had been a seminary professor here, and here met and married Harriet Beecher. Ephraim's personal contact with the professor, and his ability to lead studies on the book, soon resulted in invitations from several churches and discussion clubs. Once more he had a platform for the passion from his youth for fearless, truthful knowledge unbounded by superstition or orthodoxy. This new fire, combined with

Sarah's willingness to convert, rekindled his missionary zeal. Why couldn't all Jews see the light? He began to send articles to the Melioration Society's journal.

It was at their evening meal on return from one of his Bible discussions that Ephraim's daughter announced she was ready for baptism, if he thought so too. He regarded her tenderly: small, gifted, bright, energetic, her eyes so blue in her sincerity, her flower-sprigged summer gown fresh and graceful. How Mama must have been like this when she was young. How he did love having a woman of his own family in the house. 'So you have examined your soul and mind, and communed with the Lord. The spirit is with you. Amen!'

'I thought, as my godparents – Dr and Mrs Greyer?'

Ephraim's solemn face lit with a smile. 'Of course! Amen, amen. My dear, dear girl. The word had to come from you, but Pastor Blake told me weeks ago that he found you well ready.'

'Not the Baptists.'

'Not the Baptists!'

She waited as his smile faded. 'The Methodists, Papa.'

'Not the Baptists? But you have spent more time in Pastor Blake's Baptist fold. It is the true baptism, as our Lord had it. My dear, I am perplexed. Now Pastor Robinson... it is true we have benefited from his Methodist breadth of vision. Is there something in particular, some point of interpretation that calls to you? Think carefully.' He covered his dismay with the inquiries. From the moment she had declared her interest in Christianity – and even before – he had seen her by a body of water arrayed in white robes, submerged to the old life, joyfully risen in the new, as he had been. As all Christians should be.

'A point of interpretation, yes. I prefer to be sprinkled by the Methodists than immersed by the Baptists.'

'Sprinkled!' Ephraim raised his voice in disbelief. 'That is the reason?' He stood abruptly, chair legs scraping across the floor boards. 'You object to complete immersion? But you know it is the only way, the true way, to salvation!'

She looked down at the willow-ware patterned plate at her place. He had begun pacing on the other side of the table. 'How can you not recall that Jesus himself said – and I quote: "with the baptism with which I am baptized, you will be baptized." ' She nodded her head slightly but stopped as he paced on, voice ringing with Biblical cadences. 'And the actual event in his life, in Matthew! "Jesus, when he was baptized, went up straightway out of the water: and, lo – " ' he paused expectantly in the midst of the drama, then went on: ' "The heavens were opened unto him, and he saw the Spirit of God descending like a dove, and lighting upon him." ' Still, she kept her eyes down on the plate. She would not give in. 'You must pray over this, Sarah Epstein. And so shall I. I am going to my room now. I will stay and pray until you come to your right mind, with the Lord's help.'

She cleared and washed up dinner alone; she bid him goodnight through his closed bedroom door and received silence. Ephraim refused to come down to breakfast, only snatching a slice of bread from the tray she'd left outside his room when he did not respond to her knocking. On his return from work at midday and in the evening he went directly to his bedroom. When she knocked he opened the door, silently accepted a tray of food and shut the door after briefly studying her face. Alone on his knees, he felt his heart breaking. This daughter of his, she was her mother's daughter too: as stubborn, as willful, as selfish. He could not fathom how she could disagree with the plain truth, the clear and obvious truth of Christian baptism by total immersion. He prayed to the Lord for her soul.

Traces of sunset still streaked the sky when he heard a knock at his door and a new voice. 'Dr Epstein, may we talk?' Helena Greyer, his daughter's friend.

He donned his suit jacket, quickly smoothed his hair and invited her in – Sadie stood beside her but remained outside the open door. And so began the peace-making. Gently and rationally Helena led him to weigh her friend's point of view. No one could doubt that his daughter was an ardent, educated Protestant convert, she said. Perhaps Dr Epstein, having converted so long ago, had forgotten how eager she might be to leave behind Jewish ritual. Sadie had told her much about Jewish ways – of course his daughter believed cleanliness was essential to life, but she also believed it should not be confused with cleanliness of spirit. Had he considered that total immersion was to his daughter too close to the Jewish mikvah? Ephraim listened, stock still, struck by the truth Helena uttered. It was the old ritual-bound Judaic laws she was trying to escape.

He said nothing, but Helena, reading his features, continued: how praiseworthy the Greyers – and, she believed, Dr Epstein himself – found Sadie's coming to the light of Christ, not spoon-fed or forced. Could she not have her own relationship with the Lord, in her own way? He nodded slowly, feeling the sudden awful realization that he was turning into his father – shutting himself away, not listening to other views, demanding to be obeyed. All this while Ephraim was seeing but not-seeing Helena, her blue eyes and fair hair, so like his daughter, yet behaving reasonably.'

The young woman spoke on, saying she realized that baptism outside the Baptist church could be an embarrassment to Dr Epstein's standing in that congregation. He wanted to deny this, but the same pride that had indeed been hurt by his daughter's choice kept him from admitting Helena was right, and meanwhile she was suggesting that the Greyers would be honored to sponsor the ceremony in their own church. To everyone this non-immersive baptism would be completely natural, she soothed, Sadie and her father having attended and having grown so close to the family. He nodded again, and Helena said she had one further, very personal observation, if he would allow it? She said that she found Sadie truly remarkable, being so new in the faith, to have such strong belief in a few drops of baptismal water as sufficient to sanctify her.

Ephraim absorbed a prickling of shame. Perhaps his daughter's faith outshone even his. He prayed to God this was so. He closed his eyes and nodded, went to the door and caught up Sarah's hand, kissing her on the forehead and drawing her into the room. He took Helena's hand too, saying, 'Let us pray,' and the three fell to their knees. He began with the Lord's Prayer, and then a psalm of thanksgiving and a blessing and concluded with the New Testament: 'And now why tarriest thou? Arise, and be baptized, and wash away thy sins, calling on the name of the Lord.'

What Ephraim did not guess Helena had suspected and Sadie's gratitude confirmed: proud and glad as she was to become Christian, Sadie did not want their Cincinnati Christian friends and the entire Greyer family to see her streaming wet, sputtering and in disarray. Rift healed, the ceremony was held early in September amid rejoicing at the German Reformed Church.

Something else, something momentous, happened that day. After the baptism, at the collation where the new Christian and her young hostess held court, Ephraim suddenly saw Helena. In his body and soul he saw her as he had never done before: body and soul, she was a woman – fair and small, bright and pretty, gifted and energetic, gentle and wise. Struck to the core, he knew. Impossibly, inevitably, Helena was the one.

24

EPHRAIM IN LOVE
Cincinnati 1871-72

What to do, what to do? Ephraim watched Helena through September, October, into November, the two young women reading and singing together, laughing and talking with his medical tutorial students, walking and playing games with the Greyer family. He paid courteous attention to both, taking care not to single out Helena. How would she feel? She was Sadie's own age, half his own. How would Sadie feel? He prayed to the Lord for guidance. Should he speak first to Helena herself, to Sadie or to Dr Greyer? He found himself reading the cries and joys of the Psalms and then the lyrical love of the Song of Solomon. And then Paul, echoing Genesis: 'Therefore a man shall leave his father and his mother, and shall cleave unto his wife, and they shall be one flesh.' This became his consolation. He was meant to marry and God had directed Helena into his pathway.

So long had he been unhappily married, so long focused on his patients, his theology, his God. All of that had helped him quell unseemly longings of the flesh. Except for that one time... he pushed away the memory of his transgression. Now he was free, free to marry. Sweet Helena... so kind to Sarah, such a good friend and the daughter of his own respected colleague. Even the Greyers' emigration from Germany created a closeness of understanding. And as a doctor's daughter, she knew how a doctor's household needed to be run. And: she was young and healthy. He did so much wish for children.

By December 1871, though he risked Helena's rejection, rebuttal, even horror, Ephraim knew he had to speak to her. He sent for some new sheet music, and after the cake and coffee he regularly shared with his ladies and students before his evening appointments, he asked Helena if she would come to him to look at the contents of the package. Birthdays needed surprises, he said to the group in the parlor, and there was something the next birthday celebrant here among us – meaning Sadie – could not know yet. In the book-lined consulting room he ushered Helena to a chair.

Instead of sitting behind the desk he took the companion chair. She looked eagerly toward the folder and he handed it to her. From New York, Benjamin had sent a Brahms duet, the overture to Wagner's Paris *Tannhauser* for piano, a new hymn, *Pass Me Not, O Gentle Savior,* and a newly popular minstrel tune. She paged through them and exclaimed, 'They're lovely! I can't wait to play them. Which one is the surprise?'

'My dear Helena. I apologize for the subterfuge, but the surprise is not music. It will come as a surprise, though. I hope not an unwelcome one.' He paused and drew breath. 'You know that I admire your family, and you, with all my heart. Having come to know you through your kindness and friendship to my daughter, I have grown to see you in another light.'

She went still, eyes on the music in her lap.

'My dear, please do not answer me now. But feeling for you the way I do, might you ever, could you think to ever become my wife?'

She looked up at him, his gray-blue eyes and dark whiskers, his grave face, anxious and hopeful. She opened her mouth to speak and then closed it.

His heart sank. He looked at the music, and her white fingers, so delicate, grasping the paper. 'I was afraid of that. I have been too sudden. I am an old man, old enough to be your father. I should not have presumed. Please, let us forget—'

'No!' she cried out. 'I'm sorry, I must be upsetting you. It's the surprise. I need time. And Sadie...'

'Time, yes. I have patience. I have time. Please, take all the time you need to consider. Of course I cannot court you like the young men, but,' he dared to touch her, one gentle touch with two fingers to the back of her hand, 'I can be ardent.' She studied his face and then looked away.

'You do not forbid me to hope?' She shook her head. They agreed to say nothing to anyone. He offered to say nothing more to her until two months had passed. They chose *Pass Me Not* as the surprise for Sarah's birthday. Helena would learn and play it for the celebration day next month.

It was ridiculous. For the first time in his life Ephraim was a romantic in love. He embarrassed himself, blushing when Helena entered the room, going hot and cold. As if all the years of repression, of the life of the mind and soul, had built up his tenderness and longing for affection, and now the floodgates opened. He kept close watch on himself, living in fear that everyone could read him: Helena's parents, her brothers, Mercy and most of all Sadie.

Christmas came and went, and finally came the January day of Sadie's twenty-fourth birthday. The party was at the Greyers' with all the family, including Uncle Jacob and Tanteh Esther and other close Cincinnati friends. The tall gray-blue wooden house was trimmed with white cut-out woodwork like a German fairytale cottage in a forest. Mrs Greyer, plump and friendly, ran home, husband and children with a firm rule. Ephraim approved of her. The foundation of happiness was a solid family life, and now perhaps this would be his, if Helena could marry him, an old man. She had suitors, he knew from Sadie's chatter, as Sadie herself had suitors. But he took hope because Sadie confided in him that they were just boys.

Helena played and sang the hymn beautifully, Ephraim bursting with pride. He looked from Sadie to Helena, Helena to Sadie. Two pearls, two beautiful young fair women. His own daughter and – dared he to hope – his life partner. Sadie joined Helena at the piano for the Brahms, and then all gathered round and sang *Little Old Cabin* and old favorites. Over the dinner table there had been champagne and a toast to Sadie's happiness. Ephraim had risen to toast both girls.

Amid the hubbub of routine life in the two families Helena contrived to be always busy, never near Ephraim for long. Since his proposal only once had he exchanged a private moment with her, caught alone by chance when she sat waiting for her father in the carriage outside the Court House. She allowed him to press her hand, and he implored with his eyes, until she lowered hers. Had he any hope at all? Who was he – an old man. But: vigorous! He knew he was vigorous. And he could give her the life she had grown up to deserve: a doctor's wife, a Christian, educated, cultured, familiar with her parents' German background.

Finally the waiting time was up and Ephraim, with a bouquet of early violets, skirted patches of thawing snow to walk to the Greyers. His brief note asking to call on Helena had not been rejected and he chose a time when Sadie was at the Methodist Sunday school teachers' gathering. Helena opened the front door before he knocked, and the moment he saw her he knew the answer was yes. She silently laid a finger on her smiling lips and led him to the front parlor where a fire glowed in the grate. She took the violets, inhaling their fragrance. 'They flower in hope,' said Ephraim. 'Like myself, if you will accept me, dear Helena.'

'Ephraim. Can you accept me, a mere girl, so ignorant compared to your experience, so young for your wisdom. So new in the spirit compared to your faith and learning.'

He fell to one knee before her. 'My dearest, you, in the first bloom of life. I can offer you the full flush. I promise you my strength and all my deepest love in the face of the Lord. Thank you, dear one. Are you certain?'

'Yes, Ephraim, I am.' She gazed steadily into his eyes. They remained like that for an eternity, until she said, 'Sit by me.'

He took her hand in his, dazed and full of joy. The hint of spring to come, the warmth of coals in the hearth, the violets in her lap, the blue of her gown, he felt he should be etching all this on his heart, but his pressing concern was to claim this wonderful woman for his own. 'Does anyone know? Have you confided in – '

'Not Sadie. I had to be certain between us.' She looked at him and laughed gently, 'What if you had changed your mind?'

'Never.' He lifted her hand and pressed his lips to it, and her cheeks grew pinker. 'And your father and mother, they don't know either?'

'Well, I perhaps gave a small hint to Mother, talking about the life of a doctor's wife. But she may have thought I meant George's friend Oliver. Though I spoke too of the church.'

'You have made me so happy.'

He spoke to her father that day and, startled, Dr Greyer questioned him on his earlier marriage. For the first time, man to man, Ephraim explained the circumstances of that marriage and its resolution in divorce. He promised to produce the papers to Dr Greyer's satisfaction, but this was brushed aside by Helena's father as he called in his daughter and saw her happiness. The problem remained of how to tell Sadie. Nothing would be announced until Sadie gave her permission too.

Getting ready to approach his daughter Ephraim felt as if he were preparing for a delicate surgical operation. With a prayer and high hope, he chose that very evening's walk home from his talk at the Baptist church. She had come because he had reached a new section in his history of the Bible books, one on Moses, which she knew had particular meaning for him. They agreed, as they made their way under the clear winter night sky, that the lecture had gone well. Before Ephraim could clear his throat to open the topic burning within him, Sadie asked: 'Is marriage any closer for you, Papa?'

Startled, he squeezed her arm to his as they continued walking and then replied, 'Yes. I am happy to say yes. My hopes and prayers are answered, she has accepted me. But only if you will accept her.'

Sadie stopped short. 'How kind to think of me! When will I meet her?'

'You know her already.'

'I thought so!' she crowed. 'It is Miss Pettifer!'

'It is Helena Greyer.'

There was a sudden deep silence before her puzzled response. 'But she's my friend.' She dropped his arm, her aghast, stricken face turned away from him.

'I am sorry if it is a shock to you. I realized my feelings for her only a little while ago.'

'Helena!'

'Do you find it impossible?'

She shook her head in dazed amazement, but not denial. He tucked her arm back into his and they strolled on as he continued: 'I know she is young. And,' he gave a wry laugh, 'she knows I am old. But not too old to be a husband to her. And she, as well as being your friend, she will be a

THE EXTRAORDINARY DR EPSTEIN

wonderful wife.' Sadie remained quiet. 'However, she will only accept me if you will accept her.'

'What about her father, what will he say?'

'He has given us his blessing.'

'Already!'

'I pray you will accept Helena as my wife, Sadie. It is a resurrection of my life the Lord has provided. I feel surely I am graced to have this. I vow to make her happy.' Sadie was silent, so he went on. 'If you will grant us this joy.'

They had arrived at the front path to their house when she burst out, 'But what about me?'

He hugged her to him. 'My dear child, you are my daughter forever. After those many years of separation you will always have a home with me. You two will be like sisters. As close friends as ever – and more. Won't that be good?'

Ephraim had a restless night filled with joy, anguish and prayer. His dear, perfect Helena to be his wife! But he risked alienating his daughter. He prayed that she could forgive him this new wound on top of the years of fatherlessness. He prayed to be freely allowed this new life.

In the morning Sadie's smile and an embrace flooded him with relief. At the breakfast table he apologized for upsetting her as, inwardly, he restrained himself from shouting hallelujahs of delight and racing over to see Helena. He gave every appearance of listening as Sarah murmured forgiveness and best wishes for their happiness. And then she dropped her bombshell.

'For myself, I shall be going to Charleston as soon as it can be arranged.'

'Charleston? South Carolina? Why?'

'Do you remember Uncle Jacob's offer last summer, his friend who needs teachers? I will talk to him this morning.' She hurried on to forestall Ephraim's protests. 'It is time that I cease to be a burden on you. I always promised to support myself.'

'But why not here? You have two students preparing for the conservatory, and you're teaching French to little Sarah. If you want to do more... Cincinnati is a good city.'

'Papa,' she gave him a stern look. 'Please be understanding. I want to give you and Ilenka the peace of your engagement.' As she used her own Russian pet name for her best friend he began to wish for Helena the peacemaker to mend this rift. She continued, 'He said there were Jewish families who wanted tutors.'

The previous summer Uncle Jacob, who still traded all over America, had told the Epsteins and even the Greyers about the southern port's flourishing reconstruction, about Charleston's cosmopolitan sophistication, its colonial heritage, the good families, the opportunities for trade, for physicians, for educators. At the time Sadie had no reason to be interested, but now Charleston was the perfect solution.

'Jewish families!' Suddenly a different level of alarm alerted Ephraim. 'You are missing the old ways, you would forsake Christ?'

'No Papa, I promise you, I am a Christian. I will go to church. I will write to you and I will continue my Gospel studies.'

He was unsure, and let her know he was displeased. But he had to let her go. After all, she was a grown woman of twenty-four. What's more, she had granted him his heart's desire: his dear, dear Helena.

25

DOCTOR AND FAMILY MAN
Cincinnati 1872-74

Over a flurried few weeks engagement congratulations mingled with preparations and farewell parties for Sister Sadie, as Helena now called her. And then all too soon came the carriage ride to Cincinnati railroad station. As Ephraim went off to tend to his daughter's baggage a disorienting wave of homesickness swept through him. Leave-takings were so much part of his life, yet now he was the one remaining behind. On the platform he saw the two young women from afar, blonde, pretty, embracing, sharing tears and promises, his Sarah and his Helena. And shimmering with them, his own Mama, fair, small, full of love. For a moment they merged into one – who, which, was he marrying? Helena turned to him with a question on her lips and tenderness in her eyes, and the strange sensation faded.

On the way home Helena confessed uneasiness to Ephraim. She worried: did Sister Sadie go to Charleston because she was embarrassed at the idea of Helena becoming her step-mother? She hinted delicately: was Sadie perhaps jealous over the loss of her father's attentions? Ephraim held Helena's hand and dismissed her frettings; Sadie would be fine, all that mattered was their own future as husband and wife.

Ephraim's life began anew in the white-painted house with its window boxes and cherry tree – he loved the way Helena so readily took his daughter's place, playing piano for him, listening to his sermons, reading over his medical and theological articles, presiding over coffee and cake with his students. They hoped to be married in four months, a June wedding, and when not at his house, Helena was busy with what seemed to him endless readying for marriage: sewing bed and table linens with her mother and cousins, buying dress fabrics, having fittings. For the very latest in hats and shoes a party of Greyer women even traveled to Chicago as that city recovered from its devastating fire of the year before.

There was only one cloud: the lack of a specific wedding date. This was because Dr Greyer did, after all, want more information about the

Jewish divorce. So bemused was Ephraim by love and joyful anticipation that he took no offense and willingly translated the formal Hebrew of the get, explaining the laws and traditions. To be sure no blot would affect the marriage, he wrote to Kathy in Heidelberg, sharing his happy news and asking Abraham for further papers to confirm the divorce as legal in the eyes of the state. He left it to them to tell – or not tell – his father; since his return to America and Christianity father and son had no communication. Warmest congratulations came back from Kathy and Abraham – but no papers. Wedding delayed, the engagement stretched to five months and Ephraim's untypical patience began to wear thin. He telegraphed Abraham, politely but urgently.

On the professional side Ephraim's annual quarter-year on the hospital wards came and went, reducing his income and demanding his time. Helena's concerns about Sister Sadie began to dissipate. She missed her sister-friend and hoped she detected in the letters from Charleston that she had truly been forgiven for being loved by Ephraim and daring to love him in return. Sadie sounded well-settled, having easily found a post teaching languages at a girls' school, and private students too, thanks to Ephraim's Freemason connections and Uncle Jacob's introductions. The people of Carolina were hospitable in a way different to Ohio, she wrote. There were concerts, assemblies and lectures as in Cincinnati, but the social air in Charleston was more cosmopolitan. 'It seems ridiculous in this wilting summer heat,' she said, 'but tell Papa that living here reminds me of home – of Russia and Germany, that is. Many Charleston residents are foreigners, and the entertainments are often European, with many parties that help friendships flourish.'

Finally, in September, the Heidelberg divorce evidence arrived, and the happy couple named the day after Christmas for their wedding. But before they could write the news to Sister Sadie, a well-wrapped packet addressed to Dr Epstein arrived from Charleston. Calling to Helena, Ephraim opened it to find a portrait of his daughter. She sat straight, the posture her mother had drilled into her, head high, neck long, shoulders relaxed and straight. The calm gaze of her light-colored eyes held a hint of humor. She wore the diamond earrings and the cross Ephraim had given her upon her baptism, its velvet ribbon and gold filigree handsome against the white bodice of her dress. The photographer had posed her against a painted backdrop: filmy magnolia branches and, hazy in the distance, a pillared plantation house. Helena noted Sadie styled her hair in the newest London fashion, blonde curls against her shoulder, burnished, touchable.

She sighed, and Ephraim agreed, Sister Sadie was beautiful – 'but no more beautiful than you, liebchen,' he smiled and took her hand in his two hands. After a moment they remembered to unfold the letter enclosed with the photograph. At a glance Ephraim saw it was surprisingly short, no more than a note: 'Dear Papa, Mama will never see this portrait. I learned by telegram yesterday that she took ill and died of dysentery last week. May she rest in peace, and Lord Jesus have mercy on her soul. I hope this news will not distress you. Perhaps there is comfort in it, for now you are widowed as well as divorced. She was happy these last years, I think, and she has left an inheritance for me. It feels strange not to sit shiva for her, but those times are over of course. With all my affection and the Lord's blessing, to you and my sister Helena, your daughter Sarah.'

Rachel, dead and gone. The news shafted through Ephraim and rested in his belly like a leaden lump. His once-wife, his cousin, his annoyer, seducer, betrayer, aggravator, mother of his daughter. All their past, now truly past. He sat quiet and pale, brooding, and Helena took his hand in hers – was he devastated? Would he feel differently about her and marriage? He stirred, and said, 'Let us say a prayer for Rachel. Let her be safe in the bosom of Abraham and may Christ Jesus shine his light upon her.' He reached for the Old Testament, and together there in the family parlor they read from the Psalms: 'God is our refuge and strength, a very present help in trouble...' Afterwards Ephraim closed his eyes and recited the burial Kaddish in the language of Rachel's faith: Yitgaddal veyitqaddash shmeh rabba. B''al'ma d'hu 'atid l'ithaddata... May His great name be exalted and sanctified...

And so it was deemed proper to delay the wedding, for Sarah's sake and for propriety. One last time Rachel interfered in the course of Ephraim's life. The ceremony was on 29 April 1873, at the German Reformed Church in the joyful presence of friends from the Greyers' wide circle and from all of Ephraim's congregations and the Freemasons. In the church bliss and pride consumed him; verses rang continuously in his head and heart, some woven into the service, others spilling from his long, deep scriptural knowledge. 'A perfect wife, who can find her? She is far beyond the price of pearls. Her husband's heart has confidence in her...' 'how beautiful she is! Her gown is made of gold thread, she is led to the king followed by her bridesmaids...'

As to the bridesmaids, of course Sarah-Sister-Sadie was chief among them. Pale mauve ribbons on her cream gown were the only remaining sign of mourning for the first Mrs Ephraim Epstein. Uncle Jacob and his eternal fiancee Mrs Tobleroff teasingly wrapped a wine glass in a white napkin and urged Ephraim to crush it underfoot – and he just as teasingly declined. He had once performed that ceremony of Jewish marriage, and the marriage itself had broken, and he himself had broken with the past. Their mazel t'ovs blessed him and his new marriage.

Other verses from the songs of Solomon thrilled through Ephraim during the dinner and dance, 'How your eyes shine with love behind your veil, your hair dances, your lips are like a scarlet ribbon... how perfect you are!'

And finally on the wedding night itself when they came together in fulfillment, he lived more from the Song of Songs, 'My sweetheart, my bride is a secret garden, a walled garden, a private spring...' Helena, in their intimacy, met him too in the spirit of Solomon's words: 'My lover is handsome and strong; he is one in ten thousand...'

Before their honeymoon – to New York and Boston, where Ephraim intended to dazzle old friends with his beautiful young wife – Helena, Sadie and Ephraim took time together as in days before, riding by carriage up to Eden Park, strolling in the burgeoning green of spring, pausing at the wide views over the city and the Ohio River and beyond to Kentucky.

'The sun is much kinder here than in Charleston,' said Sadie as they began to circuit Mirror Lake. 'That heat!' she fanned her face with a hand against the Cincinnati spring sun.

'I thought you liked Charleston!' exclaimed Ephraim.

'Mmm. It is very nice, but the Southerners... They're well-mannered and gracious yet there's an edge. Geniality like cut crystal, beautiful and hard beneath the charm. Also, the Jewish thing, our name. I think the Christian ladies want to flick me with a fingernail to see if I ring true.' She laughed ruefully.

'I'm so sorry, dear girl. Are you unhappy, do you want to come home?'

'Home? Here? No, Papa. It is lovely there, and I have my own life, and I like it. Even in the hottest days there is always a breeze by the harbor in the evenings, and ships coming in and the wonderful wide sea. You both must come visit, soon!'

Ephraim pushed further. 'And friends? These many cultured people you write of?'

'I like best the foreigners like myself. And some of the Americans.'

Helena linked her arm through Sadie's, 'All these friends, what about beaux? You haven't mentioned a one!'

'I have friends. No particular beau. Maybe... one or two special friends.' Sadie laughingly refused to be drawn into any revelations, and said that time would tell.

Ephraim felt at last the Lord had blessed him fully: a beautiful young wife, a lovely independent daughter, a community of souls about him, the serious work of healing the sick in body and preaching and teaching the message of Christ Jesus. His practice and his reputation in Cincinnati continued to grow.

Early in 1874 this bounty was crowned by the birth of a son. A son: William. To Helena's surprise Ephraim did not turn to the New Testament, nor the Old, but instead wanted him named for that brave, brilliant admiral,

Wilhelm von Tegetthoff. She had read her husband's poem, seen the medallion in its velvet box; she too thought it was the best possible name for their golden boy.

For many men the birth of a son is a great thing, and for Ephraim perhaps especially so. He knew what it was to be the first born son of his parents, the longed for male, and this joy in a son was bred in his bones and could not be denied. Equally undeniable was consideration of circumcision. He himself was circumcised, of course – by a mohel at the bris at eight days of age, as all Jewish boys were. For the first time since Rachel's gossiping in Turkey, Ephraim's faith, his personal life and his profession constellated in a crisis, for of late circumcision for health reasons had become a debated topic in the professional medical world.

With his surname, Ephraim was forever being taken as Jewish. He'd experienced this assumption and prejudice everywhere in the world, and even had feared his name would be an obstacle to Helena's acceptance of his marriage proposal. She too would suffer the prejudice, along with their children. She scolded him for mentioning the issue, for she loved every aspect of him. This was just as well, for never had Ephraim entertained changing his surname. Epstein was a fine old German Ashkenazy Jewish name meaning a place of wild boar and stone, the marker of a fierce creature that slashed left and right, determined on its own ends. What name more apropos for him: the wild boar of his powerful mind going after truth ruthlessly. Besides, it was his father's name, and his father's father's and many generations further back.

If Ephraim had his son circumcised would colleagues take this as a return to his Jewish loyalties? Just as he was weighing the issues a leading medical journal spurred him into action. 'Have the Jews an Immunity from Certain Diseases?' – a letter by a Christian physician published in the *Medical and Surgical Reporter* – lit Ephraim's ire at tedious, intolerable assumptions about Jews by some in his profession. The wider Jewish community were caught up in the general debate – some notable American Jewish leaders were pleased with pro-Jewish medical accolades, others objected.

Tuberculosis was the main subject here, and the Jewish race came up for praise: physique, intelligence, general vitality and immunity to disease. Thinking fast and furiously about Jewishness, health, his profession, his faith and his son, Ephraim fired a salvo, published in the same journal a month later. After rebuttal over supposed immunity from tuberculosis, he expanded:

I am sure I have observed no Jewish immunity from any diseases, venereal disease not excepted. In common with others, once I believed that circumcision offered protection against venereal diseases, but my practice in Vienna and in this country since 1862 persuaded me fully to the contrary.

190

But what to do about William? To Ephraim, having grown up among his circumcised brothers and cousins, and having treated many uncircumcised Christians from sailors to gentlemen, lack of the foreskin, though not preventing sexual disease, seemed simply natural and cleaner. If his Christian-born son were to be circumcised it should be done early. It would be a medical procedure, as done by many physicians these days; he would perform it himself, and soon. On the other hand, the operation was essentially an ancient ritual tradition, smacking of superstition and tribal exclusivity, and now overlaid with modern medical suppositions tainted with prejudice.

Ephraim's medical letter-fight received a vicious response. The answering physician tried to demolish the arguments of the 'Eastern European Jewish doctor' and said categorically that circumcision was an Egyptian ritual which Moses, himself an Egyptian priest, brought to the Hebrews. The man was now purporting to understand Judaism itself. In reply, on the whole issue of Jewish 'superiority', Ephraim concluded his *Medical and Surgical Reporter* battle with fiery outrage against assumptions:

> *The singular perseverance of the Jews in health is a mean fiction propounded either by those who are not acquainted with the Jewish race in this country or by certain Jewish enthusiasts who have a special axe to grind.*

And on the personal level? Ephraim conferred first with Dr Greyer, physician to physician. Then he explained the predicament to Helena and together they read St Paul: 'Here there is no Gentile or Jew, circumcised or uncircumcised... but Christ is all, and is in all.' In the end he decided no: his boy and his brothers, should he and Helena be so blessed, would carry their manhood uncircumcised, as Christian men. He himself would teach them cleanliness.

The christening of William could have been another occasion for Ephraim to exercise his scruples, but in fact Helena's wishes were an easy concession for him. Their son was baptized by a pouring on of water in her family's church, because her husband's preferred Baptist total immersion was only for those old enough to state belief.

As they celebrated their first wedding anniversary Ephraim rejoiced in contentment at last, and thanked the Lord for his rich life. However, something rankled from the recent letter-battle. Worse than the presumptions about Jews was the presumptuousness of Jews themselves. Would they never see the truth of Jesus Christ? Ephraim vented his annoyance through the Melioration Society journal. And he decided to begin a close study of Moses. In the story of the man who led the Israelites out of slavery he would find evidence for his own efforts to lead today's Jews to the truth.

26

PERJURED
Cincinnati 1874

While their darling boy flourished, Helena and Ephraim grew ever happier in domestic life, and in June 1874 they eagerly awaited Sister Sadie's visit to meet their young prince. In a bustle of parcels and prettiness she arrived to duly admire the bonny four-month-old who was her half-brother.

Helena had an inkling that there was more afoot than a family visit and was not surprised the next day when Sadie took her aside and showed her a thick envelope tied with ribbon and sealed with wax. It was addressed to Ephraim. Her smile full of secrets and hopes, Sadie promised to tell all if dear Ilenka would be sure to have her father read it this very afternoon. Helena made the arrangements and with baby William they wandered over to the Greyers' house. Along the way, and again with further embellishments to the delight of Mrs Greyer, Sadie told the tale, a story that had played out over nearly two years. That portrait of her, the photograph: the man who had taken it was the brother of Sadie's friend, a Russian woman. He had taken up the new craft of photography and was so pleased with the results that he begged to keep a copy of Miss Epstein's portrait for himself. Sometime after Sadie was amazed to receive a letter from a complete stranger, covered by an introduction from the photographer begging forgiveness if this act was too impertinent. Alexander Franz Zur Hosen, of St Petersburg and Kaluga Oblast had seen her portrait. He was utterly taken with Miss Sarah Epstein of Charleston, South Carolina. Their mutual friend vouched for his background and character; Mr Zur Hosen had been informed that her intelligence and education matched her beauty. He would like to correspond, might she agree?

For a year their letters crossed the ocean. He asked her to describe life in America, the aftermath of the war, the methods of growing, the trade, the people. She begged from him to know about Petersburg, Moscow, Paris, London, Berlin. They exchanged favorite Bible verses. He sent her music. She did watercolors of American flowers, and wrote him the lyrics of some amusing American songs. He sent her a book of poetry by Goethe. He sent a portrait of himself in court dress. He told her about his family's estate, about his family, his sisters, his brother, his parents. About the balls and the hunting, the ice and snow of the ferocious winters which she so much missed in the claustrophobic humidity of the south.

Finally he sailed to meet her, stopping to visit friends in New York and Philadelphia, and arrived in Charleston. When they met nothing disappointed, all was wonderful, everything was possible. Within a week, on bended knee, he asked if she would agree to be his wife.

'Oh, Sadie, back to Russia? What about...' After all the exclamations and sighs, Helena tried not to let her own feelings interfere with the joy Sadie clearly felt. What about your father, Helena had almost said: Ephraim would miss Sarah-Sadie, Helena herself would too. But most of all Helena feared her marriage to Sadie's father had caused this plunge into romantic adventure. 'Are you sure?'

'Yes! A thousand times yes! It will be St Petersburg, completely different than funny old Brisk.' Sadie took the baby from Helena's arms and cradled him in her own, smiling down on him. 'Alexander sailed right back home to ask his family's permission, and now he asks Papa to grant the same. All the financial and legal marriage settlements are in the proposal, Alexi says. He is so handsome!' Sadie handed William back to his mother, 'I have his photograph hidden in my case – now I can show you!'

Ephraim greeted them at the back door, held out his hands, drew Sarah-Sadie to him and kissed her on the cheek.

Helena smiled. 'I thought so! Oh, my best, best wishes!'

'I must talk to Sarah alone,' he said, his use of her true name a signal.

Helena's face turned to puzzlement. Surely congratulations were in order.

In his consulting room Ephraim asked, 'Do you love him?' He looked up from the letter and was struck again by the fair beauty of his daughter. How composed she was, how serene and independent she'd become during the time in Charleston.

'Yes, Papa, of course I do.'

'Why of course? You are not obliged to love him.' She looked as lovely as the photograph she'd sent home, the same photograph the wealthy Russian had fallen in love with.

She lowered her eyes. 'Of course – or I would never have let him write to you. I would never give encouragement to someone I did not care for.'

He looked at the letter again. 'It is a handsome settlement he offers. Remarkable. God is smiling on you.'

'So you give your permission!' She beamed.

He shifted in his chair. 'There is a problem.' Sarah's face fell. 'Your

Alexander Zur Hosen says his family needs to be assured that you were born Christian.'

Sarah's hands flew to her mouth in shock. 'He never said...'

He levelled his gaze at her. 'What has given him this idea, that you were Christian since birth?'

'I don't know.' Her eyes glistened with tears, 'He just assumed it, seeing me in Charleston, going to church, living among gentiles, I mean Christians. Of course with our surname he asked about you, and I said you had converted when you were twenty, which is true.'

'Twenty-one,' said Ephraim grimly.

'By then he was in love with me, and I could tell all along that he thought I had been raised in the faith.'

'So you let him believe that.'

'We never spoke of it. I never told him that.'

'But you did not disabuse him by telling the full facts.'

Her cheeks flamed. She shook her head.

Ephraim said: 'I cannot lie. I am a minister of the cloth. You were born Jewish.'

'But then... oh!' his daughter rose from her chair, saying oh! again, and ran from the room.

Helena put glasses of lemonade before them, a lemon wedge floating in the translucent liquid. The table cloth was one the two girls had embroidered together with pink roses and green leaves on pink gingham for Helena's dowry. She had feared that Sadie's stitches were done in duty and resentment as much as love. Helena put her arms around the desolate Sadie, her best friend, her step-daughter. 'We will find a way,' she murmured. How to bring Ephraim round she did not know – before God he could not lie – but she had to make it happen.

Sarah stayed in her room for dinner that night. Ephraim took this behavior in silence. He ached for his beautiful daughter. She would be upset of course, but she would understand. Helena had spent time with her, he had heard voices and sobs. Now at the dinner table his wife was quiet, and during the Bible reading, subdued. For two more days Sarah remained in her room. Finally Helena went to Ephraim. 'Please, is there nothing you can do? She is heartbroken.'

'I too am heartbroken.'

'This is her life Ephraim!'

'This is my life! And this is my God, the son of God our lord Jesus Christ. I cannot lie about such a thing.'

Helena said: 'I will pray.'

Ephraim started in amazement. Helena, defying him? Praying against his own obligations, his own truth and faith? He wanted to say, I forbid you. But how could he forbid anyone to petition the Lord? He looked up from the Bible. 'I will pray, too.'

The next day Sister Sadie left the house after a short conversation with Helena. Ephraim hoped she was coming to her senses. Already twenty-six, she was proving to be as stubborn as her mother, so finding a husband might be difficult. Never mind, holy matrimony could not be founded on a lie. She was lovely and talented, there would be other men. They might not be rich Russians, but perhaps that was for the best. Perhaps going to Russia was not God's will for her.

Ephraim prayed, and preached mightily about adhering to the faith and to the truth of God. He was pleased to see Sarah slip into church, her bonnet with its blue feathers so pretty in East Coast fashion. Surely she would find a suitor soon. Perhaps his daughter should return from Carolina, come to live with them again; he had thought once that young George Greyer had shown an interest in her.

She rode home with them in the buggy, and joined them at the Sunday lunch table. Roast chicken and dumplings, one of Helena's favorite recipes. Afterwards Sarah asked to speak to her father in his office. She refused a seat and so Ephraim stood as well. 'Papa, please will you write the letter so that Alexander and I can marry?'

'You know I cannot.'

'I think you can. And you must.' She spoke evenly, reasonably, though on the last word her voice trembled.

'I cannot swear to – '

She held up a hand. 'I have found a way.' She went to his desk, picking up several of the books there, found the one she wanted, and hurried through the pages, opening the book flat at her destination. Ephraim watched dubiously. He took a step toward the desk, and she said, her back to him as she scanned his bookshelves, 'Not yet.'

She took a book from the shelf, found a page and opened that on the desk. Finally, under his glowering eyes, she opened the New Testament.

'I can prove to you that I was born Christian. How did it happen to Lord Jesus, the son of God? Listen.' She began to read out the verses, and Ephraim joined her, word for word. He ended in perplexity. She nodded and smiled.

'See? Yes. Now.' She picked up the other book, *The Making of a Christian*, by Elias P Jones. She read out: 'the new Christian comes naked and unclothed like the babe newborn, his soul refreshed, renewed, pristine, unstained, his new life begun. He has had no life before, just as the babe from the womb is a new creature under God, the Father, a true son or daughter, like our Lord Jesus who himself was born a Jew.' She began to read out the next paragraph, but Ephraim stopped her.

'Elias Jones. I know the text. How did you – '

'Wait, there is one more.' She picked up the order of service for the Baptist church and read out. 'From the Service of Baptism: And the new child of Christ shall come from the waters born again into Christian life,' Ephraim's voice joined hers in the familiar words, 'to live and work and bear the fruit of a true Christian, as witnessed by his brothers and sisters in Christ. Amen.'

Silence held between them. Sarah-Sadie sat now, her skirts softly rustling as she took her place. Ephraim moved to his desk and looked at the open books again.

'So you can say, in truth, that I was born Christian,' she said.

'A Jew would believe you – but not a Christian. How did you gain this sophistry? It is like the arguments of the Mishnah,' he said grudgingly. 'I cannot agree, but it is ingenious.'

In fact, she had sought the advice of Uncle Jacob, once again the fount of new life. Despite the influence of his orthodox Esther, the incorrigible free spirit still followed laws of the heart, and had no compunctions about helping Ephraim's daughter. 'I AM born Christian. You can say it is true. I returned to my old faith to support my new faith – Uncle Jacob sends his regards. He says he knows you will do the right thing.'

'The right thing, under God. Which is to tell the whole truth. Not to put my name to a lie.'

'Father. You must.' Her voice rose as the rancor of the first twenty years of her life spilled out. 'You have always done what you want. It is always your way. You abandoned Mama and me. You were dead to us and we were alone. Papa, the Lord wants me to have this life. If God has to punish you for an argued truth – for it is a truth – then so be it. God is on my side as well.'

'Out! Leave this room.'

She was shaking in righteous anger. 'I have written the letter for you. You only need sign your name.'

After an hour Helena knocked quietly on his door and entered. Ephraim slumped in his chair, deep in thought, his face etched in sorrowful lines.

'This daughter wants me to condemn myself to ever-lasting hell. Lie! I cannot perjure myself! Not even for her!' He heard his mother's tears again, saw her begging, clinging to his knees. He had forsworn Christ once, because of her. On his soul, he could not testify before God falsely again, ever.

'Will you let her marry?' Helena said softly.

'How can I?'

'She has told me of the disputation. It is very...'

'Very Jewish,' said Ephraim in bitter wryness.

'It does carry conviction. You too were born again into Jesus Christ.'

Her voice soothed, she sat down opposite him, and he looked at her calm, loving face.

'But it is not the same. Not what the Zur Hosens mean. How can I...'

'She needs you. Sign the letter. No one in America will ever know.'

'Almighty God will know!'

'It is only for his family. She is Christian. It should not matter. And his family are only exercising the centuries of prejudice against your people. The same prejudice you lived with. The same we still experience with our name. Jewish, Jewish – what matters it? She has come to Christ. Release her to her new life.'

He pulled the letter toward him listlessly. She dipped the pen in the inkwell and he took it, poising above the paper. Suddenly he shot her a look of sheer doubt – was she the temptress, Satan in disguise? Helena looked to the letter and his hand. He signed his name.

'We will never speak of this,' he said.

'Amen,' Helena answered.

That same year, on 12 December 1874, Sarah Epstein married Alexander Franz Zur Hosen of St Petersburg, at the German Reformed Church in Cincinnati in the presence of her parents. Sister Sadie's fair hair was adorned with a bridal crown traditional in Belarus, of gleaming evergreen myrtle. The many friends and family of the Epsteins and Greyers flocked to the railroad station to wave the handsome young couple off on their return to Russia, thrilled with the high romance.

27

THE DARKNESS
Cincinnati 1876-78

By the time Sister Sadie Zur Hosen sent radiant news in 1876 that she had given birth to a boy, Helena and Ephraim were the delighted parents of a second child, a daughter. They named her Selda, a German variation on dearest Mama's name. It bemused Ephraim to think that within one single year he had become both father and grandfather. If only his mother could have known. In his prayers, in dreams sometimes, he was sure that she did know. He felt her presence often. Not continents, not oceans, not faiths, not even death separated them; they still communed. It pleased him to see how like his mother Helena sometimes looked, the wisps of blonde hair, the light blue eyes. Especially when she was a little tired. Not that he wanted her to be tired. She was strong, of such good stock. He thought of that every time he visited her family, which had now expanded to grandchildren, so that the little cousins ran about the lawns of the Greyers' spacious home. Their health, vitality and play conjured up the happiness of his own childhood.

Helena put the framed photograph of Sadie and baby Shurek next to the Charleston portrait of Sister Sadie that had seeded her future. It gave her an excuse to take down the Russian wedding portrait in its gilded frame, given pride of place since Sadie had sent it along with a stream of assurances as to her happiness. She had included a yard of finest French lace from the dress she wore at the grand celebration of the marriage given by her new St Petersburg family. Initially, joyful for her friend's good fortune, Helena proudly hung the picture of the handsome couple on the wall. They looked like they could be a Count and Countess. But she caught Ephraim from time to time studying the photograph closely, frowning. Better for him not to see this reminder of the untruth he had committed, Helena realized, and so she now put the picture aside in her dowry chest with her personal girlish things. The romance of it all still thrilled her, yet she was absolutely sure that she, Helena Greyer, was as lucky as Sadie, as happy, being the wife of Dr Ephraim Epstein.

William was the apple of everyone's eye, and Ephraim marveled at his brightness even in the toddler years. He babytalked his son in the sounds of the Hebrew alphabet – alef, bet, gimel – as well as in English and German. At four Ephraim introduced him to the sweetness of learning just as he had been at home in Belarus: the very first time his son sounded out his first word in the Bible, he gave him a taste of honey. 'In the beginning…' would always be sweet to William, because learning is sweet, sweet as honey.

As he savored warmth and family love in these years of fulfillment, a backdrop of troubles touched Ephraim's consciousness. The places of his missionizing, Saloniki and Monastir, were part of the Christian struggle to get free of Ottoman Turkish domination. Since 1876 the whole of Western Turkey – including Bulgaria, Serbia, Montenegro, Herzegovia – was rocked with shocking slaughter. Russia and European powers tried to broker peace with the Muslim empire, but finally in April 1877 the Czar declared war on Turkey. The freed lands would be Orthodox Christian, and Russia would rule them. Known both as a Russian and a proselytizing Christian, Ephraim's insights were sought in lively, concerned discussions among informed Ohioans. Sadie's letters provided further personal illumination, for military gossip swirled through St Petersburg society.

In America there were battles, too. Indian and white atrocities arose from the clash of cultures as the far West drew settlers and Dakota Territory drew gold and silver prospectors. Sioux were among the tribes Ephraim had observed in Leavenworth, the Sioux who were viciously defeated in the Black Hills in 1876. He thought of them in his Moses study, noting again that the wandering tribes of Hebrews were not unlike these tent-dwelling natives, and how he should like to bring them to Christ, if he were still a missionary. He wondered about their gods and rituals, thinking of the perplexing, detailed instructions for the sacred tent Moses commanded the Israelites to build.

But he was not a missionary, he was a successful physician and preacher, blessed in July 1877 with yet another new light in his life. Helena gave birth to their third child, another daughter, Frieda – named for a favorite aunt. Helena's confinements were at home as almost all births were, far safer from the dreaded puerperal fever which still could strike and kill, even in Cincinnati's up-to-date University Hospital. Their housekeeper Mercy lived-in over the period, acting as nurse as well as housekeeper. When the time came Ephraim called on a trusted colleague to conduct Helena's deliveries, wanting to spare her the indignities she would need to reveal to him. He was there to comfort and rejoice, confident in the knowledge that he could intervene should anything go wrong. But nothing did go wrong, Helena was strong and healthy, well-made for bearing children, an ideal mother, the blessed helpmeet, wife and lover he had always longed for.

One day early in 1878 the eldest of the three children – four year old William – fell ill, a listless feverishness of the kind children often suffer. Helena put him to bed, gave him broth to sip and bathed his forehead in cool water. Ephraim examined his tongue and ears, sounded his chest, and went out to see his patients. By the time he returned the fever was raging. Helena had sent Mercy with toddler Selda to her mother's house and wrapped William in wet sheets. Ephraim wrote out the prescription: three grains of quinine to manage the high temperature, in an infusion of roses to sweeten the bitter taste. He raced with it to the chemist himself, pacing inside the dark paneled store with its comforting smell of eucalypt, alcohol, camphor, peppermint. Mr Maxwell hurried the brown bottle out to the doctor. Many a time he'd filled Dr Epstein's prescriptions but this was the first urgency for his own child. Ephraim dashed off, driving the horse wildly on the return journey. They had to get the fever down and provoke the sweating.

In the bedroom the little boy lay unclothed, his pale skin showing blue veins on arms and ankles. His fair curls spilled over the pillow, and Helena fanned him, wet cloths in a basin by the bed.

'William,' Ephraim said gently. He put his hand under his son's head to raise it slightly and put the spoon to his lips. The boy's mouth tightened against the intrusion. 'William, open and take this medicine. It will help you.' The child wrenched his head way, his eyes opening wide, knocking the spoon and its life-saving contents onto the sheet.

'William, please,' Helena begged. The little boy called out to her. Ephraim refilled the spoon and handed it to Helena to try. But the boy was rigid with the terror of delirium and pushed her away at the same time that he was calling to her.

'Mama, take William in your arms,' Ephraim instructed. She did, and he clung to her, settling a bit. Ephraim crouched by her, humming a soothing hymn. This time the elixir went in. In ten minutes the boy went limp and peaceful. Ephraim lifted him from Helena's lap and laid him on the bed. Together they smoothed the sheets and Helena caressed the forehead of their little one saying, 'Sleep now, sleep, hush now.'

They stood, Ephraim's arm about her waist, at the foot of the bed, taking one last look. 'He'll sleep, we'll repeat the dose in four hours.' He raised his voice and praised God, and thanked him for his mercies. Helena went to baby Frieda's cradle; she too was sleeping peacefully. She thanked God with her own prayer, for the mercy that her husband was a doctor, and her father too. Her children had so much better chance than ordinary people.

She slept in the chair by William's bed. In the night she woke, sensing something was wrong. The time – by the half-heard chimes of the grandfather clock – midnight. Shouldn't they have dosed William again? She looked at him – his eyes open, dazed, dreamy. 'Mama? Abba.' He called his baby name for Ephraim, the Hebrew word for father, used before he was able to say Papa.

'William, yes, Mama's here. Sweet sleepy one. I'll be right back.'

She went to their room and roused Ephraim. 'Isn't it time for his medicine?' He started. 'Yes! How is he?'

'Calm, lucid. He seems – Oh,' she suddenly broke, burying her face in her hands. 'Oh, I think he is better.'

In his nightshirt Ephraim came to William's bed.

'Abba?'

Ephraim bent and kissed his son on the cheek, in tenderness, and to check his temperature. Good. The quinine would soon provoke the sweat. The boy's eyes were shiny-bright, but he seemed comfortable. This time he did not resist the spoon, docilely opening his lips. He sighed and closed his eyes before another word was spoken. Father and mother bent to kiss his forehead and smooth the bedcovers.

'I will sit by him,' Ephraim said. 'You go and sleep. Everything will be all right now.'

Early birdsong woke Ephraim, and the gray creeping light of predawn. Good, the child had slept through. But the sweat should have begun. He reached for the boy – and died. At that moment his heart and soul evaporated. His beautiful son, his William lay with his eyes staring wide open, his face fixed in death.

He cried the boy's name, twice, with a sound that came from deep in his gut. He seized William, snatched him to his chest, breathed into his mouth with his own. Looked at his face, shook him. By now Helena had come flying in, the baby in her arms, and Mercy hovered in the hallway. 'William, William,' was all Ephraim could say. Helena thrust the baby at Mercy and reached for her son. She had to force her way through Ephraim's embrace of the boy. She too cried his name, then adding – 'What happened? Ephraim, what's happened? He's gone!'

'This is wrong, this shouldn't be. He... he was mending. The sweat was due. It was working.'

Eloi eloi labach sabactini... My god, my god, my god. He tore at his hair.

'My baby my baby my baby,' Helena crooned, rocking the sturdy little boy in her arms. She had closed William's eyelids, so he looked now as if he were sleeping, his yellow hair curling against her bosom.

Ephraim knelt by her and the boy, arms half around them. He prayed. He raised his voice – 'Mercy, fetch Dr Greyer, please.'

My William, my William. Wracked with shock and grief, Ephraim could barely think. As he paced the room Dr Greyer confirmed the death so that he could sign the certificate. He too, had called out and cried: his darling grandson. Everyone's darling, suddenly gone. Why? Ephraim moved the basin of cloths they had washed the boy with. His foot kicked against a wooden block that had spilled from the toys on the shelf. He had to restrain himself from a sudden urge to kick it hard. Instead, he picked it up, turning it in his hands A, B, C, apple… and placed it on the shelf with the others. His dulled gaze caught the dresser with its crocheted mat, and the medicine, the brown bottle and silver spoon. Why hadn't the quinine worked? To the depths of his being, beside his depths of faith and duty, he was a questioner. The driving force of his life was to question. This came the more so in his shock and grief – the need to know why. God may know why on God's terms but, in fleshly, earthly terms, scientifically, medically – why? He picked up the bottle and stared at it as if brown glass and handwritten label could answer him. Absently Ephraim opened the bottle and sniffed at it. The sweet smell of roses – a strangled sob seized him. He touched his fingertip to the bottle, tilted it, then licked his finger. Where was the bitter undertaste?

'Dr Greyer, taste this, will you? It is not quinine.' His colleague concurred, and Ephraim poured some into the spoon and swallowed. Definitely not quinine. He stared unseeing at the bare branches outside the window. Within five minutes he felt a wish to sit, and took the chair by William's body. Over the next five minutes he felt his muscles relax.

It was morphine. The subsequent coroner's investigation revealed the course of the tragedy. The prescription held by Mr Maxwell was perfectly legible – written by Dr Epstein himself, it stated three grains quinine. But somehow in the panic and haste the pharmacist, who adored little William as did everyone, had in error provided three grains morphine. An amount that would ease a full grown man to pain-free sleep or even coma. Enough to kill a child in two consecutive doses.

Now came the darkest days of Ephraim's life. Everything he had undergone, the hardships of Jewry, departure and disconnection from his family, the loneliness of years without love and companionship, medical horrors, were as nothing to this black pit. At the funeral Ephraim and Helena, stunned and stoical, held each other up by their straight bearing, surrounded by their community. Only when the first handful of earth dropped onto the little coffin six feet deep in the ground did they break. Helena, then Ephraim bent to pick up and release the brown soil of Ohio, and at its thud and crumble on the wood Helena was wracked by a huge sob. Ephraim wrapped his arms around her, his face contorted with tears. They clung to each other silently as the others added their token handfuls of earth and flowers. At the last, Dr Greyer shepherded the Epsteins away.

Ephraim withdrew into himself, holing up in the consulting room. He refused the food trays Mercy and then Helena brought him. All patients were directed to Dr Greyer. Every day Ephraim walked the fifteen minutes to his Baptist church alone. He knelt and prayed, then walked home unseeing. After one or two attempts no one, no brother or sister of the church, no neighborly acquaintance, dared speak to him. It was too cruel. The man was devastated.

His God had punished him. This was all that Ephraim could understand. To take his first-born son, his shining boy, a gift of God. Helena despaired, not only of her boy – that was a numbness, a happening beyond belief she could only suspend. She could see it as a fact, but not know it in her heart, it made no sense. But she had Selda and baby Frieda to nurse. She could go through the motions of mothering, they needed her. The further loss was Ephraim. No longer the upright, strong man of faith, he was an empty husk. He was shattered, wasted, and gave her no comfort. And then, two-year-old Selda fell ill.

At last, roused by Helena, Ephraim stirred. He felt the child's forehead, took her pulse and wordlessly left the room where she lay in her crib.

'What does she need? What can it be?' Helena followed him down the stairs. 'Dear God, what's wrong?'

'Call your father. I cannot touch her,' came the curt reply and Ephraim shut himself in his consulting room again. Helena stood before the door staring at the oaken grain of the wood. He was utterly closed to her.

She sent for her father and sat by Selda's bed, sponging her forehead from time to time, but this was no fever. In the short time before Dr Greyer appeared all the world shrank to this bed, this little girl, this second dear child. He examined her pale and floppy limbs, looked into her dull eyes, then paused to consider. Surely, Helena pinned all her hopes on her father, surely Selda will recover. But at that moment the toddler convulsed. Her eyes rolled back, the tiny body arched and then she was gone.

Ephraim offered Helena no comfort. He did not grieve and mourn. He was a stick of wood. He stood by the gravesite, the second grave, sister to William, now side by side in death. He did not cry this time. Did not speak prayers either, except to say Amen.

At home, dark forces wanted possession of his soul. The end of all things was in his heart.

28

GOD FORSAKEN
Cincinnati 1878

Helena came to the surface of sleep. A small cry carried her to a place where she nestled. It insisted: a squall from the cradle by their bed. She opened her eyes to see Ephraim in his nightshirt holding their eight-month-old baby by the neck.

'Stop! Stop it!' She hurled herself at him, snatching Frieda. Ephraim let go and threw his strength on Helena, pinning her to the bed. She tried to fend him off, one arm protecting the baby as she screamed his name.

He shouted over her, 'It is the only way. Guilty, guilty. It is my guilt – I was tempted, Lord God! This is the price. The sacrifice, oh my God, my God – ' broken snatches came from him, his eyes staring wide and wild. But he loosened the pressure on her shoulders.

Slowly Helena pulled at his hands, moving them away, looking into his face, breathing hoarsely. 'Ephraim.' There was pity in her voice, and love. Frieda startled with a cry next to her and he turned his head, the yell seeming to wake him. 'The baby?' he asked, bewildered. He stood up fully and looked at his hands as if he did not know them. Helena sat forward rubbing at her shoulder. She pushed back her golden hair and watched her husband as he sat heavily on the bed next to her, burying his head in his hands and groaning.

'I have done wrong. I have sinned against God and there is no health in me.'

Frieda began a steady cry and Helena eased off the bed. 'The baby needs me,' she said to the room. 'Frieda needs me,' she emphasized the name, holding the infant and stepping around him. 'Go downstairs, Ephraim.' He seemed mild, dazed. She thought of the delirium of William. Relieved and blank and still fearful, she prayed to God wordlessly as she suckled Frieda and settled her, extinguished the candle by her husband's bedside and went to brew him a chamomile tisane.

'So that is how it is.' Uncle Jacob could think of nothing more to say.

Helena bowed her head. 'Since last month he is worse. I have to take meals to him in his room. Oh – his room!' Her voice broke and she wiped away tears. 'I have done everything I can think of. I've gentled him, I've scolded him. I've prayed for him. My father talks to him, Reverend Blake. Nothing, nothing. Maybe you can bring him back.' A torrent of grief burst from Helena. 'He doesn't seem to notice – William was my son, too! And Selda, my Selda...'

'I can only try,' said the old uncle. He went to the door, knocked and pushed in. Ephraim lifted his head, but did not rise to greet him. 'Jacob.' He sat in the dimness, curtains drawn. The bookshelves were ghostly, their contents reversed, spines to the wall.

'What are you doing?' said Jacob in their old Brisker tongue.

'I have no life left.' Ephraim replied dully in the same sibilant, strongly consonanted language.

'Come outside.' He led a docile Ephraim out of his room into the back of the house. The smell of roasting chicken filled the kitchen, and he turned his head away in disgust. Jacob pushed him through the door to the porch. Something touched Ephraim – the old language, or Jacob's benign authority stirred from long ago, or perhaps it was just that time had run its course. The sunlight dazzled and made Ephraim blink and he pulled away from his uncle. 'Where is Helena?' he asked, bewildered.

'Upstairs, with the baby. You know you do have a baby.' Ephraim frowned, and Jacob continued, 'And a wife.'

White sheets lifted in the breeze, and he watched them, like breath falling and rising, he thought. And so the spirit moves and goeth where it listeth. He took a few steps onto the grass. Jacob watched, then followed. He stood still, cocking his head as if listening. Ephraim's beard was grizzled now, straggly, and his thick hair silvered and awry, a tangle.

'Wake up, Ephraim. Choose Helena, choose life.'

He did not respond, just watched the sheets, felt the sun on his back, the breeze on his skin. 'There's Helena to think of. She deserves life. And the little one, Frieda needs you' – and there's your God, Jacob thought, but did not say.

Instead, Ephraim spoke in English: 'And there is our Lord, who gave his only begotten son that all who believe in him shall not perish.' He turned, as if seeing his uncle for the first time since his arrival. 'Jacob. What shall I do?'

The old man smiled and shrugged. It was over, he was back in this world. 'Come inside.'

Helena joined them as they sat at the kitchen table. Ephraim had sluiced his hands and face at the sink. His beard was now wet and bedraggled, his hair where he had run his wet hands through was partly smoothed, but still stuck up in tufts. Helena put Russian glasses of tea on the table, amber, fragrant, highly sugared.

After a time Ephraim got to his feet. 'Thank you for the drink, Mama,' he said to Helena. To Jacob he said, 'I have no patients. I must find work.'

Jacob waited for the quote, Samuel probably, or Proverbs, or the Jewish Christian Paul, something on the bounty of creation. But none came, only a great space within Ephraim which they all felt. Ephraim bowed slightly, formally. As he left the room Helena said, 'Shall you take the meal with us tonight? To honor your uncle's visit?'

The bedraggled doctor stiffened his posture. 'If God wills it.'

He came to dinner that evening, and ate well. And he had looked in at Frieda, even picked her up, holding her high, looking into her eyes. Helena had watched, relieved – at last, at last he was himself again. She longed to tell him of baby's smiles, of how she fed. More, she longed to say how she herself had missed him. How she needed him. He said grace in the usual way. He complemented the food as he had always done. But he was still abstracted. Over the peach pie Helena had raced to bake, to tempt him, to please him, to make tonight special, as well as normal, Ephraim paused, fork halfway to his mouth. 'I cannot go on doctoring.'

'Oh, but' — Helena stopped herself.

He put down the fork still laden with pie. He looked at his hands. 'How can I trust myself? How can I know who may die, at these hands.'

'Ephraim,' she murmured, trying to banish his thought with soothing.

'I am cursed, cursed, God has punished me. I cannot heal, I kill.'

'But it was not you! It was Mr Maxwell's mistake.'

'But my hand wrote the scrip!' he roared as he stood up, making the chair fall over, and left the room. Jacob comforted her, patting her arm and urging her to give him more time. At least he was returned to them.

Ephraim had made a long decent into hell. In his darkest hours of torment sins descended on him as twisted demons. Christ's last words repeated endlessly: Eloi eloi labach sabactini. My God, my God, why have you forsaken me? He knew he was being punished, as King David was – David coveted Bathsheba and took her to wife, and their first son died. The causes stalked his brain, the logic of a vengeful God: Helena was the sin – he had coveted his daughter's friend, and William was therefore taken. He could not bear to look at her, and when he did, the lusts of the flesh came to curse him, the soft smile, softer skin, blue eyes, blue silk dress, the parted thighs and mounded breasts of another woman, a sinful forbidden woman. The once, just the once in Vienna. In clean, civilized Vienna, he had trusted the paid women of the house off Alser Strasse. Just the once, on the night of the Emperor's award. Then came the vengeance for his pride and lust: news of Mama's death the next morning. He had prayed and prayed for forgiveness. But no, William was the punishment, William and Selda.

Endless circles chased through Ephraim's head to the point where he loathed himself, his mind, his body, his very sitting in one place. So he would get up and pace. And then he loathed that, and forced himself to sit still. Mama, Mama – his mother kept coming to his mind, her pains, the pain he had caused her, and the pains of her mourning her Anna. Now Ephraim knew the agony she had suffered at the loss of her first-born. How angry and powerless Ephraim had felt as a boy, wishing he could save that long-gone sister, save her to save Mama's sorrow. And now he himself was the butchering physician, the incompetent charlatan who had caused his own child's death. He wanted to claw his face, writhe on the floor, get outside himself, be anybody but himself. William, poor, dear, beautiful William. The round of blame and guilt moved on.

Ephraim could not pray, he could not bear to see the Bible, and put it on the floor outside his room. He could not curse God, but he could not reach out to Christ. A buried part of him flinched in guilt and terror: the wrath of God Almighty had smote him. Vengeance is mine said the Lord. The God of Abraham and Jacob was a jealous God. For turning to Christ from the old God of Judaism, this was the revenge. Not once but twice he had become kofer, he still was apostate! God was telling him – this is the sacrifice, your first-born son, dedicated to me, now you must return to me. The need to pace seized Ephraim at these times and he circled, circled, circled his room. The lie attacked him – he had lied, on oath before God and the people, he had sworn the lie that Sarah had been born Christian. This was the punishment, the vengeance of the wrathful God. But why William? This small and brilliant innocent, this babe, and punishing Helena too. And Selda, not one but two taken. It was not like Job, seven sons and three daughters and all his living destroyed by God, for Job was a good, God-fearing man. Ephraim was not good, he was a hypocrite, a coward, a worthless worm deserving of all kind of punishment. Like King David who coveted Bathsheba, and their first son died – the cycle of furies repeated, twisting and crossing. Jesus was God's son. God the Father had allowed his Son to die – how could that be, why? To live. To bring life to all. How could that be? How could it be allowed? The pity of it, the pain, the injustice, the sorrow, the guilt.

Now and then, through his torment, music penetrated. Helena, in the parlor across the hallway, played. Sometimes a painfully sweet Schubert song, or Brahms – the lullaby that made Ephraim weep behind his closed door. Helena wept too as she played. Sometimes hymns, words they both knew: Frail children of dust, and feeble as frail, in thee do we trust... and another stirring hymn of praise to the Almighty, full of worship and vigor with the verse they'd taken as their own particular favorite at the height of their romance: Truth in its beauty and love in its tenderness, These are the offerings to lay on his shrine.

After Jacob's visit Ephraim's mind and self shakily rejoined the world. He went to church daily, spending hours on his knees in the empty building and by the two little graves, hours more alone with his Bible and his books. The solace of others could reach him now. He spent time with Christian brethren and attended Freemason meetings once again. Though he was often silent around the house, and did not go anywhere near medicine or medical texts, he did begin to read the newspapers, and venture into conversation.

By invitation he preached at one church and another – sometimes fiery with conviction, other times deeply scholarly, occasionally fumbling in his rhetoric. He took to reading out Old Testament passages in three versions: the common English, the Greek, and the Hebrew, interpreting himself the two ancient languages into English. He insisted the differences mattered, Exodus chapter 26, verse 1, for instance. Moses transmits the Lord's instructions to make 'the tabernacle' in English, 'the dwelling' in Hebrew and 'the tent' in the oldest, the Greek, text. Ephraim's followers had long admired his learning, but these sermons left them puzzled. It was as if he was debating an unseen opponent. He also repeated two verses obsessively in public and within himself, for their comfort. From Luke, as laid down by the Law of Moses: Every first-born male must be consecrated to the Lord. So he was, so he was, William was consecrated to the Lord. And King David: Could I bring the child back to life? I will someday go to where he is, but he can never come back to me. It was, Ephraim later thought, like converting himself to Christianity all over again. He wrestled with God, and God won, again.

In the meanwhile, Helena was getting very worried about money. Her father helped with household expenses, but there were other bills to pay and their accounts – which she had begun keeping for the practice soon after their marriage – were perilously low. They were scraping a living on Ephraim's preaching bursaries; Helena began to bring in dollars by giving piano, French and German lessons. This was not the life of the physician's wife she had expected. That life had its hardships – long hours, late-night calls, insights into losses and tragedies – but there was also medical camaraderie, the community of physicians she'd grown up with. However, the change of vocation was what Ephraim needed, no matter the sacrifice.

Ephraim too had some private pupils, tutoring in foreign and ancient languages. But he also took long hours alone in his library. He resumed his work on Moses, determined to make sense of the instructions for the holy tent in the desert that had caught his curiosity. Six chapters of the entire forty in Exodus, 199 verses by his count – surely there had to be some reason for this emphasis. Yet in his readings no scholar or theologian to date had satisfactorily calculated how the tabernacle was constructed. With pen and paper and ruler and the ancient Hebrew and Greek texts in their variations, he began to work on the puzzle. Helena, calling him to dinner or offering coffee, would find his arithmetical figurings, his geometric diagrams, sheets of paper folded in L-shapes and triangles. Once he asked her for a length of cloth, another time she discovered him in the back yard, sawing and weighing planks of wood. As he mused and calculated he began to consult his Freemason brothers; Helena began to fear this was an obsession.

However, Ephraim also spent time writing poetry and translating the Song of Solomon. He wrote articles as well, and sent them off to scholarly and theological journals. The publication of his poems could bring income, and his anguish find an outlet. If his poems could touch others, and bring them to seek God, this would be a recompense for his sinfulness. Along with the few acceptances and many rejection letters the mail brought Sister Sadie's missives, fascinating glimpses of her life that she illustrated with little sketches. As further illustration she included generous lengths of ribbon or fine fabric; once Helena had simply treasured these, now she found them extremely useful. The packets from Russia were a mixed blessing of brightness for Helena and bitter reminder to Ephraim of one of the sins for which God had cursed him. And so all correspondence with Sadie was now conducted via Helena.

Alone and together they prayed for guidance. How to make a living? He refused to practice medicine, and for all his theology he fled from pastoral work: baptizing, leading a flock, ministering to the poor in spirit – how could he, he was poor in spirit himself. He still hardly counted the death of his second child, so grief-stricken was he over the first.

Ephraim sank into gloom frequently. Helena led prayers sometimes. The 23rd Psalm especially seemed to relieve him – though I walk through the valley of the shadow of death, I will fear no evil. She played a favorite hymn – Father, hear the prayer we offer, not for ease that prayer shall be – to prod him from depression. Finally she suggested he visit Andover Seminary. She proposed it in the guise of new learning but her hope was that he would find someone at his old school who could assuage the weight on his spirit.

PART 4: THE TERRITORY

29

PROFESSOR EPSTEIN
Tiffin, Ohio 1878-79

A professorship? The offer came from Heidelberg of all places. But this Heidelberg was not in Germany where Ephraim had stayed with Kathy and Abraham Sack during that fraught time of reconciliation, divorce and return to Judaism. Named for the ancient famous university, this Heidelberg was a college founded by the German Reformed Church and established in Tiffin, Ohio.

Ephraim agreed to consider the idea during his visit to Andover. Helena thanked God that he regarded it as a gift from heaven. Still battling depression, he would not doctor but perhaps he could allow himself to take a teaching post. Privately she thanked her father, for he had pressed behind the scenes to bring about the appointment without hurt to Ephraim's pride. After a year he would be offered tenure, a permanent place to settle, a home on the campus. Tiffin was a day's travel north through smooth and fertile land, still close enough to friends and family, but a new start, a new house. Close enough to visit William's and Selda's graves. Far enough to never have to see Mr Maxwell the druggist again. Recall of the scrip, the medicine bottle, of spooning the medicine into his golden son still wrenched Ephraim. William, dead, it was wrong, wrong, wrong. It should not have been. But he stopped himself – again and again he stopped himself – from going further in that direction. He would pull himself up short, say a quick prayer, and go to look at little Frieda in her cradle.

Helena's instincts were right. The trip east renewed Ephraim, and not only did he come back ready to agree the position as professor of German, Hebrew and natural sciences, he brought news. Through Andover connections he would also serve as a minister in Tiffin's Episcopalian church. A far cry from his preferred Baptist practice, it was nevertheless an established, formal denomination he respected – and the timing of the two situations coming available surely was a sign of mercy and meaning from the Lord.

The semester would begin in October 1878, and they had to hurry to find a house to rent, to pack up, to bid adieu to Mercy, who wanted to stay near her own family, and say farewells to their friends, so glad to see Dr Epstein rally. Amid the bustle Ephraim was surprised by the return of desire. Helena was worn by grief, but as Ephraim improved and returned to normal her face filled out and softened. Her golden hair, her blue eyes, her goodness... He thought of Job and all his sons and daughters slain, yet in the end Job emerged with faith, and with all joy restored – sons and daughters and faith. Ephraim finally reconciled himself with God's mysterious might and will.

To mark the commencement of his professorship Ephraim gave an address in Heidelberg's recently finished red-brick hall, its Greek revival style signifying enlightened scholarship. The title: 'The Pyramids in the Bible'. His fascination with Moses and the riddle of the holy tent had shaped itself into ideas on practical mathematics in the Bible. The months of obsessing emerged in rational form, his rhetoric on linguistic references became clear. He calculated cubits, he quoted Euclid and the Pythagorean Theorem, he said there should be no fear of scientific exploration of Biblical text. Scientific truth was the Lord's truth. This liberal arts college was also a theological seminary and Ephraim's startling marriage of his subjects provoked lively interest in the learned Christian-Jewish professor.

The new start in Tiffin was happy and invigorating. Sadness lay behind and once more Ephraim relished a challenge. Academia had long ago in Brest-Litovsk been a vocation he'd dreamed of pursuing and he plunged into it wholeheartedly. He read reams of texts, delved into the college's library, ordered books and equipment, chaired meetings. He expounded in Hebrew and Greek in his sermons for the Episcopal church. And he determined to shape his work on Moses and the holy tent into a book, to be titled *The Construction of the Tabernacle*. Surely it would be published, for his inaugural lecture had created such a stir that Ephraim evolved a monthly gathering of the brightest students to discuss science and scripture.

Ephraim loved a following, not for the adulation and respect, though these were very pleasant, but because he loved to set minds and hearts alight. This work – pleasure – was not unlike his proselytizing to the Jews, a passion to which he now returned. The visit to Andover had brought him close to brothers of the Melioration Society from those early days, and he resumed regularly writing articles and letters to persuade stubborn Jews to the truth of Jesus. Meanwhile here at Heidelberg these fresh-faced Christians had to overcome resistance to the truth of science. Of course Charles Darwin's *Origin of Species* became a focus of discussion. The general public still misconstrued Mr Darwin's thinking and feared it. Mankind descended from the ape? Seven days of creation took more than seventy times seven eons? What about Adam and Eve and Noah? Dr Epstein encouraged his students to intellectual honesty and to glory in the wonders of God Almighty. Evolution and the Bible, scientific analysis and the Bible: never fear the Truth. Unlike the Jews, they should have faith enough to test their faith and to grow it.

As the warmth of the seminars grew, Ephraim gathered objections and solutions into a series of articles which were first published in the college newspaper. Through this the townspeople became interested, which by March lead to monthly lectures for the public at the Episcopalian hall where Christian men and women of all ages and several denominations came to question and discuss. Helena's father Dr Greyer and some Cincinnati Freemasons travelled to attend several of these, and word of Dr Epstein's open lectures spread. Helena took part by playing piano to lead hymns at the start and end of the sessions.

Another facet to this settled period was the full renewal of marital life with Helena, and delight in little Frieda, treasuring her all the more against the pale shadow of the two small graves in Cincinnati. News came from Sister Sadie that he was a grandfather again. Sarah Zur Hosen had given birth to a girl, Ljuba, and Ephraim was content to see his patrimony increase. Summer came, and as he crossed the campus to the splendid new red brick College Hall with its Gothic-styled tower Ephraim wished that his old mentor Professor Stowe were alive to savor his protégé's strides into academia. Students flocked to his lectures and he was honored and proud to be shaping the minds of future pastors, professors and contributors to America. This afternoon the principal, in his end-of-year interview, would award him the promised tenure and house in this small and peaceful town on the Sandusky River – a permanent home and an ideal place to raise children amid an atmosphere of learning. It was an outcome, he used an Episcopalian phrase, most wholly to be desired, for to his joy Helena had just declared herself with child.

Ephraim left the interview fuming. Tenure was offered – conditionally. The principal, a righteous man he had never felt fully comfortable with, began by complimenting Dr Epstein on his successful series of extra-curricular seminars, then cleared his throat and requested that they cease. The principal said that as an enlightened Christian he felt this was a shame. Of course educated theologians all knew that the Bible was written by many authors, that it contradicted itself, that it required exegesis as to the historical, cultural and linguistic background of every chapter and verse. But talking up Darwin's evolution, bringing square-roots and geometry into Moses, splitting hairs in Hebrew text – this was far too distressing and scholarly for ordinary people. Heidelberg was beginning to seem like a hotbed of radical thinking, so that the best students would not be attracted. Furthermore, the college's benefactors objected to the controversies that

Dr Epstein's openly scientific approach to scripture attached to the college. And benefactors, essential to the good of the college, must be considered.

To have his knowledge, his faith and his passion put under a bushel basket – it was worse than an insult. It was criminal. Ephraim seethed. But he understood: the request was a demand. He ached to put in his resignation, but reined in his response and accepted the principal's cloying sympathies. The hypocrite dared to urge Ephraim to pray, and to think of all he was achieving with these hungry young minds. The man prattled on about how much Dr Epstein had to give as a tenured professor at Heidelberg: his experiences of missionary work, of Hebrew life and learning, his many languages and of course the natural sciences. Ephraim left the principal with a handshake and an agreement which they both knew was tenuous.

Helena expected a joyful countenance on his return, and Ephraim did not know how to tell her this upsetting news. He could hardly ask her to uproot herself for the second time in a year, and with a baby on the way. In any case where would they go? Tiffin had been a golden opportunity. He came home determined to conceal the situation. With pretended satisfaction he told Helena that there would be some changes to his work and they would soon be in a larger house. He buried himself behind a newspaper.

His wife, of course, knew immediately that something was very wrong. Ephraim should be glowing, he should be reading Bible passages and conducting a prayer of thanksgiving. He should be asking her to play *Praise the Lord!* and speculating about the new house. She sat near him for a while, sewing, feeling his unhappiness gather strength. Finally she asked, 'Ephraim, what is it?'

He told her, concluding with a bitter outburst, 'They are crucifying me. They want me to keep silent. It is not my truth, but the truth. God's own truth. Jesus did not say "speak not the truth." Science is God's creation. How can knowledge be any threat to faith?'

Helena joined his outrage: 'The college will look so foolish. This makes a joke of learning and your teaching. And not just in Tiffin, what about the people who come from Cincinnati to hear you?'

'They will have to stay in Cincinnati.' He raised the newspaper again, exercising his willpower to remain calm.

'You must resign.'

His shoulders sagged in relief at the permission her words gave him, but still he said, 'How can I? We have Frieda and the baby. No. I will bear it until the baby comes and then search for another position.'

'Ephraim, you can't. You will not be able to live with yourself,' she said gently, also thinking how hard it would be for her to live with him under the circumstances. 'You will have to take up medicine again. Thank goodness father can help. George has been wanting to go back and train in eye surgery.'

'No! In the name of William I cannot.' He thundered out of the room, into his library.

Helena knew it had been a risk. But he had been so fine, and so happy all the year. She thought surely he would be ready to return to medicine.

Ephraim took his meals in the library for two days. With wisdom gained in her other experiences of his storms Helena decided to proceed with plans for a summer visit to her parents and to leave him behind to wrestle with God. They would pray for him in Cincinnati.

Wrestle he did. In the past he had rebelled against authority, avoided hypocrisy, and sought his truth by moving on, whatever the cost. Even the trauma of William's death he had solved by moving on. Now though, he was trapped by the family he loved and had always wanted. The pressure brought to mind the day of his seventeenth birthday and Grandfather Zayde. Suddenly he felt a kinship with the patriarch: the burden of family. Seventy people – seventy! – had depended on Zayde. And here, he, Ephraim, was finding himself forced against his will by only four, including himself and his dear Helena and the child yet unborn. Medicine? Never. He had sworn under God that he would never practice again. How could he, he who had caused the death of his own son. But stay here as a silenced teacher? It went against every tenet of his being. If he agreed not to speak Truth he was denying Christ.

He could only pray, and it was in the Old Testament, the Psalms, which the Hebrews called one of the Books of Truth, that he found most comfort. Keep me safe, my God, for in you I take refuge.... I will praise the Lord who counsels me... You make known to me the path of life...

Something began to ease, but answer came there none. Counsel. The word made him think of Uncle Jacob, his shrewdness, his experience. They had seen less of each other since Esther Tobleroff monopolized him, and since he had supported Sadie in her born-Christian sophistry and since the move to Tiffin. But Jacob had come when Helena asked for help with Ephraim; his down-to-earth presence was ever a saving grace. Ephraim shut up the house and set off for Cincinnati.

'Daniel in the lion's den, nephew!' Jacob beamed, embracing Ephraim. 'Sit, sit, eat with me. How long since you had gefilte fish?' They were in a kosher restaurant in the Jewish area of Cincinnati, white tiles gleaming, a striped awning shading the interior from glaring summer sun.

'Cold borscht. Just the thing for this weather.' Ephraim said, studying the menu. His mouth watered, and his mother's dining table came to mind. 'And pickled herring and brown bread.' Though Helena's German-influenced cooking provided many familiar tastes, it had indeed been a while since he'd eaten kashrut at the table of Jacob's red-haired fiancee. After ordering, he had to ask, 'So your Esther doesn't want to see me? Is that why we meet here?' They sat opposite each other in a corner of the bright, clean, quiet establishment.

'You are not exactly a favorite in the community, Dr Israelite Indeed.' He smiled as he said this.

Ephraim smiled in return. 'Glad to know that my letters to the Jews are getting through! You remained unconvinced, I take it.'

'Unconvinced, unconverted,' Jacob replied cheerfully. 'It's true she doesn't approve of my missionizing nephew. But that's not why she left me.'

'She left you?'

Jacob cocked his head to one side. 'The Tobleroff ran off with an older man. No, no –' he brushed away Ephraim's sympathies '– tell the truth I badly missed being a bachelor. I even let her keep the diamond.' He gave his wry smile. The waiter set the food down and they began to eat amid chatter and clatter, for several tables were now occupied. 'Interesting that you are teaching Hebrew to Christians; you never know, they might go the other way. And very clever, the tabernacle and all those numbers.'

'So you've heard about that. What do you think? The word, Qeresh,' he said it in Hebrew. 'Unique, doesn't exist in the language. I say it means vertical planks of wood. Not boards, not woods, not tenons, not armlets, as the sages, even the great Maimonides, would have it. You agree?'

'Plank. Qeresh.' Jacob considered. 'Could be. Certainly possible to load them onto four ox carts, like it says, and trek around the desert.'

Ephraim, expecting no quibbles, was ahead of him. 'But the numerology of its Hebrew letters... there has to be a meaning.' He gestured, and the image in the large mirror across the room caught his eye: himself with grizzled hair and neat beard sitting with a stocky frizzy-haired older man, the tables of diners with their earlocks and yarmulkas. For a moment he felt an echo of old times, of beth midrash and the intricate back-and-forth of Torah interpretation.

Jacob took another bite of his fishcake and seemed to be thinking over the tabernacle riddle. 'What are you trying to prove, Ephraim?'

Ephraim paused, clarifying his thoughts and frustrations before he spoke. 'That truth is the Lord's message. Un-afeared honesty,' he said firm, and quiet. 'Truth is the Way.'

'That will carry you through,' he airily dismissed the subject. 'You like the herring? How is little Frieda? And the pretty Mrs Epstein.'

Ephraim told him about the baby on the way, and then plunged into his turmoil, ending, 'I can't be a physician, you know I cannot. But I cannot stay on as a silenced teacher.'

'The Jews don't like you because of your Jesus. And the Christians don't like you because of your truth.' Jacob laughed gently, shaking his head, 'Do you ever think of keeping quiet?'

Ephraim started to object, then joined him in laughter which then turned to a heartfelt plea. 'What can I do? What would you do?' Now that they were both mature men the gap between them had narrowed, but still Ephraim hoped his uncle's quarter-century seniority would show him a path.

'Ephraim, don't be meshugeh.' Jacob gave him an appraising and reproachful look. 'You and I, two very different people. You and your truth, and a family to support. Me – footloose and fancy free. I'd spin the dreidel and see how it fell.'

Though there was no answer from the uncle who had opened doors for him before, Ephraim felt renewed in faith. He rejoined Helena at her parents' house and immersed himself in the family, in his studies and in prayer. Within the week he came across a newspaper he'd brought among his papers from home. The ways of the Lord are mysterious: a path appeared. Consulting with Helena, he applied to six advertisements in *The Baptist Times*: three to colleges, three to churches. Teach or preach, north, south, east, west. Let the Almighty decide.

30

A VOICE CRYING IN THE WILDERNESS
Yankton, Dakota 1879

At the age of fifty Ephraim's relationship with the Almighty took a new turn. His sojourn with Episcopalians in Tiffin had gently eased him into pastoral ministry after the bleak hiatus of William's death. But the limitations on scripture interpretation by college trustees recalled him to his earlier home with the free and forthright Baptists. Their practice allowed for a wide range of beliefs with no centralized orthodoxy; the sole authority was the Bible and the believer's faith. Ephraim, with his Old Testament Hebrew, New Testament Greek and new ideas now knew he required this freedom. Only one offer came of his applications to teach or preach within the Baptist denomination: pastor in Yankton, the capital of Dakota Territory. Back to the wild West: the Lord Almighty could move in ironical ways.

Ephraim accepted the post with grim determination. Yankton was the riverside base for a new frontier far more raw than Kansas and he feared it would be rollicking with the kind of riff-raff he'd seen in Leavenworth. He also had to quell fears about the Indians: only three years earlier, in 1876, Sitting Bull and Crazy Horse led their braves to kill General Custer and his troops at Little Bighorn. Native resistance seemed to be no longer a problem, but there were the realities of the territory's distances and its climate: droughts, bitter winters, searing summers, tornadoes, locusts, prairie fires. Nevertheless they would go. Helena did not demur. As a woman and wife she accepted as the very air she breathed her task to be helpmeet, to have an orderly household, meals on the table and a pleasant countenance, just as it was Ephraim's task as a man and husband to provide for his wife and family.

At first appearance Yankton made Leavenworth seem a veritable metropolis. Its grid of ten dusty roads was bordered on the south by the Missouri, with a range of limestone bluffs along the river to the west of the town. All around lay vast prairie emptiness. But the very newness made Yankton more civilized in spirit than the Kansas outpost, and Ephraim was relieved to find the ethos here upright, God-fearing, hard working. The Dakota population boom was in full swing: those miles of prairie plateau were rich and ready to homestead, railroad lines were pushing in, the Sioux Lakota tribes had been driven back, the buffalo herds were nearly extinct. Invited immigrant settlers were pouring in from back East, and from Germany, Russia and Scandinavia. If they didn't want to farm or trade in farm goods or develop businesses to serve the new settlers or work the railroads, those seeking new lives and fortunes passed through Yankton on their way west to seek gold in the Black Hills.

Earlier in the '70s the railroad had reached Yankton, and now the train came regularly, bringing mail and goods from the East and dropping and collecting passengers. This was how Ephraim, Helena and two-year-old Frieda had arrived, a long journey of ten days from the farewells of Cincinnati through the ripe fields of Ohio up to Chicago where they broke the journey. Advised by other pastors' wives in the Baptist circle, the pregnant Helena stocked up on bed linens and shoes, having been told those were difficult articles to come by in Dakota. And sheet music – they assured her she would have no dearth of piano pupils. The rail trip continued through fertile and increasingly flat farmland until they crossed the Missouri, which looked just as wide and muddy as the mighty Mississippi they'd crossed earlier.

While homesteaders round about lived in sod huts until they could buy timber to build barns and houses, life in Yankton itself was far from makeshift. The town had been laid out twenty years before, its curve of the Missouri forming an ideal port for steamboats and the best base for access to the Territory beyond. It had ten churches with resident clergymen; Ephraim was taking over as pastor of the longest established Protestant congregation. Education was a prime concern in Yankton, evidenced by half a dozen purpose-built school buildings, including a high school, which boded well for the Epsteins to be able to find pupils for private tutoring. It was a thriving place, with lumberyards, blacksmiths, a brickwork, several breweries, some hundred goods stores, including wholesalers, and a clutch of hotels. The white painted timber two-story territorial capitol building was a major center of activity and there were all the accouterments of the capital of a vast territory: courthouse, post office, three banks, physicians, lawyers, accountants, a daily newspaper and several weeklies, including the German-language *Freie Press*. There was even, as solace for Helena, a brand new brick building commissioned in the latest Italianate architecture for the German club, with a hall for entertainments and social gatherings. Ephraim's linguistic skills were a perfect fit among the Dakota settlers, and he also found a welcome in Yankton's newly fledged Freemason's Lodge.

No longer a warrior fighting the good fight, forging ahead, daring to defy, Ephraim buckled down to the compromises of maturity. Duty and necessity took the place of his former zeal and passion. His salary was even less than that of an untenured college teacher, but at least this position had a house with it. And a house indeed they needed, for a sister for Frieda, Julia, was born in March 1880 six months after they arrived. As if there were some kind of heavenly scoreboard, a month later a letter from Kathy arrived informing Ephraim of their father's death. 'Though he would not speak your name, he sorrowed for you still. On his deathbed he called Aaron to him, our little brother the good son who still lived with him, and blessed him as eldest, and when the time came Aaron said the Kaddish.' Involuntarily Ephraim's lips moved. Yitgaddal veyitqaddash shmeh rabba, May His great name be exalted... in the world which will be renewed and where He will give life to the dead and raise them to eternal life. The orphan's Kaddish.

He left the letter on the table when his baby daughter gave a brief cry, picked her up from the cradle and cuddled the warm bundle of sweet, helpless life. The prophet Jeremiah's praise came to him: I am Israel's father, and Ephraim is my firstborn son. How glad his father must have been to have a son at last, after three daughters. The irony: his father had given him the second name Menachem, meaning consoler. Instead he had become his father's disappointment. He kissed Julia's head but he was thinking of William. He loathed his superstitious feeling that he would never have the joy of a son, a punishment for leaving Judaism. He prayed blessings upon Julia, tucked her into the cradle and rocked it. Well, he would not be tearing his clothes for his father. But he did feel sorrow and regret. Too late, too late now to convince the stubborn old man of Jesus, the Christ, son of God. A spark of anger flared – if only he could have made his father see. And his mother. And all the Jewish nation.

The new life was hard for Helena, hard for both of them, for Ephraim was away two or three days at time. He had to cover an enormous area in his new post, riding ten or twenty miles on horseback or horse-drawn buckboard – or even sleigh or on foot – in the circuit beyond Yankton. The subtly undulating land reminded Ephraim of the prairie he'd seen beyond Leavenworth, and even of the miles of marshes in Belarus where he'd gone fishing with his uncles. But those were lush with greenery compared to the endless waving grasses and flat croplands here in Dakota Territory where trees grew only along the bottom land in the river valley. Huge skies, dramatic clouds and wind dominated. A man was just a speck in God's great dominion. In this solitude Ephraim struggled to renew his relationship with the Almighty and to justify his worthiness to be a pastor when he still felt so empty. He clung to a section of a psalm – I shall not die, but I shall live, and recount the deeds of the Lord. The Lord has punished me severely, but he did not give me over to death. The Lord and Helena were his solace, Frieda and baby Julia brought moments of pleasure, but of joy he felt none. He was indeed in the wilderness.

On his visits to outlying homesteads, where he stayed overnight, he encountered a sheer hunger for human contact, and for the world. Sometimes the homes were just a sprawling log cabin or a single turf room expanded by lean-tos, sometimes a new-built timber frame house. In Medicine Hat he was the first visitor they'd had for two months. He brought letters and newspapers, for which he was much thanked. They were keen to talk, though taciturn at first, as though the very idea of speaking their thoughts had atrophied. Except for reading the Bible nightly among themselves they spoke little – there not being much to say amid the wind, the cattle, the growing crops. Ephraim's long-ago experiences in farm work created bonds; occasionally he exercised his Hebrew, Greek and Latin, for scholars were among those creating new lives in the Territory, but generally plain English or German, sometimes Russian, were sufficient.

As for Charles Darwin and evolution, no one asked, so Ephraim didn't raise the subject. Not that he considered himself gagged, but he took on board Uncle Jacob's teasing about keeping quiet and decided to rest. Deep thinkers relished exegesis, these children of God needed simple, straightforward edification. And so he was pleased to bring a dozen believers for baptism by total immersion at the Tent Festival come July. That was a heartening day: the Missouri momentarily become the River Jordan, with the fringe of cottonwood, elm, oak and willow on the bank a splendid shady place for the picnic and the singing Helena led.

In the time when he was not performing his Baptist duties Ephraim taught Latin and Greek to the brightest of the local children, wrote and sent off theological articles and tried to tease out the rest of the tabernacle puzzle. By now he knew through linguistics, arithmetic, geometry and sheer practicality that the key to the holy tent's framework was the right-angled triangle – the mathematical law defined by Pythagoras six hundred years before Christ. But the time of Moses and the sacred tent was some thousand years earlier. And then there was the mystery of the text's unknown Hebrew word – Qeresh.

The Hebrew alphabet gives letters numerical values and after much pondering Ephraim's mind went back to those lonely years in Vienna when he had found meaning in the mystical world of the Kabbalah. Perhaps...? The letters of the unknown word Qeresh were the numbers 1-2-3. He applied kabbalistic numerology starting with a right-angled triangle, labelling the sides 1-2-3. The puzzle was how to turn these into the correct Pythagorean ratio: 3-4-5. He tried adding up around the triangle sides, substituting letters for numbers, moving on a side, then back into letters: a new word, a new hint, new numbers to try. Finally the numbers arrived at the correctly proportioned right-angled triangle: 4-3-5. Thau, Shin, Hey. But they made no Hebrew word. Yet the numbers were right, so they had to mean something!

The riddle became a constant background gnawing. Ephraim's scripture calculations of cubits, right angles, planks and cloths made sense beyond all other scholarly theories. And he'd proved it in his model-making. But he needed evidence in the actual Bible text. He brooded during the long Dakota distances until one gentle starlit night, in the jouncing of the buckboard, the clopping of horse-hoofs, the never-still wind soughing in the grasses, he heard a whisper: Mem, Shin, Hey... Mou-Sh-eH! Moses! He laughed and stretched his arms up to the starry heavens and shouted out Mou-Sh-eH! Mou-Sh-eH! Moses!

For Mem also represents 4, and the shift in digit-meaning transformed the 4-3-5 triangle into the name of Moses in Hebrew.

This was the secret of building and measuring that Pythagoras himself had learned in Egypt as a geometric law. A millennium earlier Moses, from Egypt, used the unique word Qeresh as a coded message for his own name and the theorem for the construction of the holy tent. Eureka, riddle solved!

Elated, Ephraim arrived home, shared the good news with Helena and set about finishing his book. He had discovered a solution for a unique Hebrew word mistranslated, misunderstood and misapplied for thousands of years. His scholarship would not only enlighten Christian readers, but also be a means of reaching Jewish circles, his never-ending mission. In high hopes, he sent the manuscript to a Chicago publisher.

31

ORION RISING
Yankton, Dakota 1880-81

The seasons turned, the constellation of Orion began to climb in the starry heavens and Ephraim continued to find solace in the great book of nature as well as in his studies. Autumn of that first Dakota year brought a thrill of social intellectual stimulation, because, as the best season for travel, both the Baptists and the Freemasons held their major annual territorial gatherings in the capital. Indeed many Baptists were among the Freemason brotherhood, movers and shakers of the Territory. Discussions and presentations of papers covered topics ranging from the geological history of Dakota to Tolstoy's books to concepts of the steam engine and trestle bridges. Darwin's theory of evolution was among the lively, open topics, and so was Ephraim's 'The Pyramids of the Bible', a simplified approach to his discoveries on the construction of the tabernacle.

One of these convocations brought Ephraim to the attention of the influential Thomas Kettering, and so began a friendship that was to lead, in very little time, to another change in fortune. Round-faced, balding, unbearded but with a thick, wide black mustache, Mr Kettering was an early Dakota settler who had carved a career for himself: scout for Custer's cavalry, railway construction worker and manager, factory owner, a spell as sheriff of Clay County, elder of his church, railroad agent, business investor. With no formal education himself, he was campaigning to improve education facilities in the Territory. Yankton's first territorial legislature in 1862 had passed an act authorizing a university, but no institution yet existed. At an address to Baptist pastors he expounded: 'Now that Dakota has been homesteaded for twenty years there is a crying need to educate the brightest young minds to a higher level. We are building the next state of these United States, we must provide a liberal and practical education necessary to life's pursuits and professions. And necessary to morality, happiness and good government. We need Territory-born-and-raised spokesmen, not East coast carpetbaggers who come intent only on profit and political power.'

Kettering's cheeks flushed with enthusiasm, his brown eyes shone, his mustache bristled with emphasis. Ephraim listened intently, glad to find someone in authority with vision, principles and energy. Kettering outlined the situation. 'As designated founding trustee I have secured preliminary funding from the current legislature towards the University of Dakota. The education act deems it is to be located in Vermillion, just down the river. University of Dakota! Doesn't that sound grand! The ninety-nine counties in the Territory stretch from the Black Hills to the Missouri, from Canada to Nebraska. And the bylaws require local demand and financial support from a minimum of fifty counties. Thus far we who are devoted to education have forty counties committed and signed. Only ten to go! We are on the brink of success – gentlemen, what say you?'

Ephraim was hooked. Education, fine minds, the good of all – this work had to be done. He offered to join the campaign, for his Baptist circuits provided an ideal opportunity to build support. Mr Kettering gladly welcomed the respected, highly-educated Dr Epstein, pastor of the first Baptist church in the Territory. He introduced Ephraim to the two other founding trustees, Colonel Coddrington, a distinguished retired US Army officer from Vermillion, and Mr Franklin Hendricks, Yankton's major grain merchant. They were tough, intelligent men and Ephraim savored working with them as equals conferring over petitions, deadlines and charter requirements. Among all the education campaigners the new recruit and the spearhead founding trustee made a striking pair, Dr Epstein the salt with his graying patriarch's beard and bemused wisdom, Kettering the younger pepper with his bushy black mustache and exuberance.

With a cause to fight for Ephraim became fully his old self. His dispirited determination ceased, his bouts of gastric pains and burps dwindled, his withdrawals to his desk were now charged with energy. Helena rejoiced in his zeal; at last he was the confident, enthusiastic man she had fallen in love with.

Ephraim had barely begun his educational proselytizing when the Territory intruded. In early October 1880 a freak blizzard hit. He waited it out and then resumed his circuit, for snow did not deter the dedicated pastors of Dakota. The river froze solid as it did every winter, keeping steamboats in port until the spring. Huge drifts blocked the railways bringing in supplies. No sooner had they been dug out than more snow fell, and as the digging out began there came another storm, and another. No supplies could get through. Territorial Governor Nehemiah Ordway, newly installed by the President of the United States, sought relief supplies from the army. Yankton residents in the meanwhile helped each other and rationed what food and fuel they had. Ephraim offered his church as a distribution center and he and Helena called on the needy.

After this terrible winter finally came hints of spring. Late in March 1881, returning from a visit to western Yankton county, Ephraim brought the good news that the river ice showed signs of melting. They relaxed and looked forward, glad when after church the next Sunday the frozen river began to groan and crack. But three days later panicked shouts pulled Helena and Ephraim from their house. They dashed out to see a mass of giant ice cakes moving in the rising current. The town itself was safe, but warehouses, steamboats and dwellings on the bottom land were at risk of flood. Fortunately people had warning enough to evacuate, for the Missouri rose, and rose... and then subsided. For two days the river halted and resumed, ice creaking, grinding, tossing up chunks bigger than houses.

And then the ice jammed a few miles downriver. Floes built up layers high, back upriver toward Yankton. The mighty blockage held in ominous creaking silence that broke with a terrible roar after twenty-four hours of suspense. The force moved forward and waters rose higher than ever, making a river ten miles wide. Amid snowflakes and freezing weather, Ephraim and Helena wrapped up the baby and four-year-old Frieda to join others viewing the flood from the higher bluffs beyond town. In a hellish scene haystacks, barns, tree trunks, houses – some with people clinging to the roofs – swept by. The massive flow carried huge chunks of ice, sometimes bearing frantic pigs, chickens and dogs; horses and cattle floundered in the current.

Worse came as they stood watching: a mile or so opposite Yankton on the Nebraska shore giant ice cakes bore down on low-lying Green Island, surrounding it. The residents had fled, but Ephraim, Helena and the others clasped hands to their faces in horror as the whole village, home to 150 people, was smashed and swept away. Then incredibly the village church, tall spire and all, was lifted from its foundations. In a weird farewell the church turned and floated calmly downstream amid the ice and debris for a whole mile before disappearing around a bend.

Noah's Flood, apocalypse, Armageddon, the end of times... the power and destruction was beyond believing. In all, by mid-April a 400 mile length of the Missouri River had been inundated, and the worst destruction was in the twenty-five miles between Yankton and the downriver town, Vermillion. That entire settlement was wiped out just as Green Island had been. Vermillion! What about the new university! But higher education was of little matter now; throughout the whole valley residents lost homes, grain, timber, thousands of cattle and other livestock. Miraculously only a very few people lost their lives.

Pastor Epstein led his congregation in prayers of awe at the Almighty's power, thanksgiving for their survival and mercy for the unfortunate. He and the town's other ministers opened their churches and homes and rallied the citizens to help victims with food, shelter, warmth and clothing. Amid the work, compassion and tiredness, Helena, making and serving out bread and soup, glimpsed a wonder – Ephraim using his healing skills. Quietly, routinely, as he encountered the need he cleaned and sewed wounds, set bones, soothed pains. The necessity, the urgency, the rows of camp-beds sent him back to the smallpox crisis in Monastir and the time he and Rachel had lived and worked in accord. How different to have Helena by his side, how good that she did not press him over acting as physician. Helena within herself gave thanks. Her Ephraim had gained a measure of inner peace lately, and certainly he drew strength from his association with Mr Kettering. She hoped her husband was healing himself as he healed others.

Perhaps she was right for, as the weather improved and the mails became regular again, Helena was surprised by Ephraim's equanimity when his book was rejected. He grumbled for a day, and then sent the manuscript to a California publisher, Thomas Wilson, as suggested by a brother in Freemasonry. For although the book was perfectly clear and open to all interested in scripture, Hebrew, mathematics and geometry, it also could be deeply understood by Freemasons.

Ephraim's task for late spring 1881 was to rouse his flock to find the faith, energy and funding to start over again. Besides banks, some money came available from the federal government; Governor Ordway had negotiated funds with the President. In turn, Kettering negotiated with the Governor, and assured Ephraim that the catastrophe would bring nothing but good to the university. The whole of Vermillion town would be rebuilt on the bluff above the river – and the University of Dakota would be at its heart. But still, now more than ever, they needed popular support. Mingled with his ministry, all summer and autumn Ephraim carried on his university proselytizing in public talks and one-to-one conversations. His accent now was thoroughly that of an educated American from somewhere west of the East coast, his linguistic abilities having tuned his ear and smoothed out any tinge of Russia. His voice was pleasant and engaging, his enthusiasm captivating. He persuaded via intellect or charm, or both, as befitted the audience, meeting lukewarm interest in some places and genuine support in many others. He worked with a passion, gathering petition signatures and financial pledges.

By December 1881 Kettering had his essential county demand, and both he and the Baptist churches gave special thanks and praise for the outstanding effort of Dr. Epstein. Ephraim was credited with personally bringing in four counties, including the vital final one. He glowed with satisfaction and harbored hopes that he would be invited to advise on the university's curriculum, and, while remaining a pastor, to do some teaching when it was formed. But he had no need to ask, for in Kettering he had found another Judge Sherman, another Professor Stowe. Though younger than those early mentors, like them the education campaigner was perceptive and keen to progress the best interests of his bright and learned friend. In a quiet conversation after the celebration dinner for all united in the cause Kettering said that, with permission, he was suggesting Ephraim's very wishes to the other two trustees.

Two further thrilling events came towards the end of this year of upheaval. As the new season's snows began the Epsteins had another daughter. In his faith and renewed energy Ephraim called her Zelda, so close to the name of the little one sleeping in the Cincinnati cemetery, but a name Ephraim wanted in his family, his mother's name. Now that his father was gone the child was a remembrance of both parents. Before the new baby's birth came momentous news – the acceptance of his manuscript along with a contract and a banker's draft for thirty dollars. By Christmas *The Key to the Construction of the Tabernacle* became a real book he held in his hands after five years of work. He felt pride, ambition, justification, defiance; it held mystery, scholarship, skill, and even humor. He mailed a copy to Jacob in Cincinnati, to Benjamin in New York, to Heidelberg College, to Andover and to theological journals for review. If it sold, a bit more welcome money might be forthcoming.

Another book was stirring, something more about Moses, and Psalms. Truth was woven into the grammar of the scripture, the truth that the coming of Jesus Christ as the divine Son of God was fore-ordained. Ephraim knew he could make people understand; Christians would be interested, Hebrews enlightened. It would be a complex argument requiring deep study and delicate linguistic proofs; he relished the long winter ahead when he could justify extra time at his desk.

But the new year turned out not to favor scholarly delving. On the second of January 1882 came a knock at the door of the Epsteins' clapboard Baptist house. Full of good spirits, dusting off snowflakes, Kettering entered to wish them the New Year and admire the baby. Then, his smile accentuated by the bushy mustache, he proudly informed them that the University of Dakota was officially sanctioned. 'You are now looking at the president of the university's Board of Trustees, appointed along with the Colonel and Hendricks by the Territory's Board of Regents.'

'Well deserved! Congratulations, my dear Kettering!' Ephraim pumped his hand, and Helena added her compliments.

Kettering demurred, crediting the many who had helped the cause, and then said, 'But there is more. I am pleased to tell you, Reverend Doctor Epstein, that the regents have delegated the trustees to invite you to be Founding President.' Kettering beamed proudly as he stood by the warmth of the iron stove. Astonished, Ephraim had no words. Kettering filled the gap. 'Of course you have commitments to the Baptists, but I think they would...'

'They would be honored,' Ephraim found his voice. 'As I am, deeply. But are you certain? I believe in the cause and have fought for it, but I always thought...' He'd thought that Kettering, though unlettered, would run the university, or if not him, some Eastern academic appointee.

'No, no, no. No one has worked harder than you. No one has your distinguished intellect, no one could be more appropriate,' Kettering insisted. 'Are you game for it? I can see you now, just right to continue promoting the university and recruit students – people trust you, believe in you. Within the year I know you can establish its curriculum. Its library and staff. Of course we have more fund-raising to do, more trustees to get in and there's the building program. I'll worry about those. By October of this very year you will be teaching our first students.'

Helena's face registered surprise and doubt. Kettering slowed his grand planning. 'I can see you are concerned. True, it will be a prodigious amount of work. And you – and the three children – will have to move to Vermillion. It will be raw and muddy for a while.' He paused as she looked to Ephraim. She could see he was absorbing the idea, the spark kindling. She looked back to Kettering who waited politely. She gave a nod of assent, and Kettering glowed with excitement: 'For the good of Dakota, Dr Epstein? There is, by the way, a handsome annual salary. And a presidential residence. Do you accept?'

'Is not the gleaning of the grapes of Ephraim better than the vintage of Abiezer?' Gideon's Old Testament words spoke the irony for which Ephraim thanked the Lord: to be silenced by the trustees of one higher education institute, and commissioned founding president by another. From being outcast, his virtues had triumphed. He swore to the Almighty and to Helena that no inquiring mind would be silenced in his university. This institution would be free from the restrictions of faith; the only faith was Truth. He would ensure that it was written into the bylaws of the university. Its motto would be *Veritas*.

32

VERITAS: PRESIDENT AND FOUNDER
Vermillion, Dakota 1882-83

Father of a university. Ephraim was fired with purpose – he had faith and trust in the cause, and the cause had faith and trust in him. It was the first position since he abjured medicine that fully utilized his mental powers, experience, qualifications and knowledge. Indeed he saw it as the first post in his life in which his complete personal authority was fully recognized. The Baptists, pleased that their former pastor was central to the Territory's university, accepted his resignation and kindly allowed the family to remain in the Yankton residence until their new home was ready.

The town of Vermillion, so named for the red color of the bluffs along this stretch of the Missouri, lay some twenty-eight undulating land miles east of Yankton. It had been a busy place since the great flood of 1881. Within a month of Vermillion's utter devastation its businessmen had decided to move and rebuild the whole town three miles inland along the railroad line, safely on top of the bluff. The townspeople agreed unanimously, road layouts were settled – allotting acreage for the intended university – and building commenced at such a pace that by autumn 1881 much housing was established and businesses and hotels had opened on the new Main and Market Streets.

In March 1882 before the snows of winter had disappeared the salt and pepper pair – Ephraim and Kettering – took the short train ride from Yankton to Vermillion to meet the university's Board of Trustees at the university's site. Frozen mud underfoot, beneath louring gray clouds, in cutting wind, amid sawing and hammering as workmen raised up houses, stores, offices and churches they marveled at the recovery powers of mankind. Where construction had not begun people lived, worked and traded in a canvas city, and pegs and rope marked out rectangular lots. Ephraim and Kettering made their way to flat, empty land bounded by a line designated Clark Street. There, a group of four top-hatted men stepped forward to greet them, revealing a neatly painted white and black sign planted in the earth: The University of Dakota.

'Gentlemen!' hailed Kettering. 'What a fine and glorious moment!' After general salutations he said, 'And here is the man who will bring our vision to life, Dr Ephraim M Epstein. Well known to two of you, of course. And you others certainly know of him.'

Handshakes and introductions proceeded. Decreed by the Territory's supervisory Board of Regents, the trustees had now expanded to six members. Joining droopy-mustached Colonel Coddrington and the bulky grain merchant Hendricks were two newcomers. Mr William Turnstall, a tall man with a thin, serious face, was a banker from Bismarck. Mr Charles LaSalle was a curly-haired lawyer from Vermillion. As a pastor and university campaigner Ephraim had encountered them briefly at various functions in Yankton. A final new trustee was not yet in place.

Kettering unfurled a plan of the site and the party of six walked the boundaries along Clark, up Plum Street, left along Cherry and left again back down Dakota Street. Then, all of them thoroughly chilled, he mooted an adjournment to the Hotel Meriwether for warmth, refreshment and planning. But they did not depart until Ephraim spoke. He stood by the sign, stocky and proud in his sober dark suit, his top hat, his grizzled beard riffled by the harsh wind of the plains. 'Gentlemen, I am deeply honored by the trust you have placed in me and the faith you have in my abilities. Don't you feel the exhilaration of the hope and energy of Vermillion? That same hope and energy – and more, that of the whole Territory – will carry us through the creation of our university. I pledge myself fully to the success of our endeavor. For Dakota now and into our children's children's time and on into the future.'

The first concern of the trustees was University Hall, and plans were already in place. It was to be of Dakota gray stone, two to three stories tall, mounted with two cupola'd towers. It would have eight classrooms, a lecture hall, a theater for speaking engagements, a library… and allowance for expansion. In the same stone, at a slight distance across the campus would be West Hall, a men's dormitory, soon to be matched by East Hall, for women. President's House would be just off campus on North Yale Street, a residence suitable to the dignity of the institution. It would provide spacious family accommodation and hold an office large enough to be a meeting chamber for university business. Two other smaller houses would follow for academic staff homes. All this was on paper and in budgets, which could now be released. Amid the discussion of plans and contracts Ephraim and the trustees agreed there would be no delay in opening, for Vermillion's Judge Kidder had offered space in the Court House for classrooms. Ephraim and Colonel Coddrington, who lived here in Clay County, would enlist homes and boarding houses to provide rooms and meals for students.

Students! Books! Learning! Without these there is no university, and through the spring and summer of 1882 while Kettering and the others progressed things in Vermillion Ephraim traveled the counties by rail and horse and carriage to recruit students and urge Dakotans to educational aspiration. One of his first executive actions was to secure Joseph Brown as a tutor and as treasurer for the university. A fellow education campaigner, the mild, sandy-haired Pennsylvania Congregationalist had been teaching at Yankton's high school. Brown was well qualified and Ephraim found in him a kindred spirit, someone with whom he could discuss the details of education, instead of the bricks, mortar and benefactors of the trustees' concern. Ephraim himself at this stage would head the Liberal Arts, and with Brown as his assistant teach Latin, German, mathematics, grammar, composition and history. They determined that speaking and a non-credit course of musical participation would round out the two-year degree.

In September, except for some finishing details, President's House was ready. Ephraim and Helena took possession with heady delight. For the third time since leaving Cincinnati Helena wrote to Sister Sadie describing new surroundings. The town itself was laid out on a grid and surrounded by treeless plateau much like Yankton, but much smaller of course, she said. Though still a-building the new Vermillion had four churches, four hotels, numerous general and specialist stores, two banks, apothecaries, barbershops, a newspaper and of course the usual hostelries, mills, hardware suppliers and farm outfitters. Ephraim broke in as Helena sat writing – he generally left the family correspondence to her, but this time he insisted: 'Have you told her about our front parlor? The stained glass from Chicago? Tell her I sent for textbooks from Cincinnati!'

Helena smiled and agreed. The house was clapboard, gabled, three stories high, with white-painted gingerbread woodwork, a bay window, a deep wide veranda. She added a snippet of the striped wallpaper Ephraim liked. For several happy afternoons Helena, Colonel Coddrington's wife and Ephraim had pored over mail order catalogs selecting items for President's House... a solid, generous home, wonderful for Frieda, Julia and Zelda. She described the handsome front parlor, and the place near the piano where she had hung the most recent Zur Hosen portrait. Sadie, Alexander, their son Shurek and little daughter Ljuba: such a good looking, well-to-do family.

Their correspondence had flown across the distances since the dreadful news of Russia after the assassination of the Czar in 1881. In Kiev and then in Warsaw, so close to Brest, incited mobs rampaged against Jews. Mad, inhuman treatment, inexplicable blame. Their houses and businesses were wrecked and set on fire, women, men, even children stripped naked, attacked. Most recently the May Laws of 1882 had been decreed by the Russian government against Jews: no new property allowed, regulations on trading, renting, settling. Sadie had said she'd heard that the situation was not too bad for the family in Belarus, no violence in the city, but the repression, yes, that was hard. She said she prayed to Lord Jesus Christ for mercy. Ephraim and Helena had read news accounts and said prayers and were grateful for her personal reports. Kathy's letters, too, from Heidelberg, sent outrage at the events and reassurance about the family. Ephraim gave thanks that his father and mother were at safely at rest, thanks too that his daughter had seen the light and come to Christ.

Helena was relieved to know Sadie continued healthy, happy and safe in Petersburg where life was normal. As to the velvet-trimmed, beaded, lacy green gown Sister Sadie had so kindly sent in her last parcel, Helena delighted to say that it would not be dismembered to create various articles of clothing, but put to direct use for formal occasions in her role as President's wife. She signed with fondest love, promising to tell her all about the ball for the October opening of the university's first year – nothing so magnificent as in Cincinnati, nor certainly St Petersburg – but a grand event it would be nonetheless, to honor the new students and welcome the Governor, mayor, trustees, regents, councilors, townspeople and their wives to the new university.

That first term the passionate campaigning of Ephraim and his fellow educationalists around the Territory had resulted in an enrollment of sixty-nine students. With University Hall not yet ready, on a clear blue-sky day in early October 1882 the University of Dakota's classes opened in Clay County Court House in Vermillion's Main Street with Ephraim, Brown and an assistant the only teaching staff. As President, Ephraim also maintained the university's records, correspondence and its budding library and ordered textbooks for the students to purchase.

The crowning joy of this first academic year in Vermillion came in June 1883 with the opening ceremony for University Hall. Six-year-old Frieda Epstein, in a new white dress, led a cortege of twenty children strewing daisies and pink roses to carpet the path to the hall. Top-hatted dignitaries including Governor Ordway and a beaming Thomas Kettering followed. Then, straight, dignified and shining with pride came President Ephraim M Epstein. Academic rules required him to wear the robe of his most recent degree, pale blue hooded with deep green, connoting medicine. For Ephraim the reminder of his former vocation did not now conjure the pain of loss but richness of learning.

In due solemnity – and with a smile – he led his double row of first year students. Their seats were reserved at the front of an audience of hundreds who cheered and applauded the inaugural speeches. *Veritas*, Truth: the theme of Ephraim's oratory rang with his fervor. 'You and I, these young people, all of us here today are part of America's destiny. This university, this Territory is part of the greatest of all experiments in establishing a just country, with Truth, freedom and opportunities for all!'

This spirit carried on into the champagne reception where Ephraim was rewarded with fulsome praise by the Governor, who took time to jovially reminisce about their relief work together during Yankton's blizzards. Governor Ordway was flush with new victory: earlier in the month, after bitter political battles and underhanded maneuvering, he had succeeded in moving the Territory's capital from Yankton to Bismarck, an upstart town 450 miles north where new railway rights had developed. For Ephraim this was of little matter, except as an indicator of the dismaying wheeling and dealing that nearly always accompanied land, money and ambition. New powers were at force in Dakota as its economy developed and statehood came in sight. Privately, Kettering reassured Ephraim that the trustees had secured new loans and funding for the university's expansion, and new benefactors had emerged, keen for the prestige of association with such an honorable cause.

Hovering around the Governor was a cluster of Dakota's key people, and Ephraim made sure to exchange pleasantries with each, performing introductions to any of the trustees not yet known to them. Members of the press were guests at this great occasion too, and Ephraim invited men from *The Bismarck Tribune*, *Sioux Falls Argus*, *Fargo Forum*, and *Yankton Daily Press* to come on a personal tour of University Hall. In a final flourish of courtesy, he and Helena led them across the campus and down the new-built street to the presidential residence. The newspapermen glanced over the five bedrooms and wide oak-plank upstairs hallway, admired the front parlor and Mrs Epstein's piano, lingered in the President's office and even briefly sat at the long Board table to see the colored glass of the windows to best advantage. *The Tribune* promised to photograph President's House to add to the story of the Territory's coming of age with its own university.

University business followed the next day. The Board of Trustees was joined by five additional faces around the highly polished meeting table. They were members of the Board of Regents, nominally from Bismarck, the new capital, actually from counties across the Territory. Kettering introduced them – a railroad magnate, a mine owner, a physician, a farmer, a newspaper editor, a banker. Ephraim had met several through the Freemasons.

Founding President Epstein welcomed the newcomers to the first full academic year's session of the university Board. 'How right and proper it is that good men appreciate learning. You value the immeasurable import of education for the benefit of Dakota, our future agriculturalists, entrepreneurs, preachers and educators,' he gestured in turn toward each representative of these needs of the growing territory and then included the bankers, saying, 'And our financiers, who, along with the Lord, make all this possible.' In the first order of business he praised Kettering and outlined the progress of the university to date, then projected student intake and plans for adding natural sciences to the curriculum.

The agenda moved to financial reports. Acting Treasurer Joseph Brown summarized the accounts, and as the newcomers pored over them questions began. How had this sum been acquired? How had that amount been allocated? Who had authorized these expenditures? Calm, sandy-haired Brown had answers for them all. The topic moved to anticipated future costs and to fund-raising. Ephraim sat back during all this, benignly overseeing the conduct of business. His role – the academic establishment, development and probity of the university – had been impeccably achieved. This had been recognized and praised before the Board had moved along to business. He spoke again when future plans were the topic, naming projects dear to his heart – among these, a school of medicine.

In high summer corn is ready to pick, and corn on the cob at its peak of perfection was Ephraim's favorite American food. Joseph found him in his vegetable patch at the back of the house on North Yale Street under the wide blue sky, schooling Frieda in the discreet peeling-back of the wrapper of green leaves to see if the kernels were plump and blond and ready.

'Corn tonight, Joseph! How is yours coming along?' He let Frieda check another ear, stopping her before she picked it. 'Not yet! Run tell Mama it's corn tonight. We'll pick it when the pot is boiling.' She scampered off and he began to extol the prairie soil, 'So rich, so fertile – the corn practically grows itself in this heat. Those were years I don't regret, you know Joseph, when I was a farmhand. Then and now it brings me to thank the Lord for his goodness.' Joseph nodded agreement and reached over to pull a weed from a row of bush beans as Ephraim expanded, 'His goodness to me and my family, and to the blessings showered on Dakota Territory and our place in it, yours and mine.'

'Ephraim,' Joseph interrupted, his ruddy face strained. 'There are difficulties.'

'What?' the effusiveness slowed. 'What difficulties?'

'Turnstall and Bervan.'

'The bankers,' Ephraim identified a trustee and one of the regents. 'They're not mooting a change of treasurer! And they came to you directly instead of me! I will defend your – '

Joseph shook his head, but then said, 'Yes, they want a professional financial man as university treasurer.'

'One of their men no doubt.'

'No doubt.'

'This is ridiculous. I will not allow it. Does Kettering know? These carpetbaggers are riding on our coattails. There are three original founders, they'll fight it. Or – ' Ephraim noticed that Joseph did not join in his outrage. He interrupted himself, speaking gently to his friend – 'Do you wish to step down in any case? It has been so much extra work for you, along with the teaching.'

'I don't know. But it's not that.' He hesitated, looking at Ephraim and then away. In the distance, afternoon cumulus clouds towered over the mysterious bump in the prairie called Spirit Mound. 'They want you to step down as President.'

Ephraim startled, bewildered. He considered the words. Step down as President. His stomach lurched and at the same time his hackles rose. 'I don't understand.'

'Nor do I. Something about the Board of Regents.' He continued to avoid Ephraim's eyes.

'Does Kettering know?'

Kettering was in Washington, DC. When he returned Ephraim and Joseph urgently informed him of the troubling challenge and called for a private meeting. At the Board table it was instantly clear that Kettering already knew.

'This is outrageous!' said Ephraim. 'As if something is amiss!'

'Amiss?' said Kettering mildly. 'Surely not. As written, the Board of Regents approve the trustees and the university executive. They have found a splendid President in John Wesley Simonds.'

'Mr Kettering, I am President of the University.' Ephraim managed to keep his voice low and steady, containing his fury. 'Where is it written?'

'Ah, well, Founding President! An excellent one, indeed! Just as I knew you would be,' Kettering hurried on through the smile on his lips, 'It is in the Act of Education 1862. We are now established as a public body. In fact, I have good news! President Simonds is not able to come west to take up his post until after the new year, so I am sure you will be delighted to know that the regents have allowed that you shall stay on as Acting President. And continue to live in this fine – ' Kettering looked around the room '– this very handsome President's House.'

'You sanction this… this implication that I am not…?' Ephraim could not bring himself to speak further. He was beyond anger, completely winded by the blow.

'No implications, Ephraim. Heavens!' Kettering was at last discomfited enough by the situation to take a handkerchief from his inner pocket and mop his perspiring forehead. 'The regents are completely impressed with you, a brilliant teacher, excellent scholar! Such a following! They simply want their man in place to make everything watertight. You know up in Brookings the Agriculture College is trying to steal the march on us? It all comes down to finance, and influence. If the university is to grow the regents say we need these new men to have a hand in the making of the institution. To pick up where we, and our Founding President, began,' he bowed slightly toward Ephraim. 'With absolutely no hard feelings over this inevitable step.'

'I know they want a new man to be Treasurer,' said Joseph, 'I accept that.'

'But not through any suggestion of ineptitude!' insisted Ephraim.

'Well, that is very good of you, Joseph, very percipient,' said Kettering smoothly. Joseph's face flushed as he faced Kettering. 'I have no stomach for influence. We have done our part in the struggle and glory of founding this institution. I am content to teach and assist...' he hesitated over the title, 'Dr Epstein.'

Kettering nodded and addressed Ephraim with earnest new energy, 'Of course the regents are convinced you must remain as Head of Liberal Arts.'

'Thomas Kettering,' Ephraim thundered... and halted. He looked at the balding, smug pepper pot with whom he had worked so hard. A man he trusted. A man who had put his faith and trust in Ephraim. 'I will not resign.'

Kettering raised his eyebrows and nodded. 'I am sorry.' He rose from the table and they went to the door. Kettering extended his hand to Ephraim who looked him in the face and shook hands firmly, gritting his teeth against his outrage, determined to scrutinize every paragraph and amendment of the Education Act 1862.

Forced out. Ephraim vowed to Joseph he would fight this, all the way. Did they not know the scriptures that Jesus quoted to the chief priests and elders? 'The stone that the builders rejected has became the cornerstone.'

33

THE STONE REJECTED BY THE BUILDERS
Vermillion, Dakota 1883-85

The second academic year of the new university progressed, a bittersweet time for Ephraim. Though soured, he came to accept that the Board of Regents would have its way; a codicil to an amendment to the Education Act was buried in business pushed through under Governor Ordway in his first Bismarck legislature. The regents would install their own influential carpetbaggers from the East, men who had no particular pride in Dakota or the West. Men given favors in exchange for favors who could in turn curry more favors. It was political chicanery, in light of the prospect of statehood. The Board of Regents needed Republicans in place – unfortunately.

Ephraim certainly could not regret that the institution was flourishing and his imprint was on every aspect of its success. The first year's intake had re-enrolled and a new cohort of students had more than doubled the student body. The curriculum had expanded to include natural sciences, headed by a man named Culver from Wisconsin. University Hall bustled with energy and purpose. But each day through the first term of 1883 as he crossed the threshold of his office, Acting President Epstein had been acutely aware of the gleaming brass door knob under his hand, the oaken solidity of the door, the spaciousness of his room and the adequacy of the shelves he had caused to be built. When the rays of the declining sun shone through the central window, its green and rose glass cast tints on the patterned carpet, and the faceted circle the children called the jewel glowed amber. All this he would be losing. Ephraim and Helena – and all six trustees – had been particularly proud of the house's details. Truly, they had agreed, worthy of a university's presidential seat

'I have seen all the works that are done under the sun; and, behold all is vanity and vexation of the spirit.' Biblical words helped: continuing to live here was a daily moral scourge Ephraim put to spiritual use, drawing on both Old Testament and New. 'Lay not up for yourself treasures upon earth where moth and rust doth corrupt... for where your treasure is, there will your heart be also.' After all, what did he truly value – the title, the honors, the expensive house? Of course not. Helena and the children mattered most, and *Veritas*: inspiring young minds. And Lord God Almighty, Father, Son and Spirit. So, come spring 1884 he endured the arrival of the new President, Simonds. He gave up the humiliating title of Acting President and the family moved to a newly built professorial house further down North Yale Street, next door to Joseph Brown. It had three bedrooms, a study, front and back parlor and was handsomely constructed, but not on the fine scale of the presidential residence he passed every day on his way to University Hall. The new man was qualified and decent enough, conscious of the awkwardness, and they managed to avoid each other as much as possible. Head of Liberal Arts, very much still the teacher, valued by staff and trustees and beloved by his students, Ephraim turned to the Lord more and more. Helena did all she could on the domestic front to soften her husband's pain and anguish. She loathed Kettering, and saw him as a snake, shedding one skin, slithering in a new one. She chose not to tell Sadie of this fall in fortune, crowding her letters with Vermillion doings, weather, filtered university anecdotes and family events.

Now it was August and in the stifling heat Helena's groan sounded through the house. A baby was arriving. Though muffled, in this smaller house Helena's birthing agony reached through all the rooms. Ephraim had led his daughters to his study to read the day's lessons. Even the youngest, three-year-old Zelda, knew to stay quiet for prayers and lessons. Suitably, the Old Testament was Jeremiah: 'Before I formed thee in the belly I knew thee; and before thou camest forth out of the womb I sanctified thee.'

The sound of labor intensifying meant it was time to have Frieda take the young ones over to the Browns where they would stay until the baby came. At seven his eldest was familiar with the pattern. Mrs Brown would take care of Frieda, Julia and Zelda just as Helena had cared for the Browns' youngsters when their mother was confined.

After hours more alone in his study Ephraim lifted his head to the squall of the newborn. Hallelujah! Relief and joy broke through him: a strong and healthy baby! He hurried up the stairs, knocked and entered – how was his dear Helena? She smiled wearily at him, her fair hair mussed against the pillow, that smile of happiness and accomplishment, tremulous with the effort and the pain. Dear God, dear God, he loved her so. What she went through for him. A nod from Dr Davis indicated all was well and he leaned over to kiss her brow. The birthing had been helped by chloroform – so much kinder, praise God.

Ephraim took the small wrapped bundle in his arms. 'And we shall call – '

'Her,' said Dr Davis, 'a fine girl.'

'Naomi,' said Helena.

'Your favorite book of the Old Testament.' Ephraim agreed as he examined the perfect morsel of humanity, deep down finding he was glad she was not a boy, for there could never be another William. 'Naomi: she was strong and clever, and inspired loyalty. Although she had difficult times.'

'Pleasant, her name means pleasant,' Helena smiled, taking back her baby girl.

'Amen.' Ephraim kissed Helena again. What good stock she was, what fine children she bore. And he, a man of fifty-five, still fathering them! And feeding, clothing and sheltering them.

At the Browns, Joseph congratulated Ephraim heartily, shaking his hand at the doorway, leading him inside, inquiring for the mother's well-being.

'A blessing that the house will fit another one in,' Ephraim joked, accepting the coffee and cake Joseph's wife put before him. 'I hope they have behaved themselves,' he said, hearing his girls at play, and received assurance that they had. Mrs Brown went to gather them, promising to keep secret the surprise of whether they had a baby brother or sister.

In the quiet of the porch as twilight gathered Joseph cleared his throat and said, 'There is something I have to tell you, and I am sorry it comes at this happy time.' Joseph's tone and expression duplicated his demeanor of last summer's awful revelation. Dread filled Ephraim even before the next words. 'They think the housing of the founding president was irregular.'

'Irregular? What do they mean?'

'I don't know. Treasurer Bervan has asked me to prepare an affidavit.'

'Affidavit!' Ephraim bellowed. 'The six founding trustees agreed everything. There was nothing done wrong!'

Joseph nodded. Both men considered what might be meant by this. None of the other housing was questioned, nor the Hall. None of the expenses of the classrooms. Nor the other teaching staff. Joseph had a month in which to prepare this affidavit – to which, the two of them agreed, there was nothing to add or change. The dubious regents already knew and had access to everything. Angry and perplexed, they had no one in power to turn to for support since Kettering had proved himself a Judas. Joseph agreed to keep this situation to himself; Ephraim did not want Helena worrying at the moment of nursing a newborn and recovering her strength.

He returned with his girls to the family now expanded by one. The joy and cooing was balm to his heart, and the sight of Helena, who had had time to sleep and to feed the baby. That night uneasiness took hold. He sat late in his office, shirt sleeves rolled as relief from the August heat, thinking through the early days of planning, ideas and organization. He turned up the flame of the kerosene lamp to page through folders of letters and minutes from those times. Everything was fully set out, everything in order. What could be irregular about anything to do with the presidential residence?

The month of affidavit preparation passed and the 1884 academic year began with yet another increased flock of students. Ephraim taught with more love and passion than ever, his internal ire imbuing every lesson with *Veritas*, Truth. He poured his fire into sermons, too, preaching more now since he no longer had the duties of President, returning to his earlier practice of using his Hebrew and Greek, adding his own *The Key to the Construction of the Tabernacle* as a text. He still did not confide the ripple of doubt about the presidential house to Helena. He and Joseph tiptoed round each other as no further word of irregularities was heard. The snow flurries of late autumn began and Ephraim continued to brood on the situation. To have an accusation of irregularity under his leadership. How could Joseph or any of the trustees have done anything in the least bit questionable? Or, unknowingly, unwittingly, had he himself spoken or ordered something untoward? He searched his soul. He had always acted in the university's highest, best interests. He prayed and read his Bible. His old pains and burps returned. His nights were broken by dream snatches: the pediment of Andover Seminary, the cupolas of University Hall, the lecture theater of his medical school, the jeweled pointer of the scroll in synagogue – a long time since he had thought of that. Familiar things, but out of place. Helena finally remarked upon his restless sleep and he told her some fragments of dreams.

'That sounds odd,' Helena said, straightening the bedcover, finishing their moment of privacy before descending to the breakfast table and family life.

'Yes,' he agreed, still not confessing the cause.

She went to her husband and took his hands in hers, kissed them and looked into his face. He was tired, his skin lined, eyes shadow-smudged. 'Take it to the Lord. This too shall pass.'

When the semi-annual full Board meeting approached he decided to tell her there was some niggling over the presidential house, so that it should not come as a shock to her. 'They have Joseph's affidavit, it's a mere formality, nothing to worry about,' he said with confidence he did not feel.

But there was everything to worry about. The Board of Regents said the presidential house had incurred significant debts. Ephraim called on his fellow founders, reminding them to look at the papers laid out on the long table, 'We decided together, look, the signature of every trustee is on every university plan.' The trustees nodded agreement, but a regent pointed out that only Dr Epstein's and Mr Brown's signatures were on the accounts for the presidential house. And, already duly noted, Joseph Brown had resigned as Treasurer. This was suggestive of something, the regents intimated. Further investigation would continue. Ephraim appealed to Kettering for defense and got only evasiveness. Joseph remained shrunken and miserable, unable or unwilling to fight. Ephraim, by contrast, rose and thundered with pulpit rhetoric. As he did so the sharp familiar chest pain seized him as never before – he would not, could not pause, but forced himself onward through the piercing agony. Before the initially cool and dubious, then startled and finally indignant eyes of the Board of Regents, he called on God Almighty as witness to his character.

After the Board meeting, sickened with anger but determined to battle, Ephraim had to tell his wife that his probity was being questioned. Distressed and protective, Helena knelt to pray with him. Ephraim opened with the fiery lament of the old prophet Jeremiah. 'I hear so many disparaging me… Denounce him! Let us denounce him!'

Rumors circulated, arousing doubts and suspicion among incomers, outrage and support among Ephraim's trusted friends. The first winter blizzard struck. Innuendos brewed and newspapers re-ran photographs of the grand details of President's House, with editorials of varied intensity depending on the politics of the paper. It was the house's colored glass that did it, commissioned and imported from Chicago. The Boardroom had a panoply of colored glass even more splendid than University Hall, and a Venetian mirror over the hearth. Showy glass in the presidential office, too. Nothing in Yankton or Bismarck had anything like this. At the time of planning, Kettering had insisted it takes money to make money. In those early days he had pointed out to Ephraim the efficacy of this policy, how it helped to attract wealthy, astute trustees.

Several rounds of reports and meetings drove Ephraim into an internal rage of injustice. The doubt was about him and only him. Not Joseph, nor Kettering nor any other founding trustee, only Ephraim. Further objections to Ephraim Epstein's propriety arose over his profession of faith. He preached too often from his book, with its convoluted Euclidian proof of the mathematics of the tabernacle. As for the Bible, he insisted on reading in Hebrew or Greek, and then interpreting in his own words, instead of an acknowledged translation. Just as in Tiffin, Ohio, the university could not afford to be associated with such controversial religious views. Truth and freedom were all very well and good, hinted the regents, but there were unwritten rules meant to have been 'understood' by a President, even by a Head of Department.

In public Ephraim managed to keep his stern, calm presence. In the Baptist pulpit he roared. At home, however, he plunged into despair. After his teaching and business of the day as the issue dragged on he strode home and went directly to his study. There he prayed on his knees, or when not praying paced. It happened to the prophet Jeremiah, it was happening to him now. 'Friends are watching for me to stumble... we can prevail against him and take our revenge on him.' The idea that he was guilty of something, of feathering his nest, of miss-spending trustee funds, ate at Ephraim – how could this be? Yet somehow there always lurked a splinter of guilt. He must have done something wrong. On his knees he begged for forgiveness from the Lord, absolution from the Son of God. Whatever the wrong was, he did not know. There was nothing he could apologize for, admit or explain. The anguish was unbearable.

Helena brought food on a tray to his door. At her knock and her voice he would open to take it. But three hours later when he emerged to do necessary work or to try to sleep she would find the tray barely touched. He grew gaunt, endured his old pains. She wanted Ephraim to protest at the machinations, so far from the earnest, honest, aspiring days of the start of the university. Kettering to her now was a writhing, twisting boa constrictor killing Ephraim in his coils, and the regents were vultures gouging his flesh. But Ephraim was shut up in himself and with his God. She tried to keep the children quiet so as not to disturb Papa, and for the same reason curtailed her piano lessons. This too was a hardship: they needed the money she earned, for a reduction in salary had come with Ephraim's reduction of post.

After three awful months, early in 1885, Ephraim called Helena into his study. 'I am going to resign,' he said without preamble.

'Why?' she cried out. 'They have accused you of this... whatever it is. You've done nothing wrong!'

'No. I have done nothing wrong.'

Silence fell between them. Her long white housekeeping apron showed smudges from the gingerbread which she and the children had been baking.

'You must continue. You founded the university. It is your university.'

'They do not want me anymore.' He sat down wearily on the chair next to her.

'You have done everything, given your all.'

'But now they want – I don't know what they want. Yes-men. Republicans. Their own kind.'

'You are one of their own, better than any of them. As much as Kettering or Turnstall or Bervan or...' then her mind fell on Kettering, on Governor Ordway and his capital cronies. And then she said the thing he meant – 'It's your name, isn't it. Epstein. Our Jewish name.'

'They are philistines.'

'You are Christian. More Christian by a thousand miles than any one of them. Than all of them put together.'

'By God, I have done nothing wrong!' The words burst from him in passion. He banged his fist into his palm. 'There is nothing irregular in anything I have done!'

'What will we do?' Helena said, immediately regretting she had let the thought escape into words.

'My babies, my children!' Suddenly he shook with a great sob. 'My babies. What have they done to us?' he held his head in his hands, sobbing harshly, a man's unfamiliar grating tears, wracked from his depths.

She moved closer to press his grizzled head against her, and he circled his arms about her hips. She said nothing, just stroked his hair as he quieted, then started to hum a hymn they had come to love. 'Amazing grace! How sweet the sound...'

'I'm sorry,' he said into her skirts. 'I have failed you.' She hushed him. 'So many moves, uprooting you every time. It is true, I am the wandering Jew.'

'Ephraim,' she said in a gentle scold. The babble of baby Naomi reached them. 'Whither thou goest, I shall go,' she quoted the Book of Ruth, then hesitantly confirmed his unspoken intention. 'You will not stay on here...'

He raised his head. 'Damnation, no! The territory of Dakota can rot in hell.'

She flinched. 'Ohio,' she said, settling things matter-of-factly. He went back to the chair at his desk as she continued. 'You can write to Andover and they will find you a pastoral post. I wouldn't be sad to get out of the West.'

'Helena – you never said – '

'Shsh now, whither thou goest...' She resumed efficiency, reaching both hands behind her back to re-tie the apron strings. 'And think, we'd be closer to William and Selda. It would be nice to be able to visit their graves.' Her face down-turned in concentration, he heard a wistful note emerge.

'Ohio,' Ephraim said uncertainly.

PART 5: THE GLEANER

34

RESURRECTION
Bethany, West Virginia 1885

The farewell speeches in Vermillion in June had been generous, praising Ephraim's scholarship, his teaching gift, his zeal in recruiting academics and students. But the ceremony was perfunctory, with an underlying odor of bitterness. Here was a man hard-done by, supported by his loyal friends; here was a man well-got-rid of, to the relief of thrusting powers. Ephraim rose above the moment, buoyed with vindication: ahead lay a secure and satisfying destination. The publication of his *The Key to the Construction of the Tabernacle* in 1881 had resulted in a lively correspondence from many quarters. No fan was more enthusiastic and like-minded than the president of Bethany College in West Virginia. Ephraim's mere mention, in one of their exchanges, that he was leaving Dakota brought an offer of a professorship at this small, well-established college.

En route to re-settling, the Epstein family planned to stop for a month of respite with the Greyers. There would be plenty of catching-up to do – besides accounts of life in the raw Territory, Helena and Ephraim had departed from Ohio with one child, and now they had four. Naomi was too little to share in the excitement – or the anxiety – but whatever trepidation Helena felt about starting their new life she made the prospect of the east a great adventure for eight-year-old Frieda, and for Julia and Zelda at five and three. She promised them the joys of many Ohio cousins, a grandmama and grandfather, and even a funny, wise old Russian uncle.

Uncle Jacob was one of Ephraim's first ports of call in Cincinnati, initially alone, when he freely poured out his rancor over the Dakota university treatment. Jacob had always seemed old to Ephraim and now in his eighties he had grown wiry and more wrinkled; paler, too, a consequence of anchoring himself in Ohio. But he was still vital, mischievous, mysterious and still the same good listener. The guttural Brisker Russian of their old home city helped Ephraim give full voice to his hurt and anger. Jacob heard out his nephew until the storming passed and responded with his shrewd, sage shrug. It said *Such is life*, and Ephraim, spleen vented, met him with a wry smile.

'How are the mighty fallen. Ah, Ephraim, you were slain in high places,' Jacob quoted the Prophets, shaking his head in sympathy.

'Amen,' Ephraim responded, feeling in his heart the words of Saint Paul: 'I have fought the good fight, I have finished the race, I have kept the faith.'

'But the weapons of war have not perished! You are going to be Herr Professor again, this is good. And you have four children! You are on the way to out-doing your parents, maybe?'

Ephraim laughed and said he wasn't half way there yet. He embarked on a brief, fond character sketch of each child: Frieda, perceptive and quick, Julia sunny, Zelda determined not to be overlooked and Naomi, almost walking. He promised Jacob the torment of a Suwanee whistle concert by the children the next week.

Being back in Ohio was not so difficult as Ephraim had feared. Though anti-Darwin attitudes still prevailed in some circles he was a welcome guest preacher at his old Baptist church, and the Presbyterian and Methodist too. It was good to talk medicine again with the Doctors Greyer, father and son, to see the familiar reference books lining their shelves, clinical journals lying about. The scientist in Ephraim could not resist browsing the German and French publications for European developments, and he seized on the *Journal of the American Medical Association*, new since his time in practice. He was particularly absorbed in one article when he looked up to catch Helena's father observing him from the other wing chair in the study.

'Is that the piece discussing alkaloids?'

'Indeed. So that's the name they've given to active principles. Remarkable progress! They've succeeded in isolating the alkaloid of monkshood, calling it…' he glanced at the page again, 'aconitine. I cherish the day when all plant remedies are reduced to their active principles. Then we will know exactly what we are administering.'

'Mmm. But it can be risky, these alkaloids are powerful. After all morphine is an alkaloid of the opium poppy,' he said blandly. 'In general, I prefer to give tincture of opium to relieve pain.'

Was his father-in-law deliberately tormenting him? Ephraim gazed quietly at Dr Greyer. Morphine, the killer of his son. Morphine, the perfidious friend of delicate ladies, the degrading addiction of sleazy physicians. Morphine, the ultimate drug for dying patients. Ephraim said only, 'There is risk in all medicines.'

'I left that journal there hoping you'd pick it up,' said Dr Greyer, and Ephraim knew, then, that this was a deliberate challenge. 'There's a fellow, Shaller, here in Cincinnati taking this alkaloidal medicine further, would you like to – ' he was cut short by Ephraim's icy stare.

'You know I cannot.'

His father-in-law shifted in his seat impatiently. 'Time has passed. You are so gifted a physician. I thought you might be ready.' He left space for response but Ephraim withdrew into memory even as he closed the journal and shook his head.

Early in their visit Helena had the children gather gold and pink zinnias from her parents' garden and, with Ephraim, all the family visited the cemetery where the two little markers stood side by side. Several times she went back to sit and commune with her darlings, to remember the innocent years when she was young and untried. On the day before their departure Ephraim went alone to the graves. He squatted by William's white stone, leaning to trace his fingers in the indentation of the letters. So awful, his death, so unreal, so unjust. Even with four children he still had a black hole where William should be. A child, a child, its only function in love was to receive it. Where should all this love he held for his son go? Nowhere. For seven years he had lived with emptiness and prayers. 'Such things will always happen – but how terrible for the one who causes them!' said Jesus. Today Ephraim felt bidden. He knelt and opened his hands to heaven, raised his head and with great effort brought the chemist Maxwell to his mind. The man had taken William's death even harder than Ephraim, losing himself in alcohol and morphine, his business sold, family abandoned. They heard he had gone to Portland, Oregon, or perhaps San Francisco. 'How many times do I have to forgive him?' Ephraim asked the Lord as the apostle had. His heart burned – in terror, he realized. There were two people he had to forgive, Maxwell and himself. He did not want the reply, he did not know how to let go of this ache inside him '...to forgive him?' He cried out and buried his face in his hands as the answer reached him: 'Not seven times, but seventy times seven.' The effort hurt but the pain lightened. He remained slumped on his knees in the summer sun in relief, dwelling with the words of Christ. The work of forgiving had begun. He rose with the words of the mourning King David in his mind and bid goodbye: 'I will someday go to where he is, but he can never come back to me.' Sleep well, little son, God bless. He touched the other stone, You too, sweet Selda.

From dry, spare prairie to cradling, green hills, the jolt was as if the Epsteins had been picked up and put down by a tornado. Bethany lay in the northern panhandle of West Virginia not far from Ohio, at the beginning of the Allegheny Mountains. 'He maketh me to lie down in green pastures, He restoreth my soul.' Indeed, as in the comfort of the 23rd Psalm, the tiny town was a place Ephraim could lay down his burden and find new life yet again. The college, founded by the free-thinking Disciples of Christ who believed in no sects, no denominations, was the ideal academic home for his strongly literate and independent style of Christianity and teaching. Ephraim's position, however, paid far less than a territorial university professor's, in fact almost as little as a minister's, with fewer of the privileges a preacher and his family generally received. The house for the Epsteins was a further diminishment. The three older girls crowded into the master bedroom, the marital bed was squeezed into a smaller bedroom and a box room held a crib for the littlest. The single front parlor served as Ephraim's library, crammed with his desk and his many books, side chairs, a settee and the piano as well. The Epstein children did their studies at the dining table in the back parlor, which was also where the family gathered morning and evening for prayer. It was a far cry from the grand days of living in a presidential residence.

Still, they started out happily enough, welcomed warmly by colleagues and reveling in the lush late summer foliage. The house, which fronted directly onto quiet Main Street, looked out from its porch up towards the college spread over a hill, and then to the ridges of higher hills beyond. A large well-planted plot at the back gave them a view down over trees to the valley of Buffalo Creek. Fertile alluvial fields, some stooked, some awaiting harvest, stretched beyond a river that was endearingly tame and narrow after Dakota's mighty Missouri. Ephraim and Helena blessed the professor who had departed this house, for he had sown and tended a thriving vegetable garden. Corn on the cob, green beans, squash and more were coming ripe, even tomatoes. There was plenty to feed the family and enough over to preserve and keep on the pantry shelves for winter. In the woods, blackberries, blueberries and huckleberries were free for the picking, and Ephraim and the older girls were in good time to sow late crops of carrots, parsnip, collards, beets and rutabaga. More than a moral discipline and teaching device, now the kitchen garden and chickens and Helena's domestic skills were a financial necessity.

Despite the deprivations, Bethany began to emerge as a fortuitous move. As in previous academic posts Ephraim taught Greek, Hebrew and Biblical exegesis and the latter was his heart's joy: his own translations of the Old and New Testaments, direct from their ancient languages. He found freedom and support he had missed since the heady days of his break into Christianity and the years at Andover Seminary. The campus itself was a refuge, focusing on a cluster of handsome redbrick gothic-styled buildings, including an imposing four-story turreted clock tower and double-height Commencement Hall. Tucked into a dip of hillside was the old founder's house, a gleaming white-painted mansion. On a further rise stood gothic-trimmed Pendleton Heights, the residence named for the second college president and Ephraim's patron, William K Pendleton. This calm, erudite Christian, with his pale eyes, stern brows, white beard and full mustache, looked the epitome of the Southern gentleman. But in fact his house had been a station for escaping slaves and, when Ephraim asked, Pendleton willingly told him his personal versions of Mrs Stowe's famous novel. In turn, he was eager to hear of the warmth and intelligence Ephraim had found as a seminary student in the bosom of the Stowe family.

By the time the reds and golds of autumn blazed the hillsides President Pendleton and Ephraim were meeting regularly in a mutual seminar. Like Judge Sherman in those very early days, and like Professor Stowe, the older man took a shine to Ephraim, responding to his fierce convictions and deep knowledge, his quick wit and response to life. They re-explored Ephraim's translation of Exodus for his book, its details of the tabernacle's cubits, timber and craftsmanship surely reflecting the universal truth of divine order.

One afternoon as the sun slanted in through the bay window of the President's study, Ephraim felt safe enough to reveal his current fascination: the three names used for God in the first five books of the Bible: Elohim, Yaweh and Adonai. He tested his premise on Pendleton, beginning with a question, 'Why did Moses use the plural form of the Hebrew – Elohim – for the name of God, so that it is, in effect Gods – yet almost always with the singular verb? It's like saying "the Presidents is".'

'Some say Moses was a complete myth,' Pendleton mused.

Ephraim halted, nonplussed. Then he saw a twitch of laughter under the white mustache, and smiled in wry agreement, eager to continue – of course Pendleton followed the latest scholarly Biblical squabbles. 'Yes, yes… whoever or however many wrote the text, or texts, there has to be a reason. I say it lies in the actual language.'

'But surely – '

'The plural Elohim is used in hundreds of places with the singular verb.'

'And what of – ' the President tried again.

'Hundreds! I have gone systematically through all the Old Testament.'

'Plural with singular. Distinctly ungrammatical.' This time Pendleton chose to follow the argument of his fiery professor.

'Exactly! So it has to be intentional!' Ephraim smacked his fist into his palm, then laughed: 'Whatever else may not agree in this disagreeing world, a verb must agree with its noun.'

'Amen to that!' Pendleton laughed, too. 'So your proposition is that this strange repeated error is a message?'

'My first premise,' Ephraim nodded. 'It signifies a plural deity. Christ is embedded in the Hebrew right from the start – and yet the Jews rejected him. But I am still building my edifice.'

'Ah! So, more to come.' Pendleton paused, then spoke sternly. 'I want it published this year.'

Ephraim's hackles rose. It was a repeat of the old authoritarian pattern:

bedazzling a figure who bestowed encouragement, and who then made demands. As in Dakota, as in Tiffin, as when a missionary, as with his father. Or betrayed, as with that devious Kettering. To cover the silence Ephraim bent to pick up a pencil which had fallen to the rug, feeling his ire. He had vowed never, never again, to dance to another's tune. Ready to defend his independence, he faced Pendleton, only to see him gazing out the window into the distance, oblivious to the gap in conversation. 'I would so love to see it published in my time...'

Ephraim heard a dreamy note and realized that his employer was an old man, and frail. This was no order, no threat, just a wish. 'God willing,' he said gently. 'I am in close study on the second of the three Mosaic names. The library here is a splendid resource.' They fell to talking about Hebrew grammars and German Bible scholarship until they bid each other good evening.

That night Ephraim blessed the Lord for his good fortune in both patron and place. With Helena he chose to read the Gospel of John where Christ raised Lazarus from the dead in a village called Bethany. It was a place of resurrection, as was this West Virginia Bethany for Ephraim.

35

STILL FULL OF SAP
Bethany, West Virginia 1885-87

And then winter hit. November alternated between stretches of mild days and assaults of freezing weather until finally the freeze remained and snow began. The family was used to hot summers and harsh winters, but West Virginia's nearly perpetual cloud cover and the mists that clung to hills and rested in ravines created a depleting chill that penetrated to the bones. Neighbors and colleagues said the weather was worse than normal, small comfort when the house proved itself thinly built, drafty, damp and cold.

The middle daughters felt the effect first. Julia came down with a fever and sore throat that turned to a cough and Zelda followed. Once Ephraim ascertained they had no serious condition, he and Helena dosed them with honey in hot water and syrup of squills, administered light mustard plasters, fed them broths and light meals. The girls' hacking night and day kept everyone wakeful and irritable, casting a pall over the Epsteins' first Christmas in Bethany. When school resumed in the new year big sister Frieda came home with stomach ache, vomiting and diarrhea. Within days she was better, but the illness went through the family, first the littler girls, then the baby – which vastly multiplied the laundering for Helena and the hired girl. Even Ephraim caught a touch of it, and a flare-up of his old gastric pain followed. At least he had his Hoffman's Anodyne and carbonated water to ease him through.

Runny noses, earache and repeated coughs continued through that miserable winter, with the most awful time being in the depths of February when both Zelda and Naomi developed croup. For three days Helena and Ephraim helped each other through the rasping inhalations of their 4-year-old and 18-month-old, cuddling and comforting them to ward off crying which could trigger the spasms. They tucked them in their double bed, getting their own sleep as and where they could. The barking coughs of night were worst, when they took turns to sit with child on knee under a sheet tented over a basin of steaming water to soothe the airways. Ephraim felt nearly overwhelmed by tenderness and helplessness when Naomi's head, her blonde baby curls wetly straight, pressed against his chest, when Zelda croaked out her word for throat, her hair damp and cheeks unnaturally red. Tender, helpless and worried, of course – Ephraim could not let go of fear and remorse. What if, what if? Though he knew croup was a typical infantile illness and not usually threatening, he was concerned by their pulse, rapid breathing and temperature – 103 degrees – besides the dreadful cough. Finally he would not trust his own judgment and insisted on calling in the local physician, despite the expense. He had met Dr Richard Caldwell only once at a college event, a pleasant-seeming gentleman. Ephraim was well aware that it was probably a fool's errand. The children would be fine, and his old fears meant the man had to travel from the town of West Liberty through miles of rutted frozen roads.

'I agree, Dr Epstein, it is no more than croup. But so distressing for the little ones – and their parents.' The fair-haired young physician re-fastened his shirt cuffs after examining the children. 'Mrs Epstein, may I have a jug of hot water, a glass and tablespoon, please?' Dr Caldwell turned to his medical bag and extracted a small cork-stopped wooden container and two silver spoons.

As Helena hurried to the kitchen, Ephraim's question about the medication was interrupted when Zelda muttered and tossed restlessly on the bed. He managed only to say, 'I was anticipating turpeth mineral,' as he laid a soothing hand on his daughter's hot head.

'One used to use it. This is much kinder, no vomiting required.' Helena entered and he selected an item from his case. 'Iodized lime. Remarkably effective for croup, I have found.' Ephraim watched him measure two tablespoons of water into the tumbler, then drop in two white tablets.

'Mother, Father, will you kindly divide this between Naomi and Zelda? By spoon. They will find it pleasant enough.' To reassure his medically knowledgeable client he added, 'It is reliably prompt. I gave it to my son just last week. We should see improvement within the hour.'

'Only an hour!' exclaimed Helena. She and Ephraim each bent to a child, urging them to sip.

'But the fever...' Dr Caldwell said, taking the empty glass and turning to his bag again. 'Aconitine.'

'Ah! I read of it just recently. You're for alkaloids, then.' Ephraim watched as the young professional ladled out hot water counting under his breath. When asked, Ephraim confirmed the children's ages and saw the doctor add three granules and stir.

'A teaspoon each. I make the time to be eleven o'clock,' said Dr Caldwell checking his watch as he stood over the sickbed observing Helena and Ephraim give the medicine. 'Ten or fifteen minutes and we repeat.'

Helena smoothed Naomi's hair and her bedcovers, then offered the doctor a coffee and went to brew it while the two men stayed with the children. For the moment they were quiet, and Ephraim glanced around the room, seeing it as a stranger might: the marriage bed, cheerful in its quilt of patchwork squares, jammed next to the single bedside table, Helena's walnut-framed mirror on the wall, her hair brush and ornaments on the narrow shelf beneath. Wind rattled the window and the muslin curtain stirred.

'So you are of the eclectic school of medicine?' said Ephraim, straightening the sheet under Zelda's chin, seeing his little girl's bright glazed eyes follow his movements.

'Of no particular school. I will take whatever medicaments are effective, safe and pleasant in use — eclectic American plants sometimes, the recent alkaloidals, the regular old Galenic medicines. May I ask – '

But just then Naomi was racked with a gasping, croaking cough and Ephraim bent to lift her to himself. Helena came in to take over, saying the coffee was ready, and they gave the second doses before the men went downstairs.

In the kitchen by the heat of the stove Ephraim served slices of Helena's apple crumb cake still warm from cooking. The young man's mustache was as yellow as his hair, and he wore his chin clean-shaven. He liked Dr Caldwell, felt a sense of confidence and trust, despite their difference in years. 'It has been a long journey in the cold, I am grateful for your trouble. You will stay to eat with us, I hope.'

'Five miles? Sometimes I go twenty or thirty, not easy in this mountain country.' He smiled and praised the cake and accepted the offer.

Helena added dumplings to yesterday's stew in honor of their visitor and opened peaches preserved from their own little orchard. Frieda and Julia, when they came home from school, were delighted at the unexpected treat. Upstairs Zelda and Naomi slept peacefully, breathing and pulse regular. Helena was impressed and, not only as mother, but as physician's daughter and wife – once upon a time – she wished to know more about this rapid successful treatment. Between Ephraim and herself she avoided talk of all medical subjects, a sore spot best left alone. But here at the dinner table she could ask.

'What is an alkaloid, Dr Caldwell? They certainly seem to work.'

After a glance at Ephraim, whose nod meant he should proceed, the young doctor launched into an answer. 'An alkaloid is an active principle of a medicinal plant.' He noticed that Frieda was listening and addressed her, 'You know that many medicines are made from plants?'

'Like… peppermint?' said Frieda, thinking of her recent tummy ache medicine.

'Good. Peppermint's active principle is a volatile oil, but it is still a good example for explaining. Think about making up a peppermint tisane. You strip the leaves, dry them carefully, pour on boiling water, cover it for ten minutes and then sip it. Or for a tincture, which a doctor can keep on his shelf or put in his bag ready to use, you soak the leaves in alcohol for two weeks, press them and there's your tincture. Good for your tummy pains.

'But! You know how gardens grow – say, carrots.' His followers indicated they did indeed. 'You know that some plants grow vigorous and healthy, and some are thin and weedy. And some get ripe before others. And some grow strong in the middle of the row and some straggle at the ends. And after they are harvested, some get withered, and some stay fresh. Well, when you macerate a pound of, say, peppermint, how do you know what you are getting? Weak peppermint, strong peppermint? What is in the medicine?

'But when you isolate the active principle – that is the part of the plant that specifically treats the problem – then you know what you have.' He turned to Helena, 'It is particularly the very toxic, but very useful, plants whose active principles are alkaloids. Aconitine, for instance, which brought down the little ones' fever, is from monkshood. Yellow jasmine, which grows in some warmer spots here, is another example – potentially poisonous, but an excellent pain killer. Now we can use its pure, measured active principle, the alkaloid gelseminine.' He sat back, smiling, 'When you can isolate the active principle, then there is less guessing. And we doctors prefer less guessing.'

'Thank you, Dr Caldwell – for the lesson and the children's health!' Helena responded. Like Ephraim, she felt at ease with the young physician.

'Do people have active principles? Do I have one?' asked Frieda.

'Yes!' said her father, smiling. 'The spirit of the Lord is your active principle.' And he followed with Amen, which all round the table echoed.

By the time Dr Caldwell was ready to leave, Ephraim hoped he and Helena had found new friends among these West Virginia hills, and they gladly accepted the invitation to call upon the Caldwell family when the roads cleared. In the front parlor, as they settled the bill, the young man hesitated and then said, 'If I might ask, Dr Epstein... you took your medical degree at Columbia? And you have chosen academia?' Ephraim nodded warily. Dr Caldwell paused, expecting an answer. When none came he continued, 'A pity, this region has need of good physicians.' Still Ephraim made no response, so he hurried on, 'Ah, well, our loss. Lighting minds is an admirable vocation.'

'Indeed, a calling.' Ephraim gestured toward his overflowing bookcases. 'But, of medicine...' now it was his turn to hesitate. No, he would not reveal the tragedy that haunted him. 'Speaking of medicine, I have great respect for your use of alkaloids. I think – I hope! – they are the future of medicine. Myself, I was of the regular school of physicians, though never comfortable with heroic therapeutics. At the other extreme, I presume you do not hold with homeopathy?'

'At least it does not make patients suffer,' said Dr Caldwell, and cut short Ephraim's frown by continuing, 'but it does not make scientific sense.'

'Indeed! We are of the same inclination.' Ephraim beamed. 'Thank you so much for today, such a dramatic improvement! I dare say that you would approve a cod liver oil regime for the little ones as they recover, to strengthen the constitution?'

'Folk wisdom of the eclectic school, sir, and I heartily approve. For the whole family, I suggest?' He laughed at the face Ephraim made and added, 'The real tonic you need is a change of season.'

Fortunately for all the family spring comes to West Virginia earlier than in Dakota or even Ohio. In March the last crusts of snow melted and day by day Ephraim on his way to lecture diverted his uphill walk for the pleasure of the shy trillium pushing its three green leaves, then its bud, then three-petaled white flower above the dead brown leaves of the woodland floor. One day he found clumps of violets in such abundance that he picked a bouquet for Helena, harking back to that happy moment when she agreed to be his wife. The children glanced at their Mama and Papa curiously when he presented the violets, as for a moment Ephraim and Helena were in a different world, smiling into each other's eyes, the Song of Solomon in their hearts: My sweetheart, my bride is a secret garden, a walled garden, a private spring.

Soon white dogwood blossom and the vivid pink of redbud trees bloomed on bare boughs in the forest underlayer. Veils of green covered the trees, the family's ailments abated and the earth became warm enough to plant the vegetable garden. Along with mists and rain and mud the sweet balm of spring eased in.

The change of weather was welcome for other reasons, too. Helena had already taken on as many piano students as Bethany offered. With improved travel conditions she found pupils in West Liberty who had their own pianos, and others she tutored in German, including Dr Caldwell and his wife, Elizabeth, whose friendship became a great boon. With two boys conveniently close in age to the Epstein middle girls the five miles soon seemed no distance at all, and their households became mutually welcoming, be it the small Epstein or the large Caldwell home. Besides quilting (Helena and Elizabeth) and informed conversation (the men) the families shared outings to streams and special glens, to vertiginous climbs and glorious views. Not yet a year here, Ephraim and Helena relaxed into the sense of settling in.

Ephraim too did extra tutoring, and as his intriguing background and insights became known he became guest preacher in West Liberty and further afield, in Wellsburg ten miles northwest via the winding Bethany Pike. But he still held most dear the Baptist denomination for its practice of mature baptism by total immersion, and to reach this congregation he had to travel the best part of a day south to Wheeling, where he also preached. Until recently the state's capital, Wheeling was where he met his brothers in the region's Masonic lodge. These ventures – for both Ephraim and Helena, who sometimes accompanied him – highlighted the weaknesses of their cozy backwater. The college was the major force in a town with little else but a few service stores. In Bethany, even in West Liberty, there was no newspaper, no industry, no bustle of political business, no hospital, no German club, no concert hall.

However, with a growing family and a satisfying environment, sophisticated stimulation was not a driving need for Ephraim. He took advantage of his calm retreat to throw himself into his study of the names of God. He had already analyzed the plural/singular paradox of Elohim. Now he moved onto the second step in his scholarly argument: the four letters spelling out the sacred name as given to Moses by God himself. In Hebrew it was IVHV, which scholars pronounced Yaweh and Christians pronounced Jehovah and Jews superstitiously would not pronounce at all.

The King James Bible and most others translated the four letters of God's name to English as 'I am that I am', strong and enigmatic. But, again using grammar, Ephraim went back to basics: Hebrew has no word for 'to be' or 'am.' But it does have a future tense, so he determined that the correct translation is: 'I shall become that I shall become.'

There came the day, with grammars and Bible concordances spread around him, that Ephraim felt the thrill of victory. He could confidently say that true worship for Jew and Christian was for the God of Becoming: God in essence ever becoming what the creatures he made need him to become. Including Himself in human form, Jesus the Christ. Now he was free to analyze the third name, Adonai, Lord.

The year turned amid writing, teaching and preaching, amid cultivating, cleaning and cooking, amid morning and evening prayers around the family table, letters to and from Cincinnati, St Petersburg, Heidelberg. Summer brought the thrill of a visit to Ohio. The children loved the adventure by horse and carriage alongside the Ohio River and across to Steubenville, the bustle of its railroad station, the rocking rhythm of the steam train ride to Cincinnati. Ephraim and Helena too relished their spell of citified pleasures.

Come Christmastime the household was deep in Helena's German traditions. For weeks she had been baking gingerbread hearts, gingerbread boys and girls, and set the children decorating them with icing sugar. The rich smell of spice cake and yeast-bread filled the house. With Frieda, Julia,

Zelda and two-year-old Naomi, Ephraim tramped through the woods to find a fir tree, wielding his ax with skill he'd acquired long ago in New Jersey. In Vienna, when he was Jewish, he had seen decorated trees but Christmas at the Greyers' house had introduced him to the whole warm ceremony of fetching the tree, installing it, preparing the decorations and the joy of lighting the candles.

That first December long ago in Cincinnati Ephraim and Sadie had told Helena how the Epstein family celebrated Chanukah. Though the Jewish festival of lights was based on history and the northern German tradition muddled up Christianity with pagan folklore, the two celebrations had in common the deepest faith of all – the miracle of light in darkness. On her fifth Christmas Ephraim told his eldest the story of Chanukah and now for all the children it was a tradition of Christmas day. Along with prayers and readings from the Gospels of the story of the son of God born in a stable, they heard about the candelabrum and the oil for one day which lasted for eight in the Temple in Jerusalem. Jesus would have known this story too, Ephraim made sure they understood. Chanukah gambling for small coins, as Ephraim had done with his sisters when he was growing up, he no longer approved of. But now, as then, there were presents for each person – bright mittens and scarf, rag dolls, embroidered handkerchiefs, paper and pencils. Helena always gave her husband a book, for no gift could delight him more. There was plenty of singing round the piano and, more recently added to tradition, Ephraim's dramatic reading of *T'was the Night before Christmas*.

Housebound by a blizzard soon into the new year of 1887, Ephraim tried to raise the family's spirits by looking forward a repeat of last summer's visit to their cousins in Ohio.

'Oh, I don't know, I hope the cousins will come to us this summer,' said Helena as she sat sewing by the stove. 'They'll see waterfalls and streams and mountains like they've never seen before.'

'They'll get to have the long train ride,' said Frieda with a pout of disappointment.

'Can we have a picnic down by the creek? Can we climb up to the top of Old Baldy?' asked Julia.

'Certainly, some time soon we must introduce them to the joys of West-by-God-Virginia,' Ephraim said, quoting the fond phrase fellow citizens used of their home state. But at the same time he cast his wife a quizzical look, knowing how she had enjoyed last year's trip.

'You can guess the true reason for not traveling this summer,' Helena said that evening in the quiet of their bedroom.

In an instant Ephraim wrapped her in his arms. 'Liebchen! When? How long have you…'

'It will be July, I think.' She pulled back a bit to search his face, 'You are truly happy? Another mouth to feed...'

'Dear one, you bring me such joy. A father again! I will be fifty-eight this March!' He held her tight once more and tears welled in his eyes. 'Still bearing fruit when I am old, still green and full of sap,' he echoed the phrase from the psalm with wonder.

The joy was even more in July when Helena gave birth to a son. A son, a boy! No child could ever be William again, but – to have a male child! They chose the name Leo, because he looked a fine, brave, healthy baby, and Uncle Jacob's middle name was Leon. If further reason were needed, as a preacher Ephraim liked the forthright evangelist Mark, whose symbol is the lion. To be the father of four girls and a boy, how rich, how proud he felt.

'Abba! Abba.' The child's voice calling for Daddy in the night came to him clear and strong. Ephraim jerked awake, lay there on the pillow with eyes staring wide open into the dark. Daddy, Daddy: Jesus's own name for his Father. He listened to the room – some noise by baby Leo, perhaps? From the cradle came an infant snuffle and silence. Helena slept peacefully, her breathing regular and soft beside him. His left knee ached, a touch of arthritis that came and went, sometimes in one knee, sometimes the other, or an ankle. The child's voice, as if in this very room, was still alive in his head. He felt an incredible urge to say the Lord's prayer, the Savior's own words, his instructions on how to pray. He slipped out from under the covers and knelt, flinching when the bones of his knee took his weight. The carpet was thin, the autumn air cool through his nightshirt. He clasped his hands, checked that Helena slept on, and closed his eyes to address his God. 'Our Father in heaven – Abba – give us this day...'

After Amen no other thoughts or words came to him, and though wide awake, he slid back under the covers and lay listening to the sleeping house. So simple: daily food, forgiveness of wrongdoing, deliverance from evil ways. This is the kingdom of heaven.

When he woke, all was clear. Ephraim understood his God-given duty to return to medicine. William, William, William – was this a message from the beloved boy? Had he called in forgiveness or chastisement or a re-birth out of the birth of a boy child? Somehow a miracle of trust had occurred. Ephraim saw that he had let his own doubts stand in the way of God's will, arrogant again, and now he was humbled by a child. He had only to trust in the Lord and all would be well. Yet he was terrified, how could he dare to practice again? Beyond this, he did not know if he was capable; so much had happened in medicine since 1878. He struggled between faith and fear, and between conscience and pride, for Helena was a further worry. He was a fool, a coward, he'd run away from medicine and forced these wandering years on his loyal, loving wife. After all her sacrifice, could she forgive a turn-around?

He took his turmoil up the hill to Pendleton, and this too was an issue of loyalty, for the wise educator had rescued Ephraim from Dakota. He had shown faith in Ephraim and surely it was ingratitude to seek another path. The older man heard Ephraim out – his fears and guilt and doubts – and they prayed together, then sat again in the book-lined room by the fire.

'You know that I am leaving Bethany,' said Pendleton. Ephraim did; health failing, he had been made President Emeritus and soon another would be confirmed as head of the college. 'I do so want to see your Mosaic names of God to completion. Such scholarship, it needs to be published.'

Ephraim hung his head, 'It is my earnest desire, my oath under God, to finish the work.' In silence, he meditated on the current state of his researches and felt the pain of the two equally strong forces pulling at him: proclaiming the truth of Christ, answering the call of the Lord to medicine. 'I am now analyzing Adonai. If the Jews read Hebrew correctly – which they prefer not to – then they have been praying to Milord, son of God, far before Jesus actually came. Christ himself argues the point with the Pharisees using Psalm 110. And then there's Psalm 2.'

'Ah, yes: Thou art my Son,' said Pendleton, by now familiar with his protégé's favorite texts. 'I hope you intend your work for wide readership, Christians as well as Jews. Your God of Becoming interpretation is an immense truth for both.'

'Amen.' The quiet rested on Ephraim. 'So you advise me not to proceed to medicine. You are right. I am too old, I have been away from it too long. And I have this flaw – of doubt in myself.'

Pendleton looked at him and cocked his head. 'Doubt. Perhaps an advantage, Dr Epstein, to have humility.' He acknowledged Ephraim's rueful smile. 'You will indeed have to refresh your knowledge, but for you that will be no problem. Your professional confidence, however, is another matter. I see it will take time.' Again, Ephraim nodded ruefully. 'I have a proposal that may satisfy us both. It is in my gift this parting year to appoint a Bethany scholar of honorary degree. I want that person to be you – to continue your names of God analysis with both Jewish and Christian implications... and continue some teaching and – when licensed – to be consultant physician to the college. Would that suit?'

That night, in a quiet marital exchange Helena brushed away Ephraim's apologies for the years of wandering and bolstered his belief in his ability to learn. Next day they sent for the medical books he had left with Dr Greyer, apologizing for the inconvenience of their nine years' storage. In West Liberty, Dr and Mrs Caldwell delighted in welcoming Dr Epstein to the medical community. Within a month Ephraim had applied to the state of West Virginia for his medical license.

36

WHITHER THOU GOEST
West Virginia 1888-92

Ephraim's faith in himself as a physician returned gradually, supported by his faith in God and by the modest nature of his practice. He saw only the few Bethany students and staff who fell ill, only the local people to relieve Dr Caldwell. As a professor he still taught Greek and Hebrew, and he worked hard on his names of God thesis. Of course there was an enormous amount of medical catching up to do; he subscribed to a clutch of journals and plunged into Dr Caldwell's library of recent issues. He delved in Dr Greyer's library on summer visits in 1888 and 1889 and absorbed information from conferences at Cincinnati University Hospital. The ill health of humankind continued as ever: tumors and gunshot wounds, epilepsy and syphilis, pneumonia and cirrhosis, scarlet fever and ulcers, tuberculosis... for many conditions treatment was much the same as he'd used before. However there were advances, too. His old enemy from Monastir and Pola remained a scourge, but at least smallpox vaccination was becoming more accepted by the public. Yellow fever still broke out in port cities, but the search for its microbes was narrowing. Childbirth, as always, presented risks, but Ephraim was pleased to read that puerperal fever was less common, and to see poor old Semmelweis praised, his theories of cleanliness taking hold. Lister's carbolic acid solution now swabbed most surgical procedures, and a recent article said a solution of iodine had proved a good antiseptic.

These developments happened in the far off world of cities and university hospitals, rewarding to read about, but of little direct relation to Ephraim's backwater. He had only a small consulting room in the college infirmary and, with no pharmacy in or near Bethany, had to travel down to Wheeling to purchase materia medica: senna, ginger, coltsfoot, quinine, alcohol and more. And, of course, morphine. The situation of having to make his own remedies was another factor in allowing Ephraim to trust himself as a physician. In addition, he sent to Dr Caldwell's source in Philadelphia for the tablets of medicinal alkaloids which the younger man so trusted.

Helena had resumed the familiar role of doctor's wife and was glad to see her husband grow in confidence. She continued to take on piano and German students, freer now as Leo emerged from infancy. They needed the income, for the scholarship bursary barely covered Ephraim's drop in teaching hours, and his earnings from medical practice were small. Just as the new way of life settled into a regular pattern an upheaval announced itself, and late in 1889 Helena gave birth to a son.

A second boy! Ephraim held the tiny bundle of life and stroked the petal-soft cheek, marking the contrast with his own sixty-year-old hand. He looked over to Helena, exhausted yet also calm and radiant in their bed. He lived with her as the blonde, pink-cheeked girl he married, but now he saw her afresh: his Helena was all the more beautiful in the blossoming maturity of true womanhood. Together they chose the name George, a sturdy Hanoverian German name from Helena's side of the family; equitable, Ephraim considered, as Leo's name was from the Epstein side.

With four girls and two boys life was full, purposeful and joyful – except for the very crowded house and the cost of six children's endlessly outgrown clothes and shoes. At least, as they grew up, the older girls helped more and more around the house. But increasingly the very fact of the girls growing up was a worry, which came to a head in 1891 one summer over evening prayers.

'In the beginning God created the heaven and the earth,' Ephraim began the reading in his sonorous tones. This bountiful mid-summer day the satisfaction of seeing their late-season sowing sprout had inspired him to choose Genesis in praise of the marvel of creation. For Ephraim the Bible was a story that told tales, and it was also the truth. It conveyed truths within, below, above, between the words, if the soul would hear. Morning and evening he tended the souls of his family around the dining table when they sat to read scripture and to hear Papa's prayers and say their own. He checked the faces of his loved ones, each intent on their pages as he ended the passage, '...And God saw that it was good.'

He nodded towards Naomi, her mass of fair curls reminding him of his mother and that lock of her hair he had carried so long, now tucked away with her memorial card. He still felt their deep connection despite the separations of time, distance, faiths and death. His six-year old continued from her Bible, 'And God said, Let the earth bring forth grass, the herb yee...?' She looked up and he nodded, encouraging her. '...yielding seed, and the fruit tree yielding,' her piping voice strengthened with confidence and she hurried on, 'fruit after his kind, whose seed is its seed, upon the earth: and it was so. And the earth...'

Ephraim frowned. 'Not seed is its seed! Seed is in itself. Frieda, continue. With less haste than your sister.'

'And God said, Let the earth bring forth grass,' his eldest began.

Helena shifted in her chair, startled, and Ephraim barked, 'Frieda, you are not following – again!'

At her daughter's panicked, guilty face Helena reached over and tapped the correct verse on the page of Frieda's Bible. 'Sorry, Papa. And the earth brought forth' – but he stopped her.

'You have missed your turn. We are at verse twelve. Our Lord wants an attentive mind.' He looked around the table at fully alert faces. 'Zelda, you go on.'

And so it went around the table, with no one foolish enough to lose track again, and even Frieda given another chance, until Mama read the final verse of the chapter, 'And God saw everything that he had made, and, behold, it was very good...'

That night Helena laid the problem before Ephraim. Their bedroom walls were thin, and the girls asleep – perhaps – in the next room, so she kept her voice low as they turned down their quilt. 'What are we going to do about Frieda?'

'Frieda? So inattentive, not what we expect. Is she unwell, perhaps? Or her hearing, that earache she had?' He frowned, distracted by concern for a similarly ill student in the infirmary.

'She's fine.' She stopped brushing her hair and turned to him. 'The absent-mindedness – her head is full of many things. She is growing up! No, I meant school, she has a good mind and she will be a good teacher.' She turned back to her vanity mirror and hairbrush, watching his face in the reflection. He was listening fully, and she launched her proposal. 'She goes to Normal School next year.'

'Yes. How did she suddenly get to be fourteen?' He sat on the edge of the bed as their thoughts went back to Cincinnati and the house of Frieda's birth that had been so happy, and then so unhappy. And then that vision of her strewing flowers in her white dress in Dakota.

'I've been thinking – she could lodge with the Caldwells during the week. She could help with their children and be useful in the house.'

'She doesn't need to live out,' Ephraim protested. 'It's only five miles and back to West Liberty. Besides, you need her here.'

'Liebchen.' Helena, now in her white nightgown, sat next to Ephraim. 'I think it's time she sees a bit of the world.'

'West Liberty... not much more worldly than Bethany,' he said wryly.

'But some. And she is ready for it.'

Reluctantly – how could they let go of their first nestling? – Ephraim agreed to explore with their friends the possibility of taking in a young and helpful lodger. He got a response that turned everything upside down: Dr Caldwell was moving to Wheeling, and he gave Dr Epstein first refusal on taking over his West Liberty practice, house included.

Ephraim walked the five miles back deep in thought – a full time country practice, did he want this? Half of him leapt at the chance, the other half shrank; he had a good, calm life with freedom to think, write and teach, as well as practice medicine. Though stretched, their income was sufficient and the family was content.

But still: to be a physician fully, not hiding away. The words of Jesus to his disciples admonished him: 'Neither do men light a candle, and put it under a bushel, but on a candlestick; and it giveth light unto all.' Dare he? He would be physician to the whole area between Wellsburg and Wheeling... his gut clutched at a stab of the old anguish: a physician who caused his own son's death. He strode on through the late afternoon. The ground was wet with earlier rain, and mist lay low in ravines along the way. Droplets clung to leaf-tips, a late low sun broke through turning them to tiny bright crystals.

Being alone in the midst of nature always brought Ephraim closer to God. He would have liked to stop and think and pray, but he had to reach home by nightfall. The rhythm of walking provoked perspective. What did he really want all his life? So many moves, always moving on. So many bullheaded people, opposing what surely they had to see was right. When they wouldn't see, or worse, when they wouldn't let him see things his own way, then he had moved: from Russia to America, from Jewish to Christian, from doctor to minister to professor. There was no rest, no satisfaction for long. Because eventually things went wrong, or else he himself needed to change and grow; he was always seeking God and Truth, and testing the limits he met. Or God was testing him. And now in Bethany he had a God-given respite of peace and fulfillment. On what basis could he want to give this up? No, it was wrong; other physicians would bid for Dr Caldwell's practice, younger men more suited to it than a sixty-two-year-old.

As he emerged from the covered bridge over Buffalo Creek and began to mount the hill towards home a startling self-knowledge struck him: it's not enough – I am bored. I need this challenge, I need more than peace and safety. And then it dawned on him that, probably because he no longer fought an opposition, he wished – oh irony – to be in his grandfather's position, with prestige and wealth. He had two sons and four daughters to clothe and feed and educate, and the most wonderful supportive wife who deserved liberation from work and worry. He would never be, never want to be, like the domineering Zayde. But he had an obligation to be a better provider to his family and, as Christ said, to let his light shine.

'Back to full-time medical practice,' Helena wrote to Sadie in March 1892, once more describing a new post for her father, giving a new address, depicting a new home: '...a big, warm clapboard house, a fine kitchen garden, a stable – we hardly know what to do with ourselves. Leo and George have a nursery together, Frieda and Julia share a bedroom. Zelda pouted when she was demoted, as she felt, from being a big girl with them to sharing with Naomi. ('But she's only seven, Mama!') To sweeten things I let her have first choice of rooms. Very pleased I am too, to have a spare bedroom, a place to leave my Singer sewing machine and materials to hand. It was a nuisance putting it away every time in order to set dinner on the table. Your father's consulting room and study suits him to a T – quite like the Cincinnati arrangement. We have the luxury of a good parlor where I've put the piano and your family portrait (showing off my pretty sister to my students). And then there's a dining room and a family parlor. Everything is hunky-dory, as they say.'

There was no need to go to lengths about their surroundings, for West Liberty was very much like Bethany. True, the Allegheny foothills were somewhat further off and there was no river in sight (but plenty of streams) and they saw more fields and fewer woods than from their other home, as the land was gentler. But still, there were many hills and even, as before, above the town a college. The brick buildings of West Liberty State Normal School sprawled on the hilltop in the view up from their back yard. The town was a bit bigger than Bethany, with two churches, a post office and general store and a feed store, but the layout was less condensed, so in some ways West Liberty felt more rural. They dearly missed the Caldwell family, but over the years the Epsteins had secured many friendships in both towns, and living on Van Meter Way – named for an early Dutch settler – they saw plenty of activity, for the physician's house was on West Liberty's main road, and the main road was the route between Bethany and Wheeling.

Sadie's reply from St Petersburg was long in coming. Ephraim and Helena began to worry, for recent news of Russia was bad. But at last it arrived, in the form of a parcel. Sister Sadie still annually indulged the American family in a miniature treasure trove, giving them a glimpse of her life. Every time, when the brown wrapping was folded back, the scent lingering from Sadie's own household – lavender, orris root, bergamot – seemed to bring her right into Helena's presence.

Out of relief, Helena did not wait for Ephraim and the younger children before opening the box, as they usually did. Only Frieda happened to be at home. This time beneath the inner tissue paper lay a light purple-colored gown. Before the letter was read or other items heeded, Helena let her eldest reverently lift and hold it against herself. She had reached the age where notions of grand balls, waltzes and hand-kissing gentlemen danced in her head.

'Oh, Mama! It's lilac. Look at this lace, and the draping!'

'So the front of the skirt is slim, all the interest at the back,' Helena commented. 'Gone are the days of the full crinoline,' she sighed. 'Though it hardly uses less fabric, I am glad to say for our purposes.' She was calculating that she could get two dresses for her girls from this one, and a shirtwaist, let alone make use of the trimmings. 'However does she keep up? A new style must be on the way, if she is letting this go to us.'

Frieda swooped about the parlor humming. 'Do we have to cut it down? Can't I wear it myself? There is a dance at the end of the first year...'

'It is far too sophisticated – that waist!' Helena took back the dress and now she held it to herself, for a moment imagining her friend and sister in it. The pale purple was an hourglass shape against the white apron that protected her green print dress. 'Just think of the corset it needs. Your father will be in a complete fret about Sister Sadie's health, wearing that silhouette.'

'Is there anything else?' Julia's voice surprised them from the doorway. And there was, indeed: a chemise for Helena embroidered by Sadie, a lacy crocheted collar, and a length of wool which would make breeches for Leo, now that he was old enough to wear them. Finally, as usual, a Petersburg newspaper for Papa and bright paper figures of animals and flowers for the children to cut out and paste in their commonplace books.

All must be well, Helena thought, but a glance at the letter made her decide to wait to read it until Ephraim was back. When they digested it, they had each other for comfort. Sister Sadie and the whole Zur Hosen family were fine, but her shock in the aftermath of the Czar's revised, even more repressive May Laws of 1891 was clear:

'For ten thousand, possibly twenty thousand, Jews to suddenly, on no notice at all, have to leave Moscow! To have to go back to live within the Pale, in places like Brest-Litovsk, Kiev and Warsaw. With the horrible madness of attacks against Jews to fear, let alone leaving everything behind after years of successful businesses, social lives, position. And already the laws kept all but a few per cent of Jewish boys from attending university. We hear that Moscow is like a ghost city. Here in Petersburg we still have some Jewish friends with leave to stay on. We pray for the Jews so cruelly uprooted.'

Between the lines Ephraim read, at last, genuine gratitude from his lost-found-and-lost-again daughter. She truly forgave him for his Christianity despite the years of abandonment; she blessed him for bringing her to the light of Christ. Within himself he still was not sure, had hers been a conversion of convenience? To win his favor or to guarantee a husband or to save herself from persecution... he would never know. Sarah-Sadie was after all her mother's daughter, and Rachel... Rachel had always been duplicitous. The streak of bitter feeling caught him unawares. The antidote was to kneel with his true and beloved helpmeet and pray for friend, sister, daughter and her family. And for Jews under the Czar. He yet again beseeched the Lord to wake all Jews to Jesus as the Christ.

Being a physician in full time country practice felt inevitable and right to Ephraim. He kept his own horse – a steadfast brown mare they called Sheba – and buggy in the stable behind the house, with a hired man who came in to help tend her and muck out. Determined to do his best, Dr Epstein traveled widely to patients to build his clientele. As time went by he often took one of the children on the long rural rides, for company and to talk with them to improve their minds, to give them insights into the lives a doctor is privy to, the pain and struggles that much of the world did not see. The horse and buggy also allowed easier travel to Wheeling where Ephraim continued to purchase materials to make up many of his own medicaments, for West Liberty, like Bethany, had no pharmacy. The trips became more frequent, often with Helena or one of the older girls: to call on the Caldwells, catch up with concerts, lectures and shopping, and to keep up with the Baptists and Freemasons.

There was only one regret: a curtailment of time to prepare *The Mosaic Names of God* for publication. The thesis itself was done – and had earned him the promised Master of Arts degree. The commencement exercises had been a touching and fitting conclusion to his time at Bethany. But the manuscript required changes before sending it out into the world. Ephraim's long hours meant that too often he found himself asleep over the text, and gradually he worked on it less and less. He wrote a long apologetic letter to Pendleton in his Florida retirement, galled at failing his patron and himself, vowing that someday he would see it published.

This thorn aside, Ephraim entered a rare time of fulfillment, and Psalm 16 became his inner anthem: 'Lord, you alone are my portion and my cup... therefore my heart is glad and my tongue rejoices... you make known to me the path of life.'

As if to bless their new West Liberty life, Helena felt the familiar quickening of pregnancy. Late in 1892, the same year they enrolled their eldest daughter in the education that would provide her a career, they were parents to a new daughter. Seven living children they had now: Ephraim praised and thanked the Lord. He could not help a flare of amazement and pride – once he had feared he was too old for his bride; and here he was, still ardent. Helena turned again to her favorite book of the Bible to name their baby. She was Ruth, after the loyal wife who said, 'whither thou goest, I shall go.'

37

THE LAST CAUSE
West Liberty, West Virginia 1893-95

'It's educational.' said Frieda. 'And I will write a report and present it for school.'

'There's a whole separate Woman's Building, filled with women's work and achievements. Just think...' mused Helena.

'Please can we go on the Ferris Wheel? Pretty please?' begged Zelda.

'The boys will love the entertainments,' Helena said decisively. 'And we can leave Ruth at home with Mother.'

Ephraim had teasingly resisted attending The Chicago World's Fair, but in fact he was eager to go. The whole nation was abuzz with the exposition to celebrate the 400th anniversary of Christopher Columbus' landing in America. What better way of celebration than to show off the newest and best in American society, business and culture. So, in summer 1893, in a variation on their Ohio family visits, the Epsteins settled the baby with the Greyers, added Uncle Jacob to the party and boarded the train for Chicago.

The huge city bustled with foot traffic, horse-drawn wagons, carriages, with elevated passenger railways and cable streetcars, with new tall buildings made of steel and stone. The midwest's thriving center of trade and transportation was better than ever after the dreadful fire twenty years before. Even more amazing was the Exposition spread over 633 acres of reclaimed marshland in the South Side along Lake Michigan. The family planned to stay for two days, but so enchanted were they, so astonished and torn by all there was to see, that they extended to four days. At the center of the fair the White City shimmered: complete with domes, pediments, turrets and pillars, fourteen grand white stucco palaces ranged around a fountain and enormous reflecting pool. The family wandered in and out of the gleaming halls agog at the latest in electricity, machinery, transport, industry, agriculture. They took in lectures on history, displays of livestock, botanicals, meteorites, ostrich skeletons, a woolly mammoth, a diorama of sea lions. They dipped into smaller outlying state pavilions and others that showed ways of life from foreign lands. Among the 8,000 works in the

Palace of Fine Arts they lost Julia and Naomi for a whole worrying hour, and when the lost sheep were found, all rejoiced with a treat of fresh doughnuts and lemon-ginger drink chilled with shaved ice. Even just sitting by the water and watching people was a spectacle. Throughout, to keep the younger ones on best behavior, was the promise for the last day of the zoo, the Ferris Wheel and Buffalo Bill's Wild West Show.

Despite the surging crowds, their visit was an utter success. To end with a flourish, they decided on the viewing balcony over the White City and its waterways. Ephraim and his uncle trailed the others, for Jacob, still bright and lively, still dressed in layers of black, walked with a stick now, and had to take the stairs slowly. The sky was pale twilight as the two men emerged to see the others at the railing taking in the scene.

'A fine family, nephew. You have done very well.'

Ephraim murmured, 'Praise the Lord,' and paused as Jacob rested. Helena, slim and fair, stood in profile, a perfect cameo, and Frieda, also blonde and already her mother's height, twirled her parasol knowing she made a fetching picture. The long, flounced summer dresses of all five females shone luminously white in the dusk, and so did the boys' sailor suits.

'But I have no regrets,' Jacob said. 'Or if I did, they are long gone.'

No regrets about being a bachelor, Ephraim had to assume. 'Shall we sit?' They made their way to a bench at one end of the terrace.

'I am so glad to have seen all this, thank you for bringing me.' Jacob winced as he sat and then waved his walking stick over the view. 'The new world, eh. What would old Columbus have thought? Electricity... a map of America entirely made of pickles!'

'I have to say, seeing that iron-clad ship at the pier, and seeing the Sioux village and the Wild West show, it felt like a review of my life!' joked Ephraim.

'The future, too. You watch out for those bicycles and moving sidewalks and electric streetcars – they could do a person damage! Like me with my knee.' He laughed wryly, 'But of course things happen anyway, it was a horse that did me.'

Suddenly they stood at the sound of gasps, oohs and aahs. The Magic City appeared as darkness fell. One by one the stately buildings were illuminated, and then the grounds, all festooned with thousands of electric lights. Reflected in the waters, it was a glowing fairy-land vision. Soon the night sky came alive with piercing, moving spotlight beams, until finally came the whoosh, bangs and brilliance of fireworks, their adventure's dazzling finale.

One May afternoon in 1894 on a visit to re-stock medical supplies Ephraim decided to look in on a patient of his at Wheeling City Hospital. The impulse had repercussions that would last the rest of his days.

He waited for the consulting physician in a reception room, wilting in the humid spring heat. Children's voices floated a hymn sweetly through the open window and he relaxed into reverie. Being here reminded him of his days in other hospitals when he'd done ward rounds – Cincinnati, Vienna, even back in New York City, trailing along with other medical students. Such changes since then; this hospital, with its cherrywood balustrades, broad corridors and hygienically tiled operating theater met with his full approval. Every room had one or more windows giving light, airiness and sweeping views of the Ohio River. Some things rankled: it was not a research hospital, for there was no university in Wheeling. And Dr Epstein, with his country practice, could not be an attending physician. He could only refer patients here, as he regretfully had to do when Mrs McKinnon's diabetes progressed to requiring the amputation of her foot. The children's chorus, from a wing across the courtyard that was home and school to orphans, concluded the song of Daisy's bicycle-riding suitor and fell silent. A pile of printed matter lay on the table next to him and Ephraim idly picked up a journal he'd never seen before, *The Alkaloidal Clinic*. Within minutes his browsing became riveted attention – this was about alkaloidal medicines, but their use in a new way: the dosimetric method. On he read, gripped.

'Dr Epstein?' The voice startled Ephraim back to the present. He rose and shook hands with a stout, dark-haired professional man. 'Dr Frissell, good afternoon. A remarkable concept!' He gestured to the journal.

'That? Tosh. Another of these crack-pot quack companies.'

'Do you think so?' Ephraim reined in, choosing not to challenge the hospital's medical head. 'It looks reasonable to me – uses alkaloids.'

'Ad hoc by the physician? In tiny doses? It's as ridiculous as homeopathy. Don't say you believe it.'

So Ephraim didn't say, and they went to visit his patient.

But that night he would be seeing his ally in alkaloidal medicine; surely Dr Caldwell would consider the dosimetric method. The young physician had established himself well in Wheeling and frequently attended his private patients at the city hospital. Their families were still close and on this visit, after the monthly Masonic meeting, the two physicians strolled through the balmy evening to the Caldwells' fine house on Chapline Street. The younger man did indeed favor the innovative dosing concept, and went directly to his copies of *The Alkaloidal Clinic*. Not only had he subscribed to the new publication but also he had begun to use alkaloidal granules ordered from the journal's publisher in Chicago.

Ephraim put on his spectacles and flipped through the journals. His colleague disappeared and returned with a pitcher and glasses, refreshment on this spring evening. 'Compared to our other supplier?' Ephraim wanted evidence.

'Very satisfactory. And a chief factor is the method.'

'Yes! This is what strikes me. The difference is the very small doses of an alkaloid, little by little til it shows effect.'

Caldwell poured them each a cool, sweet, spicy sassparilla and sipped. 'Dr Frissell and other regulars just won't have it. They still think the best way is to give a big dose of... whatever it might be... to whack the illness – and the patient! – on the head with it.'

'If the patient survives the treatment, he'll survive the illness,' Ephraim said lifting his sassparilla in an acknowledging toast to Caldwell. 'But this dosing method of Burggraeve's sounds much more efficient – and safe!'

'Convenient, too, I find. Regrettably some – like Dr Frissell – condemn it as homeopathy, because of the little-by-little approach.' The young doctor sighed in frustration. 'It's an unfortunate confusion. Dr Burggraeve studied under Buchheim in Russia, he's a professor of medicine, published. His dosimetric theory is accepted in France.'

'How can Frissell object? Clearly this is not watered-down plants in sugar-pills, it's alkaloids: measured, isolated active principles. It is new, it is progress, a God-send! I, for one, am most eager to try dosimetry.'

'Old school. He lumps it in with patent medicines and their secret recipes, and the charlatans who sell them.'

'Oh, I see. He stands the same on any medical treatment that's not mainstream, I expect.' When Caldwell assented Ephraim added, 'A Republican, no doubt.' That too got agreement; medicine now had a political edge. 'You are not going to challenge him on this?'

Caldwell looked at him askance, his blond hair gleaming in the comfort of the gas-lit parlor. 'In my circumstances that would not be wise. Meanwhile,' he sighed again, 'he can't prevent me using dosimetry on my own patients.'

'But this is what every doctor needs!' Ephraim burst out. 'If every physician in the land used dosimetry, no patient could ever be over-dosed!'

Before the month was out Ephraim wrote to the Abbott Alkaloidal Company for a subscription to their journal and got with it, free, a leather-bound pocket case containing nine vials, each filled with one hundred alkaloidal granules. Among his choices: aconitine for fever, digitalin for heart and circulation, codeine for pain, coughs and intestinal distress, morphine sulphate for pain. A month of using the dosimetric method – how easy to handle, how pleasant for patients, how efficient, how effective! – and Ephraim knew this was a cause he must champion.

His passion drove him to action. He wrote to the editors of the journal: 'never was I so certain of myself as after I became thoroughly acquainted with this method.' He said he had substantiated his positive opinion by reading *Annales de Traitement Dosimetrique*, the French journal that followed the book of the same name by Dr Burggraeve. So strong was his conviction that he said he wished to help to spread news of it. But there was one problem: the name. In the letter he begged forgiveness if he might be so bold as to criticize. Dosimetry, named by Burggraeve, smacked confusingly of homeopathy with its emphasis on small doses. Dr Abbott, by bringing dosimetry into this country, should clarify the facts of the method with a new name. As a linguist and scholar as well as a medical man, Dr Epstein proposed: alkalometry. An American name for an American interpretation, the term alkalometry would avoid the hint of homeopathy, and promote the facts of medicinal alkaloids and measured precision. Ephraim posted the letter with hope and determination: this ethical, scientific form of medication had to be the future of medicine. He would do all he could to make it so.

In her private prayers Helena thanked the Lord for her husband's increased confidence in practice. She knew William, their darling golden William, stood behind his new-found enthusiasm, for in this new medicine Ephraim at last had a way to fight the ghost demon of the tragedy. If the medication had been a tiny dosimetric granule they would have seen it was not quinine by the response – and saved their son's life.

With the children Ephraim was as strict as ever over Bible-reading and morning and evening prayers. He still supervised them in the vegetable patch, insisting they learn the practical, moral and spiritual lessons of cultivating the soil. By now Naomi, Leo and George were the main recruits, for Frieda, at 17, was tied to finishing her teacher training. Julia and Zelda when not at their studies had to help in the house with sewing, cooking, cleaning and supervising their siblings. But as the youngsters hoed, pulled weeds and picked off beetles, they could sense their father's good mood when he hummed hymns with them. Sometimes he even repeated stories from his life before he'd met Mama: working on tightwad Ackerman's farm, his improvements to Judge Sherman's livestock, showing the newly Christian Hebrews in Harrison how to plow. Even tales of the perilous ocean voyage and the glorious sea battle.

He was in just such an agreeable state of mind when Frieda came home from Normal School with her friend Alfred, who had a camera. 'He'll take a photograph of us, Papa. Mama says we can send it to Sister Sadie, won't that be good? He even has a scenery cloth. May we do it?'

'Your mother says that, does she?' Ephraim, sitting with a book in a rocking chair on the back porch, studied his eldest for a moment – a young woman now, the age he was when he had been made to marry. Come autumn she would be teaching a classroom of children. Alfred, ruddy-haired and freckled, hung back uneasily.

'Pretty please? And he wants to do a portrait of me, too.'

'All of us are at home?' Ephraim rose and placed his reading on the chair. They followed him indoors and found Helena, her apron thrown aside, busily wiping rice pudding from Ruth's hands as she told the others to wash their faces and for heaven's sake to put a brush to their hair. Husband and wife exchanged a glance and a smile and Ephraim went to the front parlor where Alfred's camera stood, a wooden box on a tall tripod. The young man hurried to unroll his canvas backdrop and explain where he wanted to place it when Ephraim said, 'No. Stop.' He frowned at the painted scene: a Corinthian column, a park-like row of trees.

He turned back to the kitchen, calling out, 'Mama, put your apron back on. We will have the family portrait in the vegetable garden.'

'For Sister Sadie?' Helena paused in smoothing stray locks into her bun. Frieda too, standing behind her father, was taken aback. In her heart she hoped that a rich, handsome Russian would see the photograph and fall in love with her. It happened to Sister Sadie, and now Shurek, her own cousin, was just a bit older than her, he would have friends. She longed to see the world, and not to be seen in a cabbage patch.

'Indeed for Sister Sadie. We are proud for all of Russia to see the way an honest, hardworking, Christian American family live, are we not?' There could be no opposition to Ephraim's tone of voice. 'We play piano and speak foreign languages, we know our Bible, I am a physician, my daughter will teach. And we grow our own vegetables. It is all part of the American promise.'

And so Alfred took the photograph Dr Epstein wanted, all of them in a row, dressed just as they were. They stood very still for minutes at a time in the sunshine. Ephraim took the right end, cabbages and corn sprouts in the foreground, bean poles in the background. With his wavy white hair and square-bottomed full beard he looked like a neatly groomed Old Testament prophet, slim in his brass-buttoned waistcoat and white shirt. He struck a patriarchal stance with a twinkle of humor, one hand resting atop a hoe handle, the other arm akimbo. He wanted Helena next to him in her long white apron and ruffled shirt-front; she held blond baby Ruth on her hip to prevent her toddling off. Zelda and Julia stood behind, and in front of them Leo, who demanded a hoe like Papa had, and Frieda, apronless because she'd come from school, little George to the other side of her. At the far end – Alfred's idea, to complete the composition – Naomi, right hand on hoe, left hand on hip, echoing her father's pose.

When Alfred brought the photograph to the Epsteins, Ephraim scanned it – yes, his fine brood of seven, his good crops. He approved, and even asked if further copies could be made. He wanted to send one to Joseph Brown, still keeping his head down in Dakota, and one to Benjamin and Susannah in New York – they'd smile to see him, at sixty-five, with his own little ones their grandchildren's ages. One for Kathy in Heidelberg, as well; widowed last year, surely she would be amused and interested to have an image of her American brother and his tribe. Helena would send one to Petersburg, along with the portraits of Frieda and Julia they so desired, posed by the painted classic column, dressed up in gowns Sister Sadie had sent.

He would not say so, but Ephraim hoped the family group somehow would be seen by his brothers, sisters and cousins in Belarus. He wondered if they knew he had returned to Christianity, if they imagined him living a life of gold and freedom in America. The news coming out of Russia and Poland was not good: the Czar was ailing and who knew what would happen to Jews when the Czarevich took the throne. If they were sensible they would come to America now. But they were not sensible because they would not recognize Jesus as the Messiah. He prayed for them. If he urged his family to come would they even open a letter from him? He left their fate in God's hands.

That same autumn of 1894 Dr Epstein's letter to *The Alkaloidal Clinic* was published, to his delight, and a lively correspondence with the editor and founder of the firm ensued. Dr Wallace C Abbott warmly welcomed Ephraim's enthusiasm and even commissioned a translation of whatever French dosimetric item Dr Epstein deemed of interest. However he declined the name 'alkalometry,' though he valued the sentiment. Dr Abbott removed the sting of refusal by granting Dr Epstein permission to use the term in his practice and among his colleagues. Congenial letters continued, and over the months so did paid commissions.

They progressed naturally to the idea of a personal meeting, and Ephraim expressed himself keen to see the changes in Chicago since the World's Fair closed. So in summer 1895 with Cincinnati again the convenient midway point, the family embarked on a journey of rediscovery. Though there had recently been workers' upheavals, political unrest and a national depression, Chicago continued to grow and grow. The South Side exposition site had become an oasis of groomed parkland and home to a new university. In the city's frenetic central Loop a third elevated passenger railway had opened, although there was still no L for the North Side, location of Dr Abbott.

Ephraim left Helena and the big girls shopping in State Street and wove through the hot, crowded streets to board a cable streetcar. Grateful when a young man gave up a seat to his senior, Ephraim settled in for the long ride as they clanged through the madness of traffic. The bustle dwindled by the time he approached his destination, and Ephraim could glimpse spacious side streets with courtyard residential buildings, handsome family houses, brick row houses and greenery. This new Lincoln Square area even had tastefully planned commercial sections. Finding his way to the address he had written to so many times Ephraim sensed a calmness, a tang in the air that could only come from a large body of water, though the great lake's shore was some three miles east.

The Abbott company office was based where it started, in Dr Abbott's own apartment above his pharmacy. Ephraim eagerly rang the bell and at the top of the stairs a smiling Wallace C Abbott extended a handshake. They inspected each other with warm regard: Dr Abbott in his mid-thirties, stocky, round-faced with glinting spectacles and a dark walrus mustache, and Dr Epstein, nearly twice his age, white-haired, vital. The visit began with a tour: the kitchen was Dr Abbott's laboratory, where he had made the dosimetric granules for five years, and it was still his experimental lab.

'But something had to give when sales grew and I took on the journal. You can imagine! I've built a new house for the family nearby, and moved production of the granules to a building around the corner. You'll meet Dr Waugh there later. This is all offices now –' he broke off to introduce Dr Epstein to a young woman at a typewriter – 'accounts, materials, some storage. The journal I put together in here.' They entered what had been a back bedroom, with windows looking onto green backyards of the terraced rows. 'And I am building a library,' he paused, seeing Ephraim's face light up, 'Come see.'

They sat in Dr Abbott's office, its window looking down on the street, and talked of several cases – asthma, typhoid fever, pre-eclampsia – where Dr Epstein had remarkable successes with alkalometry, the term he continued to use.

'You are saying dosimetric alkaloidals can do miracles, it seems!'

Ephraim checked himself, about to launch into exhortations again – he thought for a moment, then gave a laugh. 'Who am I to convince you! You are right, I do sound like a madman. Of course the granules don't cover every situation. And only the Almighty can make a miracle. But I dare say it's criminal for a physician not to use alkalometry.'

Pleased to have a willing audience, Dr Abbott expanded on his ideas for the future; he was getting inquiries from California, New York, London, even India. 'But first we need to persuade all of America. I envision a team going out with the dosimetric message – like missionaries!' Ephraim flinched inwardly at that word: his first years as a professional proselytizing physician, that exciting but difficult time.

The library, so-called, was a disappointment, merely taking up one wall of Abbott's office, smaller than Ephraim's own. Still, he spied some volumes he would have liked to spend time with. Dr Abbott assured him that he planned to grow the library and eventually, when they were successful enough, it would have its own room and be open to researching physicians and chemists.

'Splendid! But no Abbott Alkaloidal medical school?' Ephraim raised the notion tentatively, hoping this visionary did not plan to join the ranks of patented therapies a practitioner could only learn from one source, with its own treatments, texts, schools and diplomas.

'A school has never been my intention,' Dr Abbott frowned, to Ephraim's relief. 'Dosimetry is not a new system of medicine, simply a method of administering medicine.'

Their conversation turned to the new attempts at synthetic alkaloids, then on to their own trainings. Ephraim recalled to Dr Abbott his old mentor from student days as an origin of his support for dosimetric granules. 'Dr Cable, may he rest in peace, from the very start insisted physicians in his training learn to dispense their own medicines – with a pen-knife blade as a powder measurer if need be! And believe me, in Turkey and in the Austrian Navy I sometimes had such a need.'

On they talked, circling back to Ephraim's latest reading in German, French, and British journals. By the time they parted a lifelong friendship was sealed, each man feeling enlarged by the other. Ephraim returned to West Virginia knowing his contributions to *The Alkaloidal Clinic* would always be welcomed. America might be in turmoil over laborers' conditions and fat cats, unions and strikes, the economy could go bust and boom and bust again, pogroms, wars and famine would funnel waves of immigrants to Ellis Island, and through it all humans would fall ill, have accidents, be born, need medications, surgeons and physicians. And medicine would advance.

38

THE GLEANER
West Virginia 1896-99

In his country practice, traveling miles by horse and carriage in all weathers, Ephraim began to feel the toll of West Virginia's misty autumns, snowy winters, cloudy springs and humid summers. Unhappy with the way he tired easily he decided to investigate, and self-diagnosed mild diabetes. Fortunately, with Helena's culinary cooperation, he successfully managed it in the usual way, reducing sugars and fats in his diet. Still, at the end of a day of rounds, he sometimes would come home dog tired and lie on the couch with a newspaper to rest. Helena would come and sit in the room quietly, sewing. Sometimes one of the children crept in and curled up nearby reading, or sat by the end of the couch and stroked his hair. He would doze, the house hushed for Papa.

Nevertheless, Ephraim contributed to *The Alkaloidal Clinic* nearly monthly. He wrote of his own cases, his observations, his ideas and provided translations and summaries from European medical journals. His other correspondence was lively, too – to Andover Seminary on theological matters, to Jewish Melioration Society missionary friends all over the country, and to medical colleagues. *The Mosaic Names of God*, however, remained untouched, but he continued to preach at the Baptist church in Wheeling, and by invitation at churches in Wellsburg, Bethany and West Liberty; his preference for translating the Bible directly from the Hebrew and Greek still impressed congregations.

Then in late November 1898, heralded by the stuttering ring of the telephone recently installed in the Epstein house, a crisis struck. Would the doctor please, please come out? Mr Boynton had collapsed. He had angina pectoris, this was urgent. Though it was a cold, wet day, Ephraim backed Sheba into the carriage traces, tucked a lap robe around himself and set off. He had inherited old Boynton from Dr Caldwell's time, and seen him in sickness and in health; he lived eight miles away, off the hilly road to Bethany.

Ephraim returned in darkness six hours later, jolted into aches and pains and chilled bone-deep. He had treated the collapse with caffeine half hourly, then digitalis and had to wait – albeit by the warmth of Boynton's daughter's stove – to see how the medication took hold. He promised to visit again the next day, and so he did, after making two other calls, despite a sleety rain that gusted into his face all the way home. Old Boynton's progress was not good, and Dr Epstein commenced a course of sparteine with strychnine. A fierce freeze descended the next day, and snow the next, turning the rutted road so perilous Ephraim had to descend and lead the horse on foot. By the seventh day of fighting weather and road, and the patient rallying only to sink again, Ephraim came home in the afternoon so exhausted that he obeyed Helena's insistence that he go to bed. As he sank into warmth and comfort anxiety began to gnaw: he was sixty-nine years old, how much longer could he keep this up? If he could not maintain a country practice, how would he support the family? His thoughts turned to prayer…

Dressed and ready to depart next day Ephraim felt the wind shifting to the north and west, saw the bleak sky and decided not to venture out. He had left medications and instructions with the daughter; another onslaught of vicious weather might put him to bed for days and make him no good for any patient. Instead he settled at his writing desk in the warmth, guilt assuaged by Helena's relief, as the promised blizzard howled. *The great Physician bless you all and yours fraternally* – he put the finishing sentence to his article on pyloric spasms for the *Clinic* when suddenly the searing gastric pain of old tore through his chest.

He gasped and lurched to his medical cabinet to find the treatment he relied on to get him through these familiar attacks. He had not had one in ages. He steadied his hand to measure out Hoffman's Anodyne, and the pain eased. He sat to recover himself, but in minutes it came back. He increasing the dose, and belched – the usual welcome effect. And then the pain returned, forcing a small cry from him. Helena, sensing something wrong, entered just as he finished the entire bottle. Ephraim sat again, his breathing shallow for fear of disturbing the relief, and then he cried out in greater pain.

'My stomach, my gut! The pain!' he gasped, clutching at his chest and abdomen. Helena helped him to the couch as he stifled his groans. He clenched his jaw, clamped his mouth shut, but the tearing, knife-like pains took charge and he lost control. He groaned, cries bursting out. 'It's like a bull-dog dragging at my insides! Lord, help me!'

For two days and two nights Ephraim battled the pains. He tried again and again to suffer in silence, but minutes later as if in vengeance the pain redoubled. Snatches of prayer interjected, and moments of self-examination – was he exaggerating, was he indulging in the pain? No, no, no. He tried to use his mind to master his body, denying the reality of the pains. Tried another new technique, auto-suggestion: 'I am improving, the pains have lessened.' To no avail. The agonizing pains took him over and he groaned, clutched and clawed at himself, begging Helena and Leo to hold him down as he writhed.

Morphine, of course, would stop the agony. Another physician might use it but Ephraim held out. Even in the throes of pain he knew he did not dare to trust the treatment of his own case to his own judgment. He directed Helena to call in Dr Caldwell as consultant.

Worn and worried, Helena felt like rejoicing when she welcomed their friend at the door of the house he had sold them. He stamped off the snow and handed her his muffler, hat and overcoat, heading straight for the bedroom at the sound of Ephraim's groan. He knew, of course, Dr Epstein's history of sporadic attacks and burping remedies; he heard in further detail the differences on this occasion, examined the patient and witnessed for himself the extreme pain.

'I concur. A hypodermic of morphine is advisable,' nodded Dr Caldwell.

'Morphine!' Helena said in alarm.

Ephraim, teeth gritted in pain, nodded, closing his eyes. Blessed relief would come. Dr Caldwell addressed Helena's concern, 'No need to worry. A single dose will give respite, to allow your husband's natural strength to aid his recovery.' He turned to his medical bag to prepare the injection, continuing, 'It is curious, and a positive sign for his health, that pulse, temperature and respiration are normal.'

'Not morphine! Please!' Helena dropped to her knees by Ephraim's bedside. Only now did he open his eyes and turn his head, seeing close-to Helena's anguished face, her welling tears, disheveled hair. He could not stop a grunt of pain emerging. He put his hand over her clasped ones and squeezed them, bearing down, his knuckles and fingers turning white, closing his eyes again. She endured his strength.

When Ephraim's grip slackened Helena turned her appeal to the other physician. Morphine had killed their son. It must not ruin their lives again. 'Please, no. Too many take it, just the once, and then the habit begins. Especially among physicians.' She drew breath, 'And there is always the risk of... of... error.'

Ephraim clutched himself and stifled a sound. He looked at Helena, still kneeling by him, and then to the hovering Dr Caldwell, then to his wife again. Nine trials of labor she had undergone in birthing their children; he would suffer this pain for Helena. He spoke to her, 'Thy will be done. No morphine.'

Dr Caldwell slowly shook his head in disagreement. 'I understand. And I acquiesce... but if this continues another six hours it will break your body and your mind. In that instance, I would say that you are not capable of decision, and will intervene. But, I assure you both, only in extremis.'

And so the case was managed. In fourteen days of piercing pain Ephraim gave way to morphine three times. In between he and Dr Caldwell tried every other painkiller they knew, and all the dosimetric granules relevant to digestion, intestines, spasm and pain, but in vain. The old heroic evacuation remedies produced results, but no relief. A week into the ordeal Ephraim agreed with Dr Caldwell's suggestion to call in a colleague from Wheeling for further confirmation. Experienced in digestive and intestinal conditions, with careful examination Dr Schwin diagnosed diabetic gastrointestinal aggravation and inflammation. Internally he prescribed nothing other than what was already underway, but externally he recommended blistering plasters on the chest and lower spine. For two days these provided pain of another sort which did indeed diminish the internal agonies. But not entirely. Mercifully less frequent, less strong, the pains lingered day and night. In the third week they no longer made Ephraim cry out and contort himself. Gradually the intervals of peace increased until he could sleep a whole two hours at a time, eventually a whole night.

By Christmas Ephraim could shuffle around the house, and though a cloud of gloom blanketed the season, there was also thankfulness. Helena played the piano again and tender, soothing Brahms and Schubert filled the house, along with *Stille Nachte*, *O Tannebaum* and their old favorites *Amazing Grace*, *Pass Me Not* and *O Worship the Lord*. Frieda and Julia battled the weather to visit from their teaching posts and managed to conceal from both Papa and Mama their shock at how thin and fragile their father had become. Helena planned a special surprise, asking each child to select a favorite Gospel story about healing. They recited these on Christmas night, seven from Jesus's many miracles in Matthew, Mark, Luke and John: the healing of the man with the paralyzed hand, Peter's mother-in-law, the deaf-mute, the pool of Bethesda, the many by the Sea of Galilee, the man born blind, the woman who was bleeding ... 'thy faith hath made thee whole.' Ephraim, seeing Helena's pride and their shining, sincere faces in the lamplight nearly broke down in tears. After a prayer of thanksgiving he spoke a psalm from memory, including them all in the sweep of his gaze: 'Blessed is every one that walks in the ways of the Lord, for happy shalt thou be and all shall be well with thee. Thy wife shall be as a fruitful vine upon the walls of thine house, thy children like olive branches round about thy table.'

In the January midst of Ephraim's convalescence a small packet arrived, bound with black ribbon. Opening it with sinking heart, he found a black-bordered card – Uncle Jacob had died, nearly the age of the century. The wise old, funny old shaper of those several main steps in his destiny. Without Jacob would he have been bold enough to go to America, brave enough to cross Europe and the Atlantic, to find his way around New York? And why ever would he have gone to Cincinnati but for Jacob – and there met the love of his life? Gone, now, gone to the bosom of the God of Abraham, the God of Isaac, the God of Jacob. But the incorrigible Jacob Leon Finkelstein had left a sparkle in his wake. In the packet was a lawyer's letter and a black velvet drawstring pouch. Inside, two matched diamonds. Precious jewels at last for his precious, deserving wife.

Another month passed before Ephraim was strong enough to resume his practice, now always taking one of the children or Helena with him to drive Sheba. Bumpy as the journeys were, he usually nodded off on the way home. He hoped and prayed and willed himself to fully recover, but could not avoid the reality of approaching seventy and the equal reality of the need for income. Zelda would soon find work, but now Naomi should start Normal School. Then there would be Leo and George, and Ruth was still only eight. He began to brood. Perhaps they could sell the practice and move to Wheeling, where travel would be easier. Perhaps he could assist Dr Caldwell, or be a locum. Or possibly he could find some employment in Cincinnati at the University Hospital or through the doctors Greyer. He had his wits, but had lost strength. He hated being an old man. He mulled these possibilities, unwilling to share this with Helena until he had no other choice.

On the 17th of March 1899 morning prayers were especially heartfelt, but family festivities for Papa's seventieth birthday would be at supper time. Ephraim saw that Helena had put the day's mail on his desk. He opened the journals first, slitting the brown wrapping with his paper-knife and unrolling the furled flimsy paper. The *Clinic* would have his interpretation from the French journal *Le Concours Medical* on infectious tonsillitis. But it was his habit to wait for the papers to flatten so he did not have to fight curling pages as he read. He rolled the journal in the reverse direction and weighted it under the crystal bowl from Dakota University, given after his first year before the vultures arrived. He'd been standing, but now realized how fatigued he was, and sat to open the next publication, from Columbia University. It would have news of some of his alumni colleagues perhaps. He still hoped they would publish his new piece on alkalometry, but it would not be in this issue. There was a third publication, from the Methodist Union – they'd recently run an article of his on converting Jews; there would be letters printed in response. His eye fell on the envelopes as he reverse-rolled the last journal. Bills, bills, replies to queries, a slim one from Abbott. Containing a banker's draft he hoped. The payment for the translations was a Godsend, and the appreciation by Dr Abbott of his own and Dr Caldwell's campaign for alkalometry was balm to his soul. With good fortune the letter would have the acceptance of his account of his diabetic storm, as he and his colleagues had decided to term the gastrointestinal attack.

He opened the envelope, grunting in satisfaction at finding the banker's draft — Helena had said the coal bill was due. And then as he read the letter his hands began to tremble. He put the letter on the desk and clapped his hands to his lips. Praise God, Lord Jesus, merciful Father. Looking at the letter again he went to the door and called Helena.

'Is something wrong?' she hurried from the back parlor where she had been darning socks as she watched over Naomi helping Leo with his arithmetic. She looked at him with alarm, 'What is it?'

'It was — not now,' he changed his mind. 'I wondered if you would come out for a walk with me later.' Ephraim saw that she was distracted and busy. He wanted to savor this moment, and to please her. He would tell her the news gently, in a pleasant setting.

Puzzled, and relieved that it was not an emergency, she said, 'Fine. Just before supper? We can come back to sauerbraten, torte and celebration.' She smiled, pleased that he wanted to walk out when so often he needed to rest. 'I'll get the girls started on the potatoes and then I can come. Would you like another glass of tea?' He accepted the offer.

The sky was pale lavender shading into twilight blue, with one wisp of orange cloud left from sunset. Ephraim looked for the evening star and pointed to it, a ritual with them, no need for words. She hugged herself to his arm as they walked on beyond the last house on the road and past an empty pasture, its split-rail fence zigging and zagging. Underfoot they negotiated mud ruts and hoof imprints. There were woods ahead where trillium was hiding and violets would soon appear. By day the distant treetops showed the faint blur that meant leafbuds swelling.

'I think it will rain tomorrow,' said Helena. 'I can smell it. Spring is really on its way.'

Where the woods began Ephraim stopped and turned to look back on the town. The foothills of the Alleghenies were a barely visible dark blue line far beyond the houses. He took both Helena's hands in his and chafed them, bent to warm them with his breath, and kissed them, feeling her work-roughened skin.

'How would you feel about moving away from here?'

'Why?' she pulled her hands away, startled. 'Something is wrong. Not the death of old Boynton? You knew you could not save him. Please don't accuse yourself —'

'Not that. I have had the most generous, wonderful, timely offer from Dr Abbott. It would mean living in the city — Chicago.'

'Chicago!'

'A permanent editorial post. He wants me to run the library and contribute articles to the journal. I am saved! We are saved. No more call-outs on freezing nights, no long rides into the districts.'

'The city, a journal... and think of the opportunities for the children! How did this happen?'

'God's own mercy. I had no idea. Praise the Lord.' Ephraim pressed Helena to him as she murmured a thanksgiving. 'What's more, I'm to have a regular column translating foreign medical articles.' He gave a little laugh of wonder, 'You will be amazed at his name for me – from your favorite book of the Bible.'

She pulled back to see the musing smile on Ephraim's face. 'This is the end of our wandering. Yet I am to be known as the Gleaner in Foreign Fields.'

EPILOGUE: RAVENSWOOD

Ephraim M Epstein lived the rest of his life in Ravenswood, Chicago with Helena. Of course his character and the habits of a lifetime did not change: he continued to champion causes both medical and spiritual. In 1903 a streetcar accident damaged his right knee, leaving him not only in debilitating pain and permanent need of a crutch, but also with a quest. 'What the pathological condition of the tissues in and around the knee is would be interesting to know... Sprains are meagerly treated of in text books.' He requested the dissection of both knees after his death, directing that the injured and the normal be photographed, colored and compared in a furtherance of medical knowledge.

In 1907 his *The Mosaic Names of God and What they Denote* was finally published. Within a year a letter from his long-lost younger sister Pauline Wengeroff arrived from Heidelberg with news of the successful publication in Germany of her book *Memoirs of a Grandmother*. Desperate for money she asked Ephraim to help her get it published in the United States. A well-matched opportunity, he set about translating the two volumes from German to English. The Jewish Publication Society came close to accepting the book, but in 1910 they learned who the translator was and dropped the project. They would have nothing to do with the man known nationally in the Jewish community as the notorious missionizing Dr Epstein.

As the upright Christian writer, educator and medical man, Ephraim continued to be a warmly respected member of the editorial staff of *The American Journal of Clinical Medicine* right up to his death in January 1913, in his 85th year.

VERITAS

These *Veritas* notes indicate truths and where I have invented or varied major events in this documentary novel. The main characters are real, and there are also many real historical characters; some characters are completely fictional. I have imagined everyone's personalities, inner emotional responses and action scenes. Dialogue, of course, is invented, though a very few dialogue lines come from Ephraim's writings. Overall the entire 'bones' of the incidents of Ephraim's life come from his article 'Why do I live so long?' published in *The American Journal of Clinical Medicine* in 1908. Further facts come from his other writings, and from research and documents.

In the notes I use the following initials to refer to frequently used sources; these are listed in Acknowledgements and Sources.

EE – Ephraim M Epstein
PEW – Pauline Epstein Wengeroff, his sister
HGE – Helena Greyer Epstein, his second wife
NEW – Naomi Epstein Waddell, his daughter (my grandmother)

PART 1: FROM RUSSIA TO AMERICA
Chapters 1 – 13, 1846 - 1859

CHAPTER 1: AS WAS THE TRADITION, *Belarus 1846*
CHAPTER 2: THE COUSIN-BRIDE, *Belarus 1849*

The Epstein family and homes. Fact: grandfather, father, mother, sisters, friends and daughter names, and the arranged unhappy cousin marriage. Food, studies, the yellow house and apartment also are fact. [EE, PEW] I have had to invent a name for Ephraim's bride, and imagine their conflict. Daughter Sarah's exact birth date invented.

The Haskalah, Jewish Enlightenment movement. The true historical Dr Max Lilienthal, Czar Nicholas's instructions, the impact on Jews, on Brest-Litovsk and on the Epsteins are well-chronicled by PEW.

Uncle Jacob Finkelstein. Factually, Ephraim sailed for America with 'an old uncle' and he mentions him only once later, in regard to Cincinnati [EE]. I have imagined Jacob's name, personality, occupation, involved role and other reappearances.

Publications. True publications available at the time, but I have imagined them into Ephraim's hands: German-Yiddish newspapers with articles from the new world by emigrants, Johnson's dictionary, a book of English poetry by Byron (ideally the adventurous *Childe Harold's Pilgrimage*).

O Lord, you have enticed me. Jeremiah 20:7 (NRSV)

CHAPTER 3: THE PERILOUS JOURNEY BY LAND, *Hamburg 1849*
CHAPTER 4: THE PERILOUS JOURNEY BY SEA, *The Atlantic 1850*

Cecilie and husband. Fact: Ephraim truly had an older, married sister of this name [PEW]. I have invented Lipman, his role and their living in Hamburg.

Mitzvot and minhag. Rules, rites and customs of Jewish life.

The journey. EE says he landed 'at New York early in 1850 after a perilous journey of some weeks over land and a more perilous voyage by sea in a damaged sailing vessel wherein we preserved our lives in a nine-weeks' struggle with waves, hunger and thirst.' The voyage was normally three weeks long, so I invented the urgency and Liverpool stop; however, historically there was a brief threat of British naval aftermath to the 1848-49 revolutions in Europe. Fact: Ephraim Epstein is listed as a passenger on the *Howard* out of Hamburg, arrived in New York 11 March 1850.

O Worship the King. Hymn 433, The New English Hymnal.

Can you pull in leviathan. Job 41:1 (NIV) The encounter with Christians and Ephraim's reaction is completely fictional.

Kashrut. The set of Jewish dietary rules.

Castle Garden. This setting is fact. Ellis Island was not created as New York's immigration depot until 1892.

CHAPTER 5: NEW YORK, NEW YORK, *New York City 1850*
CHAPTER 6: AMAREKA, *New York City 1850*

Tomorrow we find you work. 'I spent but a few short weeks in New York, trying to earn a living' [EE]. I have invented all his job search attempts.

Benjamin Berman. 'In New York I met a playmate of my childhood and early youth who went to France long before I crossed over to the United States, and who a short time before me had arrived here' [EE]. I have invented the name. PEW says the friend's living was crafting wind instruments, a fact I chose to develop. Historically, the Muller workshop in Paris saw major improvements in the clarinet.

Ephraim's recital in Brest in honor of Crown Prince Alexander's marriage. Fact, as stated by EE.

The fort at Brest… every brick stamped with our initial. PEW says the Epstein brick factory supplied millions of bricks for the city ramparts.

Work, a job, at last! 'Though never inured to manual labor… still the ideal nobility of labor was cherished by me ever since in my youth my mind became liberated from the trammels of Talmudic haughtiness which makes its devotee presume himself to be superior to the common laborer' [EE]. Thus we see Ephraim's economic struggle to find work was also an expression of his impatience with his orthodox faith. Making bricks in New York is fictional, as is timing of his desire to be a physician.

Lilienthal. Never mentioned by Ephraim, PEW records his disillusioning meeting with the influential Jewish leader; I've changed her timing to after Ephraim met the boyhood friend. Names of the brothers-in-law are fact [PEW]. Fictionally I have Ephraim trying to impress with his advanced learning: Rabbi Yisrael Salanter was a 19th c breakthrough rabbi who emphasized moral teaching; Ramchal was an 18th c Italian rabbi who wrote a mystical guide to self-improvement.

CHAPTER 7: THE COUNTRY BEYOND, *New Jersey 1850*
CHAPTER 8: I WILL PUT EPHRAIM TO THE YOKE, *New Jersey 1851*

Hackensack. All fact from EE's life account: crossing to New Jersey, being a farm worker and the attitude towards manual labor, learning the English language, time at Squire Ackerman's, learning farm work, moving on for more pay, blind Judge Sherman of the Marine Court, wife and mature Christian daughters, and very kind treatment.

Ephraim is a trained heifer that loves to thresh. Hosea 10:11 (NIV)
And God said unto Moses, I AM THAT I AM. Exodus 3:14 (KJV)
Think not that I am come to destroy. Matthew 5:17 (KJV)

Hebrew, the language the first Christians prayed in. Jesus's common language actually was Aramaic, related to Hebrew.

CHAPTER 9: THE ROAD TO METUCHEN, *New Jersey 1851*
CHAPTER 10: MELIORATION, *New York State 1851-53*

Is he trying to convert you? Conversion cannot have come lightly to Ephraim. I have imagined the readings with Judge Sherman as a way in based on the fact of Ephraim's deeply Jewish background and his strongly inquiring mind. Further ground-laying for change was Ephraim's teenage opposition to his father and the parental restrictions on wider learning [EE, PEW]. Directly EE says only that he attended a Christian meeting-house for the first time 'in the country one Sunday' with his boyhood friend. 'It proved for both of us a turning point in our lives.' [EE]

Behold, I will do a new thing... Isaiah 43:19 (KJV) In the Jewish Bible (Tanakh) Nevi'im is the Old Testament books.of the prophets.

Moses and the prophet Elijah stood on a mountain talking to Jesus. Matthew 17:1-9. This is called the Transfiguration of Christ.

Saul, Saul, why do you... Acts 9:4 (NIV)

American Society for Meliorating the Condition of the Jews. This is a true organization Ephraim was early associated with, though I can only imagine he encountered it at this stage. In a 1908 listing of his missionary service EE states: 'missionary of Society for Melioration etc, 1851-56, summers'. In the 19th c there was a significant movement both in the USA and England to convert Jews to Christianity, along with a belief that Jews were closer to Jesus Christ than were Christians.

A fortnight in their upstate New York camp. There is a gap between Ephraim's baptism in Oswego in 1851 [HGE] and his seminary matriculation 1853. The accounts of EE and PEW conflict, which suggests to me that he spent the missing two years with the society and that he did not reveal his conversion to his family right away. PEW says he had 'a little farm of his own about twelve miles from New York... a new circle of friends,' and that he attended church for lack of other sources of religion and then that the boyhood friend led him to convert. EE says he and the friend became Christians at the same time and 'Friends began to increase,' which I would take as Christian and Melioration Society friends.

Church summer camps existed in New Jersey, so I've put one in Oswego, per the '1851-56 summers' missionary work EE states. Some missionary movements tried to convert Jews in Europe, promising them farm training in America, so I have put the experienced farmhand Ephraim in this setting for the missing years. Susannah and Solomon Levi and Paul Cassell, society director and president, are fictional.

CHAPTER 11: AT ANDOVER, *Massachusetts 1853-56*

Andover Theological Seminary. Upon becoming Christian and gaining friends there was 'no lack of means to pursue an educational career with the ultimate object of graduating as a physician, previous to which however I greatly desired to study Christian theology.' [EE] Andover was the United States' first ever graduate institution and is America's oldest graduate seminary. As sources of subjects, teachers, living expenses, bursary and Ephraim's graduation thesis and ceremony I have copies of Andover Theological Seminary course program and commencement exercises from 1856.

I set my king upon my holy hill... Kiss the son... Psalm 2: 6 and 12. (KJV)

Calvin Stowe. As described Stowe was the main teacher of first year students at Andover; the facts about him are true. EE in a 1908 letter says that he translated a German work for Professor Stowe. I have imagined their closeness.

O my son Absalom... II Samuel 18:33 (KJV) King David's grief over his son who had rebelled to the point of battle; David had ordered Absalom not to be killed, but he was; David's grief nearly ruined the kingdom. In the full listing of commandments apostasy from Judaism to another religion calls for the apostate to be completely cut off from the Jewish community; he is no longer recognized as a living person. The parental response to Ephraim's Christian conversion is imagined based on PEW's account.

Initial diagnosis scarlet fever... intestinal inflammation. The severe illness is fact, as is Dr Howard [EE]. Ephraim describes the doctor as more open to new medical trends than I have fictionalized, but I am using this episode to illustrate the state of medical theory and practice at the start of Ephraim's career. Imaginatively and psychologically I have linked Ephraim's enormous collapse to the semi-fictional utter rejection by his family.

Published barely two years before, the fame of Uncle Tom's Cabin and Harriet Beecher Stowe was sweeping the nation. True. An anecdote says that later, on meeting her, President Lincoln said, 'So you're the little lady who started the war.' Ephraim's knowing Mrs Stowe, sharing Stowe family life and the person of Clara Stowe are all fictional. I have no facts as to Ephraim's exposure to or thoughts on *Uncle Tom's Cabin*, slavery, abolition and the Civil War; he was a lifelong Democrat, according to family lore [NEW].

Letters. Correspondence with Ephraim's wife, daughter and family is fiction.

The Doctrine of Atonement in the Theology of Modern Judaism. Fact, Ephraim's thesis title is given in the seminary's Order of Exercises, August 7, 1856.

CHAPTER 12: BELLEVUE, *New York City 1856-57*
CHAPTER 13: REVEREND DOCTOR EPSTEIN, *New York City 1858-59*

New York's College of Physicians and Surgeons. Fact. In 1860, the year after Ephraim graduated, its name changed to Columbia Medical School. I have researched and fictionalized true descriptions of medical education and practice. Dr Cable and friend Andrew Burns are imagined.

Arise, shine, for your light has come... Isaiah 60:1 (NIV)

The Israelite Indeed. Fact: a bi-monthly newspaper, New York, begun 1857 with editors Gideon R Lederer and Ephraim M Epstein. Printer John Grey. It ran until 1867.

The fever that comes after childbirth. The weather and deaths I attribute here to 1858 actually happened in 1857.

Dr James Rushmore Wood (1813-1882). Historically true, as described. As is Dr Alonzo Clark.

Mama's pains... Anna had died. Ephraim's mother's gastric spasms and her first child's death aged seven from hemorrhaging leech bites are true [EE], but I have conflated them as a psychological impact on young Ephraim. I have imagined his early motivation to be a physician, along with the doubts about 'regular' medicine and heroic therapy. Anna's name is fiction, but the dates 1814-22 fact. [PEW]

An excruciating pain in his upper left mid-chest. This, the lifelong mystery of it, and 'eructations of gas from the stomach' are true, [EE] but the teasing is imagined.

Kingston, Canada. Fact: as stated in EE 1908 listing of his professional study; I have assumed that he attended Queens College Medical School although he and HGE state simply study of medicine at Kingston, Canada without naming the school.

Missionary of the Presbyterian Synod of Canada to the Jews in Saloniki, European Turkey. Fact: as stated in EE 1908 listing of his missionary service, also Monastir, both together as dates 1859-62 [also HGE].

PART 2: THE MISSION AND THE VICTORY
CHAPTERS 14 – 20, 1860 - 1866

CHAPTER 14: A MAN SHALL CLEAVE UNTO HIS WIFE, *Saloniki 1860*
CHAPTER 15: THE TASTE OF LEARNING, *Saloniki 1861*
CHAPTER 16: EPIDEMIC, *Monastir 1861*

Saloniki. Today called by its old and current Greek name, Thessalonika. This city began in the era of Alexander the Great, flourished in Greek, Roman and early Christian times and from 1453 (or before) to 1922 was within the Ottoman Empire. Areas west of Constantinople (now Istanbul) were called European Turkey by westerners.

The end of a matter is better than its beginning, and patience is better than pride. Ecclesiastes 7:8 (NIV)

Mrs Rachel Epstein. Ephraim's first wife's presence in European Turkey is imagined, as is her entire personality, actions and denial of access to their daughter. PEW says his wife joined him in America and Turkey, and the marriage was unhappy; she also says there were two children but one died. EE never says what became of his wife and never mentions a second child by her. NEW says his wife joined him in the USA and Sarah was born afterwards, then 'She (the wife) died and Papa and the child kept together. All that part of their history is blank to me until they all landed somehow in Cincinnati, Ohio.' I should say it's blank! This is an instance which well may be one of the 'secrets I will take to my grave' of which EE wrote in his life account.

Brother Albert Jeffers. A fictional character, and the operation of the mission is imagined.

St Andrews had welcomed him with joy, Reverend Machar. Ephraim was ordained 6 October 1859 at St Andrews Presbyterian Church, Kingston, Ontario, Canada [HGE]. Church records say the minister from 1827-63 was The Rev. John Machar. Ephraim graduated 31 Oct 1859 from NY College of Physicians & Surgeons [EE, HGE, other records].

Mr Goodyear's patented rubber. Thick and clumsy, Goodyear's rubber condoms were first produced in 1855. I imagine that as a medic Ephraim would have been aware of such developments.

The mission needed a school. PEW says that after his trainings Ephraim 'was called to the Balkan peninsula and lived there for several years, but his missionary work was unsuccessful. He was denied the means for a missionary school, whereupon he abandoned this activity.'

Sweetness of learning... degeneration of superstition. These letters are imagined by me, but the passion and wordiness modeled on Ephraim's own writings. Direct inspiration:

un-Christian Jew...Superstitious ignorance... fatal blindness of the Jewish Rabbis and ecclesiastical authorities... degenerated reverence all from *The Mosaic Names of God. The trammels of Talmudic haughtiness* from 'Why Do I Live So Long.'

Semmelweis's theories. True as described. Ignaz Philipp Semmelweis (1818-1865) was a Hungarian physician in Vienna. Devastated at thousands of lives needlessly lost because his premise was not followed, he died a broken man in 1865. Pasteur (1864) and Lister (1867) eventually proved him right, but not yet in our story. I have imagined that this practice was taught at Kingston Hospital and indeed that Ephraim particularly focused on childbirth or acted on the theory.

Monastir. Today called by its old name, Bitola, it is a large city in the Republic of Macedonia, as it was in ancient times. Like Saloniki it went through Greek, Roman, Christian and Ottoman rule; post World War I Monastir was in the large multi-ethnic nation Yugoslavia, which in the 1990s broke up into what is now some nine different countries.

Smallpox. I have invented this epidemic because Ephraim encounters management of this horrible disease later, in Pola, and because I have no indication of why he moved on from Saloniki to Monastir. Reverend Blackstone and the presence of Rachel are fiction, as is Ephraim's disobedience to mission orders. An unidentified family account says he fought a cholera epidemic in Constantinople but I have found no substantiation for this.

Zayde's legacy. PEW says that early in the 1860s their grandfather died and left an inheritance to Ephraim and his wife; I have imagined this timing. The name Zayde (Grandpa) is fictional.

CHAPTER 17: EPHRAIM FEEDS ON THE WIND, *Heidelburg 1862*
CHAPTER 18: THE GET, *Heidelburg 1862-63*

Ephraim feeds on the wind; he pursues the east wind all day. Hosea 12:1 (NIV) This whole chapter of the Old Testament is about the Israelite unfaithfulness to God. In Ephraim's case the question is which God?

Mama, Papa, Abraham Sack, Kathy, Sarah. PEW says the family reunion occurred in a German city but does not say why. Abraham Sack (a true person, true name) was actually a banker, eventually in St Petersburg; his wife (Ephraim's sister) Frau Catherina von Sack was resident in Heidelberg in 1915, according to HGE. So for story reasons I chose Heidelberg and made him an academic; I have imagined Sarah's presence.

Yom Kippur, Day of Atonement, the solemn highest holy Jewish day. *Sukkot,* Feast of Booths, follows soon after and is celebrated by the building of a temporary hut outside the family home representing the Israelites' forty years in the wilderness; meals and prayers are held there during this joyful festival.

Apikoros, kofer ba-Torah. Jewish law divides heretics into three categories, each with subdivisions according to the nature of the transgression.

Heileggeistkirche. Church of the Holy Spirit. It truly was divided in half and shared by Catholics and Protestants until the early 1900s; it is now fully Protestant.

And Pharoah said unto Joseph, In my dream... Genesis 41:17-18 (KJV)

Divorce. PEW says Ephraim's parents arranged a Jewish divorce at the time of this family reconciliation; she says his wife kept one child, and that there had been another which died. EE makes no mention of any of this anywhere.

Precipitation of arsenic. This was discovered by Robert Bunsen in 1833; by the time of Ephraim's fictional visit Bunsen was a full professor at Heidelberg University and had already perfected what came to be called the Bunsen burner.

Jesus told his disciples. Jesus said to the man who said he would follow him, but first wanted to go say good-bye to his family: 'No man, having put his hand to the plough, and looking back, is fit for the kingdom of God.' Luke 9:62 (KJV)

On the Origin of Species. By Charles Darwin, published in England 1859. Fact: Heinrich Georg Bronn, professor of natural history at Heidelberg University medical faculty published a German translation in 1862 with additions on controversial religious connotations.

His mother threw herself at his feet. PEW: 'a painful, heartbreaking meeting... our old mother fell at her son's feet and swore that she would not rise until he had returned to the faith of his fathers, and would never, during her lifetime, return to America. My brother promised.' Neither EE nor any other source mentions this return to Judaism.

Soweit der Osten vom Westen. 'As far as the east is from the west so far hath he removed our transgressions from us.' Psalm 103:12 (KJV)

He put into Ephraim's hands a journal, Tevunah. Fact: Rabbi Salanter (1810-1883) whom the fictional Ephraim boasted of to Lilienthal in New York in 1850 came to Germany and began publication of this mussar (ethics) journal by 1860 and a significant mussar movement developed. Abraham and Ephraim's interest is fiction.

CHAPTER 19: FIERCE AS A LEOPARD, LIGHT AS AN EAGLE, *Vienna 1863-66*

Vienna General Hospital. EE says that after European Turkey he went to Vienna, 'to attend the clinics there.' PEW says, 'My brother went to Vienna to deepen his medical skills.' I have imagined him in the two posts I give him at this world class hospital. For Semmelweis see notes for Chapter 15. Fact: after completing the novel another great-grandchild of Ephraim, George Pohlman, provided me with a certificate translation of the Royal Imperial General Hospital, Vienna, stating Ephraim's service there, April 1863 – May 1866, and that he was on surgical, medical and then Diseases of the Eye wards.

Kabbalah, mussar. I have imagined Ephraim's period of Jewish mysticism based on this eulogy by his colleague A.S. Burdick (*The American Journal of Clinical Medicine* 1913 p255): 'Dr Epstein's mind turned constantly to the great mysteries of life, death and immortality. He was essentially a mystic, seeing in the books that he read and in the greater book of nature many things of subtle significance... Next to the Bible, which he read constantly, I think his favorite author were [sic] that rare old middle-age mystic, Jacob Boehme.'

Also, in Ephraim's *The Construction of the Tabernacle* (1911, p47) he says: 'I was familiar with cabalistic numerics, mystically called G[e]matria... the ancient Israelites thought in a way that anticipated the Cabala...'

Finally, during his separation from Christian practice Ephraim's deep spiritual nature and seeking character must have demanded nurture: he could well have found it in Kabbalah, mussar and *Mesillat Yesharim*. A guide to perfection of character, it is studied to this day in Judaism. It is by Rabbi Moshe Chaim Luzzatto (1707-1746), also known as the Ramchal, taken from his initials. The fictional Ephraim in 1850 used this name to boast to Lilienthal. Benjamin Franklin's *Autobiography* (1771) lists the Thirteen Virtues he cultivated.

This was just as Jesus had done! In John 9:1-16 Jesus heals a man on the Sabbath, just one example among many where he broke Jewish religious rules.

Be fierce as a leopard, light as an eagle... etc. From Ramchal's sixth step, The Trait of Zeal, in *Mesillat Yesharim* (Pirkei Avot [Chapters of the Fathers] 5:23)

Stephen Wright and wife are invented, based on EE saying: 'In Vienna I fell in with some American friends who gave me letters of introduction to their friends at Leavenworth, Kans.' Bleeding Kansas and pastor Beecher's Bibles (rifles) are true events. Developing telegraph and newspaper communications enabled European centers to get fairly speedy news of American Civil War events.

Wilhelm von Tegetthoff. His leadership in a naval battle with the Danes at Heligoland resulted in Emperor Franz Josef promoting him to Rear Admiral by telegram. Denmark lost the duchies of Schleswig and Holstein to the German Confederation.

The Crimean War. This bloody conflict ended in 1856, just as Ephraim began medical school. Florence Nightingale's influential book was published in 1859; her establishment of the first school to train nurses gained effect in the 1860s. Ephraim's thoughts on this are imagined.

University Academy of Vienna. A medical commission in the Imperial Navy, a literary academic examination, surgeon aboard the *Feuerspeier Battery* and the *Seehund*: true. [EE, hospital document described above, Austrian War Archives]

CHAPTER 20: BATTLE, *Adriatic Sea and Vienna 1866*

Battle of Lissa, 20 July 1866. EE gives a short, vivid account of this historic battle which I have augmented with further research. Today the Croatian island of Lissa is called Vis.

Ephraim's poem. Alas I have not been able to find this poem, but EE says Admiral Tegetthoff thanked him in a letter and 'said it reminded him of Byron's description of a sea storm in his Don Juan.' So I have adapted Byron's sea storm (*Don Juan* Canto the Second, 11-53) to convey some of Ephraim's poem.

The battle had been won – but the war was lost. Europe in the 19th c is an incredible complex of politics, diplomacy, territory, armies, navies, alliances and sneaky treaties. After Napoleon's 1815 defeat Europe went through many upheavals, including the 1848 revolutions that impacted on Ephraim's earlier travels. By the 1860s not only Austria, Prussia (which became Germany) and Italy but France, Hungary, Serbia, Croatia, Russia, Britain and smaller countries in between were caught up in events. These tangles led to World War I (1914-18), and then WWII (1939-45), and even to the 1990s Bosnian War.

Supervisor of the naval smallpox hospital, Pola. True, as reported by EE: 'I had on an average sixty patients all the time, with some very severe confluent cases. The mortality did not amount to one percent. The treatment was *pro re nata*, but the external application to the exposed parts of the body was plain cold water, which answered very well.' He also says that people in that region were generally 'ignorant antivaccination fanatics' so I fictionalized this into another of his active causes.

The Emperor's prize. I knew of this from family legend, EE reports it as a present of three hundred dollars, PEW says 'the Kaiser rewarded the rhyming doctor with an honorarium of 600 florins.' Equivalent in dollars now would be around $6-7000.

The Dalmatia. EE says he was at the smallpox hospital for two months, then ordered onto this side-wheel steamer 'for some months' before applying for dismissal to return to the United States.

Mama's death. PEW indicates the dates for Zelda Epstein as c1801-c1863. The death date, however, does not fit with Ephraim's known time in Vienna and as naval surgeon; surely the reason he stayed in Europe was his promise not to return to the USA until after his mother's death [PEW]. I have slightly rearranged the timings of Ephraim's post-Lissa events for story-telling sense and invented the award ceremony and ball.

For God so loved the world... John 3:16 (KJV)

PART 3: THE PURSUIT OF HAPPINESS
CHAPTERS 21 – 28, 1867-78

CHAPTER 21: AMERICA REGAINED, *Leavenworth, Kansas 1867-69*
CHAPTER 22: HOME SWEET HOME, *Cincinnati, Ohio 1869*
CHAPTER 23: SADIE, *Cincinnati, Ohio 1870-71*

Leavenworth, Kansas. Fact: through unnamed friends Ephraim gained contacts, opened practice and continued 'for some years' [EE, HGE]. EE also describes his severe gastritis, bed rest and relief by use of carbonated water. Otherwise I have entirely invented Ephraim's personal and professional experience of his time in Leavenworth.

Majors, Russell and Waddell. As a born Waddell from the line of Naomi Epstein Waddell I cannot resist including this. From 1855 the firm transported US Army supplies, ran passenger stagecoaches and carried mail by Pony Express (1860-62) until completion of the transcontinental telegraph connection.

Hoffman's Anodyne. Also known as Compound Spirit of Ether, this was a well-established digestive pain reliever of the time. EE describes his use of the remedy and I have chosen to introduce it here.

Uncle Jacob's invitation. EE says 'An old uncle who came over with me on my first trip to this country and then located in Cincinnati learned of my second arrival and began to urge my coming to that city and offered to afford me every facility to open a good practice.'

Masonic brotherhood. EE's obituary and other sources affirm he was a Freemason but I have not been able to trace when and where he began, so decided to put it here. The Kansas Lodge says Leavenworth was not a full lodge, but rather a lodge under dispensation, and that EE was a charter member and a senior warden.

Cincinnati... greeted him with open arms. As stated in Part 1, Jacob's character and involvement beyond EE's statement above is imaginary. Besides the bare fact of practicing here for nine years [EE], I have fictionalized his medical and Christian life in Cincinnati.

Sarah/Sadie. True [EE, PEW, HGE, NEW]. But whether she was a factor in Ephraim leaving Leavenworth and whether she joined her father here and now is my invention backed by the family accounts that Sister Sadie and Helena were close friends [NEW]. When and how Sarah became Christian is imagined by me, and is part of the secrets and blanks in Ephraim's and family accounts, but it is true that she was Christian. The doings of Ephraim's first wife are fiction.

As the Father hath loved me, so have I loved you... John 15: 9 -12 (KJV)

Helena Greyer. Fact. HGE herself spells her name variously as Helen and Helene,

EE as Helena. A photograph in family possession is identified by NEW as 'my mother 4 years' with three brothers taken in Hanover. Visually: George is the eldest, Wilhelm older than Helena, Julius younger. For fictional purposes I invented a fifth child, young Sarah. HGE gives her parents as Wilhelm and Julia, and her own birth date as 3 April 1850, born in Hanover. A tribute to Ephraim in 1913 refers to a Dr Julius Greyer, the basis for me making HGE's father and older brother doctors.

Origin and History of the Books of the Bible, both Canonical and Apocryphal. True. By Calvin Stowe (Hartford, 1867). He married Harriet Beecher in 1836 when they met in Cincinnati where she lived with her father, head of Lane Seminary. In correspondence EE 1908 says he did some translation for Professor Stowe at Andover, which I have expanded to include translation help on this book.

Prefer to be sprinkled by the Methodists than immersed by the Baptists. This is an anecdote reported by EE's daughter Naomi: 'Papa believed absolutely in immersion for salvation, so when I wanted to become a member of church and said I'd just as soon be sprinkled by the Presbyterians as immersed by the Baptists in Wheeling where he was a member and often preached, my father was really broken up. Left his room to make calls on patients. Mamma sent his meals up to him. I think he felt he had failed in his religious teachings. Anyway, *I* gave up not *he*. I was immersed in the Wheeling church and joined Presbyterian church in W. Liberty.'[NEW] For my story, I gave the rebellion to Sarah-Sadie and let her win.

With the baptism that I am baptized with shall you be baptized.' Mark 10:39 (NRSV)
Jesus, when he was baptized, went up straightway... Matthew 3:16 (KJV)
And now why tarriest thou? Arise, and be baptized... Acts 22:16 (KJV)

CHAPTER 24: EPHRAIM IN LOVE, *Cincinnati, Ohio 1871-72*
CHAPTER 25: DOCTOR AND FAMILY MAN, *Cincinnati, Ohio 1872-74*
CHAPTER 26: PERJURED, *Cincinnati, Ohio 1874*

Ephraim and Helena. 'Sister Sadie, as the family called her, became a close friend of Helena Greyer and thus Papa met Mamma' [NEW]. A twenty year age gap seems rather worrying in our time, but was more common in the eras before modern medicine when many a widow or widower remarried with such gaps, and when a single woman had few career options but to marry or be part of her father's or brother's household. Post-Civil War scarcity of younger men might be a factor too.

Therefore a man shall leave his father and his mother... Genesis 2:24 (KJV)

A Brahms duet, the overture to Wagner's Paris Tannhauser for piano, a new hymn, 'Pass Me Not, O Gentle Savior,' and a newly popular minstrel tune. The Brahms duet I am thinking of is *Two Sisters* (1874), ironic as it is about sisters vying for one suitor. *Pass Me Not*, by Crosby & Doane was published in 1870 and *The Little Old Cabin in the Lane* (ironic too as it is an old man's lament), by W.S. Hays in 1871; both became extremely popular.

God is our refuge... Psalm 46 (KJV)

Sadie and Charleston. A family account says: 'Sadie was a linguist and went to teach at a girls' school in South Carolina. She was also very beautiful...' I've chosen Charleston for her destination; as a long established seaport it would have international cross-currents and it had a thriving Jewish population, both of which fit her story.

Helena and Ephraim's wedding. I assume here that the church for their ceremony is the one where in fact Sarah's took place a year later; the date 29 April 1873 is fact [HGE]. Delays due to divorce papers and first wife's death are imagined.

A perfect wife Proverbs 31:10-11; how beautiful she is!... How your eyes shine... my bride is a secret garden... My lover is handsome and strong... From Solomon or The Song of Songs 4 and 5 (GNT).

William. His birth date is a likely guess; as to his character: 'He was an unusually bright and beautiful boy right from his birth.' [EE]

Circumcision. I do not know if Ephraim's sons (William, Leo, George) were circumcised or not, and have imagined not. Whichever, EE's hotly defensive letter published in 1874 is fact and shows that Jewish ways and circumcision were clearly on his mind this same year of his son's birth. From around this time until late mid-20th c circumcision of all boys became routine practice, now no longer the case.

Here there is no Gentile or Jew, circumcised or uncircumcised... Colossians 3:11 (NIV). Paul says that under Christ background, including circumcision, does not matter.

Sadie and Alexander Franz Zur Hosen, of St Petersburg. The photographic portrait of her and the ensuing romance are family lore. '... courted by a Russian member of the Czar's court. He saw a photograph of her which a friend, an American who lived in St Petersburg, had, and fell in love with her' [NEW]... 'and began a correspondence with her. As it grew more serious he asked her to prove to his satisfaction that she was not born a Jewess' [unidentified family account]. Though Zur Hosen was not a nobleman but a merchant, this romance is backed by an article in *The New York Times*, 24 December 1874, which also states they were married that same month at the German Reformed Church, Cincinnati.

If he had managed to stop Sarah's marriage Ephraim might well have saved her from the difficulties of the Bolshevik era. The lie as to Sarah being Christian-born may well be one of the 'secrets I will take to my grave' of which EE wrote in his life account. His resistance and guilt about this is fictional.

The Making of a Christian, by Elias T Jones, I seem to have invented this and its quotes.

CHAPTER 27: THE DARKNESS, *Cincinnati, Ohio 1876-78*
CHAPTER 28: GOD FORSAKEN, *Cincinnati, Ohio 1878*

Shurek, Selda. Fact, although not exact as to dates [HGE, NEW and other sources].

The Russian wedding portrait of Sadie and Zur Hosen. 'We used to have a large framed (gilt) picture of them hanging on our parlor wall. They were both beautiful and distinguished looking... They were quite wealthy' [NEW]. Where is it now, I wonder?

Frieda Epstein. Fact: birthdate 16 July 1877. I imagine that Helena gave birth at home given that this was common practice until the 1940s or later.

William's illness and death, and Selda's. EE himself describes the tragedy of William's death: 'by the accidental administration by a druggist of three grains of morphine instead of quinine.' He says his son was five years old, yet HGE says the death was in 1878, and that Ephraim began teaching (ie, gave up practice) in 1878. Unless Helena was already pregnant with William when they married 29 April 1873 [HGE], he must have been four years old at death. The family account [NEW] says Selda died of convulsions after William's death; HGE says both died in 1878; she spells the name with Z, but NEW uses S, so to differentiate from their later daughter I use S.

The darkest days of Ephraim's life. The descent into hell, the thoughts, depression and possible psychosis is my invention based on the following: 'It [Willliam's death] came near to breaking my heart and ending my life. I could not practise medicine any more.' [EE]. The druggist's name is invented.

Frail children of dust, from Hymn 433; *Truth in its beauty,* from Hymn 52, New English Hymnal.

Moses and the tabernacle. Exodus 26:1. Fact: publication of Ephraim's *The Key to the Construction of the Tabernacle* in 1881 (and revised publication, 1911). I have imagined Ephraim's fascination with the tabernacle as beginning with Moses in the circumcision correspondence (Chapter 25 and see notes above), and continue it as a near obsession. I also have chosen to begin here his challenging insistence on linguistics; it may well have existed earlier but from this period onward 'religious disagreement' [EE] occurs in his career and I am guessing that language interpretation was the issue. This is because linguistics is very much the basis of his books, and was part of family life [NEW].

Every first-born male must be consecrated to the Lord. Luke 2: 23. *Could I bring the child back to life?* 2 Samuel 12.23 (GNT)

Though I walk through the valley of the shadow of death... Psalm 23:4 (KJV)

PART 4: THE TERRITORY
CHAPTERS 29 – 33, 1878-84

CHAPTER 29: PROFESSOR EPSTEIN, *Tiffin, Ohio 1878-79*
CHAPTER 30: A VOICE CRYING IN THE WILDERNESS, *Yankton, Dakota 1879*
CHAPTER 31: ORION RISING, *Yankton, Dakota 1880-81*

Heidelberg College, Tiffin, Ohio. Fact: the 1878-79 professorship of German, Hebrew and natural sciences [EE, HGE]. EE 'took a place as Minister in an Episcopalian church via his Andover Theological Seminary training' [NEW]. I have invented the trip east and Ephraim's Darwin interest and controversy. Of his departure EE says only, 'A religious disagreement with the faculty, which was theological at the same time, made me sever my connections from it.'

Keep me safe, my God, for in you I take refuge... Psalm 16:1, 7, 11 (NIV)

Daniel in the lions' den. Daniel, Chapter 6.

Qeresh. This word, its uniqueness, the translation and the urge to make sense of it are all directly from Ephraim's book *The Construction of the Tabernacle* (1911) in which he analyzes the instructions in Exodus, Chapter 26 for the structure of the Israelites' sacred tent. He uses linguistics to solve the Qeresh puzzle which appears in Exodus 26:15-30.

Yankton, Dakota Territory. In 1804 the USA acquired from France land stretching from New Orleans to Canada; it was carved into administrative territories to be gradually settled. I have invented the way in which Ephraim found this post, and his feelings about it, but the fact that he held it is true [Baptist records].

Julia Epstein. Fact: birth date 27 March 1880 [NEW].

I am Israel's father, and Ephraim is my firstborn son. Jeremiah 31: 9 (NIV)

I shall not die, but I shall live.... Psalm 118:17-18 (NRSV)

Kabbalistic numerology. Ephraim's use of this, in much more detail, and the anecdote of his ecstatic discovery of the solution appears in *The Construction of the Tabernacle* (p 49), though for EE in reality this occurred in Ohio, not Dakota.

Thomas Kettering and the campaign to open Dakota University. Kettering is an invented character, but the campaign, opening dates and building of the university are fact. Ephraim's involvement is also true; Baptist records say: 'Early in 1882 Dr Epstein resigned as pastor at Yankton, and spent several months traveling over the southern counties of the territory. By public addresses and personal interviews, he awakened an interest among the people in the contemplated university.'

This terrible winter. These descriptions are based on true historical accounts of Dakota's 1880 extreme blizzards and the great flood of 1881.

Governor Ordway. A true person; I imagine Ephraim, being quite highly placed in the territorial capital, would have encountered him.

Zelda Epstein. Fact: birthdate 27 December 1881 [NEW].

The Key to the Construction of the Tabernacle: the 47th of Euclid. Fact: published by Thos Wilson, Oakland, Calif 1881. Revised and republished in 1911.

Is not the gleaning of the grapes of Ephraim better... Judges 8:2 (KJV) Two tribes were quarreling over glory in battle and Gideon's words assuaged them.

CHAPTER 32: *VERITAS*: PRESIDENT AND FOUNDER, *Vermillion, Dakota 1882-83*
CHAPTER 33: THE STONE REJECTED BY THE BUILDERS, *Vermillion, Dakota 1883-85*

Vermillion. Descriptions of its rebuilding after the great flood of 1881 are based on historical records.

Father of a university. True. [EE, university records, Baptist records.] The University of Dakota (1882) became the University of South Dakota when the huge territory gained statehood as two states, North and South, in November 1889. The structure of the university's governing body is imaginatively based on fact; names of trustees and regents are invented. Teacher Joseph Brown is invented. University Hall and President's House are based on fact – though not in detail.

Sadie's parcel and news from Russia. Parcels from Sister Sadie were a feature of Epstein domestic life: 'They were quite wealthy. Used to send Mamma boxes and boxes of clothing and materials which Mamma had fashioned for we girls into beautiful apparel.' [NEW]. The assassination of Czar Alexander II in 1881 and the repressive anti-Jewish May Laws of 1882 under Czar Alexander III and other Russian developments are historical fact.

First academic year. Fact: the place, date and EE's duties. The university's archives say: 'he conducted most of the classes, kept university records, and sold textbooks to the 69 students enrolled... Epstein was an excellent teacher who enjoyed inspiring young minds..' The courses taught were Latin, German, mathematics, grammar, composition, history and speaking and non-credit musical participation.

Veritas. This motto is so much in Ephraim's character that I have imagined he originated it. Fact: the seal of the University of South Dakota continues to this day: the word *Veritas* beneath a depiction of a book on which stands a lighted genie-type lamp, a hand pouring oil into it.

The Bismarck Tribune, Sioux Falls Argus etc All are true newspapers of the time.

Ousted. Specifics are imagined, but the general facts are true: 'whose first president I was till sectarian and political chicanery ousted me' [EE]

From university archives: 'but [he] held controversial religious views. Eventually Epstein was removed as president due to political motives by certain members of the Regents of Education when the territory assumed control of the university in 1883. There was also speculation that Dr Epstein had amassed a significant debt for contracting a house in Vermillion.'

Further information from the university: While Ephraim was re-hired for the school year 1883, he had been replaced as principal/president by John Wesley Simonds. A science class was added in 1883, taught by Garry E Culver (University of Wisconsin Masters degree).

A Baptist historical report says trustees, students and citizens were satisfied with Dr Epstein, but 'The one to whom above all others credit was due for the successful establishment of the school, and its first prosperous year, was removed from the office of president, and another one, a stranger from the east, was chosen in his place. Many friends of the institution deeply regretted the discourtesy and ingratitude exhibited towards its founder.'

I have invented the hint of anti-Semitic prejudice; family lore and EE never suggest it, but I feel it is quite possible. On the other hand, perhaps he simply was too independent and outspoken for the Regents, or they wanted the eastern connection.

The stone that the builders rejected... Matthew 21:42 (NRSV)

I have seen all the works that are done under the sun... Ecclesiastes 1:14 (KJV)
Lay not up for yourself treasures upon earth... Matthew 6:19-21 (KJV)

Before I formed thee in the belly... Jeremiah 1:5 (KJV)

Naomi Epstein. Fact: birth date 6 August 1884 [NEW]. Naomi is the mother-in-law of Ruth in the Book of Ruth; she changed her name to Mara, meaning bitter, in the hard times. She is the grandmother of the author of this fiction version of the true life of Ephraim M Epstein.

Friends are watching for me to stumble. "Perhaps he can be enticed, and we can prevail against him and take our revenge on him." Jeremiah 20:10 (NRSV)

'*Whither thou goest, I shall go,*' Ruth 1:16 (KJV) See Naomi above. Ruth is the daughter-in-law who loyally insisted on following Naomi to an unfamiliar land.

PART 5: THE GLEANER
CHAPTERS 34 – 38, 1885 – 1899

CHAPTER 34: RESURRECTION, *Bethany, West Virginia 1885*
CHAPTER 35: STILL FULL OF SAP, *Bethany, West Virginia 1885-87*
CHAPTER 36: WHITHER THOU GOEST, *West Virginia 1890-92*

How are the mighty fallen... weapons of war... 2 Samuel 1:25, 27 (KJV)
I have fought the good fight... 2 Timothy 4:7 (NRSV)

Journal of the American Medical Association. JAMA began publication in 1883. I have invented the article Ephraim reads, but the facts are true: the alkaloid from monkshood (aconite, a deadly poisonous plant) is aconitine, then used medically to reduce fever and as an analgesic. The earliest 'active principle' – morphine, from the opium poppy – was isolated in 1804 by a German chemist. The word alkaloid came into use by 1820. Throughout the 19th century chemists worked to make drugs precise, specific and safe – leading to modern medicine and Ephraim's final career.

Shaller. John M Shaller, M.D. is real, although I have put him in Cincinnati possibly earlier than reality. He is author of a medical text I draw on for much of the alkaloidal technicalities of Ephraim's life. He was former Professor of Physiology and Clinical Medicine in the Cincinnati College of Medicine and Surgery.

*Such things will always happen...*Matthew 18:7 (GNT)
Not seven times, but seventy times seven. Matthew 18:22 (NIV)
I will someday go to where he is, but he can never... 2 Samuel 12:23 (GNT)

He maketh me to lie down... He restoreth my soul. Psalm 23:2, 3 (KJV)

West Virginia. Originally included in the state of Virginia and settled since pre-Revolutionary times, during the War Between the States this western mountainous region split to form a new state and stay with the northern Union states (1863).

Even tomatoes. Tomatoes were not common American food until very late 19th c.

Bethany College. The college continues to the present, founded in 1840 by Alexander Campbell (1788-1866). He would have been a kindred spirit to Ephraim; he so disapproved of differing Christian sects that he abjured all man-made institutions and insisted on worshiping only in the words and practice as written in the New Testament.

The second president, William K Pendleton (1817-1899), is a real person as described, but I have imagined the tabernacle book being the connection that led to the offer of professorship at Bethany and likewise fictionalized their close relationship. College records say Ephraim taught Greek and Hebrew.

Whatever else may not agree in this disagreeing world, a verb must agree with its noun. This is a direct quote from Ephraim's *The Mosaic Names of God and What They Denote*, eventually published in 1907, first in *The Monist* and then by The Open Court publishing company, Chicago. If indeed he encouraged Ephraim Pendleton did not live to see it.

Very closely argued, with much fire and some humor, Ephraim's main points are woven into the story from this point forward. For ease of reading I have used Elohim (Gods) instead of his spelling AeLouHeeIM in which he shows the Hebrew consonants in upper case, and the vowel sounds in lower case (there are no written vowels in Hebrew).

The study of developments in languages as indications of actual historical developments of a culture or people became a cutting edge category of scholarship (philology) in the 19th c. This is evidence of Ephraim's dauntless questioning continuing from his teens; though God-fearing he was in no way afraid to see the Bible as a historical collection of writings fit to be analyzed.

Christ raised Lazarus from the dead in a village called Bethany. John 11:1-44. Coincidentally, after this miracle Jesus withdraws to a town named Ephraim.

And then winter hit. I have imagined the family's woeful health, all too likely in the conditions EE describes as 'a very cold winter and our living in a cold house.' He actually declared he had hereditary polakisuria (known today as pollakiruia, frequent micturation), not his old gastric pain.

Dr Richard Caldwell. EE names a Dr J R Caldwell at a later point, and a separate article mentions 'an eclectic physician in a neighboring town' and conversing with him about the satisfaction of using alkaloidal granules. So I have conflated these into the young physician who attends, and eventually has an effect on Ephraim's future. The medicines he uses I have taken from Shaller's medical text.

My sweetheart, my bride is a secret garden... Solomon or The Song of Songs 4:12 (GNT).

Guest preaching, Masonic lodge. This is imaginative assumption on my part.

Wheeling, West Virginia. This city had been the capital of the new state of West Virginia. No sooner had Ephraim arrived than the capital was moved two hundred miles south to Charleston, West Virginia.

I am that I am. In *The Mosaic Names of God and What They Denote* Ephraim says that 'to be' (am/is/are) does not exist in Hebrew, whereas the words 'becoming' or 'became' occur 3,354 times in the Old Testament. Exodus 3:13-14 (KJV)

Christmas and Chanukah. The nativity accounts: Matthew 1:18-25 and Luke 2:1-21. The Chanukah story: the Temple in Jerusalem had been desecrated by a Syrian ruler about 200 years before Jesus's birth. Jews rebelled, reclaimed it and the re-dedication required holy oil which took eight days to prepare, when only one day's supply was to be had; miraculously it lasted. I have imagined Ephraim told Jewish lore to his children.

Still green and full of sap. Psalm 92:14 (NRSV)

Leo Greyer Epstein. Fact: birth date 23 February 1887. For fictional reasons I advanced this to July 1887.

Return to medicine. Ephraim's license to practice in West Virginia is on Columbia University records as 1887. But EE says he began practice in West Liberty in the early 90s. Bethany College reports gaps in his teaching records. Therefore I have invented this interim phase-in of part-time practice in Bethany.

Medical advances. Since Ephraim had stopped practicing in 1878, the German Robert Koch had advanced knowledge of causes of tuberculosis, cholera and anthrax. From France, Louis Pasteur's breakthroughs on rabies, pasteurization and germ theory had become widely accepted. Semmelweis was praised in *JAMA* 2 March 1889.

Having to make his own remedies... tablets of medicinal alkaloids... Facts: 'A friend and generous patron during my early struggles in New York city [during medical education]... impressed upon my mind the advantage of dispensing my own medicines, even though it be with my pen-knife blade as a powder measurer... My practice in different parts of the world and on sea... made me quite familiar with medicaments and self-dispensing... when practising in West Liberty, W. Va., *The Medical World* of Philadelphia directed me to the medicinal alkaloids...' [Ephraim from 'Why and when I became an alkalometrist', *American Journal of Clinical Medicine*, ca 1906.] To build the story I have spread the self-reporting in this article over several episodes in Ephraim's life.

George Epstein. Birthdate unknown; my late 1889 guess is based on a West Liberty, West Virginia photographic family portrait.

In the beginning God created the heaven and the earth... Genesis 1:1-31 (KJV) Daily readings and requirements based on NEW's account: 'At our family prayers each morning each of we children had our own Bible opened at the same place as Papa's, he translating from the original and we following the Saint [sic, should be King] James version. We had to go along as we might get caught inattentive. We sang a hymn or two, Mamma accompanying on a small parlor organ worked with foot pedals, then we knelt at our separate chairs for prayer by Papa, ending with the Lord's Prayer.'

Neither do men light a candle... it giveth light unto all... Matthew 5:15 (KJV)

Back to full time medical practice. Fact: West Liberty practice in the early 1890s [EE; JAMA; family lore]. I have invented why, when and how Ephraim came to this. Horse and buggy were essential to rural practice and family lore told of accompanying Papa; I've invented the name of the horse.

Recent news from Russia was bad. Persecution of Jews under Czar Alexander III in the 1880s and the even more repressive anti-Semitic May Laws of 1891 led to massive Jewish immigration to the USA.

Master of Arts. In a 1908 document Ephraim writes this as A.M. (artium magister) after M.D. for his medical degree, as does HGE, dating it 1890. In correspondence with Andover Theological Seminary in 1908 he pursues the issue of getting the degree added to his credentials.

Lord, you alone are my portion and my cup... Psalm 16:5-11 (NIV)

They enrolled their eldest daughter. Fact: Frieda and Julia graduated from West Liberty State Normal School (today called West Liberty State College), and both taught before their marriages [HGE]. Normal School was the name given to teacher-training colleges when the movement toward free elementary public education was established mid 19th c. (Based on the French ecole normale, ie setting the standards of teaching norms.) Following high school, the age of enrollment was fifteen; the course generally lasted two years.

Ruth Epstein. Birth date unknown; my late 1892 guess is based on a West Liberty, West Virginia photographic family portrait.

CHAPTER 37: THE LAST CAUSE, *West Liberty, West Virginia 1893-95*
CHAPTER 38: THE GLEANER, *West Liberty, West Virginia 1896-99*

Chicago World's Fair. I have imagined the Epstein family visit to this phenomenal exposition.

The Alkaloidal Clinic. Fact: published by Wallace C Abbott MD from 1894. Though I have invented the circumstances, EE describes his discovery of it and his 'riveted attention' in his Alkalometrist article.

Wheeling City Hospital. Existed as described, but I have no evidence of Ephraim visiting it.

Tosh... a Republican, no doubt. Medicine had a political edge through much of 19th c America. 'Regular' (mainstream medical school educated) physicians were too expensive for many ordinary people and deemed elitist. 'Eclectic' physicians, their origins in home remedies and herbal medicines, were affordable for the common man, with populist and Democratic political appeal. Homeopathy, with its theories from Germany of very dilute medicines, was yet another strand in opposition to the regular school, preferred by patients who wanted gentle treatment. By 1845 the liberal spirit had even led to the end of medical licensing in most states. Thirty years later the pendulum swung back: too many charlatans, and the pressures of the mainstream, meant that state licenses began to be required again. Muddying the waters were so-called doctors who were actually promoters, dispensing medicines to which only they knew the secrets. Some of these even ran their own educational programs, sold their own texts, issued their own diplomas; small schools of followers developed.

Among his choices of Abbott's alkaloidal granules. In his Alkalometrist article EE lists the nine he chose as: aconitine, digitalin, hyoscyamine, codeine, strychnine arsenate, glonoine, brucine, morphine sulphate and veratrine. Plus Abbott's Effervescent Saline Laxative. Vomiting and purging, combined with medication, remained part of treatment well into the 20th c. For example, I can remember, as a 6-year-old with asthma in the early 1950s, being given ipecac to make me vomit, and enemas; within a decade asthma treatment turned to corticosteroids.

'never was I so certain of myself...' EE's own words, from the Alkalometrist article. Dr Burggraeve and his dosimetric method is true; he published in French, but I have invented the titles. EE's letter to *The Alkaloidal Clinic* was published in 1894, and regular correspondence and publication followed.

The family portrait and Frieda's secret wishes. The photograph exists, photographer unknown. I doubt Frieda ever went to Russia, but according to NEW: 'Frieda was the really gifted one of the family in many ways. She taught school in West Virginia, then went to Chicago and on to Cuba for the Abbott people. She married there, had three children, was divorced and finally got to Philadelphia. She died in 1963, after a stormy and eventful life.' In the course of writing this book the wife of her grandson Gordon Geist has reached me and provided helpful information.

Who knew what would happen to Jews when the Czarevich took the throne... He left their fate in God's hands. The ill Alexander III died in October 1894; his son Nicholas II (who married the British Queen Victoria's daughter Alix, April 1894) became Czar in November 1894. The Russian anti-Semitism ongoing since the 1880s continued; by 1903 pograms killed and wounded Jews and looted Jewish houses and businesses. Emigration to the USA continued. In the 1890s Zionism, a Jewish movement for a national home in the faith's original home in the Palestine region gathered strength. I have no record of EE's response to pogroms or Zionism.

From NEW's account of what became of Sarah Epstein Zur Hosen: 'There were two children, boy Shurek and girl Ljuba, both of whom and parents were lost somehow in the turbulent years of the Revolution. I know that Sister Sadie wrote Mamma that the son joined the Bolsheviks to her intense sorrow. Ljuba lived with her mother through her last illness, then letters and all communications stopped. We sent food packages, any moneys never reached them, also food was lost and stolen. I remember that Mamma tried to persuade Ljuba to come to America after her mother died, but she wouldn't do it.'

In the course of writing this book a relation has emerged through the internet, Anatoly Sack, descended from Ephraim's sister Catherine. His research shows Ljuba and Shurek in St Petersburg phone directory 1901-1917. Sadie is listed as 'a widow of the distinct honorable citizen' Alexander Zur Hosen. There is some evidence to this day of relations in St Petersburg with the name modified to Zurgosen.

Ephraim's sisters Pauline Epstein Wengeroff and Catherine Epstein Sack lived into the 20th c, ending their days in Heidelberg, Germany.

In Brest-Litovsk, on 15 October 1942, some 20,000 Jews of the Brest ghetto were rounded up by Nazi soldiers, transported northeast by train, shot and buried in pits. A search under Epstein (Epsztejn) on the Brest Ghetto Passport Archive (jewishgen.org) produces 22 names registered in November 1941. Among them are a Sara and a Menachem, born in the late 1800s. An early post-Soviet monument in Bronnaya Gora, between Brest and Minsk, Belarus, marks the total of 50,000 victims, primarily Jewish, buried at the site.

The Abbott company office was based where it started. I have imagined Ephraim's first personal meeting with the true Dr Wallace C Abbott. A 1885 MD graduate of University of Michigan, he started making and selling his dosimetric alkaloidal granules based on Burggraeve's method in 1888. His partner was William F Waugh MD. In 1915 the incorporated Abbott Alkaloidal Company changed its name to Abbott Laboratories to reflect the company's growth and the development of synthetic-based medications. In the 21st c it is a huge multinational research and development pharmaceutical company based near Chicago.

It's like a bull-dog dragging at my insides! This wording and the entire episode, including Dr Caldwell's attendance, comes directly from EE's article 'A diabetic storm of gastro-intestinal neuralgia' in *The Alkaloidal Clinic* (June and July 1899). Regarding the blistering plasters that helped, even today counter-irritation (from extracts of cayenne pepper or insect poison) is sometimes used for diabetic neuropathy.

The healing miracles. Those listed are the healing of the man with the paralyzed hand John 5:1-8, Peter's mother-in-law Matthew 8:14-16, the deaf-mute Mark 7:31-37, the pool of Bethesda John 5:1-8, the many by the Sea of Galilee Matthew 14:13-21, the man born blind John 9:1-11, the woman who was bleeding Luke 8:43-48. *Blessed is every one,* Psalm 128:1-3 (KJV)

Living in Chicago. In 1899 the Epsteins moved to the Ravenswood area, near Dr Abbott. In reality Dr Abbott first invited EE to come for a recuperative visit, and soon after offered the permanent post.

EPILOGUE: RAVENSWOOD

Editorial staff. Ephraim worked on the Abbott company journal for the next fourteen years, 1899-1913. His Alkalometrist article ca 1906 says he wrote his first article for the journal (and its successor *The American Journal of Clinical Medicine*) twelve years previously, and wrote one or more articles almost every month after that. The earliest indices for the journal that Abbott Pharmaceuticals provided are for 1899 and 1901. They list 6 entries under Ephraim M Epstein's name for 1899 and 37 for 1901.

Streetcar accident. EE himself describes the accident and makes the post-mortem request in his 1908 article 'Why do I live so long?'

Notorious missionizing Dr Epstein. Ephraim was described thus in a letter from Jewish leader Solomon Schechter in 1910 regarding possible publication of PEW's book. For this information I am grateful to Shulamit Magnus, translator and annotator of Pauline Wengeroff's *Memoirs of a Grandmother*, published 2013 and 2014 by Stanford University Press. She granted me an advance look at her as-yet unpublished subsequent article about the bumpy publication history of Pauline Epstein Wengeroff's very readable book.

Warmly respected. EE died 26 January 1913, of acute gastritis, aged nearly eighty-four. He was happy and thoroughly appreciated in his last career. In a memorial article Dr Abbott writes: 'In the passing of Dr Epstein the world loses an unusual man, one highly and broadly educated, a most unique and versatile character who, as a thinker, was far in advance of the spirit of his time.' From Dr Waugh's tribute: 'Everybody who came in contact with Dr Epstein loved him... his kindly heart, immense erudition, and keen wit.' From a colleague, A S Burdick: 'He really lived in the library – in our own editorial library and among his own books at home. He had several thousand volumes... Dr Epstein had many friends, but nowhere were there those who respected more his marvellous erudition and loved him better than right here among his colleagues of the editorial staff.' *The American Journal of Clinical Medicine*, March 1913, Abbott Alkaloidal Company, Chicago.

EPHRAIM SPEAKS, in 'Why do I live so long?'

Lastly, I look for the coming of the great, strong brother Death without enthusiasm, but also without dread. "Into Thine Hand I would commit my spirit, Thou hast redeemed me, Jehovah, God of Truth." (Ps. 31:6)

Ephraim Menachem Epstein, MD, AM, Ravenswood, Chicago, March 1, 1908.

ACKNOWLEDGEMENTS AND SOURCES

Specific information on Ephraim M Epstein's life comes from published writings by him, by his sister, by his colleagues, and from family accounts and papers. Documentary evidence of him has come through the archives of various organizations. In the search for him and his background a number of people have come forward with information or guidance whom I name below. Researching Ephraim's life and times has been a fascinating journey, and has, in addition, brought forth several distant Epstein relations formerly unknown to me. I have arranged sources by topic.

ABOUT EPHRAIM M EPSTEIN, THE MAN; HIS PUBLICATIONS

Abbott, W., Waugh, W. et al (1913). 'Gleanings from foreign fields, Dr Ephraim M Epstein.' *The American Journal of Clinical Medicine*, 250-6. Chicago: Abbott Laboratories.

Epstein, E. (1899) 'A diabetic storm of gastro-intestinal neuralgia.' *The Alkaloidal Clinic*. Chicago: Abbott Laboratories.

– (undated, ca 1906) 'Why and when I became an alkalometrist.' *The American Journal of Clinical Medicine*, 85-7. Chicago: Abbott Laboratories.

– (1907) *The Mosaic names of God and what they denote*. Chicago: The Open Court Publishing Company. First published in *The Monist* (1907).

– (1908) 'Why do I live so long.' *The American Journal of Clinical Medicine*, 522-25, 677-80. 2nd edn published posthumously 1913, 251-3. Chicago: Abbott Laboratories.

– (1911) *The construction of the tabernacle*. Chicago: Open Court. 1st edn. published 1881 as *The key to the construction of the tabernacle: the 47th of Euclid*. Oakland: Thos Wilson.

Further publications by Ephraim I was unable to access at the time of writing:

– (1857) *The Israelite indeed: a periodical devoted to the illustration and defence of the Hebrew Christianity*. Lederer, G., Epstein, E. (eds). New York: John A Gray.

– (1904) *A text-book of alkaloidal therapeutics*. Waugh, W., Abbott, W., Epstein, E. Chicago: Clinic Pub Co.

– (Dates and publications unknown) Song of Songs, and Last Words of Christ, listed by Helena Greyer Epstein in Andover Theological Seminary obituary form.

Wengeroff, P. (1908). *Memoiren einer Grossmutter*.

Memoirs of a Grandmother: scenes from the cultural history of the Jews of Russia in the nineteenth century. Wengergoff, P. Magnus, S. (tr.) (2010) Stanford: Stanford University Press. [see further acknowledgement in *Veritas* notes for Epilogue.]

Rememberings. An abridged translation of the German, 2nd edn. of: *Memoiren einer Grossmutter*. Wenkart, H. (tr.), Cooperman, B. (ed.) (2000). Bethesda: University of Maryland Press.

My brief PEW quotes in *Veritas* notes are from the Wenkart translation. Volume 2 of the Magnus translation, where information on Ephraim appears, was not available at the time of writing.

'Seventy-five hundred miles for a wife.' (24 December 1874) *The New York Times*, New York.

JEWISH AND CHRISTIAN PRACTICE

For Hebrew prayer and practice, transliterations and translations I have relied very much on the Wikipedia Judaism Portal under Creative Commons license. For particular prayers, the sources are http://en.wikipedia.org/wiki/ and then Aleinu, Kaddish, Amidah, Shema_Yisrael, Shehecheyanu. Transliterations varied within these sites, so I have altered spellings where necessary for consistency. For informal language I drew ideas from http://www. yiddishdictionaryonline.com.

Bible quotes come from various versions – as Ephraim freely translated from the Hebrew and Greek, so I have not limited myself to a single version. http:// biblegateway.com was very useful for searching scripture. Scripture quotations are identified by chapter and verse in the *Veritas* notes section, sources are:

KJV: King James Version is Public Domain.
NRSV: New Revised Standard Version Bible, copyright © 1989 the Division of Christian Education of the national Council of the churches of Christ in the United States of America. Used by permission. All rights reserved.
NIV: The Holy Bible, New International Version ®, NIV R Copyright c 1973, 1978, 1984, 2011 by Biblica, Inc. R Used by permission. All rights reserved worldwide.
GNT: Scripture quotations marked (GNT) are from the Good News Translation in Today's English Version- Second Edition Copyright © 1992 by American Bible Society. Used by Permission.

Christian hymns from *The New English Hymnal* (1986) Norwich: Canterbury Press.

HISTORICAL BACKGROUND AND SETTINGS

For general, visual and geographical orientation to the settings of Ephraim's life I am grateful to Wikipedia, Google Images and Google Maps as well as the following specific sources:

Jewish and Emigrant experience:
Feingold, H. (1974) *Zion in America*. New York: Twayne.
'Experiences of an English Emigrant', *The New York Times* – December 23, 1866.
Available at http://members.tripod.com/~alfano/castle
Howe, I. (1976) *World of our fathers*. New York and London: Harcourt Brace Jovanovich.
http://www.castlegarden.org. (The Battery Conservancy).
http://www.Jewish-history.com. (Jewish-American History Documentation Foundation).

Belarus:
http://www.jewishgen.org/databases/Belarus/brest.htm
http://brest-belarus.org

European and American 19th century:
Andrist, R. (ed.) (1987) *The American Heritage history of the confident years*. New York: Bonanza.
http://charlesdickenspage.com/perils_of_steam Same site /america
Waters, B. (ed.) (1956) *Mr. Vessey of England*. New York: G.P. Putnam's Sons.
Wood, A. (1984) *Europe 1815-1960*. 2nd edn. Harlow: Longman.

Battle of Lissa:
Detailed description of the battle, including a map and photographs available at
http://www.Cityofart.net/bship/sms_ferdinand_max.html#lissa.

Dakota:
Account of Yankton's development, including descriptions of the great flood of
1881 available at http://files.usgwarchives.net/sd/andreas/yankton. Also
Norwegian American Historical Association (1936). *Norwegian American Studies and Records*, Vol IX, Hustvedt, H. (Hustvedt, K. tr) 'The Missouri flood of 1881'.
Northfield, Minnesota. Accessed at
www.naha.stolaf.edu/pubs/nas/volume09/vol09_7.htm
Smith, E. (2002) *Historic Vermillion and Clay county*. Chicago: Arcadia.

MEDICAL SOURCES AND BACKGROUND

Carlisle, R. (ed.) (1893) *An account of Bellevue Hospital...1736-1894*. New York: The Society of the Alumni of Bellevue Hospital.
Gilman, S. (1993). *Freud, race and gender*, Cincinnati, Cincinnati University Press, 1993, p.64. 'Have the Jews an immunity from certain diseases?' *Medical & Surgical Reporter* (Philadelphia) vol xxx, 1874, pp 40-41.
Heaton, C. (no date) *The First One Hundred Twenty-Five Years of the New York University School of Medicine*. New York: New York University.
Hertzler, A. (1938) *The horse and buggy doctor*. Lincoln: University of Nebraska Press.
Journal of the American Medical Association began publication in 1883. Archives online.
http://jama.jamanetwork.com
Lamb, A (1955) *The Presbyterian Hospital and the Columbia-Presbyterian Medical Center 1868-1943*. New York: Columbia University Press.
Lloyd, J. and C. (1910) *The eclectic alkaloids*. The Lloyd Library Bulletin #12.
Accessed at http://www.henriettes-herb.com/eclectic/alkaloids/
Lyman, H, Fenger, C, Jones, H, and Belfield, W (date unknown). *The practical home physician and encyclopedia of medicine*. London: World Publishing Company. Accessed at http://www.doctortreatments.com. Urquhart, D. (2000).
Medical and Surgical Reporter (Philadelphia). 1872 – 1880 onward. Archives online.
http://archive.org/details/medicalsurgicalr26philuoft
Rothstein, W. G. (1987) *American Medical Schools and Practice, a history*. New York: Oxford University Press.
Science Museum, London at www.sciencemuseum.org.uk/broughttolife
Shaller, J (1907). *A therapeutic guide to alkaloidal dosimetric medication*. 2nd edn. Chicago: Clinic Publishing Co. Accessed at http://wolf.mind.net/swsbm/Ephemera as Dosimetrics pdf.

ACKNOWLEDGEMENTS AND SOURCES

INSTITUTIONS

My thanks to the archivists, librarians and/or curators of organizations who provided evidence of Ephraim and whose work helped me to imagine his world: Abbott Laboratories, Illinois; Andover Theological Seminary, Massachusetts; Austrian National Archives (Osterreichisches Staatsarchiv, Kriegsarchiv), Vienna, Austria; Bethany College, West Virginia; Country Doctor Museum, North Carolina; Freemason Grand Lodges of Illinois, West Virginia, Kansas and the United Grand Lodge of England; SUNY Upstate Medical University; University of South Dakota, South Dakota; Wellcome Collection, London.

INDIVIDUALS

Particular appreciation to the following helpful people: Anne Anderson, Dr Walter Blasi, Bernard Dov Cooperman, Martin Daly, Laura Durinski, Joy Isaacs, Eric Luft, Shirley Seaton McLaughlin, Sharon Monigold, Dominic Stevens MD, Diana Yount, Karin Maritato, Phillip Carter, Stephanie Zia and especially Shulamit Magnus, Professor of Jewish History, Oberlin College, Ohio.

Many thanks for support and interest from Writers at Work, NotMorely Novelists and other writerly colleagues. Much gratitude for encouragement and information during this long project from Epstein family descendants (or their spouses): Caroline Waddell Bourne, Nancy Lee Waddell, Anatoly Sack Belogorsky, Julie Ripper, Else Geist, George Pohlman, and Christopher, Michael, Richard, Jennifer and Margaret, my Waddell siblings. And, in spirit, I am grateful to Ephraim's wife Helena Greyer Epstein for completing the Andover document, and his daughter, my grandmother Naomi Epstein Waddell for her written and verbal inspiration: 'Add your imagination to all this as I remember it, and you could have quite a tale!'

And finally, deep thanks to Michael Kerr, for encouragement, patience and wisdom.

susanleekerr.com
ephraimmepstein.com

A digital edition of this book is available.

Made in the USA
Charleston, SC
15 April 2015